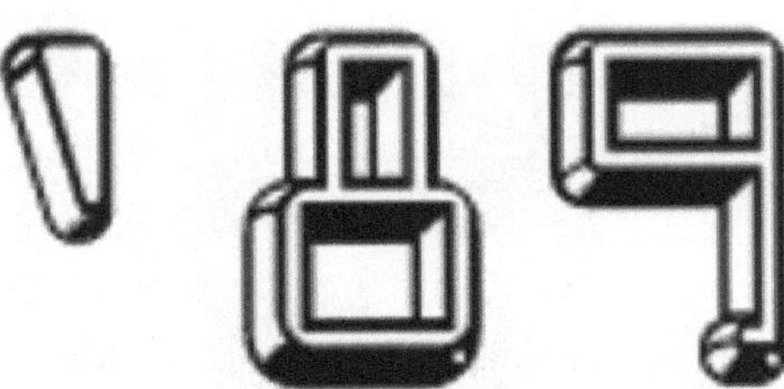

Library of Congress Control Number: 2021914343

ISBN: 978-1-7373440-2-5
eBook ISBN: 978-1-7373440-0-1

Book design by Rob J. LaBelle
Cover illustration by Ethan Shaw

This book is dedicated to the greatest decade in human history,
and to all of those who still worship it today!

AUTHOR'S NOTE

To some, the '80s were a joke. To others, it was the absolute best time of their lives (myself included).

I tried to include as many references as possible in this story, most of which I experienced during my own childhood. The rest are strictly fanfare.

I've seen every single movie referenced. I've listened to or still listen to every single band or group mentioned. I remember owning my very own Casio calculator watch. I still own an Atari 2600. (*Frogs and Flies* is my favorite game.) *Mike Tyson's Punchout* for Nintendo? Yup. I've only been able to beat it a handful of times in my life. And even though I currently own it, I still haven't beaten *Friday the 13th*.

Remember the prizes we all used to get in cereal boxes? It's too bad they don't do that anymore. I think my kids would've loved them.

As for the references that occurred after the events of this story (I do mention Steve Urkel, even though *Family Matters* debuted in September of 1989), I apologize. I added them in there because I just couldn't help myself. Still...

As I'd said before, I'm not writing to win any kind of special awards for grammar and punctuation because, again, I'm simply an independent author who enjoys entertaining people. And hopefully, by the time you're done reading this, you will have been thoroughly entertained.

Anyway, I thank you for listening. And as always...

Happy reading!

PROLOGUE

People say that when you graduate from high school, you immediately begin the slow transition into adulthood. Of course, if you're lucky enough to go to college afterward, that's not entirely true. Because, in college, you usually go to frat parties and wind up drinking yourself to death like an inexperienced teenager. At least, that's how it was back in the '80s.

As for me, I was one of my school's top track and field stars, and because of it, I wound up getting a full ride to Florida State. So both my scholarship and tuition were fully covered. And that made my hard-working parents happy not to pay for any of it. In my mind, though, I was one lucky son of a bitch. However, that's not what this story is about. You see, this story is about what happened to me during the summer of 1989, the summer *after* I graduated from high school.

My best friend Eric and I were going to enjoy the summer and go out with a bang. Since it was officially the last summer of the 1980s, and since we had both turned eighteen not long before graduation, we were going to try to be as rebellious as possible—to an extent.

Even though I was technically considered a jock, I wasn't much of a party animal and didn't really hang out with the other jocks either. I was more of a nerd than anything else. I mean, yes, I could sometimes run faster than the Flash and was considered one of the most popular kids in school, but I always got more joy out of playing Dungeons and Dragons with Eric and the rest of the nerds. While the popular kids were out partying and drinking, I was sitting at home playing RPGs, Nintendo, or just watching a movie or two, which brings me back to both Eric and me turning eighteen and us being as rebellious as possible.

Now, when I say rebellious, I mean that we were going to do something that summer we'd never been able to do before. We were going to go to the theater to see R-rated movies for the first time in our lives without our parents. Well, my parents.

When it came to R-rated movies, Eric's parents were a little more lenient. My parents, on the other hand, told me that I had to wait until I was eighteen before I could go without them. Even though they already knew what kinds of movies I watched, they still gave me some bullshit excuse about focusing on my studies. I guess they didn't want me to risk ruining my scholarship. And, I didn't blame them. But I still went behind their backs and did it anyway.

Eric and I had planned on going to see seven movies that summer. Four of them were *Ghostbusters II*, *The Karate Kid Part III*, *Weekend at Bernie's*, and, of course, *Batman*. Also, to this day, I've seen every *Batman* movie in the theaters and will argue until I'm blue in the face that Michael Keaton is still the best one. If you don't agree, then too bad. You can just plant your lips on my pasty, white ass.

I'm so sorry about that. Talking about *Batman* always seems to rile me up. Okay then, back to the story.

As I was saying, the other three movies were the R-rated films: *Lethal Weapon II*, *Friday the 13th Part VIII: Jason Takes Manhattan*, and *A Nightmare on Elm Street 5: The Dream Child*. Again, for obvious reasons, those were the three we looked forward to seeing the most.

Aside from that, we were going to go swimming, cruise around town, and possibly try to sneak into some of the casinos in Las Vegas. But you know what they say—the best-laid plans don't usually work out the way they're supposed to.

Okay, maybe that's not exactly what they say, but it's close enough.

Anyway, about a week into our summer vacation, we got invited to a birthday party for two girls who would both be turning eighteen on the same day. Before then, neither of us had ever heard of anyone by the name of Anna James or Eve Parker. Actually, come to think of it, nobody knew who they were. Apparently, they decided to invite not only their friends but also our entire graduating senior class. How thoughtful of them.

It was also at that very same party we would officially begin the most unbelievable summer of our lives. And, it wasn't until we met both Anna and Eve that we would find out why. That summer was supposed to be fun, exciting, and filled with adventure. Instead, it ended up becoming something more. Something unexpected. Something—epic.

ROB J. LABELLE

CHAPTER 1

Summer wasn't even a week old yet, and I was hanging out where I always liked to hang out. It wasn't at the movies, the roller rink, or even the mall. No. It was ten o'clock in the morning, and I was hanging out at my favorite arcade, which was located smack dab in the center of town.

The Electric Box Arcade had around two hundred stand-up coin-operated machines in there, ranging from *Altered Beast* and *Dig Dug* all the way up to *TRON* and *Xevious*. With all the money I had earned by working part-time at Johnny's Café, which also happened to be right next door, I could spend hours on end there, beating most of the games with just a single quarter.

I had called my best friend Eric from our kitchen phone the night before to ask him to meet me there so we could do our usual morning battle on one of the machines. You see, each day, we would rotate our choice of game. That way, we both got an equal chance to kick each other's ass.

When I got there, Eric hadn't arrived yet, and I was already in a fresh, heated debate with some fifteen-year-old douchebag who claimed to be "God's gift to arcade games." He said that he could beat anybody at anything. So, of course, I decided to call him out and challenge him. And as you probably could've already guessed, he didn't like that too much. So it was officially game on.

Seeing as how his smug little self thought he would easily kick my ass, he allowed me to choose the game. However, after pretending to scan the room and pick one out, it didn't take me long to choose one I knew I could beat him at.

I challenged him to a game called *Rolling Thunder,* which was released in 1986 by Namco. It was always a favorite of mine and was a side-scrolling game in which you took control of a character named Albatross, who wore red shoes, gray pants, a red, long-sleeved shirt, and worked for the World Crime Police Organization's Rolling Thunder unit.

The object of the game was to travel through two "stories," if you will, comprised of five stages apiece, all in a bid to save a female character and fellow agent named Leila Blitz. Along the way, you had to shoot many miscellaneous hooded enemies, rabid panthers, trolls, bats, and fire people, who all worked for a secret society named Geldra. There were also many doors you could enter to replenish your handgun and machine gun bullets when your ammo was low. Of course, shithead insisted that since I got to pick the game, he should go first. So he did.

To my amazement, he made it through the first five levels without losing a single guy. That was something even I'd never done before. Hell, to this day, I still wind up losing my first guy to the fire people near the end of level four.

Once he had finished the first story, he moved on to the second one before finally losing his first life on stage six. He then wound up making it through stages seven and eight before losing two more lives on stage nine. He was now on his last life and still had the most challenging stage left.

The way he played, I thought he would breeze through the last stage with no problems. That is, until he reached a group of hooded enemies, where he misjudged a shot and took a bullet to the head. Once all was said and done, he entered his initials, D.W.B., in the second-place slot. I was thoroughly amazed, as I had never seen anyone get that far in the game in my life.

My eyes widened in false amazement. "Second place? Holy shit! I've never seen anyone make it that far before," I said, trying to sound as surprised as humanly possible.

"Good luck beating that," he said while sporting a cocky grin.

After watching someone score second place while making it that far, I knew I had to play my best if I wanted to shut him up. Unfortunately, seeing him make it as far as he did, playing my best meant that I now had to beat the entire game. And that was certainly no easy feat.

After taking a deep breath and cracking all the knuckles on my hands, I inserted my quarter, hit the player one button, and began. Now, it was my turn to play.

I wound up making it through the first three levels easily. I lost my first life on level four (where I usually do) and then another on level five before making it through to the second story. Once I got there, however, I somehow managed to do something I'd never been able to do before.

Maybe it was because I didn't want to lose. Maybe it was because playing video games brought out the best in me. Or maybe it was because I simply didn't want to lose to a little piss ant like him. But whatever it was, I was now officially "in the zone."

I wound up blowing through the sixth level, followed by the seventh and then the eighth. When I got to the ninth level, I wound up losing what would've been my last life just before the end of the level. Thankfully, though, I was awarded a free guy shortly before I died and managed to finish it. However, that was all she wrote.

I plowed through the rest of the final level with ease, making it past the computer and through the weird-looking end part, which wasn't in story one. I then used almost all the ammo I had left to kill the final boss and beat the game, rescuing my fellow agent in the process.

Once I had finished, I entered my initials on the screen in the first place slot, claiming the high score and beating all the other poor saps whose initials were below mine. When that little shit saw me enter the initials W.A.T. at the top, he slowly glared at all the other initials in each of the other slots before getting a confused look on his face.

You see, when I told him that I'd never seen anyone else make it that far in the game before, I technically wasn't lying. What I didn't tell him was that I'd only seen one other person ever make it that far in my life. And that person was me.

Other than second place, which now had his initials, the entire screen had the initials W.A.T. from top to bottom. When he saw that, he looked back up at me with a very pissed-off expression. He immediately knew I played him, and he also knew that I did, in fact, call his bluff.

Knowing that I was victorious and how good it also felt to kick his sorry little ass, I looked at him, gave him a cocky smirk, and shrugged.

"Sorry, kid," I said. "Better luck next time."

"You tricked me," he said. "And I'm not a kid, asshole!"

He then followed that up with another dirty look before huffing smoke out of his nose like a dragon, flipping me the bird, and storming off.

When it was all over, I felt great for beating that little snot-nosed punk and putting him in his place. I mean, could I have taken the high road and just ignored him? Of course, I could've. But what would be the fun in that?

Besides, beating that little dick wasn't why I was there. I was there to play some games with my best friend and have a good time in the process. Although technically, I'd kind of already started without him. And by that point, he'd already missed all the fun. Oh well.

When Eric finally did arrive, it wasn't until ten minutes later, after my *Rolling Thunder* battle, that all five feet, ten inches of his average self came walking up to me.

Eric and I have been best friends since the first grade. We initially met at a birthday party that was being held for a mutual friend and have been close ever since. For the most part, we both have the same likes and dislikes, which basically applies to everything we watch, play, and eat.

Like me, he's also light-skinned. At the time, he had short, dark hair, brown eyes, wore a pair of glasses, and was always decked out in some kind of video game T-shirt, cargo shorts, and those Nike Bruin sneakers Marty McFly wore in *Back to the Future*. As a matter of fact, I also wore those sneakers because that just happened to be one of our favorite movies. Both of us have always been infatuated with the concept of time travel and have seen almost every movie based on it since the late '70s.

Up until that point, some of our favorites included such titles as *Time Bandits, The Terminator* (which we borrowed from a friend and watched when my parents weren't around), *Bill and Ted's Excellent Adventure, Flight of the Navigator, The Philadelphia Experiment,* and, of course, *Back to the Future.* There were also a whole slew of others, which would take up way too much time if I decided to list them all. To this day, we still watch every time-travel film that comes out. We even make it a point to call each other on the phone and discuss the movie afterward.

Eric didn't run track like I did. Instead, he was captain of the school's debate team and beat almost every opponent his squad had faced. And because he was so good at it, no one would dare pick a fight with him. The moment that someone began giving him shit, he would immediately start giving it right back to them, talking about things that would easily make anyone uncomfortable. And when that happened, the other person would quickly back off.

Let's put it this way…he was so good at what he did that he could sell ice cream to an Eskimo in five seconds flat. Plus, everyone knew he was my best friend. And since I was liked by, well, pretty much the entire school, they only got in his face to mess with him.

Actually, the only real difference we had and still have is that he always follows politics. In my opinion, politics can go and suck my big fat hairy balls. I could give absolutely two left testicles about any type of political matters. However, he does make it a point to keep me informed from time to time.

"What's up, dude?" Eric greeted me.

"Oh, nothing much. Other than the fact that I just got finished kicking some punk's ass in a game," I said, then huffed. "Asshole thought he could beat me at *Rolling Thunder*. Can you believe that?"

"But you've beaten that game a million times."

"True. However, he didn't know that," I said before flashing a devilish grin.

"Very nice," Eric replied while golf clapping and slowly nodding his head. "I applaud your deviousness."

"Why, thank you," I said, giving him a nod of my own. "So what game did you want to play today?"

Eric looked up at the ceiling and pretended to think about it before flashing me a guilty smile and responding, *"Rolling Thunder."*

I just laughed before he wound up picking a different game altogether.

He chose a game called *Dig Dug*, which was initially released in Japan by Namco in 1982. Here in North America, however, it was released later that same year by Atari.

In the game, you take control of Dig Dug, who can tunnel down through different layers of dirt to defeat his enemies. One of them is called a Pooka, which is a round, red creature that wears oversized goggles. The other ones are called Frygars, which are basically green dragons who breathe fire.

Dig Dug is equipped only with a bike pump and can defeat his enemies in one of two ways: he can use the bike pump to inflate them with air until they explode, or he can crush them under large falling rocks. As the game progresses, the enemies continue to move faster and faster. And, like most games, whoever has the most points after all their lives are lost wins.

We spent the better part of three hours in the arcade, both of us going back and forth while giving each other a decent ass-kicking. Once we ran out of quarters, we then decided to call it quits and head back to my house.

———————

Swanson, Nevada—a small town consisting of just about ten thousand people, was where I lived at the time. It sits on the northern border of Las Vegas and is located just a few miles from the base of Gass Peak, a mountain named after Octavius Decatur Gass, an early settler and prominent rancher of Las Vegas who died in 1924. Why I just told you that little fact, I have no idea. Apparently, the things I learned in history class seemed to have stuck with me after all these years.

Anyway, I lived on Apple Drive at the end of a circular cul-de-sac in suburbia. The name of our little community was called Swanson North, and the way it was set up kind of reminded me of how Tujunga, California, looked. You know, the town where Elliot lived in the 1982 movie *E.T.*? All the houses were close together, and there was nothing but desert and mountains as far as the eye could see.

My house was the very last one on the street and sat right in the middle of all the others. In fact, once you turned onto my road, you could drive right down the center of it and straight into my driveway without ever having to turn the wheel.

It was a two-story abode made of tan stucco, a red-tiled roof, and a one-car garage located just to the right of the front entrance. Because of the heat, almost all the houses out that way were built using the same materials. We didn't have a pool because we couldn't afford one. However, we did have a finished basement, which was where my parents spent most of their time during the summer because it was nice and cool down there.

The first floor had all the standard rooms that any house would have: a living room, a kitchen, a study, and a bathroom. Our kitchen had many yellow countertops, while the cupboards and cabinets were painted a very light brown. We also had one of those glass tables surrounded by six plastic chairs—the very same plastic chairs supported by a metal bar curved into a sideways *U.* Yup, that was us.

Our living room had a solid-wood coffee table with two side doors that opened on both the right and left sides. I don't even think a wrecking ball could've destroyed that thing. I know I definitely couldn't because I tried many times by jumping from our ugly "grandma's couch," as they called it, onto the top of it, not once denting or scratching the thing. When I did that, the only thing that got dented or scratched was me.

Other than the La-Z-Boy chair, which my father seldom left while he was home, the only other thing in there, aside from our god-awful floor lamps, was an old Zenith wooden console TV. As much as I begged them to get a new one, they just didn't want to part with it.

As for our bathroom, well, let's just say that, at the time, it suffered from a nasty case of what they used to call the Miami Vice effect. Also, if you don't know what that term means, feel free to Google it. And if you do, take caution. You may or may not like what you find.

The second floor of our house had an additional bathroom and three bedrooms. One of the rooms was my parents' room, which was practically forbidden. Another one was basically a spare room that they used solely for storage. And finally, there was my room.

My room was the very last room on the left at the end of the hallway. When you walked in, my bed was perpendicular to the wall and tucked in the far right corner. On the left side of the room was an old, brown wooden entertainment center with a twenty-inch RCA tube TV on top.

Within the wooden monstrosity was my VCR, Nintendo (with about one hundred games), my Atari 2600 (with its own massive collection of games), and my Sony stereo, which I managed to finagle and hook up to my TV, creating my very own surround-sound system.

To the left of my entertainment center, sitting in the corner, was a rickety old computer desk that I had to keep fixing every so often when one of the legs or panels decided to fall off for no particular reason.

On the desk sat my old Apple II computer, complete with dual, 5.25-inch floppy disk drives, a whopping forty-eight kilobytes of RAM, and the processing speed of a snail. We found it a couple of years prior at a yard sale, practically brand new, and got it for an excellent price because the owner simply wanted to get rid of it. And since I needed an upgrade anyway, who was I to say no?

To the right of my entertainment center was my closet, and in between my closet and my bed was an open-view, floor-to-ceiling window. Also, because the window was so big and because I sometimes forgot to close the curtains, I think the neighbors occasionally saw just a little more than they wanted to. Oops.

Eric and I were sitting on the floor in front of my bed, playing some Nintendo while Mötley Crüe blasted out of the stereo system. We were playing a game released earlier that year, and one that I still have never beaten to this day.

Friday the 13th was released by LJN in February of 1989 and was literally one of the most challenging games ever to come out. As you can probably guess, it was based on the movies and involved you running around Camp Crystal Lake as one of six camp counselors. Each counselor had different abilities, such as multiple levels of speed, rowing, and jumping, which allowed you to traverse the camp and save the other counselors and kids.

The object of the game was simple. You had to find and defeat Jason three times (which was no easy feat) before he killed off all the characters you were trying to save. Along the way, you could also upgrade your weapons, which, in my opinion, didn't help at all. The game itself was pretty basic and incredibly difficult.

"Dammit! I can never beat Jason," Eric remarked.

"Who can?" I replied. "I think the makers created this game just to watch us all get pissed off while they laugh at us behind our backs."

He shrugged. "Oh well. Your turn," he said, handing me the controller.

I took the controller and started playing as my fingers danced around it, almost like I was some kind of famed pianist.

As I continued to play, we both sat there in silence. I could tell that something was up because as I sat there, I felt two holes being burned into the side of my right temple.

The only time we were ever that quiet was if we needed to get something off our chests. The only *other* time we were like that was when we watched a movie, in which case we would still yap over the film to dissect every little ridiculous detail.

"All right, spill it," I said. "What's on your mind?"

"I can't believe you're going all the way out to the East Coast for school," Eric said.

"Me either. I'm definitely going to miss you."

"I'll miss you too. But why Florida State? It's so far away."

"Hey, I wasn't going to turn down a full scholarship. Besides, we can still call each other."

All our lives, Eric and I had always planned on going to the same college. That way, we wouldn't be alone. And even though I got accepted to many of the local colleges, getting a full scholarship to one of the best schools in the country was no joke. Eric was upset that he was staying local and attending the only school he applied to.

He was awarded a half scholarship in business by the University of Nevada, Las Vegas. With the type of speaking skills he had, his knack for conversation was remarkable. He might have been disappointed, but his parents, who vowed to throw him a party and celebrate all the money they saved, would've said otherwise.

"But talking on the phone just isn't the same," Eric said.

"I know," I replied. "But at least I'll be coming home for the holidays and summers."

"True. And, speaking of summers…any thoughts on how you want to spend this one?"

Again, with that being the last ever summer of the 1980s, I wanted us to celebrate it in style.

"Hell yeah, I do!" I said. "Do you even realize what this summer actually means?"

His eyes quickly narrowed. "You're going to have to be a little more specific."

"Dude, this is the first summer after finishing high school and the last summer of the 1980s. You and I"—I motioned to both of us—"are going to do some shit we've never done before."

"This isn't going to involve us getting arrested again, is it?"

"No. Besides, that was all just a big misunderstanding."

The moment he was referring to actually happened a couple of years prior, shortly after we finished tenth grade.

I'd gotten invited to a party that was being held at Darren's house. At the time, Darren was the star running back for our school's football team and was quite popular.

Instead of partying with all the other kids, Eric and I were down in the basement, just checking out the place while trying to distance ourselves from any of the ruckus. Even though a few of the kids were drinking and smoking, we knew better than to get involved. So we just sat down there, played some games, and minded our own business.

However, a couple of hours into the party, we heard some shouting, followed by some banging coming from upstairs. With the majority of the partygoers being jocks, we just thought they were playing a rousing game of indoor football or something. As it turned out, they weren't.

It wasn't until the cops started hauling ass down the stairs to arrest us that we realized they weren't playing football. Afterward, we found out that one of the neighbors called the authorities, complaining about a bunch of underage kids having a party and getting drunk.

Thankfully, though, when our parents came down to the police station to get us, they believed our story after the cops told them that our breathalyzer tests came back negative. We were extremely relieved when they decided to ground us for only a couple of days instead of the rest of our lives.

————————

"Okay then. If it doesn't involve the cops, what did you have in mind?" Eric asked.

I shrugged. "I don't know. But I'm sure I'll think of something."

We both just sat there while we tried to think of anything we could possibly do to make that summer epic. However, both of our minds were totally blank. That is, until Eric said something to me that would change the rest of our lives forever.

"You do that," he said. "In the meantime, I do know of one thing we could do."

"Oh yeah? What's that?" I asked, curious.

"There are a couple of girls from school who are holding a joint birthday party on Saturday. I figured we could go."

"Do we know them?"

"No. But apparently, they graduated with us."

I immediately narrowed my eyes, paused the game, and turned to look at him.

"Who are they?" I asked.

He shrugged. "No one knows. But they invited our entire graduating class."

Since I knew almost everyone in our school, I was suddenly super intrigued about who they were.

"What are their names?" I asked.

"Anna and Eve. I think," he replied.

I quickly took a moment and tapped every brain cell in my head to try to remember anyone named Anna or Eve. I mean, two girls we graduated with were throwing a party, and I'd never heard of them?

After a few seconds of intense thought, my mind was a complete blank.

"I don't ever recall meeting anyone with those names," I said.

"Me either," Eric said. "Which is why we should go."

"Hmm…going to a party for a couple of girls we don't even know. Are you feeling okay?"

I only asked him that last question because Eric has never been the type of person to just show up at some random party. Usually, he likes to try to get to know someone first before hanging out with them. But, since the entire class got invited, he probably figured he would know a few people. Plus, with me being his best friend and knowing, well, pretty much everyone, he had a good feeling he would be okay.

I then turned to him again and gave him a half-grin, just like a supervillain would when they're planning on doing something devious. But I didn't say anything just yet.

Seeing this, he leaned slightly away and was now pointing at me, a nervous expression building on his face.

"Why are you grinning at me like that?" he asked nervously.

"Eric, my friend," I said, resting a hand on his shoulder. "I think you and I are going to start this summer off with a bang."

"Again, as long as the cops aren't involved, then count me in."

"You're never going to let that go, are you?"

We argued about the one and only time the cops arrested us for about another hour or so. That was also how much longer we each lasted facing off against Jason. And by that point, we'd gotten sliced and diced so much that we decided to call it a day.

18

CHAPTER 2

The following day, Eric and I were finally going to begin our summer movie fest and start ticking off all the films on our list. Now, even though our town wasn't as big as some of the surrounding ones, we were still lucky enough to have the choice of which movie theater we wanted to go to.

The first option we had was a place called Empire Cinema, which was located in the northern part of town. It was built sometime in the early 1940s and had gone through quite a few renovations since then.

At the time, it had around ten different theaters and always showed most of the latest films. Because it was a slightly older building, it also featured a bunch of classics as well. And since it competed with the newly built complex in the southern part of town, the prices were slightly lower. We would usually only go to that one when there was an old movie playing we really wanted to see. But once the new Megaplex was built, we almost stopped going there altogether.

The Megaplex was a brand new, state-of-the-art building boasting a whopping twenty theaters. All the latest movies that came out were usually shown in multiple auditoriums, so you didn't have to worry about missing them. Since we didn't have the internet back then, you had to wait in a long ass line to buy your tickets. If you didn't get there early enough, you wound up missing out, resulting in you purchasing a ticket for a different showing.

The Megaplex had new seats, refreshment stands, carpeting, and basically new everything. The prices were a little higher, but to sit in brand-new chairs that somewhat reclined was definitely worth it. Also, in my opinion, other than that theater being brand new, it wasn't really all that different from the other one. Sadly, though, Empire Cinema only lasted a couple more years before it went bankrupt and lost out to the Megaplex. It has since been torn down and is no longer there.

The first movie we checked off our summer blockbuster list was *Ghostbusters II,* which was directed by the great Ivan Reitman, who also directed the first one.

Now, if you haven't seen this movie yet, feel free to do one of the following: either skip past this part to avoid any spoilers or never speak to me again. Yes, I know it wasn't as good as the first, but it's still a must-see classic.

Okay then. Still here? Great.

Ghostbusters II takes place five years after the events of the first one and follows the continuing exploits of Peter Venkman, Ray Stantz, Egon Spengler, and Winston Zeddmore.

In the movie, the guys had all pretty much disbanded after suffering multiple lawsuits and going bankrupt in the process. It wasn't until a river of slime was discovered underneath New York City that the boys decided to come out of retirement and fight an ancient Carpathian sorcerer named Vigo. Vigo was attempting to be reborn by taking over the body of Dana Barrett's infant son, Oscar. Of course, the Ghostbusters eventually wind up defeating Vigo while saving the city and their reputations in the process.

Just about two and a half hours later (one hour and fifty minutes for the movie and the rest previews), we emerged from the Megaplex as a couple of *very* delighted men.

"That was actually pretty good," I said.

"I agree," Eric replied. "I mean, it wasn't as good as the first one, but it was still pretty damn good."

"That part when they were in the tunnel," I said with a laugh, "with all the heads on the stakes, followed by the ghost train…that was probably my favorite part of the movie."

"That was pretty funny. Mine was when they drenched the Statue of Liberty in slime. I mean, a moving, walking statue? That was awesome!"

"Definitely a sure-fire classic."

As we headed to my car, my stomach began to growl like a hungry tiger.

"I'm starving," I said. "Are you hungry?"

"Dude! Are you kidding me right now?" Eric said in disbelief. "After all the shit you ate in there, you're still hungry?"

By the end of the movie, I was starving. I mean, there was only so much a large bag of popcorn, a large soda, a bag of Sour Patch Kids, and a box of Nerds could do. I mean, shit. I was still a teenager. In two and a half hours, I could've devoured a house.

"Hey, I'm a growing boy," I responded. "What do you want from me?"

"Got that right. At least we now know who the man in this friendship is," Eric joked before snickering to himself.

"Ha-ha. Very funny, jackass."

"I'm just messing with you," he said. "Actually, I could go for a bite myself."

"What did you have in mind?"

He thought about it for maybe two seconds before looking up at me with a grin spanning from ear to ear.

———————

Even though he loved the place and knew I didn't like going there when I wasn't working, he wanted to eat at Johnny's Café. But because I was so hungry and didn't feel like traveling very far to fill my empty stomach, I happily obliged.

Johnny's Café was located just a couple of blocks from the Megaplex. And because of its proximity, it was a very popular place for the people who didn't buy any movie snacks to eat afterward.

During the summer and on weekends and nights when school was in session, Johnny's was a trendy place for the teenagers to hang out. When they weren't taking it over, it was either half-filled with adults or pretty much empty.

The café was probably about double the size of your typical, everyday, hole-in-the-wall joint and was built in the late '50s. It hadn't been renovated since then, except for the occasional new seat, bench, kitchen grill, or whatever. And because of that, it managed to retain its old-fashioned look, which was probably another reason why it was so popular.

To the left and right of the entrance were booths. In front of those was a line of tables and chairs, which spanned from one wall to the other. Just beyond those was the counter, which basically looked like a giant *U* with barstools lining the entire thing. There were also three entrances into and out of the kitchen: one in the far back left corner, one in the far back right corner, and one directly behind the counter.

When we walked inside, the place was packed with wall-to-wall high school kids. Eric and I managed to sit down in the only two seats available—two stools, all the way on the front right of the U-shaped counter, with our backs facing the door.

On the far left wall was a jukebox, which played almost everything current at the time. There was a solid mix of rock, pop, country, and hip-hop, all dating back to the early '80s. There wasn't anything playing when we entered, as it was probably in the middle of a song change. However, no sooner did we cop a squat, "Heaven Is a Place on Earth" by Belinda Carlisle started blasting from its speakers.

And, speaking of Belinda Carlisle (also, not many people know this about me), back then, I had a *massive* crush on her. Not to mention, I bought all her tapes and CDs, including the ones dating back to her stint with The Go-Go's. Of course, now that I've told you this, you must burn the rest of these pages and never speak of it again. If you didn't just follow my instructions and are still reading this, then please feel free to enjoy the rest of the story and ignore my previous comment.

Okay, let's get back to it.

The moment we sat down, one of the waitresses behind the counter immediately approached us. She wore a blue 1950s carhop waitress uniform (minus the roller skates). She had long, copper-red hair pulled back into a ponytail, blue eyes as bright as the sky, and a smile that could light up a room. Her name was Tammy Macintyre. And while I had just graduated, come fall, she would be starting her senior year.

I met her two years prior when I started working at the café. She wasn't working there just yet, but would always come in every Friday, right after school, to do some homework. After a few weeks of working there, I noticed that she would come in more often and only on the days I worked. That was when I figured out she wasn't coming in just for the friendly service. She had a massive crush on me. And even though I thought she was gorgeous, I didn't feel the same way. There was just something about her that turned me off. I didn't figure out what it was until a little later, when I quickly discovered that she was basically stalking me.

Now, being the nice guy I am, I could never bring myself to tell her I never liked her. Instead, I just wound up making petty excuses as to why I couldn't go out with her every time she asked me. I mean, did I feel guilty about it? A little. Is it something that haunts me to this day? Not one bit.

"Hey, Eric," Tammy greeted him before turning to me and smiling. "Hi, Wes," she said, her face as red as a tomato.

"Hey, Tammy," Eric replied.

"Hey, gorgeous," I said.

Okay, yes, I always told Tammy that she was beautiful, and I also tended to flirt with her a lot. But come on. Can you really blame me?

"So what'll it be?" she asked us.

"I'll have a double with cheese, an order of fries, and a chocolate milkshake," Eric said.

"Good choice." She then turned to me. "And how about you, handsome?"

"I'll have the Reuben special and a double-thick chocolate milkshake," I said.

"Coming right up. Don't go anywhere."

She then walked away from me like she always did, hoping to get a rise out of me. And not in that way either, you pervert.

She simply turned around, threw her ass slightly out, and walked toward the kitchen, strutting like a supermodel. It was, more or less, her way of trying to make me see what I was missing out on.

"How is it that you never went out with her?" Eric asked.

I shrugged. "I don't know. I just never felt the same way about her as she feels about me."

"You do know she turns down every guy that asks her out, right?"

I quickly narrowed my eyes. "She does? Why?"

"Because she's waiting for you to ask her out, dumbass."

"Well, she'll be waiting a while then."`

"Let me ask you this," he began before pausing. "Do you really want to start college a virgin?"

"Shh!" I said, my finger covering my lips. "Not so loud, asshole. Besides, you should be one to talk."

"Hey, it's no secret that I'm holding out. But you have it easier than anyone I've ever known."

"How so?"

He answered me quietly. "Dude, if you were to ask Tammy out, you'd get laid before you guys even left her front yard."

I sighed. "I know. But I can't go out with her just to get laid."

"Why not?"

"Seriously?" I asked, suddenly thinking that my best friend, whom I'd known my whole life, didn't even know me at all. "Look, if I even have to explain it to you, then I—"

However, I never finished my thought, as Tammy swiftly interrupted us by bringing out our food.

"Okay. One cheeseburger, fries, and a chocolate shake for you," she said, placing Eric's order down in front of him. "One Reuben special and a double-thick chocolate shake for you," she finished, placing the latter down in front of me.

"Thanks, Tammy," I said with a smile and a wink.

She smiled, giggled, and turned another shade of red, which seemed to bring out the freckles on her face.

"Can I get you boys anything else?" she asked.

Eric and I both looked at each other before shaking our heads.

"We're good for now," I said.

"Okay then. Enjoy your food," she replied before turning around and leaving.

As soon as Tammy was out of view, I could feel two holes being burned into the side of my head. That was when I turned to look at Eric, who was slowly shaking his head while giving me a very disappointed look.

"What?" I asked with a shrug.

He slowly shook his head. "Man, she has it bad for you."

"I already told you I'm not interested."

"Okay," he said before facing forward and picking up his burger. "Whatever you say."

"You're never going to let this go, are you?"

"Nope."

I let out a disgusted sigh. "Fine," I said. "I'll tell you what…if I'm still a virgin by the end of the summer, I'll ask her out before I leave for school."

"Get the fuck out of here," he said, doubting every word I just told him. "No, you won't."

"Oh, yes, I will. And do you know why?"

"Why?"

"Because you're right," I said.

"I am?" he asked, shocked I would admit that.

"For once in your life…yeah. Besides, I think I've waited long enough, and I will *not* go off to college a virgin."

He grinned and gave me a slow nod of approval. "Okay then. That's more like it," he said before chowing down on his burger.

I then picked up my Reuben and held it in my hands. I stared at it and drooled before taking a monster bite. The flavor of the Russian dressing, Swiss cheese, sauerkraut, and corned beef exploded in my mouth the moment it touched my tongue. And for that one brief moment, I forgot about everything else going on around me as I focused on the goodness sloshing in between my teeth.

For me, every time I go to a restaurant, I always look over the menu to find something I like. If nothing tickles my fancy, or if I'm not in the mood to try anything new, I always order my default go-to meal—one that I know I will enjoy no matter where it's made—a Reuben. And even though this has nothing to do with the story, I just figured I'd share it anyway.

"What are you going to wear to the party tomorrow?" I asked, chomping on a mouthful of food.

"I have no idea. You?" Eric replied.

"I don't know. I'll probably wear my MTV T-shirt, a new pair of Bugle Boys, and my Nikes."

"Good choice. However, I'm still undecided as to what kind of shoes I want to wear. I was thinking of either my British Knights or my L.A. Gear. What do you think?"

"Hmm," I grunted before thinking about it. "I say go with the L.A. Gear. Definitely a better-looking shoe, in my opinion."

"Good thinking. L.A. Gear it is."

"It just sucks that I got to work," I added.

"You're only working until seven, and the party doesn't start until eight," Eric pointed out. "That gives you an hour to get home, shower, get dressed, and go."

"You do bring up a valid point."

"Your shift will fly by, and you'll be done before you know it."

"I sure hope you're right."

"Of course, I am. Besides," he said before turning to smile at me, "you always have Tammy to keep you company."

"You're such a dick," I replied, and then produced a playful grin of my own.

We spent the better part of two hours in there, discussing all sorts of things like video games, movie theories, and girls while we finished our delicious food. He also couldn't help but bust my ass about why I'd never gone out with Tammy before. Of course, the only response I could muster up was for him to simply fuck off.

ROB J. LABELLE

CHAPTER 3

The following day at work, I had to deal with the usual customers, which, unfortunately, consisted of typical, snotty, bratty teenagers. I also did my usual flirting with Tammy for a good chunk of the morning.

And I already know what you're going to say about that, so save it. You can hate me later.

Once seven pm rolled around, I finally finished my shift at the café before punching out, hopping in my tan 1987 Ford Bronco, and speeding home in record time. I wound up paying for my truck just a couple of weeks before graduation with the money I'd saved up while working at the café.

Okay, maybe my parents might have helped me out a little, but about eighty percent of the down payment was mine.

Once I stepped foot in the door, my mom immediately stopped me to ask her usual million questions about how my day was and if anything riveting happened at work.

Beverley Tucker stood about five feet, seven inches tall and had semi-long dark hair that stopped just below her shoulders. Like me, she also had blue eyes and was very much on the slim side. She and my dad had me when they were in their early twenties and did everything they could to give me the best life possible.

At the time, my mom worked at one of the local banks as a teller, while my dad, James, or Jim (which was what he preferred), worked hard labor at a nearby rock quarry. However, my dad wasn't home that night because he was at one of his friends' houses playing his usual weekly poker games with his buddies.

"Hey, Wes!" my mom yelled out from the kitchen. "How was your day?"

Although I didn't mind chit-chatting with her, I had a minimal amount of time to get ready and make it to the party.

"It was okay," I replied.

"Did anything exciting happen?"

"Not really. You know, it was work."

I tried to double-time it to the stairs, hoping to avoid any more questions. But I only managed to reach the bottom step before another one came flying in my direction.

"Wait! Where are you going?" she asked.

I quietly sighed before turning to face her. "Mom, I have that party to go to. Remember?" I replied.

"Oh, right. The one for the girls?" she asked.

"That's the one."

"What time does it start?"

"It starts at eight. Which means I have about forty-five minutes to shower, dress, and get there."

"Oh, okay. Well then, I don't want to…"

But that was all I got to hear her say. Before she could finish her sentence, I was already at the top of the stairs, stripping my clothes off, and on my way to the bathroom.

———

About an hour and fifteen minutes later, after taking one of the quickest showers of my life, getting dressed in record time, and basically speeding over to the house on the opposite side of town where the party was, I finally arrived. I was wearing my Bugle Boy jeans, my red MTV T-shirt, and my Nikes (ala Marty McFly), just as I said I would.

Oh, and by the way, the words MUSIC TELEVISION were printed underneath the three-lettered MTV logo. That was back during a time when they actually showed music videos around the clock, had VJs (or video jockeys for all you younger folks), and kept you up to date on all the latest music news. As for today's programming, let's just say I'm glad we have the internet. Fuck you, reality TV!

Anyway, I pulled up to the front of the house, which was about a million times the size of my own. Cars lined the street on both sides as far as the eye could see. Whoever lived there was obviously doing pretty well for themselves.

I pulled into the half-moon-shaped driveway and was greeted by the valet. That was the first and only time I'd ever been to someone's house and didn't have to park my own car. As soon as I got out, the gentleman handed me a ticket before hopping in, closing the door, and driving off. I won't lie. For a brief moment, I felt like some big celebrity going to a Hollywood party or something.

Once my car left the driveway and was out of sight, I turned to face this monstrosity of a house. I could immediately hear loud, muffled music blasting out through the walls. There were also two massive strobe lights, one on each side of the front walk, moving back and forth as they shone up to the heavens.

I started walking up to the front door, located beneath an overhang supported by two giant stone pillars. Once I got up there, a muscular dude, just about the size of the Hulk and wearing a security outfit, was standing there, holding a copy of our school yearbook. I was a little confused about why, but I quickly figured it out once he asked me who I was.

"How's it going?" I asked, nodding once.

"Pretty good," he answered in a low, deep voice. "Name?"

"Uh, Wesley Tucker."

Wasting no time, Mr. Muscles opened the yearbook and flipped through the pages before finding my senior picture. He then pulled out a marker and wrote in it, most likely crossing out my photo or putting a check mark next to it, letting him know it was really me and that I was already here.

"Thank you," he said, giving me a nod of his own. "Go in and have a good time."

I smiled. "Thanks a lot."

He then grabbed the shiny gold handle and opened the massive door, allowing me to walk right inside.

I entered a massive, open foyer with stairs that ran up and down the wall's left and right sides. Apparently, the upstairs was off-limits because a gate blocked access to both sets. Directly in front of me was a counter, with a couple of people standing behind it, checking jackets, sweatshirts, and any other items that people may not have wanted to bring in with them.

The room to my left blasted hip-hop music, while the room to my right blasted rock music. Thankfully, though, it wasn't too loud in there. Because, along with the soundproof rooms, the somewhat soundproof doors dropped the noise down to a low, tolerable muffle.

The first thing on my to-do list was to find Eric and see what he was up to. And seeing as how I could probably get lost in that house, I had no idea where to even begin. So I just stood there and listened to the two rooms, instantly recognizing the songs coming out of each one. After a few moments, I decided to start in the room to my left.

I walked through the doors and into the darkened room, which was big enough to fit a DJ booth, a stage, and about one hundred people. The dance floor took up about half of the room and was made up of brightly lit squares that kept changing colors on a timed rotation. In the back of the room was, in fact, a DJ. Not only was he standing behind the booth mixing, but he was also providing sound for whoever was rapping up on stage in the front of the room.

Now, I was never a fan of the late '80s, early '90s gangster rap shit, but I did love some of the more old-school, classic hip-hop. You know, artists like Run-DMC, Biz Markie, DJ Jazzy Jeff & The Fresh Prince, Salt-N-Pepa, and the Beastie Boys.

Okay, let's face it—that last one is a little on the fence because they were a mix of both rap and rock. But I think you get the picture.

Anyway, the colored lights on the floor really made the break dancers and regular dancers look like they were in one of those old-school music videos. But when I saw who was up on that stage singing, my mouth literally hit the floor. Whoever had thrown that party had enough money to hire an old-school hip-hop artist. Well, he's old school now. But at the time, he was brand new. The person they hired was someone I loved as a singer and someone I would also love later on when he became an actor.

He was semi-famous at the time, with a few hits already under his belt. Stuff like "I Can't Live Without My Radio," "Rock the Bells," "I Need Love," "Goin' Back to Cali," and "Jingling Baby." But this guy didn't really break out until a year later, when he would release his fourth studio album on August 27, 1990.

It was a small, tiny album entitled *Mama Said Knock You Out* by some dude named—I don't know—for the story's sake, let's just call him James Todd Smith. Or perhaps you know him by his stage name? That's right. I'm talking about none other than LL Cool J.

Apparently, whoever owned that house either knew him personally or paid him to perform there that night. And judging by the type of party they were throwing, they could easily afford it.

I just stood in that room for a good ten minutes before realizing that I, myself, was getting sucked into the music and the atmosphere. However, I wasn't there to have fun. At least, not yet.

So I quickly snapped out of it and exited to try to locate Eric. Next up on my search was the room across the hall blasting rock music.

The room on the other side of the foyer was set up pretty much like the hip-hop room, minus the lit squares on the floor. The back of the room had a sound booth with two guys working behind it to keep the band playing in front of the room from feeding back.

Now, everyone who knows me knows that rock music was and is my forte. I listened to a ton of different bands, dating all the way back to the mid-'70s. However, to this day, rock music of the 1980s is still my favorite.

Some of the stuff I listened to ranged from Aerosmith, Def Leppard, and Guns N' Roses all the way up to Krokus, Slaughter, and Van Halen. And I wasn't limited to just the hair bands either. Some of the heavier stuff, like Anthrax, Megadeth, and Metallica, were also favorites of mine. Of course, I would be amiss if I didn't mention my favorite band of all time—Mötley Crüe.

From the moment their first album came out in 1980, I was hooked. And while I was in my third year of college, I got their *Dr. Feelgood* logo and album name tattooed on my right bicep.

Dr. Feelgood was released on September 1, 1989, and would go on to be my favorite album of all time. I later realized that it would also be their best-selling album in the band's history. (Go figure.) But again, I digress.

Just like the up-and-coming rap icon on stage in the hip-hop room, they hired an up-and-coming rock band to play there as well. Sadly, in my opinion, the band playing that night didn't have as much success as the bands I just mentioned, but they were still one of my favorites. They were a five-piece band that released their self-titled debut album on January 4, 1988. But you might know them as L.A. Guns.

Their first album produced hits like "Sex Action," "Bitch is Back," and "Electric Gypsy." But they really scored big with their August 22, 1989 release of *Cocked & Loaded*. That had a lot of their more popular stuff on it, like "Rip and Tear," "Never Enough," and "The Ballad of Jayne."

I walked into the room right in the middle of them playing "Shoot for Thrills." Again, just like the other room, I got caught up in the music and intrigue of how the hell the party-throwers could afford those guys. But after another ten minutes of rocking out, I came to my senses and realized that I had to go and find Eric. So I walked up the left side of the wall and exited through the back of the room.

Once I walked through the door, I found myself inside one of the dining rooms. Yes, there was more than one. The other one was located just beyond the hip-hop room.

Between the two dining rooms was the kitchen, which was set up pretty much like something you would see in a restaurant. And although I wasn't allowed to go in there, I could still peek through the window in the door. I guess with the number of people who showed up to that thing, a huge kitchen and two dining rooms were needed to feed everyone.

Both dining rooms were set up pretty much as mirror images of each other. Four smaller round tables in each corner of the room held stuff like napkins, plates, cups, hors d'oeuvres, etc. The big wooden table in the middle of both, which sat about fifty chairs, each held something different.

The room I was in had all the snacks, drinks, and food. The other room had all the desserts, along with both cakes. Each room also had a fancy glass chandelier hanging from the ceiling in the middle, acting as both a light source and a decoration. However, with Eric still nowhere to be found, and although I was beginning to drool at the sight of all the food, I quickly moved on.

Also, in each dining room was a set of double glass doors that slid open and led out to a stone balcony, which ran the entire length of the back of the house. It had two sets of stairs that went down to the backyard: one on the far left and one on the far right. A white stone railing ran across the front of it, spanning from one staircase to the other.

As I scoped out the entire platform, I finally found Eric standing in the middle, leaning on the railing and looking out over the ridiculously enormous backyard. But when I went over to stand next to him, I couldn't speak. I looked out and saw something that, up until then, I had only seen in the movies.

Just below the railing was a fountain with a stone mermaid in the center of it. She wore a shell bikini top and was playing a stone harp. She looked upward at a slight angle as she spewed water from her mouth. The entire base of the fountain was completely encompassed and lit up with lights.

The rest of the backyard, which was about the length of a football field, had a rose garden with some benches. Those allowed people to sit down and relax while they enjoyed the gentle fragrance. In the far back of the yard was a small, perfectly trimmed hedge maze.

I simply could not believe what I was looking at and just muttered under my breath, the only thing that came to my mind at that exact moment. "Fucking hell!"

"Right? How awesome is this?" Eric asked me. "Who the hell can afford something like this?"

"I have no idea," I responded, still mesmerized by everything.

"Dude, where the fuck have you been? I've been standing here waiting for you for like, ever."

"Sorry. I got stopped by my mom at the house, and she just talked my ear off. You know how she is."

"The woman does like to talk."

"Plus, I got stuck inside listening to the music," I said, motioning toward the two rooms. "I mean, LL Cool J and L.A. Guns? Holy shit!"

Eric turned to face the house. "They definitely spared no expense."

"And the people. I mean, what did these girls do, invite the whole town? I thought it was supposed to be just the graduating senior class?"

Eric shrugged. "You got me."

"And, speaking of which," I curiously began to ask. "Where are they?"

"Who? The girls?"

"No. The *Killer Clowns from Outer Space*," I sarcastically remarked. "Yes, the girls."

"Again, I have no clue."

After a few moments of thought, we both just shrugged before turning and facing the backyard. As we looked out over its beauty, however, something hit me. Something began racing through my mind that seemed so obvious, I couldn't believe no one had brought it up yet.

"Don't you find it a little odd?" I asked.

Eric furrowed his brows. "Find what odd?"

"Look around you," I said, motioning to the whole place. "Two girls, whom no one has ever heard of or seen before, invite the entire senior class to a birthday party at a goddamn mansion." I held up a finger. "Which, by the way, could easily be featured on an episode of *Lifestyles of the Rich and Famous*. And yet, no one has ever seen them? Aren't they supposed to be popular or something?"

"That's what I've heard."

"Well then, where the hell are they?"

"Maybe they want to keep a low profile," a female voice rang out behind us.

Hearing that, both Eric and I immediately turned around to see who it was. However, when we did, both sets of our eyes jumped out of our heads while our jaws broke on the stone ground below.

The girl standing before Eric was thin with light skin and stood about five feet, eight inches tall. She had gorgeous blue eyes and a smile that could light up a room. Her dark brown hair had bangs that dropped to just above her eyebrows. A black scrunchie sat on the top of her head, holding the rest of her hair back in a ponytail. She also wore a pair of diamond earrings and a black mini-skirt dress with two straps that went over her shoulders, tying around the back of her neck—a pair of black high heels finished off the ensemble. Not to mention, she wasn't alone.

The girl standing in front of me also had light skin and stood about five feet, ten inches tall, just a couple of inches shorter than me. Her teased blonde hair, hoop earrings, and brown eyes worked perfectly together, while her smile practically made me weak in the knees.

She wore the same dress as her friend, except that hers was red and accented every single curve of her athletically built body. Her high heels, which made her seem just as tall as I was, were also red.

"Are you guys enjoying the party?" the one in red asked us.

But seeing those two girls standing there, staring at us, smiling, and looking all smoking hot, neither one of us could say a word. We just stood there like statues while we practically drooled all over ourselves. Even I, who was pretty popular in school and had no problem talking to anyone, couldn't even muster up a simple hello.

They looked just like most of the girls at our senior prom. But for some reason, we couldn't help but stare at them. Both of us instantly fell head over heels for these girls, and at the same time, couldn't figure out why. However, later on in this story, it eventually becomes pretty clear.

"Have you tried any of the food yet?" the blonde asked.

When we didn't answer, they both turned to look at each other, confused about why we were speechless, before turning back toward us.

"How about the music? Are you enjoying that?" the brunette asked.

At that moment, even though nothing came out of my mouth, I swear I could feel myself moving it while attempting to get some words out. But because I was still emulating a mute, the blonde quickly narrowed her eyes.

"Are you okay?" she asked. "Do you want a cup of water or something?"

And because I still hadn't responded, they shifted their attention to Eric, who pretty much gave them the same response I did.

"Are you sure you guys are okay?" the brunette asked.

And that was when Eric did something even I couldn't do.

He dug deep into his own brain and had it override the "stupid feature" currently taking over. And once that happened, he managed to give them a nod, letting them know that we were okay—in a manner of speaking.

Both girls immediately giggled at his reaction.

"You guys are cute," the blonde said.

"Yeah. We've never met anyone who's been speechless around us before," the brunette added.

Even though nothing was coming out, I just continued to stand there like a moron and move my mouth. When I did, they couldn't help but giggle once again.

"Okay, well, when you guys are ready to talk," the brunette began, "my name's Anna." She then thumbed toward the blonde. "And this is my friend, Eve."

"And since you both already know that this is our party," Eve added, "when you're ready to talk, you know where to find us."

"Until then, see you, boys."

And on that note, they each gave us one more smile before waving and turning around to walk away.

Once they were out of sight, Eric and I finally managed to break from our statue-like poses. We also managed to stop drooling on ourselves. (Figuratively speaking, of course.) After we came to, we both turned to look at each other, shocked about who had just spoken to us and what had transpired.

"Holy shit, dude!" Eric said. "That was them!"

"I hadn't noticed," I nonchalantly responded.

"And we just stood here like a couple of assholes."

"Speak for yourself."

Eric shook his head. "No. Don't give me that 'speak for yourself' bullshit. You were just as pathetic as I was."

"Not as pathetic as those shoelaces," I responded, pointing down to his feet.

He immediately looked down at his shoes before looking back up at me.

"What's wrong with my shoelaces?" he asked.

"What *isn't* wrong with your shoelaces?" I said, completely doubting his fashion choice. "I mean, neon green? Really?"

"What's wrong with neon green?"

"Dude, no one wears neon green anymore."

"What the fuck are you talking about? Everyone wears neon green."

"Oh yeah? Okay then, tell me"—I folded my arms—"what color are my shoelaces?"

Eric quickly looked down at my feet before looking back up at me. "They're white. So what?" he said.

"So what? Your shoes probably scared them away."

"Yeah, well, it was probably your face that scared them away."

"*Ooooh!* Did you think of that one all by yourself?"

He sneered at me. "Shut up!"

Of course, since we were both just messing around like we always did, it didn't take us long to shrug off our insults and return to normal.

"Also, tell me you didn't see what I just saw?" I asked.

"That depends," he said, intrigued by my question.

"Depends on what?"

"If you saw the same thing I saw."

I pointed to him. "You saw it too?"

"How could I not?"

"In that case, why don't we go find them and give it another shot?"

"You know," he said, wagging a finger at me, "that's the best idea you've had in a long time."

I quickly flipped him the bird before we left the stone balcony to begin our search for the girls. We also wanted to prove that we weren't going crazy and that we did, in fact, see something highly unusual.

CHAPTER 4

When the time finally came for Eric and me to have a conversation with the stars of the party, neither of us could say a word. We stood perfectly still like a couple of morons and said nothing when we could've been chatting up the two most beautiful girls there.

As a matter of fact, if you were to open the dictionary to the word moron, you would see our faces plastered right next to it. Of course, if that happened now, you wouldn't need an actual dictionary. You could just look it up online.

Once we left our drool spots behind and each grabbed a fresh pair of underwear, we continued our search for the girls.

And, by the way, that was only a metaphor. We didn't really need to change our underwear—yet.

We must've searched for a good couple of hours before we finally found them. The reason it took us so long was because we stopped to enjoy the live music and sample some of the delicious food.

The first room we looked in was the rock room. When we walked through the door that led in from the dining room, we somehow managed to zig-zag our way through the crowd of metalheads, who were all still rocking out. Once we got to the very back, we each took a different side (me on the left and Eric on the right) to scan the room for the girls.

However, just as we were about to leave, we got stopped by Zack Martin, a big-haired, jean jacket with patches, ripped jeans, and

Converse shoes-wearing rocker. Everyone in the school knew him because of his insanely impressive guitar skills and thought he would make it big someday, especially me.

Earlier that year, when his drummer was sick, I stepped in and jammed with him at a few of his practices while getting a first-hand look at how good he really was. I also figured that my ten years of drum lessons would finally pay off somehow. As it turned out, yes and no.

He had heard me play a couple of years prior and knew that I was good enough to get the job done. Unfortunately, after his drummer got better, I was finished.

He also said that once he graduated, his band Needle Point would finally have the time to record and put out an original album. Of course, tensions within the band soon squashed any real dream he had of doing that. Go figure.

"Yo, Wes! How's it hanging?" Zack shouted to me over the music.

"What's up, Zack!" I shouted back.

"I can't believe they got these guys to play at this party."

"Me, either."

"I'm telling you, one day, these guys are going to kick some serious ass!"

"I don't doubt it," I said, practically ignoring him to scan the room. "Hey, have you seen Anna and Eve?"

"Who?" he asked, confused.

"Anna and Eve. You know, the two girls whose party this is?"

"Oh, them. No," Zack responded while shaking his head. "Sorry, dude."

"Don't worry about it."

"Hey, awesome fact about these guys, they were—"

"Sorry, Zack," I said, swiftly interrupting him. "But I got to go. Rock on!"

"Yeah, right. Later, Wes!" he said, giving me the devil horns.

As much as I hate to admit this, regrettably, that was the last conversation I ever had with Zack.

During my senior year of college, I read a news story about a couple of local addicts who went out one night after finishing up their stint in rehab. They had partied just a little too hard and were found dead of an apparent overdose in some slum, shitty apartment. Of course, to no one's surprise, Zack was one of the locals who overdosed and died—poor guy.

After Eric and I left the room, we skipped across the main foyer, almost making it into the hip-hop room, before getting stopped by someone standing against the wall underneath the left set of stairs. The moment she said hi, we immediately knew who it was.

Sally Vennis was a straight-A student and had been ever since kindergarten. She had the most beautiful and perfect smile that anyone had ever seen. She could thank a phenomenal dentist and some braces for that. Unfortunately, the only problem was that back then, she was considered a total dork, and nobody wanted to hang out with her.

She had long, dark hair, always pulled into pigtails, brown eyes, and was dressed almost in a way that would make Steve Urkel jealous. The only two things she really had going for her, other than her smile, were her generous personality and insatiably sexy voice. She had one of those voices where, if you were to hear her on the phone and then meet her in person after having never met her before, you would agree that her voice does not go with her looks. Also, Eric and I were pretty much the only friends she had.

"Hey, Eric! Hey, Wes!" she called out enthusiastically.

"Hey, Sally," Eric said.

"Hi, Sally," I said.

"Where are you guys off to in such a hurry?" she asked.

"Well, we're looking for someone," Eric said.

"A couple of someone's, actually," I added.

"Anyone I know?" she asked.

"Yeah. Anna and Eve."

"Oh," she said, slightly disappointed.

"Have you seen them?"

She sighed. "No. I haven't seen them at all."

Because of how she responded, Eric and I shot each other a curious glance before turning back toward her.

"Are you okay?" I asked. "You don't seem too thrilled right now."

"Yeah. Don't worry about me. I'll be fine," she replied.

"Okay. Spit it out. What's the matter?" Eric asked, sounding slightly annoyed.

"Well, the reason why I haven't seen them is because I haven't seen anyone all night. You're the first two people to actually stop and talk to me."

In a way, we kind of felt bad for her. I mean, yes, we may have been her only friends, but she definitely didn't deserve to be ignored like that. Nobody does.

"Have you been standing here all night?" I asked, curious.

"Not the whole night," she replied. "Only since eight-thirty."

"Sally, the party started at eight. What time did you get here?" Eric asked.

"Eight twenty-five."

"Eight twenty-five? That's practically all night!"

"Jesus, Sally. Why didn't you come and find us earlier?" I asked.

"I don't know. I guess I didn't want to bother you," she replied.

Both of us, in unison, let out a deep sigh as we suddenly felt even worse for hearing what she'd just told us.

"Sally, I'm sorry," I said.

"It's not your fault," she replied.

"I'll tell you what…we're going to take one more stroll around this place to try and find them. Then, after we get a chance to talk to them, we'll come back and spend the rest of the night with you. We promise."

"As long as I get to be near Eric, it doesn't matter," she said, smiling shyly.

As you can probably tell from her comment, she was hard up for my best friend and had been ever since the fifth grade. The only problem was that Eric never saw her that way.

The reason he didn't see her that way had nothing to do with her flawless, smooth, mocha-colored skin or even her dorkiness. No. He didn't like her that way because she was teetering on the line of being a stalker. And yes, he was the one she stalked. Thankfully, though, it never got to the point of him getting a restraining order—kind of like how it was for Tammy and me. Both situations were basically more of an annoyance than anything.

"I'll tell you what," Eric began. "When we come back, I'm all yours."

Upon hearing his remark, Sally's eyes bolted open while her jaw practically crashed through the floor.

"Really?" she excitedly asked.

"Really," Eric responded.

She then lowered her head, turned slightly away, and cracked another shy smile at the thought of spending time with Eric. At that moment, she was probably the giddiest girl on the face of the planet.

"See you, Sally," Eric said.

Unfortunately, just like Zack, we never made it back to her and just left her standing there all by herself. Or at least, that was what we think happened. Plus, that was the last time either one of us had ever spoken to her. And it wasn't because she had died or anything. Quite the opposite, actually.

Sally left town a couple of days after the party because her parents both found new jobs across the country. Fortunately for Eric, her family had to relocate. However, about ten years later, we discovered that she became a famous supermodel and married a major league baseball player. To this day, she is still very much alive and well.

On a side note, after we found out what she became, I never missed an opportunity to bust Eric's chops about what he could've had with her. After all, she practically would've died for him. But no matter how many ribbings he took from me, I know he's happy with who he married.

After leaving Sally in our dust, we continued our search for the girls in the hip-hop room. Once we walked in there, we looked everywhere, hoping to find them while LL Cool J continued doing his thing. Not even a few seconds later, I felt a hand rest upon my right shoulder. When I turned around to see who it was, I saw Darren, the former star running back from our school's football team. And I mean former in the sense that he had just graduated.

He was about the same height as me, but was way more muscular, slightly better looking, and had light brown skin as opposed to my pale, ghostly shade of white. He was wearing his letterman's jacket, which, I swear to God, I think the dude practically slept in. And, as usual, he was hanging out with a couple other members of the football team.

With him were Tommy Mills, our quarterback; Dan Holmes, one of our offensive linemen; Justin Merlock, another offensive lineman; and Dwayne Cook, one of our linebackers.

Now, remember the story I'd mentioned earlier about going to Darren's house and getting arrested the night we went? Well, the guys I just mentioned were the very same ones who caused the ruckus that spawned the phone call to the cops.

"Yo! Wes and Eric! Sup!" Darren greeted us.

"Sup, Darren!" I replied before glancing at the rest of the group. "Guys!" I added with a single nod.

They all responded in kind with a nod of their own.

"How dope is this?" Darren continued. "They got LL to play at this party? Man, these folks must be rich or something."

I shrugged. "Must be. So when are you leaving for school?"

"Well, kickoff is August thirty-first. So I figured I'd get there sometime in July to start my training."

"I still can't believe you're going to Notre Dame."

"Yo, man, me either. My parents were thrilled I got in."

"Of course they are. That's a great school," Eric added.

"Don't worry," I said. "You're going to kill it."

"I sure hope so," Darren said. "They already got an all-star roster."

"Trust me, they got nothing on you."

What Darren was referring to was Notre Dame's plethora of stars they already had—specifically, their running backs. Of course, at the time, we had no idea how good those guys really were.

He had to compete with future superstars Ricky Watters, who was drafted by the San Francisco 49ers in 1991, Anthony Johnson, who was drafted by the Indianapolis Colts in 1990, and Raghib Ismail, who was drafted by the Los Angeles Raiders in 1991. Now, if those three names sound familiar to you, they should. There was a reason why they were drafted.

I gave Darren a quick pat on the back before I continued looking around the room some more.

"Hey, have you seen Anna and Eve?" I asked him.

"Who?" he replied, not realizing who I was talking about.

"You know, Anna and Eve?"

He still had no idea who I was talking about and just continued to stand there with a stupefied look on his face.

"The girls whose party this is for?" I added.

He nodded. "Oh, them! Nah, man. I haven't seen 'em."

"All right. Well, thanks a lot."

"No problem."

"Oh! And uh, if I don't see you before you leave, good luck," I said before leaning in and giving him a bro hug.

"Thanks, Wes," he replied.

"Look at it this way," I said as we separated. "I now have a reason to actually start watching college football."

He smiled and pointed at me with both index fingers. "You know it."

And that was it. Eric and I left him and his friends there while we continued our search for the girls.

As for Darren, he easily made the roster and played in just about every single football game during his freshman season. I didn't see him again until January 1, 1990, when Notre Dame came to Florida to play in the Orange Bowl. Even though I was at Florida State, I bought my tickets in advance and flew down to see him play.

After Notre Dame beat Colorado 21-6, I met Darren back at the hotel, where we partied just a little too hard. That was when I also learned a harrowing truth.

I found out that Darren only played a few snaps per game because of his recklessness and party habits. He was always late for practice and didn't really apply himself like he should've. And, unfortunately, that led him to get kicked out of school midway through his sophomore year.

He eventually finished his studies at one of the local state schools and graduated with a bachelor's degree in sports management. Not long after that, he got married and had two kids. Shortly after that, he started coaching one of the local high school football teams and continues to do so. The two of us keep in touch via email and text messages to this day.

———————

Inside the leftmost dining room, Eric and I got a hot tip that the girls were out in the hedge maze with a small group of people trying to see who could get through it the fastest. Needless to say, that information was false. And because of it, we spent an entire hour trying to get through that goddamn thing ourselves. I swear to you, though, from up on the balcony, it looked a hell of a lot easier than it actually was. Regardless, we still had fun.

After making it through the hedge maze, we walked back through the rose garden before stopping just outside its entrance. We looked toward the fountain and saw a big group of people standing in a circle. Since we couldn't quite see what they were looking at, we decided to move in a little closer. However, as we walked up to them, something unexpected happened—something you would typically only see in movies or TV.

As we got closer, the circle of people started to split down the middle, forming two small lines for Eric and me to walk between. When they did, we saw two female figures facing away from us. I immediately looked over at Eric, and he looked back at me, both of us confused about what was currently happening.

We slowly proceeded toward the figures, carefully walking down the middle of the two lines of people. Once we finally reached the clearing, the two females turned around and began smiling at us, almost as if they were waiting for us to come over and talk to them. It was Anna and Eve. However, that wasn't the weird part.

As we walked past everyone, we could see the people on either side of us smiling and extending their left or right hand, almost as if they were gesturing for us to continue. Once we made it to the middle of the circle, we found ourselves face-to-face with these two gorgeous angels. They smiled at us once more before a weird light started emanating from them, illuminating the entire yard. It was almost like we had just found a pot of gold at the end of a rainbow.

With Anna and Eve standing in front of us, glowing like we had just won the most heavenly prize on the face of the Earth, Eric and I looked at each other and smiled before turning back to the girls, leaning in close, and kissing them.

As soon as we did, fireworks shot off from the top of the house, exploding overhead while lighting up the night sky. The group of people encompassing us was now clapping, cheering, and whistling, just like they would right before the end credits of a movie started rolling. And once our lips separated, that was it.

I then came to and realized that we were not kissing the girls but, in fact, still standing outside the entrance to the rose garden.

So the question you're probably asking yourself is, *Did he just dream that whole sequence?* You bet your ass I did. And, if so, *When exactly did it start?* Well, it's simple. It started right around the moment we exited the rose garden.

Once we got out, I saw the girls standing there alone, which prompted me to play out some bogus, fictitious end scene of a romantic movie about them and us in my head. There was no large group of people circled around them, and no grand entrance, while everyone parted like the Red Sea. There was no kissing, no fireworks, and certainly no happiness. At least, not yet.

While I was off in dreamland, Eric just stood there, trying to get my attention.

"Dude? Wes!" he said while shaking me.

I quickly snapped out of it by shaking my head and hitching a ride back to reality.

"Huh? What happened?" I asked him.

"What happened? You left the planet for a moment. *That's* what happened," he said. "What the hell were you thinking about, anyway?"

"Uh…nothing. Don't worry about it."

Without responding, he gave me a funny look, almost as if he doubted every last word I'd just told him. I mean, come on. Can you really blame him?

Once I refocused my attention back on the girls, they were, in fact, standing in front of the water fountain. Again, there wasn't a big group of people encompassing them. They were simply standing there alone, with their backs to the fountain, just staring at us, waiting for us to come over and talk to them.

CHAPTER 5

After talking to the girls the first time, Eric and I noticed something striking and unusual about them that utterly blew our minds. So, of course, we just had to find them and get to know them a little better.

Along the way, we stopped to speak with a few of our ex-classmates. Some of them we didn't mind talking to, while others, well, not so much. We also got to hear some pretty sweet music, sample some excellent food, and get lost in a hedge maze. Not to mention my mind deciding to take a field trip to Neverland.

After a couple of grueling hours, we finally located the girls standing in front of the fountain. The hours weren't really *that* grueling. I just thought I'd throw it in there for dramatic effect. And I'll probably do it again later on in this story. Who knows?

As we stood outside the rose garden, we couldn't help but stare at them and become mesmerized by their angelic presence. Yeah, I know. I'm starting to sound cheesy. Just try not to throw up. Okay?

"There they are!" Eric pointed out.

"No, shit. I'm not blind," I replied.

"What do we do?"

I turned to face him. "I'll tell you what we're going to do," I said, using a quiet, serious tone. "We're going to march our sorry asses over there and talk to them."

"What if we have trouble speaking like the last time?"

After hearing his question, I faced forward, and with the girls still staring directly at us, I took a deep breath before letting out one of the biggest huffs of air I had ever huffed.

"We *must* speak," I said.

I then gathered all my courage, and, hopefully, a little for Eric as well, before tapping him on the arm and starting our nerve-racking walk toward them.

As we slowly took the longest walk I felt like I'd ever taken, many things started racing through my mind about what would happen once we got over there.

The first one being (and this was the most important one), *Will we be able to get out any words this time around, or will it be like a few hours ago when we just stood there like dumb statues?* The other things rolling around in my melon were more out of curiosity than anything.

Why couldn't we speak to them before? What kind of magical and mysterious powers did they have over us, and why? But most importantly, *What the hell did Eric and I see that made us so curious about them, to begin with?*

We were about to find out.

What seemed like the longest walk in history actually only took us a couple of seconds. Once we stood before them, however, it was like déjà vu. Eric and I immediately noticed the same thing about them that we had seen before. Our eyes were wide as we slowly looked them up, down, and all around, just to make sure we weren't imagining what we were currently seeing.

It was hard to explain, but to us, it looked like they had some weird, magical glow about them, almost as if a very dim light was creating some impenetrable force field around their bodies. Hard to believe, I know. But try being there and witnessing it for yourself. That was an utterly indescribable experience.

Seeing us standing there, the girls could easily tell that we looked the same as before. And while we were in the middle of staring, they made yet another valiant attempt to break us out of whatever statue-like state we were in.

"So," Eve said, slowly shifting her gaze between the two of us, "you boys going to make another go at us?"

My mouth opened, and I swear I could feel my jaw moving. Yet, nothing was coming out—again.

Anna giggled. "Still at a loss for words?" she asked. "Come on, boys. You've got to say something."

Now, I'd be lying if I said I didn't try my damndest to get a word out—any word, for that matter.

"Anything?" Eve asked.

And that was when it happened.

By some miracle, we were finally able to blurt something out. Plus, to my surprise, it wasn't me who spoke first.

"Hi!" Eric said.

The moment he spoke, the girls' eyes widened. Surprised, they turned to face each other before turning back to us. My own eyes also widened as I turned to look at him, pretty much with the same look the girls had just a split second before.

"He speaks!" Anna said. "I honestly didn't think he would."

"Me either," Eve added.

"I'm Eric, and this is my best friend, Wes," Eric said.

But I still couldn't say a word.

"I said hi. Now, it's your turn," Eric said to me.

He waited patiently for me to say something. The girls did, too, as all three of them were now staring at me, hoping I'd finally blurt something out.

"Wes?" Eric asked.

My jaw was definitely moving, but the words still seemed to escape me.

And that was when Eric did something a little unorthodox—something neither of us had ever done to each other in the past nor to this day.

He took his left hand, reached it over, and smacked me in the back of the head. My head jilted forward with such force, and since no one had ever slapped me like that before, I responded the only way I knew how.

"Ow! Dude, why the fuck did you hit me in the back of my head?" I asked him while massaging my noggin.

"You're talking, aren't you?" he pointed out.

It took me a second to understand. But once I figured it out, he was right. The words began flowing out of my mouth like raging river rapids.

"Holy shit. You're right," I replied, surprised that his little plan actually worked.

"Of course I am," he said. "Now, why don't you introduce yourself?"

I gave him a quick nod and immediately stopped rubbing my head before focusing on the girls.

"Hi! I'm Wes, and this is Eric," I said before realizing that Eric had already introduced us. "But you already know that," I finished sheepishly.

The girls giggled to themselves upon hearing my response. I quickly turned red out of embarrassment.

"Sorry about that," I said. "It's just that…I've never been this nervous around anyone before."

"Don't worry about it," Eve said. "I think it's kind of cute."

My eyes widened. "You do?"

"The way the two of you looked when you turned around and saw us?" Anna added. "I also thought it was cute."

"Really?" Eric asked.

"Really."

"We've got to admit, though, no one has ever been that speechless around us before," Eve remarked.

"Is that a good thing or a bad thing?" I asked, intrigued.

"*Definitely* a good thing."

And just like that, along with the help of a head slap, the strange, magical curse was broken as we were both now enjoying a fulfilling conversation with two beautiful women. Come to think of it, that was the first time in our lives both of us had conversed with gorgeous girls at the same time.

Upon hearing Eve's last remark, Eric and I turned to look at each other, grinning from ear to ear, before turning back to the girls.

Eric immediately held up a finger. "Could you ladies excuse us for just one moment?"

Before the girls could even get a word out edgewise, Eric grabbed my arm and dragged me back far enough so they were out of earshot.

"What the hell are you doing?" I quietly asked him.

"Dude, I think these girls are into us," he replied.

"No, shit. You think?"

"No need to be snippy about it."

"Sorry."

At that moment, and because of our private conversation, I suddenly felt like we were Anthony Michael Hall and Ilan Mitchell-Smith's characters, Gary and Wyatt, from the movie *Weird Science.*

It was the scene where they were both in the bathroom talking to each other when the girls they had crushes on came knocking on the door. The guys eventually let them in to chat for a few moments before quickly ducking into the shower. There, they quietly discussed how the girls were into them and who each of them should get.

When Eric pulled me aside and said they were into us, that was precisely how I felt at the time (minus the bathroom or the shower stall).

"Anyway," Eric continued, "if they are into us, I got dibs on the brunette."

"That's fine by me," I said. "But if I may ask…why?"

He quickly glanced over my shoulder at Anna before looking back at me. "She kind of reminds me of Elizabeth Hurley," he said.

"Who?" I asked, confused about who he was talking about.

"Elizabeth Hurley. You know, the British actress?"

Okay. Everyone and their mom probably knows who Elizabeth Hurley is by now. But back then, she didn't have many acting credits under her belt yet. And it wasn't until she starred in the 1997 movie *Austin Powers: International Man of Mystery* as British agent Vanessa Kensington that she became popular.

As far back as I can remember, Eric has always been a massive fan of British TV and film. Some of his favorite TV shows included *Doctor Who, Monty Python's Flying Circus,* and *Fawlty Towers.*

As for the movies, some of his favorites were *Lawrence of Arabia, A Clockwork Orange,* and *Monty Python's Life of Brian.* It wasn't until he saw the 1988 four-part TV mini-series *Christabel* that he absolutely fell in love with her.

Hurley played the starring role of Christabel, an English woman who marries a German lawyer in the 1930s. When bombs start falling on some of the German cities, she takes her two kids, along with her husband, and winds up fleeing to a village in the mountains. While there, she learns that her husband and some of his friends got arrested for plotting to kill Hitler. I saw the movie only once and thought it was just okay. However, Eric became ridiculously obsessed with her.

He then went back and started watching all her earlier stuff like *Inspector Morse, Rowing with the Wind* (which I actually found somewhat entertaining), and her very first film credit, a weird-ass movie called *Aria.* (Don't even get me started on that one.)

So there you have it. Eric's love for Elizabeth Hurley culminated in him calling dibs on a look-alike.

Once he mentioned the actress's name, I turned to look and stare at Anna for a few seconds before realizing that there was, in fact, a slight resemblance. What were the odds? Of course, saying that he wanted Anna because she looked like some actress wasn't the only reason why he wanted her. But I'll explain that much later.

"You think Anna looks like Elizabeth Hurley?" I asked.

"Oh, fuck yeah!" he replied, practically drooling.

I shrugged. "All right. Then if it turns out that they are into us, I promise you, she's all yours."

"You are the *best*," he said, wrapping his arms around me and squeezing tightly.

"Okay, okay," I said, trying to shove him away. "In the meantime, just try to think of a way to pay me back later."

"My brain is already on it."

I then nodded and quickly composed myself before we made our way back to the girls.

"You boys all set?" Eve asked us.

"I think we're good," I replied before turning my attention to Anna. "Oh, and uh, FYI"—I thumbed toward Eric—"he thinks you're hot."

Oh yeah. I totally just threw my best friend under the bus, so to speak. And when I did, he turned to look at me with the most hateful look I have ever seen him give me. Of course, with his face suddenly a tad on the red side from being slightly embarrassed, let's just say he wasn't too happy.

"Are you fucking kidding me right now?" he angrily asked. "Why would you do that?"

"Because it's fun," I replied. "And now"—I slowly shook my head—"you don't owe me a damn thing. The look on your face alone was payment enough. Besides, I think they can already tell that we like them."

"He's right," Eve said. "We kind of got that feeling already."

"Plus, it's nothing to be embarrassed about," Anna added. "We already feel the same way about the two of you."

I honestly didn't think Eric's face could get any redder than it already was. But when Anna said that, man, was I wrong. Of course, by that point, my face was also a slight, rosy color.

When they saw our faces completely flush red, they both turned to giggle at each other before returning their attention to us.

"You boys are too funny," Eve remarked.

"We will say this, though. There's something about you guys that seems familiar," Anna said, then narrowed her eyes out of curiosity. "Something we just can't put a finger on."

"Also, going back to what we said earlier," Eve added, "no one has ever been speechless around us before. Which leads me to ask…why were you?"

Why were we speechless? Now *that* was a question even I couldn't answer. I mean, what was I going to say? Was I just going to come out and tell them, *Well, it was probably because you were glowing, that's why.* No. That would sound crazy and just downright ridiculous.

"No reason," I nonchalantly responded. "I think it was seeing two women as beautiful as yourselves that just caught us at a loss for words."

Eric immediately leaned slightly toward me. "Good one," he mumbled under his breath.

And that was when everyone went silent because both girls' faces had also turned a slight rosy color.

"Anyway," I continued, clapping my hands together once and quickly changing the subject. "Now that we got that out of the way, I'm just dying to know…who lives here? And, how the hell were they able to afford all of this?"

The girls turned to look at each other with semi-serious expressions before turning back to us.

"Would you guys care to take a walk with us?" Eve asked.

"Not at all," I replied.

Eric and I then stood apart and faced each other. I extended out my right hand while Eric extended out his left, letting the girls know they now had the extreme honor of leading the way.

———————

Ah, the rose garden! A holiday for your nose. White, red, magenta, yellow, copper, vermilion, purple, and even apricot were just a few of the varieties they had back there. And, although I'm not a flower guy, I will say this—that had to have been one of the most beautiful gardens I'd ever seen.

The intricate paths woven between the different types of roses, along with the beauty of the flowers and their soothing aroma, definitely made it a sight to be seen. That was also where this whole conversation about who lived in the house and how they could afford it started.

I won't lie. I was curious from the get-go. I mean, we were going to a birthday party for a pair of girls that no one had ever seen around school until that very night. Yet, they decided to invite the entire graduating class. Why? What was their reasoning behind it?

First of all, anyone who went to our school wouldn't have that kind of money. If they did, they most likely went to one of the private schools in the area. But no one who attended a private school would ever invite an entire class of nobodies to a birthday party. Would they? There was only one way to find out.

"So how come we've never seen you girls around school before?" I asked, curious.

"Way to be subtle," Eric sarcastically remarked.

Eve laughed. "No, that's okay. It's a perfectly valid question. I'm just surprised no one asked us that yet."

"Seriously?" I asked.

"Yeah. You guys are the first ones we've spoken to for longer than a few seconds," Anna said.

"Holy shit. How come?" Eric asked.

Anna shrugged. "Don't know."

"We think it might have something to do with the bands and the food," Eve added.

"You mean with everything being so extravagant and Hollywood?" I remarked.

"Probably."

"And speaking of which, that brings me to another question," I continued. "Two, actually. The first one being…who the hell can afford something like this? And more importantly, whose house is this?"

"Well, to answer your second question, we don't know," Anna said.

"You don't know who lives here?"

"No."

"Well then, how about his first question? Who can afford something like this?" Eric asked.

"That part's easy," Eve said. "Our parents."

"Your parents are millionaires?"

"Something like that."

At the time, my face looked calm and collected. But on the inside, my brain was screaming. I couldn't believe what they had just told us. The only thing now racing through my mind was, *Holy shit! I finally know someone who's rich!* But that was way beside the point.

What I mean is that anyone I've ever seen with money has shown their attitude differently. More or less (and not to sugarcoat anything), they always acted like spoiled little bitches and assholes. Of course, there were always a few exceptions. For instance, look at who we were talking to.

From my perspective, they didn't seem to fit the bill of being spoiled. As a matter of fact, they seemed to be the complete opposite of that. And if that was the case, why were they so disciplined and friendly? Did their parents raise them not to be spoiled little brats? Did they make them work for a living to teach them about earning respect and trust?

"Our parents told us that since we were turning eighteen and would now be adults," Anna began, "we could have anything we wanted before going off to college."

"You guys are going to college?" I asked.

"Yeah. Why?"

I shrugged. "I don't know. I figured with what you just told us about your parents being rich and all that you would—"

"We would what? *Not* have to go to college?" Eve asked, swiftly interrupting me while sounding none too happy. "That it would be off the table, seeing as how we wouldn't have to work a single day in our lives? Is that what you meant?"

Holy shit. I honestly didn't know how to answer that. I mean, *wow*, did I feel like an asshole. And I'm not just talking about a minor asshole. I'm talking about a huge, major asshole. At that point, I could've been the one working for Dark Helmet aboard *Spaceball 1*. That was how major I felt. Hell, even Eric shot me a dirty look after I said that.

And because I didn't know how to respond, I just fumbled my words. "Well, no. I just…but I didn't mean…I only…no," I stuttered.

However, with the girls seeing me practically squirm in my now pee-soaked pants (figuratively speaking), they turned to each other and smiled before letting out the sound of collective laughter.

"You should really take a chill pill there, Captain Tight Pants," Eve said.

A confused expression immediately hit my face.

"If you could've seen the look on your face," Anna added. "We know what the majority thinks about rich people. We're pretty much used to it by now."

"I only said that to freak you out," Eve said. "And damn, was it funny."

Still confused, I perused both girls' faces, only to see that they couldn't be any more "not serious" even if they tried. I then looked at Eric, who was snickering to himself as well.

"You got to admit, that was pretty funny," he said.

I scowled at him. "Well, who asked you?"

"Come on, guys, relax," Anna said. "Anyway, back to your second question…this house belongs to a friend of my parents. They let us use it for the party."

"Is that why the upstairs is blocked off?" Eric asked.

"Correct."

"And, even though Anna and I went to the same private school, we were raised to be respectable women," Eve said.

Private school! I knew it. I thought.

"Well, that's good. Which school?" I asked.

"We went to one of the all-girl schools in Summerlin South," Eve replied.

An all-girl school? I also thought. *This night just keeps getting better and better.*

"Summerlin? That's the next county over," I remarked. "Why travel so far to have a party?"

"Dude, haven't you been listening?" Eric snidely asked. "Hello? Friends of the parents?"

"Oh, right. But why here with us? Why not have it with the girls from your school?"

"Because they're all just a bunch of spoiled little bitches," Eve replied, grinning smugly.

Eric and I also grinned after hearing her response.

"I like how you think," I replied.

"All right, I've had just about enough of this as I can take," Anna said. "What do you say we all go inside and enjoy ourselves? Because the way I see it, you guys are now officially our dates."

Holy shit. I couldn't believe what had just happened. One minute, we were simply strangers talking in a rose garden, and the next minute, we were their dates. How awesome was that?

As soon as they said that, Eric and I looked at each other, wide-eyed and grinning, before turning back to the girls and smiling. Eric stuck out his left elbow, and Anna hooked her right arm through it. I stuck out my right elbow, and Eve took it with her hand. Then the four of us walked back inside the house.

———

We spent the rest of the night having the time of our lives. We danced, we laughed, we cried while laughing, and we even pigged out on most of the delicious food. I will say this, though—I never thought I would ever meet a woman who could eat me under the table. (No pun intended.) But I was sorely mistaken.

I couldn't even begin to tell you how late we were there or how long we partied. And by the time the night was over, we all had exchanged addresses and phone numbers. After that, it was all but official—we would soon be going out on our first dates. Well, not our *first* first dates, but our first dates with those girls.

Meeting Anna and Eve was the best thing that had ever happened to us. Me, in general. Probably Eric, too. Also, after meeting the girls on that one fateful night, both of our lives would never be the same again.

CHAPTER 6

After I got home from the party, I went straight up to my room, plopped down on my bed, and passed out with my clothes on. Thankfully, my parents were already asleep, so I didn't have to worry about them burning my ears with a million questions about how my night went.

When I woke up the following afternoon, I didn't get up right away. Instead, I just folded my hands behind my head and lay in my bed, thinking about Eve and the unforgettable night we had. I then remembered that she and I, along with Eric and Anna, had all exchanged phone numbers and addresses.

So I quickly lifted my butt and stuck my left hand inside my back left jeans pocket to pull out the piece of paper on which she had written it down. Back then, we didn't have smartphones or tablets to store everything. We actually had to write things down or memorize them.

As I stared at the piece of paper with her handwritten address and phone number, I couldn't help but get lost in it. I immediately started thinking about when I should call her and if it would be too soon. After all, I didn't want to sound too desperate.

I also thought about her hair, her beautiful smile, her eyes, and just how nice she was overall. When I saw her for the first time, it was almost as if love had taken a brick and thrown it at my face—hard. It also left an impression on me that I couldn't understand at the time and wouldn't fully grasp until later.

The other thing I couldn't help but think about was the strange glow the girls were emitting. And even though I saw Eve glow, I couldn't see anything coming from Anna. When it came to Eric, however, he saw the complete opposite.

Was the light bouncing off some of the reflective surfaces? Was it the moonlight hitting them at just the right angle? Or were we simply awestruck by their beauty? Regardless, I'd find out one way or another when we went on our first date. But first things first.

At that moment, I realized that because I'd slept so late, I only had a couple of hours to get my ass up and ready for work. So I stuffed the piece of paper in the top drawer of my dresser before pulling out some fresh clothes and heading to the bathroom.

After I finished, I got dressed and went downstairs to grab a quick bite to eat. However, the instant my foot touched that bottom step, both of my parents instantly bombarded me with a billion questions about how the party was and what time I came home. And because I was so hungry, I had no choice but to sit down in the kitchen, within earshot of them both, and give them some answers.

"Good morn, *ahem*…good afternoon, Wes," my mom said.

"Hi, Mom," I said before turning toward the living room. "Hey, Dad!"

"How about that? He lives!" my dad said.

My mom was busy cleaning the kitchen while my dad sat in his La-Z-Boy chair, watching a baseball game.

As you already know, my dad worked at one of the local rock quarries nearby. At the time, he had short, dark hair, blue eyes, and a somewhat stocky build. A slight beer gut also stood out, completing his construction worker look. And although he didn't act like ninety percent of the perverted, womanizing guys that worked down there, he certainly looked like them.

"Are you hungry? Can I get you anything?" my mom asked.

"No, thanks," I replied. "I'll just have a bowl of cereal now and eat dinner at the café later."

She shrugged. "Okay."

I then reached into one of our cupboards and pulled out a bowl. I set it down on the counter before opening a different cupboard to make my selection.

Cinnamon Life was and still is my favorite cereal of all time. Don't get me wrong. I enjoy a variety of cereals from time to time and always have. But that day, I had five to choose from: Corn Flakes, Cap'N Crunch, Honey Nut Cheerios, and Cinnamon Life. Of course, those were only four of the cereals we had. However, I decided to be bold and choose something completely different. Plus, I didn't want to see it go to waste, as my mom would've had a fit if we threw it out. Then I'd have to hear her talk to me about pitching in and not wasting money on anything. As a teenager, I just never had the time for that.

So I pulled out the Nintendo Cereal System box and poured myself a heaping bowl of the berry flavor, which represented *The Legend of Zelda*. I could've chosen the fruity flavor, which represented *Super Mario Brothers*, but after last night's party, I was feeling a little on the adventurous side.

After pouring in my milk, I took my bowl into the living room to watch the game while I ate. And, in doing so, I got questioned by my father.

"Rough night?" he asked.

"Not really. Just long," I replied, plopping down on the couch.

"What time did you get in? We didn't even hear you."

"It's probably best you don't know."

I scooped up a few humongous spoonfuls of cereal and stuffed them into my mouth.

"Anything interesting happen?" my dad asked.

"Eh, not really. I mean, Eric and I just enjoyed the music and ate the food," I replied.

"That's it?"

"What else is there?"

"I don't know. Maybe, perhaps, you might have met someone. Maybe someone by the name of"—he paused, almost as if he was thinking of a random name to pull out of his ass—"for conversation's sake, let's just call her…Eve."

As soon as he mentioned her name, I quickly perked up. I mean, holy shit. How did they know about Eve? I hadn't even mentioned her yet.

"How did you know I met someone named Eve?" I asked, curious.

"She called while you were sleeping and left a message," my mom yelled from the kitchen.

"What did she say?" I asked a little too eagerly.

"She just said to give her a call back when you get the chance."

When my mom said that, I immediately looked down at my left wrist to check the time on my Casio calculator watch.

"Dammit," I muttered.

By that point, I only had a half-hour to finish eating and get to work. There was no way I could call her back before I went in. I'd have to wait until after my shift was over.

"I got to say," my mom added, "she sounded really nice. Did she go to school with you?"

"No, she went to one of the private schools," I said.

"Maybe you could invite her over for dinner."

"Jesus, Mom. I just met the girl last night."

"What he *meant* to say was he would love to," my dad said. "But only when the time was right."

My dad then turned to look and wink at me, as if somehow letting me know he just saved my ass and that I should've said *that*, to begin with. I, in return, nodded once, giving him my thanks.

"Well, until then, when's the first date?" my mom asked.

"I don't know," I said with a shrug. "We haven't set anything up yet."

"Why don't you call her back?"

"Because I have to go to work."

"You could always call her after work."

My mother was always relentless when it came to the girls I had dated, was dating, or just met. It was almost as if she was desperate for me to find someone and be happy, like her and my dad. But I always told her it would happen when the time was right. I also think that was part of the reason why I was still a virgin. Well, it was mostly my choice, but still.

Whenever I met or dated someone, my mom would continually bombard me with countless questions about how we met, whether we had shared our first kiss yet, and when we would be going out. Eventually, though, I just stopped going out on dates altogether so I wouldn't have to listen to her go on and on about it. Don't get me wrong, I loved the woman dearly. But holy shit!

"Don't worry, I had planned on it," I said, annoyed.

As I scarfed down another monster spoonful of cereal, I turned to look at my dad, who was already looking over at me with an expression on his face, almost as if to say he was sorry I had to put up with that.

My dad loved my mom more than anything else in the world. But sometimes, I think even he felt my pain when my mom decided to bombard me with questions. Although they weren't aimed at him, I think he was just as anxious as I was for the interrogation to be over with.

"Look, as much as I want to finish this conversation," I began to say before shoving in my last bite of cereal, "I have to get to work."

"Oh, okay," my mom said. "We'll see you later then."

"Don't work too hard," my dad added.

After putting my bowl in the sink, I threw on my shoes and addressed my parents. "Later, Mom! Later, Dad!"

Then out the door like lightning, I went.

I never thought I would see the day when I would be happy to go to a five-dollar-an-hour job, plus tips, just to avoid my mother's questions. I mean, they weren't all bad. But it did feel nice to go.

And, even though I was happy to get out of the house, I still had to deal with another small problem. More like, deal with another someone—someone I didn't mind being around, but someone who also annoyed the ever-living shit out of me. That's right. I now had to go to work and deal with Tammy Macintyre.

After speeding into and parking in the tiny employees-only parking lot located directly behind the café, I went through the back door, punched in, and began my shift with about twenty-five seconds to spare. Even if I were a couple of minutes late, Johnny Junior (the current owner and son of the man who originally opened that place) wouldn't have minded. He always treated me with respect and always appreciated my hard work.

I put on my apron, grabbed my pencil and order book, and made my way out onto the dining room floor to get started. However, as I looked around the room, I couldn't help but notice that it was surprisingly dead for a Saturday afternoon. Plus, everyone in there already had food in front of them.

So I stuffed my pencil and order book into my front apron pocket and decided to bus a few tables while "Walk This Way" by Run-DMC and Aerosmith quietly blared out of the jukebox.

After the dining room was all set, I brought the dishes to the kitchen and placed them over by the sink before making my way back out behind the counter. When I got out there, lo and behold, there she was.

"Oh, hey, Wes!" Tammy greeted me.

"Hey, Tammy," I said.

I will admit, though, with her copper-red hair and sparkling blue eyes, any man would've been lucky to have her. Just not me. Again, did I think she was gorgeous? Hell yeah. Would I ever go out with her? Hell no. Dating my stalker was simply never in the cards for me.

"How was the party last night?" she asked.

"I couldn't even begin to tell you how awesome that thing was," I replied. "There was food coming out the ass. And the music? Even better."

"Sounds like you had fun."

"Fun doesn't even begin to describe how badass it was."

"Well, that's nice," she said, a tiny hint of jealousy in her voice.

I personally think she was mad because we weren't in the same place at the same time. I also believe she was jealous of me because I was having fun without her. Not to mention, she knew that summer would probably be her last and only shot to try to get with me before I left for college. Oh well.

"And because it was being held at some big ass house, it felt like we were at a party in Hollywood," I said.

"I guess you did have fun," she said.

"It's too bad you're not a senior until this fall. You would've loved it."

Let me clarify that last statement for you. I only said that to be nice. I would rather have bathed in gasoline and set myself on fire than try to avoid her stalker ass all night. Well, not so much the fire part, but you know what I mean.

Anyway, by that point, "Walk This Way" had finished playing, and "Never Gonna Give You Up" by Rick Astley started playing instead.

"I love this song!" Tammy said, her eyes lit up with excitement.

"Tell me you're joking?" I asked, seriously questioning her musical choices.

She immediately placed her hands on her hips. "What's wrong with Rick Astley?"

"What *isn't* wrong with Rick Astley?"

Now, I won't lie. I never let any of my friends know about some of my own questionable music choices. That's just something I always wanted to keep private. For reputation's sake, of course.

But every time someone like Rick Astley, Madonna, Kim Wilde, Laura Brannigan, Cyndi Lauper, Men at Work, or even Steve Winwood was brought up, I always made fun of someone for listening to them. Everyone who knows me knows that I was and always have been a metalhead. Truth be told, however, I liked all that other kind of music as well. I only put up a wall so people wouldn't think I was weird. Well, any weirder than I already was. Of course, looking back on it now, I know it was wrong.

"Let me guess," I continued, holding up a finger. "You're a huge fan of Taylor Dayne and Janet Jackson as well?"

"How did you know?" she asked.

I snickered and shook my head in disbelief. "You know what? Never mind."

Just to set the record straight, Michael Jackson was completely different from his sister Janet and was also in a totally different league. I mean, there was a perfectly good reason why I didn't include him in that conversation. After all, they didn't call him the King of Pop for nothing.

Also, at that point, I really didn't feel like carrying on a pointless conversation with her anymore. So I quickly changed the subject.

"I really haven't had any time to ask you yet," I began, "but do you have any plans for the summer?"

"Not really," she replied before getting the most curious look on her face. "Why?"

I shrugged. "No reason. Just curious, is all."

"You're not asking me out, are you?"

Whoops! That really came out of left field.

"Who, me? Of course not," I replied.

"Then why did you ask it?" she asked.

"I was simply making friendly conversation with you."

"Oh, come on, Wes. Admit it. You like me."

"In your dreams."

Now, the next part of the conversation caught me completely off guard, even more so than when she thought I was asking her out.

"Then why are you always staring at me?" she asked, looking all serious, her left hip arched slightly sideways, and her right hand resting on the other.

Like I said before, did I think she was hot? Hell yeah, I did. But I would *never* want to go out with her.

"Can we not have this conversation at work?" I asked.

"You don't want to talk about it here?" she said. "Fine! Follow me."

She immediately turned to her left and stormed out from behind the counter. I also left and followed her as she walked through the kitchen before stopping just outside the back entrance.

"Okay, we're away from everyone," she said. "Now, spill it."

"Spill what?" I asked.

"You seem to have no problem flirting with and staring at me. Yet, every time I ask you out, you turn me down. Why?"

After all those years of flirting with her and not giving her the time of day, I guess she finally had enough of my leading her on and suddenly wanted an explanation. It had to happen sooner or later.

I sighed. "Fine. You really want to know why? I'll tell you. First of all," I began, "I think you're one of the hottest girls I've ever seen. But one of the reasons I won't go out with you is because you're always around. The only reason you got this job was because of me."

"That's not true," she said.

"Bullshit, it's not! You were in here all the time just because I worked here."

"Well, yeah, that's true," she agreed.

"Sometimes, I feel like you're borderline obsessed with me, which also happens to be the main reason why I won't go out with you."

"But I love you."

Shocked by that last statement? Yeah, not me. Want to know why? Because that wasn't exactly the first time she'd professed her undying love for me.

"Look," I said sternly, holding up a finger, "you may think you love me, but you don't."

"But I do," she said.

"I'm not finished. This…*obsession* that you have with me…you really need to get over it." My finger was no longer raised and was now leveled at her. "I will never date you, or go out with you, or ever love you. The only way I'd ever be with you is if I was hard up for sex."

And that was when she said the one thing that absolutely floored me.

"I mean, if you really want to sleep with me, all you have to do is ask," she said.

Immediately following her admission, my eyes shot open, and I was in absolute shock. I mean, did she really just say that? Did she just offer me the most coveted thing on the face of the Earth? And, without even trying, nonetheless? I couldn't believe it. It took me a few seconds, but I finally came to the realization that Eric was right.

He always told me that Tammy would sleep with me in a heartbeat. Even just the other day, he said that if I ever went out with her, I'd get laid before we left her front lawn. Of course, I never once believed him for a second. I guess he wasn't kidding. Also, in that very same moment, something else happened. Something I never even thought I would ever consider. For a split second, I actually thought about taking her up on her offer.

I'll tell you, being a teenager was by far one of the hardest and easiest times of my life. Plus, as most teenagers do, they can't seem to keep their hormones in check. So thoughts about sleeping with other people, sex, and masturbation are usually a big part of a teenager's ambition.

I won't lie. I always thought about what it would be like to lose my virginity to Tammy. However, after she was willing to pretty much give it up to me right then and there, I completely lost any interest I had left in her, which was very minimal to begin with. I mean, was I your everyday, average, typical teenager? In a way, yes. But for the most part, I wasn't.

You see, unlike most of the other teenagers, I didn't want to sleep with someone just for the sake of saying I slept with them. If I were to sleep with someone, it would have to be with someone I loved. And call me crazy, but I was definitely not going to give up my virginity to just anyone. They had to be special. And it also had to be someone I cared deeply about.

Now, I know that most first relationships don't last. Of course, there are a few exceptions to those who wind up marrying their high school sweethearts. And if I just happened to be one of those people where it didn't work out, then so be it. As long as they meant something to me at some point in my life, that's all that would matter.

Okay! Well, that's enough of my romanticized, puke-worthy rambling. Sorry, I kind of went off on a tangent there. Let's just get back to the story, shall we?

After hearing what Tammy had just offered me, I couldn't help myself and wound up laughing in her face.

"You really think that I'll say yes to sleeping with you?" I asked.

"If it's the only way I can be with you, then yeah," she replied.

"You really are out of your fucking mind. Do you know that? I wouldn't sleep with you, even if my life depended on it."

Okay, I'll admit that was a little harsh. That was also when I instantly wanted to take back all the bad things I ever said about her. Because at that moment, me saying that hurt her deeply. I mean, I might as well have taken a knife and stabbed her with it.

The tears that started pouring out of her eyes were unimaginable. I have never in my entire life seen someone hurt that badly and cry that much. And once it was all said and done, I felt horrible for turning her down. But I know in my heart I made the right choice.

Every day I had to work with her was like working with a jealous spouse. I'd get questions about where I was, what I was doing, and who I was doing it with, even though it was strictly none of her damn business. I regularly got tired of it and dealt with it, just to be nice.

If you recall, there was a scene in *The Goonies* when they were all in the Fratellis' restaurant, and Mouth kept making fun of Chunk's weight. Chunk then said to him, "That's all I can stand, and I can't stand no more!" before standing up and clumsily knocking over the water bottle.

In my head, I repeated Chunk's words over and over until I finally told Tammy the truth. And when people say that the truth shall set you free, they're not kidding. Because the "truth" is what ultimately got me in trouble.

"Shit," I muttered before lowering my head and shaking it in disappointment. "Tammy, look, I'm sorry. I didn't mean to…"

But that was it. I never got to finish apologizing to her as she ran back inside the café. And, needless to say, that was the last day I ever worked there.

After she ran inside, the owner (Johnny Junior) came running out to see me standing there, still shaking my head. After I gave him my side of the story, he proceeded to grill me on sexual etiquette, which I didn't understand why. After all, Tammy started it. However, he didn't stop there.

He then told me to hand over my apron, pencil, and paper before firing me right there on the spot. Four years of dedication to that place, and I got let go over a slight misunderstanding. Years later, however, I spoke with Johnny Junior over the phone after he called me and apologized for firing my ass.

He told me that a handful of other guys who worked there were also fired for pretty much the same reason I was. He then started getting complaints from some of the customers as well about Tammy's attitude. Apparently, after I got let go, she just spiraled out of control.

It wasn't until he finally put two and two together that the issue wasn't, in fact, mine or the other guys' faults, but Tammy's.

After that day, I never saw her again, nor did I want to. After Johnny fired her, I heard that she dropped out of school, bailed on her folks, and left town. What happened to her after that? No one really knows.

But getting fired that day from the café was probably one of the best things to ever happen to me. Because if I hadn't gotten fired then, what happened to me later that summer, well, I probably would've anyway.

CHAPTER 7

Getting fired from the café was probably the second greatest thing that happened to me that summer. Because suddenly, I had a lot more time to fart around and do nothing. For example…

I could sit in my room and try to beat all my high scores for every Nintendo game I owned. The same could be said for my Atari. I could also go down to the video store and rent movies upon movies of films I hadn't even seen yet. I could sleep in as long as I wanted and not have to worry about being late for anything. Of course, if those weren't just thoughts rolling around inside my head, my summer could've been a little on the dull side.

Let's be honest. I wasn't actually going to do any of the things I just mentioned. Although sitting on my ass and becoming a vegetable didn't sound all that bad. However, those things were all put on the back burner so I could do something I actually *wanted* to do.

I pulled into my driveway, parked my truck, and got out. I then hauled some serious ass inside and made a beeline straight for my bedroom, avoiding my parents' onslaught of questions in the process.

I closed my bedroom door, went over to my dresser, and pulled out the piece of paper with Eve's information on it before heading over and plopping down on my bed.

I held that little piece of paper (which, in my opinion, was suddenly worth its weight in gold) up in front of my face and just stared at it. I must've sat there and daydreamed forever before working up the nerve to actually pick up the phone and call her. In real time, it was more like five minutes.

But did it really matter? No. Because at that moment, a person who was about to commit a crime wouldn't even want to be around me. That was how nervous I was.

With my hands shaking, I reached over to the nightstand on the side of my bed and picked up the phone. I went to dial her number, but then hung up. I tried to get a grip on myself and took a couple of deep breaths before picking it up again. But this time, I managed to dial.

Yeah. I punched in one measly little number before chickening out and quickly hanging up the handset.

She's just a girl, I kept thinking to myself. *It shouldn't be this difficult.*

But I would soon find out that Eve wasn't just any old girl. She was different. She was special. She was beautiful. And, more importantly, she liked me for me.

After a couple more deep breaths (more like ten), I picked up the phone once again and finally dialed her entire number. About a second later, it started ringing.

While I waited for someone on the other end to pick up, I looked around my room at all the movie and music posters hanging on my walls. *E.T., Indiana Jones and the Temple of Doom, Return of the Jedi, Back to the Future,* and *Little Shop of Horrors* were some of the movie ones. Mötley Crüe, Black 'N Blue, Van Halen, Ozzy Osbourne, Guns 'N Roses, and Megadeth were some of the music ones.

Once I'd finished perusing my walls, I directed my attention to the phone I was using. It was one of those vintage Conair corded, see-through phones. Of course, they weren't vintage at the time, but they were still brand new and extremely popular.

Also, on an unrelated note, back then, if you had to make a phone call, you had to make sure no one was using a phone anywhere else in the house. Unless you had two separate phone lines, you could easily pick up another phone and hear someone else's conversation.

The phone rang nearly three times before someone on the other end finally picked up.

"Hello?" a female voice answered.

"Uh, hi," I nervously began. "My name is Wes. Is Eve home?"

"Is this the same Wes that met my daughter at the party last night?"

Now that I knew I was speaking to Eve's mom, I could relax just a tad.

"Yes, ma'am," I replied.

"Wow! So formal," she said, almost surprised by my politeness. "Just a moment, Wes. I'll go get her."

"Thank you."

There was silence on the other end of the line as I waited patiently for Eve's mom to tell her I was calling. Again, what was really ten seconds seemed like a lifetime while I waited for her to come and answer.

"Hi, Wes!" Eve said.

"Hey, Eve," I replied.

Even on the phone, she sounded beautiful.

"Took you long enough to call me back," she said.

"Well, I didn't want to seem too desperate," I said. "But by the time my parents told me you called, it was too late. I had to go to work."

"What time did you go in?"

"About an hour ago."

"You only worked for an hour?"

"Not exactly."

I wanted to tell her what had happened, but I wasn't sure if she would still like me. After all, if I was going to take her out on a date, I would need some money. Thankfully, though, my truck didn't consume all my savings, as I still had a pretty decent-sized chunk of change lying around.

"I...got fired," I told her.

"You got fired?" she asked, shocked by my admission.

"Yeah, but it's a long story. I'll tell you later."

"Maybe you could tell me on our date tonight."

"What date?" I asked, confused.

"The one you're going to ask me out on."

Yup. I was so clueless about what she meant that I immediately put the phone down and slammed my head into my pillow a few times, utterly disappointed by my own stupidity.

"Of course! *That* date," I responded, acting like I knew what she was talking about. "What time should I pick you up?"

"Why don't you pick me up for eight?" she suggested.

"Eight sounds good."

"Then it's a date. Don't be late."

And before I could even say goodbye or get out another word, she hung up. I also hung up the phone and just sat there in stunned silence.

I wasn't stunned because she hung up on me. I was stunned because, for the first time in a long time, I was going out on an actual date. But not just any date, mind you. No. *This* was the date of a lifetime. And also one I wasn't going to miss for anything.

For the life of me, I couldn't decide what to wear. At the time, I didn't own many dress clothes and almost came pretty damn close to wearing the only thing I had that I even considered to be somewhat dressy.

Two years prior, Eric and I went to a Halloween party with a *Pretty in Pink* theme. He beat me to it and wound up going as Blane, Andrew McCarthy's character. He dressed up in a pair of white khakis, a blue button-down shirt, and a tan overcoat.

As for me, well, I went as Duckie, Jon Cryer's character. I even dressed up in Duckie's blue suit that he wore at the end of the film, complete with the bolo tie. *That* was the somewhat dressy attire I was referring to.

But I still had no idea what to wear. I mean, I knew that Eve was rich, and everything in my closet put together wouldn't even come remotely close to costing as much as a single one of her dresses. And I didn't think she was the type of person to judge either. So I switched back and forth between both casual and "Duckie" multiple times before settling on a mix of something—different.

I threw on a pair of tan khaki dress pants and my black Converse sneakers. Now, this is where it gets interesting because I also decided to wear a plain, white T-shirt, untucked, with a black sleeveless vest over it. The vest I'm referring to was part of another outfit/costume I had.

After *Bill and Ted's Excellent Adventure* was released in February that year, I went out the following day and bought my very own Ted outfit. They were just random pieces I had purchased and put together, which I wore to school the following Monday. The other students got a kick out of it and would play the air guitar when they saw me walking down the hall.

So with me looking like a somewhat dressed-up Keanu Reeves, I looked myself over in the mirror before deciding I was ready to go. Not to mention, I was totally rocking it. Plus, a little air guitar in front of the mirror seemed wildly appropriate, which I did—twice.

Anyway, after sweating profusely, resulting in two extra showers, five outfit changes, and two wasted hours, I finally left my house and was on my way to pick up Eve for our date.

About forty minutes later, after crisscrossing my way in and out of traffic, I finally made it to Eve's house. Or at least, I was in front of the address she'd written down on the piece of paper she gave me.

I found myself in a different part of rural suburbia, very similar to the neighborhood I lived in. I was a little confused because I had pictured her house as a massive stone mansion. But when I saw that it was only about double the size of mine, a perplexed expression hit my face.

I looked down at the piece of paper, then back up at the house, then back down at the piece of paper before looking back up at the house again. I then double-checked the house number, located just to the right of the front door and on the mailbox, before confirming that I was, in fact, where I needed to be. So I simply shrugged it off and got out of my truck.

Standing on the sidewalk, I felt like a stone statue, unable to move due to the amount of nervousness coursing through my body. And with no possible way of turning back (other than bailing and possibly having her hate me), I took a couple of deep breaths before making my way up her front walk.

I arrived at her door rather quickly and immediately rang the doorbell with my left hand. I then rubbed my hands together in both anticipation and eagerness to finally get the date started. Thankfully, I didn't have to wait long because, within seconds, the front door opened, and a woman, maybe in her mid-forties, stood there.

She was about as tall as Eve, with long brown hair down to the middle of her back, blue eyes, and a somewhat slimming figure. I knew it was Eve's mom before anyone told me because I recognized her voice as the very same one I had spoken to on the phone just a few hours prior.

"You must be Wes?" she asked.

"I am," I replied. "It's nice to meet you, Mrs. Parker."

"And you, as well. Please, come on in."

"Thank you."

As I walked through the front door, I noticed that the foyer in Eve's house was much smaller than the one at the party. Instead of two sets of stairs, her house only had one that ran along the right wall up to the second floor. A single chandelier also hung from the high ceiling, adding some decor.

"Don't worry, Eve will be right down," Mrs. Parker said.

I smiled and nodded.

"So," she continued, "Eve tells me that you two met at the party last night."

"Yes, we did," I replied.

"And what did you think?"

My brows immediately furrowed as I was confused by her question. "What did I think?" I asked.

"Yeah. What did you think of the party?" she specified.

"Oh! Well, I thought the party was awesome."

"Good. And what about the music?"

What about the music? I suddenly became a little confused as to why she was asking me so many questions about the party instead of my intentions toward Eve.

I mean, usually, when kids go out on dates, parents like to ask them more "personal" questions just to get a better idea as to whether or not they'd be a good match for their son or daughter. Questions like, "Where do you work? What do you like to do in your free time? Have you ever been to jail?" You know, stupid shit like that.

But maybe she heard enough from me over the phone. Maybe she was able to judge my character just by the way I spoke. Who knows? Regardless, I just decided to shrug it off and answer her question—sort of.

"Yeah, so how were you able to get those guys to perform there, anyway?" I asked, curious.

"We know some people," she replied.

"Makes sense."

We continued to stand there in awkward silence for another few seconds.

"Don't worry, Eve will be down shortly," Mrs. Parker said.

And speaking of awkward, as I waited at the bottom of the stairs, I could feel two holes being burned into the side of my head. Out of the corner of my eye, I could see Eve's mom staring at me. I also noticed her eyes looking me up and down from head to toe, almost as if she was a terminator trying to scan me to see if I was her intended target or not.

Feeling just a tad uncomfortable, I looked over at her and smiled. When I did, she smiled back. Thankfully, though, that was when Eve appeared at the top of the stairs, abruptly ending any further awkwardness.

"There she is," Mrs. Parker said, motioning toward Eve.

I immediately looked up to the top of the stairs and saw someone standing there I almost didn't recognize. And by that point, because it had been less than twenty-four hours since I last saw Eve, her image from the party was still practically burned into my brain. My jaw crashed through the floor, and my eyes nearly fell out of my head when I saw how gorgeous she looked.

Her hair was teased and mainly fell to her left side. She also wore a sparkly, gunmetal-red dress with two straps that went up and over her shoulders and came down just past her ankles. Light makeup accentuated her facial features, and her smile lit up the room. To put it simply, she—looked—stunning.

Standing at the bottom of the stairs, I watched Eve gracefully walk down them. As a matter of fact, she was so graceful that it didn't even look like she was walking at all. She looked just like an angel floating down to the bottom, straight from the heavens. However, her looking like some sexy Hollywood actress wasn't the only thing I noticed.

As she came down the stairs, I noticed the very same glow about her I had seen the night before at the party. And since the lighting in her house wasn't all that bright, I had to ask myself, *How is this even possible?*

Regardless, with her glowing and looking the way she did, that thought quickly dissipated when she finally said hi to me. And, once again, I was speechless.

"Hi, Wes!" Eve said. "Are you ready to go?"

Just like the night before, my mouth moved, but nothing came out.

She giggled. "I see we're back to not speaking again?"

Her mom's eyes quickly narrowed as she tried to figure out what was wrong with me and why I was acting like that.

"Wes, is everything all right?" her mom asked.

"What?" I said while shaking my head and snapping out of whatever trance I was in.

"I asked if you were all right?"

I briefly glanced in her direction before turning my attention back to Eve and smiling.

"I am now," I said. I then turned to my left, opened the door, and extended my left arm out toward my truck. "Shall we?"

"We shall," Eve replied. "Bye, mom."

"Bye, honey," her mother responded.

"It was very nice to meet you, Mrs. Parker," I said.

"Likewise."

I left the house and started walking toward my truck. But as I got halfway down the walk, I decided to turn around and give her mom one more wave before taking off. As I did, I could see her peeking out through the crack of the door, just standing there, glaring at me, almost as if she didn't trust me as far as she could throw me.

Not wanting to make a big deal out of it, I turned around and continued walking to my truck. When I got to the passenger's side door, I opened it up so Eve could get inside.

"Wow! Such a gentleman!" she remarked.

As she was getting in, I glanced toward the front door once more, only to see it now closed.

Once Eve and her dress were inside the truck, I gently closed the door before heading around to the driver's side and getting in. But I didn't start the engine just yet. Instead, I just sat there, staring at Eve, thinking that she was the most beautiful thing I had ever seen in my life. The drool was practically flowing out from the side of my mouth.

"Wes?" Eve asked.

"Yeah?" I responded, still dazed.

"I love your outfit."

I shook my head and came to. "You do?"

Without saying a word, she took her left hand and put it out, almost as if she were holding the neck of an invisible guitar. She then took her right hand and held an imaginary guitar pick to her stomach. Then she started playing it while making electric guitar sounds with her mouth.

When she was finished, she smiled and said, "I love *Bill and Ted's Excellent Adventure!*"

When she said that, I just wanted to marry her right then and there. Of course, that wasn't what actually happened. Instead, I immediately bore a half-Cheshire grin before starting up my truck and driving off toward one of the most unique first dates I would ever have.

CHAPTER 8

With me being way underdressed and Eve being way overdressed, we almost looked like some otherworldly version of the odd couple walking into the movies together. However, I didn't care. Even if everyone just laughed and pointed at me all night, they could all go and suck it because I'd still have the most beautiful date in the room.

Since there wasn't a movie theater near where she lived, I drove a bit to a Showcase Cinemas, located inside Flat Rock Mall, just twenty minutes from her house.

Flat Rock Mall was about halfway between our two towns and was the only mall around at the time. It had a whopping three floors, which boasted many stores I loved to shop at. Unfortunately, most of those stores aren't around anymore. Times changed, I guess, and so did the mall.

One of the places I liked to shop at was a store called Tape World. They had an arcade game-style logo above their entrance and only sold cassette tapes. Hence, the name. TransWorld Entertainment was the creator of this concept store, and during the mid-'90s, they decided to drop the Tape World name altogether and replace it with its new name, F.Y.E.

Another place I loved shopping at was Gadzooks. They sold all kinds of weird T-shirts, which was perfect for me because, well, I was weird. I mean, I still am. But that's beside the point. Unfortunately, they eventually decided to stop selling menswear altogether, leading to bankruptcy and a buyout from Forever 21.

Sam Goody, Strawberries, K.B Toys, Babbage's (which is now GameStop), Kinney Shoes, and a whole slew of others I liked to shop at were all there. Sadly, those stores are all now gone. Regardless, we weren't there to go shopping. We were there to see a movie.

Any movie that I went to see before my date with Eve, I would see with Eric. We always went to the movies together, and this would be the first one I would watch without him. In a way, it almost felt like I was cheating on him. Like, I should feel bad for going without him or something. However, I had Eve, who was, by far, much better looking. Quickly realizing this, I felt guilty no more.

To get to know her a little better, I decided it would be best to let her pick the movie. That way, I could get a good sense of what she liked. But after she commented about my outfit and did the air guitar in the car, I knew she wouldn't let me down.

She wound up picking *Honey, I Shrunk The Kids,* a movie that focused on a character named Wayne Szalinski, who was played by the great Rick Moranis.

Szalinski plays a scientist living in suburbia who invents a shrinking machine so powerful that it only blows things up. But when one of the neighbors' kids accidentally hits a baseball through Wayne's window, it winds up landing in the path of the machine's laser, suddenly causing the whole thing to work the way it was intended.

Wayne's two kids, plus the ones next door, all end up getting shrunk to the size of ants. When Wayne goes up to his attic to survey the damage, he unknowingly sweeps up the kids along with the mess and throws them out with the trash. And that's when the fun begins.

At the very end of the yard, the shrunken kids must now make a daring journey back to the house. They wind up wading through thick grass while battling giant ants, bees, sprinklers, a lawnmower, and even a scorpion. Yeah, I thought that the last one was odd, too. Regardless, the movie was still an incredible adventure.

Eve and I made it through the entire movie, with me missing most of it because I couldn't keep my eyes off her. Right near the end, when all the kids had been found and were about to be unshrunk, Amy (Wayne's teenage daughter) and Russ (the neighbors' teenage son) held hands in anticipation of the event. That was when Eve looked over at me, flashed her pearly whites, and took my hand in hers, interlacing our fingers together.

When we held hands, shivers ran all through my body, almost as if someone was pulsing me with small electrical blasts. I tried so hard to keep my composure as I smiled back. But inside, my brain was screaming with unimaginable joy. That feeling would no doubt be surpassed later on in the evening. But one thing at a time.

Another thing I noticed was that, even in a dark movie theater, she still had that slight glow cocooning her. That was when I knew it wasn't just some freak thing and that my sleuthing skills (which were virtually nonexistent) suddenly had to come into play. I just had to find out why her body was glowing. Without being too forward about it, of course.

Once the movie was over, we left the theater and the mall altogether. We couldn't do any shopping because, by the time the movie was over, it was late, and all the stores were closed. So, with us not being able to do any shopping, dinner suddenly moved up to the next item on the date list.

We were sitting in my truck, getting ready to pull out of the parking lot, when Eve said something to me that, as far as my feelings went for her, ultimately sealed the deal.

"That was a pretty good movie," she said. "After watching it, though, I wish we would've seen *Batman* instead."

After hearing her comment, I was in utter shock. I mean, a beautiful woman sitting in my truck would rather have seen a superhero movie than what we'd just seen? At that point, I wanted to profess my undying love for her. But that would've been just a little too creepy. I mean, we'd only just met the night before. Telling her that I loved her right then and there would've surely made her run for the hills.

So I took a couple of quick, deep breaths to try to keep my composure before looking over at her and responding.

"Next time," I said.

But then I thought, *Wait a minute. What if the date goes horribly wrong? What if she doesn't like me? Will there even be a next time?*

With those thoughts suddenly rolling around in my noggin, I quickly had to find out.

"Well, if there'll be a next time?" I shyly asked. "I mean, I don't want to pressure you into thinking that—"

"Oh, don't worry," she said, interrupting me. "There will *definitely* be a next time."

She finished that statement with a flirtatious smile, causing my face to turn a colorful shade of red. I quickly turned my head away to grin like a shy schoolgirl.

After I composed myself, I took a couple of deep, shallow breaths. Then I faced forward, threw my truck in drive, and burned some serious rubber out of the parking lot.

———————

As we drove, Eve and I continued holding hands. Inside, I was screaming with excitement. I also wondered how Eric's night was going because I soon realized that I'd forgotten to call him and tell him what I would be doing before I left.

When it came to keeping secrets from each other, Eric and I were just as bad as women. We didn't keep anything from each other and always spilled the beans about everything, no matter how embarrassing it was. And since both of us saw the exact same thing when we first saw the girls, letting him know what I would be doing should've been priority number one.

Oh well. There was always tomorrow.

As we neared our dinner destination, an Italian restaurant named Linguini's, located just a few miles from the mall, our plans for the evening suddenly took a sharp U-turn.

"If it's okay with you, I'd like to skip dinner," Eve said. "I'm still a little full from the popcorn and Sour Patch Kids I ate at the theater."

She wanted to skip dinner? Was she out of her mind? I mean, even though I managed to inhale my ritualistic movie food—consisting of a large bag of popcorn, a large soda, a bag of Sour Patch Kids, and a box of Nerds by mid-film—I was still hungry. Yet, she had the nerve to ask me if we could skip dinner? There was only one possible way I could respond to that.

"Sure. We can skip dinner if you'd like?" I replied.

"Good. Because I thought we could do something a little more adventurous instead," she suggested.

Adventurous, huh? Color me intrigued.

"What did you have in mind?" I asked.

———

Fifteen minutes later, we arrived at the summit of Lone Mountain, which stands about six hundred feet above the surrounding areas and is just high enough to get an incredible view of downtown Las Vegas—especially at night.

There aren't any roads that go up to the top of the mountain, but there is a ten-foot-wide jogging trail encompassing the entire thing. Eve thought it would be a good idea if we used it to drive on, which, of course, is illegal. But we did it anyway.

So we drove up the jogging path until we couldn't go any further. We then got out of the truck and started to hike down the side of the mountain. With it being nighttime, we had to be extremely careful. One false step, and we would fall, essentially plummeting to our deaths on the jagged rocks below.

I'd been up to the top of Lone Mountain a few times myself and had never once been to the spot Eve took me to. I discovered that she had stumbled upon it one day by sheer accident while scouting around. And because of the steep decline to get down, along with the same steep incline to get back up, very few people would dare go there.

Once we made it down to the overlook, we sat down next to each other on one of the giant rocks. I looked out toward the city and saw the flickering, strobing lights of Las Vegas illuminating the night sky. It was definitely a sight to be seen.

"Wow!" I exclaimed. "Look at that!"

"It's definitely something, isn't it?" she asked.

"It sure is."

As I looked out and scanned the ever-impressive city skyline, I couldn't help but smile to myself. With the city lights brightly lit and the stars shining down from above, being up there with her felt magical. So magical, in fact, that I quickly got caught up in the moment and almost forgot about what Eric and I saw at the party. It was also something I saw earlier when I picked Eve up and later at the movies.

I quickly turned away from the city to glance over at her. And sure enough, when I did, other than seeing a smile on her beautiful face (which made my heart melt right then and there), I could see the same dim glow surrounding her body.

With it being almost pitch black, there was no way in hell the city's lights could do that to someone that far away. And by that point, I still didn't have any theories about why it was happening or what was causing it. I mean, were Eric and I really the only ones who could see it? Plus, with the relationship (I guess you would call it) being so new and all, I didn't want to scare her away by asking her about it either. Besides, I could already see how that conversation would go…

Excuse me, but I wanted to ask you something. Why does your body emit a dim glow whenever I look at you? And am I the only one who can see it?

Yeah. Those two questions would most likely produce a strange look, followed by Eve running away immediately after.

However, there was one thing I could think of to test that to make sure I wasn't going insane. Or at least I wasn't going insane just yet. I would inevitably have to do the unthinkable—I would have to introduce Eve to my parents. And that thought *definitely* made me cringe.

I wasn't cringing because I hated the thought of introducing her to my parents, or the fact that I hated my parents, which was absolutely false. No. I loved my parents and the fact that they worked so hard to give me everything I had.

As I mentioned earlier, when I had one of those rare dates with a girl, my parents would eventually meet them and ask them a bazillion questions about her life, how we met, and so on. But Eve was different. She was the first girl I'd ever felt different about right from the get-go. And since I liked her more than anyone else I'd ever dated, I didn't want to put her through that kind of pain.

Anyway, to make a long-winded story short, if my parents couldn't see the dim glow surrounding her body, then I would know, one hundred percent, without a doubt, that I wasn't insane.

Regardless, I now had to put all of that in the back of my mind to focus on more important matters. More specifically, how I was all alone on the top of a mountain with a beautiful woman. And no one was around for miles to witness it.

"I mean, it just looks so pretty at night with all the bright lights lighting it up," Eve said.

"She sure does," I remarked.

Realizing what I just said, Eve immediately narrowed her eyes and turned to look at me.

"What did you just say?" she asked.

Of course, the only thing she could see was my goofy, lovestruck, smiling face staring back at her.

"What?" I asked while shaking my head and coming to.

"I said the city looks pretty at night with all the lights," she repeated. "Wouldn't you agree?"

And that was when I realized my mind was focused only on her when I blurted that out.

"Uh…oh, yeah, sure it does," I said.

"Are you even paying attention?" she asked.

"Of course, I am."

She noticed me still stupidly grinning at her.

"Then why are you looking at me like that?" she asked, curious.

"I can't help it," I replied.

"Okay, you're officially starting to creep me out."

"I'm sorry. But it's just that…" I trailed off.

"Just what?"

I guess I had no choice but to tell her. It was now do-or-die from this point on. Well, not really. I just thought I'd throw that in there for more dramatic effect.

See? I told you I'd add some more of it later.

"Okay. Promise me you won't go running for the hills? No pun intended," I said.

She let out a small laugh. "Of course not."

"In that case, I just want to say that I've never met anyone like you before."

"How so?" she asked.

"Last night at the party," I began, "when Eric and I saw you and Anna standing behind us, I don't know what happened or why, but you're the first person in my life that I've ever been speechless around. And I talk to everyone."

"Really?"

"Yeah. And I don't know if it's because you're so ridiculously beautiful or what, but I can't explain it."

She blushed. "I'm flattered." She paused momentarily before leaning over and taking my hand in hers. "Well, if we're being truthful with each other, would you mind if I told you something as well?" I shook my head, letting her know to continue. "You're the first guy ever to be speechless around me. No one has ever had any issues chatting me up. But you…now that was something I've never experienced before."

"Why-why-why do you think that is?" I stuttered.

She shrugged. "I don't know."

With her touching my hand, all I could do was stutter. My legs felt like Jell-O, and I was basically a blithering mess. And she could easily tell.

"If it's okay with you, I'd like to try an experiment," she suggested.

I suddenly sounded like I had a speech impediment. "What kind of, what, why?"

She took her right index finger and put it up to my mouth.

"Just stop talking for a moment," she said. "You ready?"

I didn't say anything and just nodded in agreement. Eve then lowered her finger and turned her body sideways while I did the same.

With us now facing each other and one hand still holding mine, she took her free hand and immediately grabbed my free hand. And once both of our hands were joined together, *that* was when it happened.

She briefly looked into my eyes while I stared deeply into hers. Her gaze pulled me in like a black hole sucking an object into its void. She then gave me one more shy smile before leaning in, closing her eyes, and kissing me.

For a split second, my mouth was in shock, not knowing how to respond. Thankfully, my brain quickly took over and told my mouth what to do, causing me to kiss her back. Her lips were soft, almost like velvet, while her strawberry lip gloss made them taste ever so sweet.

Not just my legs this time, but my whole body felt like jelly. My heart was beating so fast that I thought it was going to punch a hole right through my breastbone. The moment our tongues met, they immediately started feeling their way around each other, almost like two sea horses getting ready to mate. That was the best, most magical first kiss I had ever had in my entire life. A few seconds into it, and we quickly found our groove.

My left hand broke away from her right as I placed it on her warm, soft cheek. I then brought our other hands up to the middle of our chests so we could each feel our pounding heartbeats against them.

But just as the moment started to get super intense, something else happened—something we couldn't explain at the time but figured out why a little later. About one minute into our lip wrestling match, the ground started to quake.

It was slow at first and had a similar feeling to a tractor-trailer driving by a house. But over the next few seconds, it gradually worsened until it felt like we were having "the big one."

The Las Vegas area wasn't very prone to getting massive earthquakes, but they were still felt from time to time. After all, Nevada is the third-most seismically active state in the nation, trailing behind only California and Alaska.

Until that moment, only seven earthquakes registering higher than a 6.0 had hit the state—the earliest dating all the way back to Pleasant Valley in 1915. So feeling them wasn't all that uncommon. But the one we started feeling when we were up on that ridge, well, again, it felt colossal. And not wanting to see her get hurt, I immediately jumped into protective mode.

I quickly stood her up and leaned her against the backmost part of the ledge we were currently on. I threw myself in front of her and folded my arms over the top of her head. As I encased her in a human shield, I closed my eyes and thought happy thoughts while we waited for this whole thing to be over with. However, no sooner did the earthquake start, it stopped just as fast.

After it was over, I opened my eyes and lifted my head to take a quick look around, just to make sure we were still in one piece. I then lifted my arms off her head so she could also look around. Once we both realized that we were, above all else, alive with no cuts, scrapes, or bruises, we turned to face each other.

"That was, um, some earthquake," I said.

"It sure was," she replied.

As we stared each other down, we realized that our bodies were still firmly pressed against each other. And once again, my heart started racing.

"That's quite a heartbeat you've got," she remarked.

"I can't help it," I said.

I thought about leaning in and kissing her again. However, I decided that it might be in the best of both our interests if we got our asses off the overlook.

"Um," I swallowed hard, "we should probably go."

She nodded fast. "You're probably right."

I then took one last look at our bodies, which were still pressed against each other, before slowly backing away.

I don't know about her, but in that brief moment, I could feel the contents of my stomach wanting to shoot up out of my mouth and splatter all over the rocks. And it wasn't because I was nervous either. I think it was because of something else—something I always thought was absolute horse shit and something I never thought was possible until that very moment. Unfortunately, my theory doesn't come into play until much later in the story. Sorry.

I hiked the ten or so feet back up the steep cliff before turning around and extending my hands down toward Eve. She quickly grabbed onto them, and I helped her up. Once we were safe and sound, we hopped back into my truck. Then I carefully turned around and drove us back down the mountain.

———————

I pulled up to the front of Eve's house, parked my truck, and turned it off. I was still nervously gripping the steering wheel as I just sat there and took a deep breath. I then turned to face her, only to notice her looking back at me and smiling.

Holy shit! I thought. *How in the world did I get so lucky?*

After all, making a fool of myself at the party, I didn't think she would want to go out with me. But she did. And it was the second-best night of my life. You'll eventually hear me talk about my first best later in the story. But for now, this was it.

I was flying high, sitting on cloud nine, feeling like I was floating in a zero-gravity environment.

"I love you, Eve," I said. "I've loved you from the moment I first saw you standing on that balcony."

"I love you, too, Wes," she replied. "I've been waiting for you my whole life."

Then we leaned in and started kissing passionately.

Of course, I was only *thinking* that's how it would all go down in my head. In reality, we were still sitting in my truck, smiling at each other.

"I had a great time, Wes," Eve said.

"This was probably the best night of my life," I replied. She immediately turned away and giggled, her face changing to a more pinkish hue. "And I was hoping we could do it again."

"Most definitely."

She then took her right hand, placed it on the left side of my face, and pulled me in for one last kiss goodnight. It wasn't the tongue-wrestling kiss we shared on top of the mountain, but it was still just as sweet. She held her lips against mine for what seemed like forever. But it was more or less only a couple of seconds.

Once she broke away, she smiled at me again before getting out of the truck. She then closed the door and leaned in through the passenger's side window.

"I'll be waiting for your call, Wes Tucker," she said.

After she turned around, I gleefully watched as she started up her front walk.

But just as she grabbed her door handle, she turned around to look at me and smile once more before blowing me a kiss. As soon as I stupidly caught it, she opened her door and went inside before closing it and disappearing out of view.

I didn't drive away just yet. Instead, I sat there, thinking about how fantastic my night was and how stunning Eve looked. And with me being me, I looked into my rearview mirror, fabricated a wide Cheshire grin, and gave myself the double finger guns. Corny, I know. But can you blame me?

As soon as I finished thinking I was on top of the world, I reached into my glove box and pulled out the cassette tape of Loverboy's 1983 release, *Keep It Up,* before sliding it into my truck's cassette player. The first song on that tape, "Hot Girls in Love," immediately started playing, and I wasted no time cranking up the volume.

With my adrenaline still in overdrive and the song now blasting out of the speakers, I started my truck, threw it in drive, and got my ass out of there, leaving some gnarly tire tracks in the road behind me.

CHAPTER 9

After leaving Eve's house, I purposely drove around and avoided going home until after my parents were already in bed. I just had one of the best nights of my life and didn't want it ruined by them asking me a million questions. Besides, I already knew how it was going to go.

I would walk in the door, and they would both ask me stuff like, "How was it? Where did you go? What did you do? Did you go to the movies? Did you kiss her? Did you hold hands? What'd you eat?" Stupid shit like that. But I just wanted to get home and go to bed while still feeling great about everything.

———

The following morning, I basically did the same thing and avoided my parents again. I got up way before they did, showered, got dressed, and jumped in my truck to head out.

I drove just a few blocks over to Flatfield Way, the street where Eric lived. Like mine, his house was also a two-story abode made of tan stucco and a red-tiled roof. He didn't have a garage, but he did have a swimming pool. And instead of living at the end of the street, his house was located in the middle on the left.

I parked my car out front and got out before making my way up his driveway and into his backyard. Since I knew that his parents were also asleep, I didn't want to ring the doorbell and wake them. If I did, and because they were basically like second parents to me, I would almost certainly feel their wrath.

I located Eric's bedroom window, which sat on the leftmost corner of the second floor. I then searched the ground for a few small stones before picking them up. I used my right hand to throw them up there, lightly hitting the glass, hoping he would hear it and wake up.

The first pebble hit the window and bounced off. After a few seconds, no movement came from within his bedroom. So I tried a second pebble and got the same reaction—nothing.

Then I tried a third pebble, which was slightly bigger than the first two. And instead of lightly throwing it at the window, I decided to chuck it at the window. Thankfully, my throwing skills weren't that great, as I wound up missing the window entirely, hitting the side of the house instead. That last thud definitely got his attention, though, because, after a few seconds, his window came flying open, along with him hanging his upper half out of it.

He looked down at me, his eyes squinting from the bright morning sun, while also looking none too pleased.

"What the hell are you doing?" Eric angrily whispered to me. "Do you have any idea what time it is?"

"I'm sorry," I whispered back. "I got to tell you something. Just get dressed and meet me out front."

"Unless it involves you winning the lottery, I'm going back to bed."

"I want to tell you about my date with Eve."

The moment I said that, he started rubbing his eyes, hoping to wake himself up a little bit faster.

"You went out with Eve?" he asked, still whispering.

"Yeah," I replied. "Now get dressed and get your ass down here."

He flashed his palms. "All right. Just give me a minute."

He then ducked back inside and closed the window. I immediately returned to my car and hopped in the driver's seat. A few minutes later, he came bounding out of his house like an excited dog, ran to my truck, and jumped into the passenger's seat.

"Sorry for waking you up so early," I said.

"It's all forgiven," he said. "Except for one thing."

"What's that?" I curiously asked.

"You went out with Eve and didn't even bother to call me first?"

I shrugged. "I'm sorry. It just happened so suddenly. I didn't have time to call you."

"Yeah, right. That's what they all say."

"Well, what about you?" I asked.

"What about me?" he replied.

"Have you called Anna yet?"

"As a matter of fact, I have."

When he didn't continue, I just stared at him, waiting for him to tell me the outcome.

"And?" I asked, motioning for him to say something.

"And I have a date with her tonight," he said with a smirk.

"Fuck yeah, dude! That's what I'm talking about!"

"Okay, okay. Enough about me. So tell me…how did it go with Eve?"

Instead of talking to him about it while sitting in my truck in front of his house, I decided that a more "private setting" would be ideal for this type of conversation.

"How about I tell you over a few games?" I suggested with a smile.

He didn't even have to say yes. All he did was grin, letting me know what his answer was.

———————

Once we arrived at the Electric Box Arcade, we went in and immediately made our way over to Eric's favorite game of all time.

Centipede was released in 1981 by Atari, and according to the original instruction manual, you took control of a garden gnome armed with a magic wand. The object was to defend his mushroom forest against an invasion of giant centipedes, spiders, fleas, and scorpions. While the premise was pretty self-explanatory, the game could be quite challenging at times.

Instead of the traditional joystick, *Centipede* used a trackball (a white ball in which you could roll in all directions) to move the main character on the bottom of the screen. The machine also had a fire button that you pressed with your left hand to make your character, well, fire.

The centipedes would move from left to right across the screen and descend one level after reaching the edge or hitting a mushroom. You could eliminate the mushrooms to make more room on the screen, but each one took four shots to destroy, and that just took too damn long. Plus, the higher up in levels you went, the more mushrooms there were. Not only that, but the fleas dropped straight down and disappeared when they touched the bottom of the screen. There were also the zig-zagging spiders, which ate the occasional mushroom to help you out. Mix those in with the horizontally moving scorpions, and it became extremely challenging.

The scorpions would turn the mushrooms poisonous upon impact. What that meant for you was that if a centipede touched those tainted mushrooms, they would immediately shoot straight down toward the bottom of the screen. If multiple sections of the centipede hit the poisonous mushrooms simultaneously, those same poisoned sections would all come down on you at once. That was why it was more challenging in the higher levels of the game. The only way you could die was when you were hit by one of the main enemies. Once you lost all three of your gnome's lives, it was game over.

Eric was a pro at that game and would kick my sorry-ass every time we played. Even though I knew I didn't stand a chance against him, and seeing as how he could go about fifteen or twenty minutes without dying, I figured that would give me plenty of time to talk while he played.

"All right. We're here, and I'm playing. Now, spill it," Eric said.

"Okay. You asked for it," I began. "Well, before my shift at Johnny's started, my parents told me that Eve called while I was sleeping. And since I didn't have any time to call her back, I had to wait until after my shift was over to do so. Oh, and, by the way, I kind of got fired."

"Holy shit! You got fired? Why?"

"Tammy and I…you know what? It's a long story. I'll tell you later."

"Tammy got you fired? Damn!"

"She didn't get me fired. I…wait, I'm the one telling this story, so shut up!"

"You're right. I'm sorry," he said. "Please, continue."

"Thank you. Anyway, after I got fired, I immediately raced home to call Eve."

"Son of a bitch!" Eric shouted as he watched his gnome get killed by a descending centipede. "Sorry. Your turn."

He stepped aside, and I took over, now controlling player two. Unfortunately, I don't have much to say about my own gameplay because, just around ten thousand points, my gnome got bombed by a flea.

"Shit," I muttered.

"Dude, that was pathetic," he said.

"You don't have to tell me."

I then stepped aside, giving control of the game back to him.

"You may continue your story now," he said.

"Oh, right," I replied. "I went to pick Eve up at her house around eight o'clock."

"Wait, you saw her house?"

"Yeah. Why?"

"What did it look like?"

"It's slightly bigger than mine and looked like any other house. Can you please try to hold your questions until after I'm finished?"

"Right. Sorry," he said.

"Anyway," I continued, "I also got to meet Mrs. Parker, who seemed very…*unusual.*"

"Unusual? Unusual, how?" he asked, intrigued.

"She kept giving me strange looks and asked me some very odd questions."

"Well, you were going out with her daughter. She was probably just being protective of her."

"I suppose. But it didn't feel like that. It almost felt like something else. Like she was…eh, never mind."

"Like she was what?"

I took a deep breath before continuing. "It almost felt like something a federal agent or maybe even a police officer would do to a suspect who was being held for questioning."

Eric laughed. "You really need to lay off the spy thrillers. Like I said, she was probably just keeping a watchful eye on you."

"Yeah, you're probably right."

"Of course, I am." He paused. "What happened next?"

"Well, when Eve appeared at the top of the stairs," I continued, "I noticed something that I had hoped would be a fluke. Remember what we saw at the party?"

Without missing a beat, Eric immediately turned to face me, his eyes wide and his jaw hitting the floor, just like a cartoon character. Plus, he turned away from his game. And he never does that while playing *Centipede.* Of course, the moment he did, his gnome died almost instantly.

"She was glowing?" he whispered, shock emanating from his mouth.

"Yeah," I replied. "I couldn't believe it."

"Holy shit."

"It never left her the whole night. And after a while, I just got used to it. Although it was a little distracting in the movie theater."

"You went to the movies? What'd you see?"

"*Honey, I Shrunk the Kids,*" I mumbled under my breath, knowing that Eric and I were supposed to go see it together.

"Wait, did you just say, *Honey, I Shrunk the Kids?*"

I nodded. "I know. But Eve wanted to see it. So I said yes. Sorry, buddy."

"What the fuck! We were supposed to see that together," he angrily reminded me before taking a deep breath and calming himself. "Well, because you were with a girl, don't worry about it. Just answer me this…how was it?"

"It was pretty good," I replied before getting a compelling thought. "You know, you should take Anna to see it. Then we can discuss it afterward."

He immediately smiled and wagged a finger at me. "That's not a bad idea," he said.

"That's because I thought of it."

"Don't get cocky."

"Whatever you say, Han."

My sarcastic reply was then followed up by a smile and a little bit of laughter from both of us. I then told him to play my game, as I was suddenly in more of a talking mood than a playing one. And once he took the controls, I continued my story.

"After the movie," I continued, "we were supposed to go to dinner. However, she didn't want to. Instead, we went up to Lone Mountain to look out over the city."

His eyes narrowed. "Lone Mountain? You hiked all the way to the top?"

"Of course not," I replied. "I drove up the jogging path until I couldn't go any further."

"You rebel!"

"We then hiked down the side of the mountain to a little overlook that I didn't even know existed."

"Interesting. I may just have to check out this so-called ledge myself."

"As we were sitting down there, we got to see the lights and the stars while we just talked and kissed. It was perfect."

Upon hearing that last part, Eric slowly turned to me with a shocked expression on his face. At that moment, he didn't even care that a centipede had just killed his gnome because, apparently, he was suddenly more interested in the fact that I kissed Eve than playing his game.

"You kissed her?" he asked.

"I did," I replied.

"How was it?"

"I can't even begin to tell you the right words."

"Come on. You must've felt something?"

"Let's put it this way, and you can't tell a soul what I'm about to say, but"—I paused to quickly scan the joint to make sure no one was listening in on us before turning back to Eric—"I think I'm in love with Eve."

After telling him that, I honestly didn't know how I expected him to react or what I expected him to say. Actually, that wasn't entirely true.

You see, I thought that maybe he would give me some bullshit about love at first sight or laugh in my face at how ludicrous that all actually sounded. However, what *did* come out of his mouth caught me completely by surprise.

"Good for you, dude," he said. "I'm happy for you."

"You want to say that again?" I asked, making sure I heard him correctly.

"Sure. I said I'm happy for you," he repeated.

I pointed at him, confused. "You're happy for me?"

"What part of that did you not understand?"

"I don't know. I guess I was expecting you to say something different, that's all."

But the moment was quickly cut short as he couldn't hold a straight face any longer. He immediately broke out into a laughing fit, which seemed to go on forever, before finally saying what I initially thought he would say in the first place.

"You love her? Are you out of your mind?" he asked, still laughing.

"See, this is why I didn't even want to tell you," I said.

"You've only known this girl for what, two days now, and you're already in love with her? Do you know how ridiculous that sounds?"

"Ridiculous or not, it's true."

And once I said *that,* he laughed even harder. In which case, I just leaned against the neighboring machine and folded my arms while I waited patiently for him to calm down.

"Okay. Just keep on laughing," I said. "When you're done, maybe we can finish this conversation like adults."

I shit you not. I waited for another two minutes before he finally finished laughing.

"Are you done?" I asked.

"I am," he replied, trying to catch his breath.

"Good. Now, as I was saying," I continued, "I tried to think of every possible solution why I would feel this way about her. And the only conclusion I could come up with is that I am, in fact, in love with her."

"Okay. But seriously. Are you sure you're not confusing love with infatuation?"

I shook my head. "No way. This is love."

He shrugged. "Well, I can't think of anything else it would be. So I guess I'll just have to give you the benefit of the doubt."

"Thank you," I politely replied.

"Anytime."

Then we went silent, as neither of us knew what to say or do next. After all, being in love with someone was completely new territory for both of us.

"So what now?" I asked.

He thought about it for a bit. "Breakfast?"

"Hell yeah. I'm starving."

"Same here."

"But anywhere besides Johnny's," I swiftly told him.

He grinned. "Sounds like a plan."

Both of us then turned around and made our way toward the front door. On the way out, however, I suddenly remembered an important detail I had forgotten to mention—something that had me practically pissing in my pants the night before.

"By the way," I said, "I couldn't find anything on the news last night or this morning, for that matter, but you didn't happen to see or hear of any reports about an earthquake last night, did you?"

He immediately turned to look at me with a confused expression on his face.

"No. Why?" he asked.

I thought about explaining to him exactly "when" it happened, but decided it would be best to tell him at another time.

I shrugged. "No reason."

He, in return, just shrugged back as we made our way out of the arcade.

CHAPTER 10

Breakfast was great. As a matter of fact (and I can't explain why), it was probably one of the best breakfasts I'd ever eaten.

We ate at a little diner on the outskirts of the city called Joe's Breakfast & Lunch. It was about the size of Johnny's but had a more modern '80s décor. Well, at the time, it was modern.

Joe's specialized in making some of the best pancakes, Belgian waffles, and omelets around. The breakfast I ordered that morning consisted of a Chocolate Eruption, hash browns, bacon, and toast. I also wound up washing everything down with a delicious cup of coffee. (Free refills, of course.)

Joe's Chocolate Eruption, or any flavor eruption, for that matter, was one of their staple breakfast plates. The Chocolate Eruption consisted of three Belgian waffles made with melted-down chocolate chips and cocoa, all stacked on top of each other. In between each layer was a coating of peanut butter, chocolate syrup, and marshmallows. Top the whole thing off with some whipped cream and more chocolate syrup, and it was like an eruption of flavor the moment it hit your tongue. Hence, the name.

However, when I flew back to Swanson for my high school reunion a few years ago, I was sad to hear that Joe's had closed just a few years before that. But hey, that's business, and life goes on.

After breakfast, Eric and I decided to go to the movies and finally watch one of the films we'd been dying to see all summer.

And by the way, this next part may be a little wordy, so feel free to skip past it. But I assure you, the subject matter is also very debate-worthy.

Still here? Great.

Batman was released on June 23, 1989, and was directed by the immeasurable Tim Burton. Michael Keaton was cast in the lead role of both Bruce Wayne and Batman. Along with everyone else, I was very skeptical about him being cast in such a prominent role. Due to his previous credits, not many people thought he'd be a good fit.

Up until that point, he starred in various TV shows, including *Mister Rogers' Neighborhood* (which was aimed toward kids), *All's Fair, The Mary Tyler Moore Hour, Working Stiffs,* and *Report to Murphy* (all of which were comedies). Some of his movie credits included *Night Shift, Mr. Mom, Johnny Dangerously, Gung Ho,* the ever-popular *Beetlejuice,* and *The Dream Team,* all of which were, again, comedies.

But to cast him in a serious superhero role like Batman, well, everyone had their doubts. However, he managed to give all of us the literal middle finger and prove everyone wrong, including myself.

Even today, the *Batman* movies remain a major topic of debate among nerds alike about which film, actor, or series was the best. But with a supporting cast like Jack Nicholson as the Joker, Kim Basinger as Vicki Vale, and Michael Gough as Alfred, the 1989 film was rock-solid. Although it strayed just a tad from the source material, it's still the best *Batman* movie to date. And I'll give you two words as to why—Michael Keaton.

Lewis Wilson was the first actor to portray Batman on-screen, in a fifteen-part serial that debuted in 1943. A second serial debuted in 1949, with Robert Lowery taking over the titular role. Adam West, who everyone thinks is the original Batman, then took over in the campy and corny (but still fun to watch) 1960s TV show.

Batman Returns, released in 1992, also starred Keaton and was just as good as the first. Then, in 1995, *Batman Forever* came out, but Keaton was nowhere to be found.

Batman Forever starred Val Kilmer in the title role and wasn't half bad. With Tim Burton no longer directing, the film wasn't as dark or successful as the first two. Because of its more light-hearted tone, the audience didn't quite approve. Plus (and no one can really understand why), nipples were added to the batsuit. Yes, you read that right. Nipples!

Its follow-up, *Batman & Robin*, replaced Val Kilmer with George Clooney. But even Arnold Schwarzenegger as Mr. Freeze couldn't save that one.

In 2005, Christopher Nolan released *Batman Begins*, starring Christian Bale. That was followed up with 2008's *The Dark Knight* (my personal favorite of the three) and 2012's *The Dark Knight Rises*. However, unlike previous movies, Nolan decided to give the latter two versions of the batsuit a voice modulator. (Don't even get me started on that.)

In 2016, a new actor would play the Caped Crusader in *Batman v. Superman*. His name was Ben Affleck. Of course, just like Michael Keaton, nobody thought that Ben would be a good fit. However, in my opinion, he was, without a doubt, my second favorite Batman. He went on to play the role a few more times in 2016's *Suicide Squad*, 2017's *Justice League*, and 2023's *The Flash*, which was also the film where Michael Keaton made his triumphant return as an alternate universe Batman. And George Clooney was in it for all of five seconds at the end of the film. (Yay.)

Oh yeah—I almost forgot about 2022's *The Batman*, which was both written and directed by Matt Reeves and starred Robert Pattinson in the title role. I must say, he wasn't half bad and is my third-favorite Batman, behind Keaton and Affleck.

So there you have it. A brief list of live-action Batmen. Or at least all the ones who played him when I wrote this. Of course, I purposely omitted all the Batman voice actors because they were cartoons. (FYI, Kevin Conroy is the best one.) Although he did play an older Bruce Wayne in the CW's version of "Crisis On Infinite Earths."

Now, whoever reads this will probably disagree with me, and that's okay. Of course, you'd still be wrong unless you went with Keaton. If you did, then you're my kind of person.

Okay then, enough of my yapping. Back to the story.

By the time we left the best *Batman* movie ever to grace the silver screen, it was just about time for Eric to leave and go on his date with Anna. Frankly, I couldn't wait to get him out of my hair because I was so desperate to find out if he would get to experience the same stuff I did with Eve.

After I dropped him off at his house, I went home. However, this time, there was no escaping it. Both of my parents were sitting in the kitchen, having some lunch. By the time I walked in and closed the door, I didn't even make it two feet, as it was already too late.

"Hi, honey!" my mom greeted me.

"Hey, Mom," I replied. "Hey, Dad."

"Late night last night?" my dad asked.

"You could say that," I replied.

Since there was no avoiding it, I went into the kitchen to join them both at the table, just to get it over with.

"Where'd you go this morning?" my mom asked. "You left before we even got up."

"Sorry about that," I said. "I had to go and talk to Eric about something. Then we ate some breakfast and saw a movie."

"Everything okay with you two?"

"Oh yeah. Everything's fine."

Then the room went awkwardly silent as I just sat there and waited for my mom to ask the inevitable question.

"So how was your date with Eve?" my mom asked.

And there it was.

"It was good," I replied.

As soon as I answered, my parents just stared at me for a few seconds, hoping I would kindly elaborate.

"Is that all?" my dad asked.

"What else do you want me to say?" I said.

"Well, for starters, how about what she looked like? Or what you guys did?" my mom elaborated.

Now, I could've given my dad a straightforward answer, and he would've been happy with it. But I knew my mom wouldn't let this go unless I gave her something a little more concrete. So I did.

"Well, we went to the movies and then took a drive," I began. "As for what she looked like, let's just say that I've never met anyone like her before."

"It sounds like you really like this girl?" my mom said.

"I do. And we'll be going out again."

"Answer me this," my dad said before leaning in close to me. "Did you kiss her?"

"Jim! What kind of a question is that?" my mom asked, slightly disgusted.

"What?" he replied, shrugging his shoulders. "I just figured I'd get it out of the way before you asked it."

My mom sneered at him. And for a split second, I actually thought about lying to them. But you'll find out why in a moment.

"Actually, we kissed twice," I said.

My dad immediately pointed at me, his face a stoic mask.

"That's my boy," he said. "That's how we Tuckers do it."

And, of course, my mom became just a little peeved by my dad's comment.

"For God's sake, Jim!" she said.

He shrugged again. "What? If the boy wants something, he should go for it. Besides, that's how I got you."

"That is *not* how you got me."

My dad immediately leaned back in his chair and folded his arms as he couldn't wait to hear what my mom had to say about that.

"Then why don't you enlighten me?" he said.

"Okay, I will," my mom said. "If I recall, you were…"

And there you have it. My dad was always, "Go for it, son. If you want something bad enough, then you should have it." But what he really meant was, "As long as it's within legal rights."

However, every time he showed his go-getter attitude, my mom would always try to shoot him down and give him some bullshit excuse about how we don't do those kinds of things around here. *That* was why I didn't want to tell them.

Rather than listen to them argue over it—well, actually, it was more like a discussion than an argument. My parents loved each other and would never argue over…

Sorry. Now, I'm just rambling.

Anyway, I quietly excused myself from the table and went upstairs to my bedroom. After closing the door, I sat down on my bed and took a breather to collect my thoughts.

I sat there and thought about Eric and how his date with Anna was about to go. *Would he have the same feelings that I had? Would he be able to see the same dim glow around her body as well? More importantly, why wasn't there anything on the news about an earthquake last night?*

Okay, I know that last thought didn't have anything to do with Eric's date, but it somehow made its way into my head. While Eve and I were up on that mountain, we felt it. I know because we both thought that we were going to die.

All right, we didn't really feel like we were going to die. See? There I go again, more drama.

But then I got to thinking—*Were we the only two people who could feel it?* I mean, while we were out last night, not a single person approached me to tell me my date was glowing. Since I was the only one besides Eric who could see it, were we the only ones who could feel it, too? And if so, why?

So the only thing left for me to do was to think about it. And the only way for me to think about it was to take my mind off it completely. And the only way for me to do *that* was to play some video games.

I went over to my entertainment center and opened the cabinet where I kept all my Nintendo games. Since I already knew which game I was going to play, I quickly located it and pulled it out.

The game I'm referring to had several versions, along with many different characters. It even spawned a sequel of a different name. Not to mention, you had to have lightning-fast reflexes to beat the end boss. That's right. I'm talking about the one and only *Mike Tyson's Punch-Out*.

Mike Tyson's Punch-Out was initially released by Nintendo in 1987. You took control of a boxer named Little Mac, whose name wasn't just a name. He also happened to be smaller than all the other boxers you faced off against.

There was a total of eleven boxers, some of whom you had to fight twice. And, of course, once you made it through everyone else, you got to face off against one of the greatest boxers to ever step in the ring—Mike Tyson himself.

You could control Little Mac by hitting the left and right arrows to dodge your opponent's punches. To block, you would hit down. You could push the *A* and *B* buttons to punch your opponent in the gut, using Mac's left and right hands, respectively. To punch your opponent in the face, you had to push up, along with one of the punching buttons. Occasionally, you would be rewarded with a star, in which you could press the start button to have Mac do a powerful uppercut.

Up until that point, I could always make it through every opponent in the game, but had never once beaten Mike Tyson. I was just never fast enough to do it. Eagerly wanting to get started, I popped in the game, hit the power button, and pressed start.

I blew through the first two title bouts, beating such characters as Glass Joe, Von Kaiser, Piston Honda, Don Flamenco, King Hippo, Great Tiger, and Bald Bull. I didn't find out until later that there was an actual secret people could use to get the upper hand on their opponents within the game itself. For example…

Bald Bull does this "bull charge" move in which he backs up to the back of the ring, ducks down, bounces for a moment, and then charges toward you like a bull. If you didn't dodge his attack in time, then he would ultimately knock you out. However, you could parry this move by punching him in the gut before he hits you, resulting in him getting knocked down for the count. Most of the time, I was able to do this at a 75/25 split. The secret that I'm talking about came in the form of one of the background spectators.

Just to the left of the upper right ring post, there would be an occasional camera flash. I didn't know it, but to knock Bald Bull down every time, you had to look for that camera flash during his bull charge. Once you saw it, that was your cue to hit either one of the punch buttons. It was a very well-hidden secret that very few people knew at the time. Once I learned about it, my games went much smoother.

After the first two title bouts, I made it through the third one, but not before taking a few knockdowns myself. In that third title bout, I faced off against Piston Honda number two, Soda Popinski, Bald Bull number two, Don Flamenco number two, Mr. Sandman, and Super Macho Man.

Another secret (which most people already know about) is building up your life meter. If you got your ass handed to you in any one of the rounds, you could press the select button during one of the cut scenes, causing your manager, Doc, to pat you on the shoulder much faster than usual. Then, once the new round began, your life meter would increase. However, the downside was that you could only do this once per match.

The final boxer in the game was Mike Tyson. His super speedy punches would always knock me out, usually by round two. The majority of the time, because his uppercuts in the first round would knock you down with just one punch, I would lose quite fast. And because he was so fast and jittery, that made me fast and jittery as well. I think the whole point of playing him was for you not to anticipate when he was going to punch you, which is what made him so difficult.

I only managed to get knocked down once during the first round, while also knocking him down. I made it through the second round, knocking him down twice while he did the same in return. During the third round, however, I was in the zone. Or at least, I thought I was.

I managed to knock him down two more times while taking a ton of damage myself. We each had just a tiny bit of life left (a couple of punches for me and only one for him). I knew that if I were to take one more hit, I wouldn't be getting back up. And, as you could've probably already guessed, I didn't.

I got so excited at the prospect of finally beating him that I prematurely moved Little Mac to the left. By the time my character was back in front of Tyson, there was nothing I could do about it. He gave me an uppercut and won the match. Even though referee Mario stood there and counted, I ferociously pushed those *A* and *B* buttons to try to get Little Mac back up. Unfortunately, that was it. I'd been beaten again.

"Shit!" I said, dropping my controller to the floor.

I would go on to beat Tyson eventually, but that wasn't the day I would do it. Even to this day, I've only managed to beat him a handful of times. Talk about your kryptonite games.

After having played through the whole game, I still couldn't think of a reason why the earthquake happened or if Eve and I were the only ones who felt it. The only thing I could do now was wait to hear from Eric about how his date with Anna went. In the meantime, there were many other things I could do to pass the time. However, I didn't want to do any of them—except for one.

So I immediately looked over toward my nightstand, reached out my left hand, and picked up my phone.

124

CHAPTER 11

"Hey, Eve. It's Wes," I said, speaking into the phone's receiver.

"Hi, Wes. How are you?" she asked.

"Better, now that I'm talking to you."

I could hear her giggle on the other end.

"You're so sweet," she said.

"Well, that's me, sweet Wes," I replied.

Sweet Wes? Really? I couldn't believe I just said that.

"Sorry," I said. "I bet that sounded really corny."

"That's okay," she replied. "I happen to like corny."

"Good. Because if you like corny, then you'll love me."

Wow! Two stupid remarks back-to-back. I was on a roll.

"Well, not love me as in *love me,* but love me as in I tend to grow on people," I nervously clarified.

She giggled again. "Don't worry. I know what you meant."

I immediately let out a silent sigh of relief.

"Hey, did you hear about Anna and Eric?" she asked.

"Hopefully, their date's going well," I remarked.

"So you did hear?"

"Yeah. I hung out with Eric this morning before he left."

"Did you happen to tell him anything about what happened on our date?"

"Of course. We tell each other everything."

She laughed. "You two are worse than girls."

"You have no idea."

"So what do I owe the pleasure of this call?"

"Oh, nothing," I replied.

"Then how come I don't believe you? Come on. No one calls someone else for no particular reason."

"That's not true. I mean, what if I just wanted to hear the sound of your voice?"

"That would be a first."

"All right, you caught me," I lied before taking a deep breath. "Actually, the reason why I'm calling you is because…"

I trailed off and froze.

"Because what?" she asked.

Of course, I wanted to hear the sound of her voice. She had the voice of an angel. I wasn't lying when I told her that. However, that was only part of it.

The real reason why I was calling her was because I couldn't get her out of my mind. Ever since I met her at the party, I couldn't stop thinking about her. If I told her that, though, she might think I was a creep or something. Damn, my thoughts.

"Wes, are you there?" she asked after not getting an immediate response.

I quickly shook my head and snapped out of the daze I was in. "Huh? Oh, yeah. I'm still here," I replied.

"Are you okay? You went silent for a moment."

"Me? Oh, I'm fine. How are you?"

"I'm…good."

Eve's last response gave nothing away. She obviously had a feeling that something was up with me when, clearly, I was just love-struck.

"Hey, what are you doing later?" I asked.

"Nothing. Why?" she replied.

"Would you like to go out with me again?"

"That depends."

"Depends on what?" I asked, curious.

"Depends on what you have in mind?"

"Do you like roller skating?"

"I love it!" she enthusiastically replied.

"Then would it be okay if I picked you up in a couple of hours?"

"Sure. But why wait? How about if you come pick me up now?"

Her response totally threw me for a loop, causing me to fumble my words. "Well, I…but I…well…" She giggled again before I was finally able to formulate an answer. "I'll see you in a little bit."

"I can't wait. Don't be late," she said and then hung up the phone.

I also hung up the phone and sat there in stunned silence, not yet really coming to terms with the fact that I had just asked Eve out on a second date so soon and in as many days. I couldn't believe it. However, no matter how shocked I was, I had no time to waste.

Because she insisted that I pick her up right away, I didn't want to spend too much time deciding what to wear. And since she loved my Ted outfit the night before, I knew she probably wouldn't care what I wore.

Since we were going roller skating, I picked out a white T-shirt with the word RELAX, written in all capital letters, which I had bought at a Frankie Goes to Hollywood concert a few years prior. I also picked out a pair of blue jeans, ripped at both knees, and threw on my blue Converse sneakers.

Once I was done, I briefly said goodbye to my parents before bolting out of the house. I hopped in my truck and quickly left, as I was now ready to go out with Eve on date number two.

———

Sometime later, I picked Eve up at her house while somehow avoiding her weird mother. Thankfully, it was because she wasn't home at the time.

Eve, again, looked absolutely stunning in her outfit. She wore a white button-down shirt that was tied just above her belly button—

kind of how a farmer's daughter would wear hers. It was also unbuttoned, just enough to show off some of her spectacular cleavage.

She also wore blue jeans (which hugged pretty much everything) and a pair of white Keds. This time, most of her hair hung down on her right side instead of her left. With her dark eyeliner, light reddish eyeshadow, and red lipstick, she almost looked like a brown-eyed version of Heather Locklear. And she looked gorgeous.

The place I took her skating was always a favorite of mine as a kid. It was located directly across the street from Lakeview Amusement Park, a typical theme park that boasted many roller coasters, Ferris wheels, concessions, and other miscellaneous booths. The place I'm referring to, however, was a little skating rink called The Rollaway.

The Rollaway was about the size of a small warehouse. When you walked in through the side entrance, the skate rental booth was right there, while the concession stand sat just on the other side of it.

The rink itself was square and surrounded by a wooden railing, supported by crisscrossing pieces that ran the length of it. Between the railing and the walls was a six-foot walkway filled with benches (for taking a quick break), lockers (for storing some of your items), and a bunch of various stand-up arcade games. In the back was a party room of sorts, with a few tables and chairs set up. There, you could eat your food, have parties, or just sit down and relax.

Along the inner top of the rink was a set of colored lights that ran the entire length of the ceiling, while a disco ball hung from the center. An impressive sound system was also installed so the DJ could make announcements and play everyone's favorite songs.

During the summertime, that place was always stuffed to the rafters with people. That day was certainly no exception.

"This should be interesting," Eve said as we walked through the doors.

"Why do you say that?" I asked. "You did say you've been roller-skating before."

"True. But only a few times. This is the first time I've ever been to one on a date."

"Well, don't worry. I'll take it nice and slow. Just follow my lead, and you'll be fine."

After I paid, we grabbed our skates and immediately walked to the far back left corner, where we found an empty locker to store our things.

I've always loved roller skating and have been doing it as far back as I can remember. I went to The Rollaway regularly and even had my twelfth birthday party there. A master skater, I was not. But a pretty damn good skater, I was.

However, as I got older, I became more interested in street skating and eventually purchased my first pair of rollerblades in the mid-'90s. To this day, I still own a pair and still love to skate.

Once we finished lacing up our skates, we both stood up and were ready to head out onto the floor. I stood up just fine while Eve seemed to stumble a bit. I quickly grabbed and steadied her so she wouldn't fall.

"You okay there?" I asked.

"Don't worry. I got it," she said.

"Are you sure? I don't want to see you fall."

"I'll take it slow. If I feel like I'm going to fall, I'll grab onto the railing."

And with that, she slowly made her way out onto the hardwood floor, holding on to the railing so she wouldn't fall. I then started to make my way out there, but soon stopped. I was now focused on Eve, who was still standing at the railing, just staring at me, sporting a devious grin.

She soon started to skate slowly back away from the railing, and as she did, I noticed that her devious grin was no more. Instead, it had been replaced by a smile, spanning from ear to ear. My curiosity immediately got the best of me about what she was doing and why she was smiling like that. So I just stood there and observed.

I watched as her slow skating picked up a little. She then turned around and started skating forward at a speed equal to what I would generally skate at, which, at other roller rinks, would typically get me thrown in the skating jail for going too fast.

She was almost finished with her first lap, and just as she passed in front of me, she twirled around twice before leaping and twirling once in mid-air. With the number of people at the rink, half of them saw what she did and applauded. I couldn't do anything but just stand there and laugh while shaking my head.

"Wow," I said. "I'll admit, you totally fooled me into thinking you couldn't skate."

"What are you waiting for, hotshot?" she said, mocking me. "Let's see what you got."

With her throwing out a challenge and me not wanting to get outskated, I wasted no time and quickly sped out onto the floor.

I started by skating forward, then backward, then forward again. Halfway through my lap, I leaped into the air to do a double spin, before landing on one foot and leaning forward. With me pretending to fly, I glided the rest of the way, stopping just a few inches shy of her.

She slowly nodded her head approvingly. "Not bad. Not bad at all."

"Well, if you think that was good," I said, "wait till you see this."

I was about to skate off and perform another trick when she suddenly grabbed my right arm, stopping me dead in my tracks.

"Let's just skate around together," she suggested.

"Good idea," I replied with a smile.

As we started to skate, "Let the Music Play" by Shannon began blasting out of the sound system.

"So, Eve…seeing as how we didn't get to do much talking last night," I began, and smiled at her. She also smiled. "Why an all-girl school? Why not a regular school?"

She shrugged. "Who knows? My mother said it was to keep me safe."

"Safe from what?"

"From boys, obviously."

"Do you think that's why you went?"

"Hell no. I think it was for a different reason."

I arched a curious eyebrow. "And what reason is that?"

She shrugged again. "I have no clue."

I then got a very intriguing thought. However, I didn't want to get my hopes up, so I decided to hold off on any excitement until she answered me.

"So then, if you went to an all-girl school," I began, "did you date other boys? Or am I your first one?"

She looked at me and huffed while shaking her head. "Typical," she said. "No, you're not my first one."

"Oh," I replied, my hope quickly deflated like a popped balloon.

"Even though I was trapped behind the walls of an all-girl school, there's a lot more to me than you think."

"Oh yeah? Like what?"

"If you stick around long enough, maybe I'll show you," she said, briefly meeting my gaze while sporting a flirtatious smirk.

Hearing that, I tried my hardest not to get too excited. So I gave her a slow nod of approval before briefly looking away and sporting the biggest smile I'd ever had. After a moment or two, I quickly composed myself and lost my boyish grin before turning back to her.

"What about college?" I asked. "Where are you going, and what are you going for?"

"I got accepted to Princeton," she replied.

"Holy shit. Really?"

"Yeah. I've always wanted to become a singer. So I'll be going there to study music."

"Well, even though I haven't heard you sing yet, I can already tell you have a beautiful voice."

"Thank you," she said while blushing. "What about you? Are you going to college?"

"I'll be going to Florida State on a track and field scholarship."

"Seriously? I'm impressed."

I narrowed my eyes. "Why do you say it like that?"

"No reason. I just never thought of you as a track and field type of guy."

"Oh, really? And just what 'type of guy' did you think of me as?"

She shrugged. "I don't know. Judging by your clothes and the way you act, I figured you to be more of a TV writer or maybe even a video game designer."

I'll tell you one thing—from my perspective, she already knew me before even really getting to know me, if that makes any sense.

"I do watch a lot of TV and play a lot of video games in my free time," I said.

"Really? I wouldn't have guessed," she sarcastically responded.

I couldn't help but snicker to myself.

"Look at it this way," she continued, "no matter what happens between us this summer, at least we'll both be on the East Coast."

Yeah. So if she broke my heart while I was sitting in class trying to concentrate, I could tell myself not to worry because she was only a thousand miles north of me. That's exactly what I wanted to think about when I went to school. Not!

"But I'm hoping it'll be more on the friendly side," she added.

"I hope so," I blurted out.

We then turned toward each other and smiled. I couldn't help but officially be in love with this girl. Although I still didn't understand why, I knew I couldn't tell her. It was way too soon. If I did, I probably would've just scared her away.

However, my thoughts were swiftly interrupted by the previous song ending and a voice emanating from the speakers.

"Okay, folks," the male voice began. "Grab that special someone, as it's now time for couples only. I repeat—couples only."

Usually, when they announced a couples-only skate, most people would clear off the floor to grab some food, play some games, relax, or even go to the bathroom. I was always one of those people. But not on that day.

On that day, I had a date. Someone I could hold hands with and skate around the half-empty floor while some cheesy, romantic song blared out of the speakers.

"Eternal Flame" by The Bangles started playing, and I couldn't help but look over at Eve and smile. I then put my left hand out, and she grabbed it with her right, interlacing our fingers as we slowly started skating around the rink.

As we did, I couldn't stop glancing over at her and smiling in the process. That was the first time in my life I'd ever skated with someone during a couples-only song. And I loved every minute of it. Again, I was always the one who would disappear during those songs to try my luck on one of the arcade games.

After several laps around the rink, I turned my body and began skating backward. As we glided around, I held Eve's hands while getting lost in the void of her vision. About one more lap around, however, I suddenly got a crazy idea.

Instead of skating around with everyone else, I took Eve and skated her out to the very center of the rink. I then pulled her in close and folded my hands around the middle of her back. She draped her arms over my shoulders, securing her hands together behind my neck. Within seconds, we began to slow dance right there in the middle of the floor.

Everyone who was skating, and some of the people waiting to come back on, began staring at us like we were covered in mud or something. It was almost as if dancing on skates in the middle of the rink was forbidden. The only thing I could think of at the time as I looked at all the odd faces staring back at us was, *Fuck them.* Because we were enjoying every goddamn minute of it.

Being on skates made it easy to glide slowly around in circles. I can tell you one thing—it definitely eliminated and hid my two left feet.

But the more we twirled around, the closer we got to each other. And the closer we got to each other, the more the rink slowly faded away.

Closer and closer we got, while less and less of the rink became visible. Then, when we were almost right on top of each other, she took her folded hands and pulled on the back of my head, bringing my lips down to hers. When they touched, and just like up on the mountain, my body turned to jelly once again.

Her velvety, soft lips caressed mine as our tongues met for the second time. With my eyes closed, I couldn't see anyone else around me. And I didn't care either. All I could do was focus on that kiss.

With the song still playing and us still kissing, everything in that place, including the floor, seemed to fade out of existence, leaving the two of us all alone. I suddenly felt like I was floating in circles instead of skating in circles. With the feeling of being weightless, I opened my eyes to make sure I wasn't dreaming. But when I did, I was in for a very unexpected surprise.

The rink, the people, the lights, the games, and everything else in there, including the building, were gone. Eve and I were just floating in a black void, surrounded by stars as far as the eye could see. The only thing that was still with us from the rink was the sound of the music. We cautiously looked around at our new surroundings, utterly shocked by what we were currently seeing.

"What the hell happened?" I whispered.

"I have no idea," she replied, using virtually the same tone.

"How is this possible?"

"Your guess is as good as mine."

"I mean, one minute we were in the rink, and now…we're in space." I then looked down at our feet. "And we're floating!"

"Okay?" she replied, still unsure what was happening or what she was seeing. "But why is the song still playing?"

"I have no clue."

We didn't say another word to each other right away. Instead, we just floated there, slowly scanning our new surroundings, amazed at what was transpiring around us.

"This is fucking crazy," I said, still taking it all in.

"You can say that again," she said.

As much as I wanted not to believe what I was looking at, I couldn't. Whatever was happening to us was really happening. I know because the song was still playing, and our skates were still on our feet. However, as quickly as the bizarre moment started, it ended just as fast.

Before we even got the slightest chance to figure out what was happening (which we couldn't do anyway), the space and stars that surrounded us slowly faded out of existence, while the rest of the rink slowly faded in. Within seconds, both of us were back, standing in the middle of the floor, just staring at each other, wondering what the hell just happened.

A few seconds later, the song that was playing had ended, and the same male voice we heard before was once again emanating out of the speakers.

"Now *that* was a show!" the voice eagerly started. "In all my years here, I have never seen anything quite like that! Let's give this couple a big round of applause!"

Every man, woman, and child in that place was now clapping from what they had just witnessed. Apparently, everyone got to see something the two of us couldn't. But what?

With everyone still clapping and us now the center of attention, we decided to just go with the flow. So we smiled and waved before finally making our way back toward our locker.

"Good luck topping that one, folks!" the male announcer said. "Okay, everyone back on the floor. It's time for an all-skate. I repeat— all skate."

The moment he went silent, "Hangin' Tough" by New Kids on the Block immediately started playing. And while everyone else was eager to make their way back out onto the floor, that was our cue to make our way off.

"That was an interesting piece of skating," I heard a woman's voice tell us.

When we looked over to see who it was, we saw a woman, probably in her mid-thirties, standing there with her son, who was about eight years old.

"Thank you," I said, still not knowing what everyone else had just witnessed.

"Everyone was amazed by the way you two did that," the woman said. "The way you moved and glided. I don't think I've ever seen that done before."

But rather than respond directly back to her, in that moment, something in my gut told me to ask the little boy what he saw. After all, kids tend to have vivid imaginations when describing specific actions. Plus, they do say the darndest things.

"Tell me, kid," I said, leaning down close to him. "What exactly did you see?"

"It was like magic," he responded.

"What kind of magic?" Eve asked, curious.

"It was like something you would see Siegfried and Roy do. Or-or-or even David Copperfield!"

Very curious about what the kid was trying to tell us, and with one eyebrow now raised, I immediately stood up and turned to my left to look at Eve. When I did, she stared back at me with almost the same expression—utter confusion.

I turned back to face the woman and her son. "Well, we're glad you enjoyed it," I politely said.

And with that, the woman smiled and took her son out onto the skating floor.

"Bye!" the kid added, waving to us.

Both of us just waved and smiled as they disappeared into the skating crowd.

"Okay, what the hell happened out there?" I asked Eve.

She shrugged. "I honestly don't know."

"This is starting to get a little weird."

"Weird, how?"

"Well, last night, it was an earthquake, and now this," I said before getting lost in my thoughts and shaking my head.

"I'll admit, with what happened last night and with everything that just happened, I'm kind of curious myself." She then placed a hand on my cheek, turning my head toward hers while snapping me out of thought. "But these past two days have been the best two days of my life."

"Oh, good," I replied. "It wasn't just me then."

She obviously couldn't help but snicker at my remark. Then she leaned in and gave me a quick peck on the lips.

"You know," she began, "since my mom isn't home, we could always get out of the public eye and go back to my house."

And, just like a clueless bastard, I responded, "And do what?"

I know, I know. You're all cursing me out for not getting that right away. Believe me, later on, I would be too.

"Really, Wes?" she said with pursed lips and a slightly tilted head.

It took me a second, but I finally got it.

"Oh!" I said with wide eyes. "I got it."

She smiled and shook her head. "You are too funny."

Needless to say, we wasted no time pulling off our skates, putting our shoes back on, and getting the hell out of there.

ROB J. LABELLE

CHAPTER 12

Driving from the roller rink back to Eve's house was probably one of the quickest trips I had ever taken in my life. (For obvious reasons, of course.)

Let's put it this way…I was going so fast that I was actually surprised the cops didn't pull me over and revoke my license on the spot. And even if they had, it would've been totally worth it.

We arrived at Eve's house in record time before parking the truck and going inside. The moment we stepped foot through the front door, you could hear a pin drop two rooms over. She wasn't kidding when she said her mom wasn't home. Which meant we had the entire place to ourselves.

I couldn't put my finger on it, but her house similarly resembled another house. Maybe it was how one of my relatives' houses was set up. Who knows? Regardless, I loved how it looked.

Anyway, as I already mentioned, when we walked through the front door, we immediately stepped into a foyer with a set of stairs that ran up the right wall to the second floor. Other than the front door, there were also three additional doorways we could walk through—one to the right, one to the left, and one straight ahead.

The one to my left led into a dining room, where a wooden table and eight wooden chairs were set up. The one to my right led into a sitting room (I guess you would call it) with a couch and a couple of chairs just waiting for your butt to sit down on and relax. The doorway straight ahead led directly into a kitchen/living room.

The kitchen occupied the left half of the room, while the living room occupied the right half. The kitchen had all marble and granite countertops. The living room had a reclining sofa, a couple of reclining chairs, and a Panasonic forty-five-inch projection TV for all our viewing pleasures. There was also a half bathroom and a mudroom just off the back left of the kitchen.

After she gave me a tour of the first floor, she offered me a drink, which I politely declined because I wasn't thirsty. As a matter of fact, I was way more interested in what was located on the second floor—specifically, her bedroom. So once we finished with the first floor, we then made our way up the stairs to the second.

Standing at the top of the landing, to the right, was her parents' bedroom, which had a master bathroom off of that, complete with dual sinks, dual shower heads, and a Jacuzzi tub. In front of us was a spare bedroom, and just to our left behind us was another spare bedroom and another full bathroom.

As we turned left and made our way down the hallway, we passed the laundry room on the right before finally making our way to the door at the far end, one that would eventually lead us into the room I'd been dying to see ever since we left The Rollaway.

We walked through the door and into a bedroom that was just about five times the size of my own. My eyes widened, and my jaw scraped the floor as I slowly rotated my head from left to right while scanning the entire room.

Around the corner, just to the left of the door, was a little nook where she had her own couch and TV. A little further in the far right corner, just past the first of three massive open view windows, sat an L-shaped desk with a very comfortable office-type chair in front of it. On the desk sat a top-of-the-line Macintosh IIcx computer with a whopping 128MB of RAM and a Motorola 68030 processing chip, making the 16MHz of speed lightning-fast.

Still going to the right brought us directly across the room from where we were standing. A canopy bed with two end tables (one on each side) sat in front of the second window. Along the far right wall sat a dresser, a white makeup vanity, the third window, and a walk-in closet, which seemed to go on for miles.

On her walls were posters upon posters of various musical groups, movies, and other miscellaneous girly stuff, like unicorns and rainbows. The bands were a well-rounded mix of rock and pop and ranged from Def Leppard, Guns 'N Roses, and Van Halen all the way up to Madonna, New Kids on the Block, and Michael Jackson.

Most of the movie posters featured teen romcoms (romantic comedies), and nearly all of them starred some teen hunk or whoever was considered hot at the time.

She had posters like *Sixteen Candles,* starring Michael Schoeffling as the handsome and popular Jake Ryan; *Say Anything,* starring John Cusack as the underachiever Lloyd Dobler; and *Heathers,* starring the hunky Christian Slater as J.D.

One of the last posters on her wall was the ultimate '80s chick flick, which is still very popular today. Of course, I'm talking about *Dirty Dancing,* which starred the late and great Patrick Swayze, who played the gorgeous dance instructor Johnny Castle.

Aside from her bedroom looking like a teenage girl lived there (which one did), it was one of the most badass rooms I'd ever seen. And after seeing everything else in that house, the party that she and Anna's parents could afford made a lot more sense as to how.

"Look at this room!" I said while looking around and admiring its sheer size. "It's fucking huge!"

"It is pretty big, "she said. "However, it does feel kind of small at times."

"Small? Are you kidding me? There's nothing small about it."

"No. I meant that it feels small because it's just me."

I immediately turned to her to try to get a better explanation. "Just you? I don't understand," I said.

"My parents might have gotten me all this cool shit to keep me entertained," she said. "But if no one's here to enjoy it with me, then what's the point?"

"Don't you have any friends? I mean, how many of those spoiled little bitches did you actually hang out with?"

She laughed upon hearing my question.

"Only a few every now and then," she said. "But not many."

I then dared to ask a question that no guy wants to know the answer to. "What about guys? Did you hang out with any of them up here?"

"Honestly? You're the first guy I've had in here," she said.

"Wait a minute," I said, flashing my palms. "No other guys have ever been in your room? I kind of find that hard to believe."

"Why do you say it like that?" she asked, her hands on her hips and a serious expression on her face. "What kind of woman do you think I am, anyway?"

Whoops! Well, that was definitely the wrong thing to say. I mean, I obviously didn't mean it the way I said it. But apparently, that was the way it came out.

Again, I was at a loss for words. "I just thought that…well, you know…but you said…"

At that moment, I had officially reverted into a blithering mess. If I could've taken my foot and stuffed it into my mouth myself, I would've shoved that thing right down my throat.

However, seeing me eat my own words, her serious face quickly turned into a smile before she started laughing.

"What's so funny?" I asked.

"You should've seen the look on your face," she said. "If I had my camera out, I would've snapped a Polaroid of it."

I immediately put my left hand over my heart and let out the most enormous sigh of relief. "Okay, you got me," I said. "Good one."

"I know what you meant," she said. "And to be honest, not only are you the first guy to step foot in my room, but you're also the first guy to step foot in my house."

"Seriously? How come?"

"My parents are very strict. Why do you think they sent me to an all-girl school in the first place?"

"Good point."

"However, you're the first guy I've ever had a good feeling about, which is why I gave you my address. And which is also why I invited you up here."

She then did something I never saw coming. She quickly put her hands behind her and slowly started to back up toward her bedroom door.

"What do you mean?" I asked.

Once she reached her door, and while still looking in my direction, she said nothing as she placed her hands on the door handle. Then she stepped all the way back, closing her door in the process and locking it almost immediately. When I heard that door lock, one side of her mouth slowly curled into a half-grin, almost as if she was about to enact some devious plan she'd cooked up in her mind. And when I saw the look on her face, I swallowed—hard.

"The party, the earthquake," she began while slowly inching her way back toward me, "the dancing in space at the roller rink. Every time our lips meet and our tongues touch, something happens that we can't explain."

I immediately held up a finger. "Technically, we never kissed at the party. We just stood there and—"

"Don't interrupt."

I quickly lowered my hand and put both of them in my pants pockets.

"Even though we didn't kiss at the party, I still felt something," she continued, still inching toward me. "So, of course, I just had to find out. And you know what I discovered?" I shook my head. "I discovered that my body, my mouth, my brain, and every other inch of me craves your touch, your feeling, and your essence."

My eyes quickly shot open, and I slowly started to raise my right hand, hoping she'd let me speak.

"Put your hand down!" she ordered.

So much for speaking, I thought, and quickly dropped my hand.

"Then I thought, how could I have these many feelings this fast?" she asked. "I tried to deny everything and tell my brain that my heart was jumping ahead. But that wasn't it. The feelings that I have are real." She then stopped moving, just about two feet away from me, and folded her arms. "So my question for you is…how? Who are you to have this much power over me?"

Holy—fucking—shit. I was absolutely, without a doubt, one hundred percent flabbergasted. I mean, how was I supposed to answer *that?* Do I tell her that I've been thinking the exact same thing? Do I reveal to her that I've been madly in love with her since day one? Not a chance in hell. So instead, I just stood there in shock, unsure of what to say.

I suddenly felt like I did at the party, where my mouth was moving, but nothing was coming out. And just when I thought the situation couldn't get any more awkward, something else happened.

With me standing there, looking like I had just taken the biggest berating of my life, Eve unfolded her arms, took one more step toward me, and laughed. She laughed and laughed and laughed. The shock that once resided on my face quickly disappeared in favor of a slightly more confused look.

"What…what the hell just happened?" I asked.

"After I just got done telling you not to take me seriously, you did it again," she said, still laughing like there was no tomorrow.

Holy shit. Did she just prank me twice in a row? You bet your ass she did. And, for some strange reason I couldn't explain, I wasn't even mad. Actually, I think I was in love with her even more.

"What?" I asked, still trying to comprehend what just happened.

"I can't believe you fell for it twice," she said.

Knowing it was all a joke, I immediately hunched over, rested my hands on my knees, and inhaled a few deep breaths. Once I stopped hyperventilating, I stood up and looked at her while shaking my head in disbelief.

She laughed for a few more seconds before stopping to catch her own breath. Once she did, she put her hands on her hips, smiled at me, and shook her head.

"You are something else, do you know that?" she said.

"I would say the same thing about you," I remarked.

"I'm really glad I met you."

"Ditto for me." I paused. "But seriously, though, was any of what you just told me true?"

Eve stood there for a brief second more and stared at me, almost as if she was wondering how to go about giving me an answer. Thankfully, I wouldn't have to wait much longer.

Instead of giving me a verbal response, she rushed up to me, cupped my face with her hands, and started to kiss me. I immediately wrapped my arms around her and returned the kiss while forcing us to fall sideways onto the bed.

We were wrapped up in each other's arms as a fierce battle raged between our two mouths. Our lips hugged, and our tongues danced as we enjoyed the warmth of each other's bodies. We groped and wrestled just a few seconds more before finally rolling over onto my back with Eve now straddling me.

Neither of us said anything as we just gazed into each other's eyes. I couldn't help but smile while my eyes took in every square inch of her gorgeous face. She smiled back as she did the same.

But then I said something to her—something I was unsure about how she would respond or what she would even say in return. Something that, after just two dates, would usually scare any sane person off.

And no. I know what you're thinking. It wasn't that.

"I've been waiting for you my whole life," I said.

Possibly a little creepy, but it was the truth. Plus, after just two dates, Eve was the only one who ever made me feel that way.

She didn't say anything back. Instead, she just kept gazing into my eyes. It didn't take long, however, before a smile graced her lips. And that was when she leaned down to kiss me again.

Just like the night before, up on the mountain, and earlier that day at the roller rink, we got into a heavy make-out session before something odd happened almost immediately. This time was no different.

As we were kissing, my body instantly felt as light as a feather. I suddenly felt like I was slowly floating toward the ceiling, with Eve still straddling me. It almost felt as if some magical force was pulling us upward. But neither one of us seemed to care. In fact, we ignored it altogether.

Soon, Eve was no longer straddling me. She was now stretched out on top of me with our arms still wrapped tightly around each other. That allowed us to intertwine our bodies and start spinning slowly in place. I then decided to take a chance by slowly moving my hands up her back and under her shirt before finding the clasp on her bra.

But just as I was about to undo it and get my first-ever look at the top half of the female form in all its glory, we heard a noise come from downstairs. Someone had just walked through the front door.

My hands immediately retreated, and both sets of our eyes quickly shot open before we noticed that we were hovering about five feet off the bed.

"What the f—" I started to say.

But before I could even finish my sentence, we shot down like bricks as we both bounced, me on the bed and Eve on top of me. She then rolled off me and sat straight up, now looking toward her bedroom door like she was in a panic.

"I thought you said no one would be home?" I quietly asked.

"No one should be home," she quietly replied.

"What was your mom supposed to be doing again?"

And that was when we heard it.

"Eve? Are you home?" a deep male voice asked.

I immediately turned to look at her. "Who the hell's that?" I asked.

"Holy shit," she whispered before turning back toward me. "That's my father."

"I take it you weren't expecting him?"

"He wasn't supposed to come home until I went off to school. He was going to fly across the country with me."

In the blink of an eye, she got up off her bed and started to frantically look around her room.

"Another couple of months? What does he do for work?" I asked.

But she avoided my question as she kept searching her room for something.

"Eve, what the hell are you looking for?" I asked as I got myself off the bed.

"Found it!" she said while rummaging through one of her desk drawers. "Quick, get down on the floor."

She then showed me a board game she'd pulled out.

"Mouse Trap?" I said, still confused. "And why are we getting on the floor?"

"Either you get down on that floor, or my father will throw you out of my bedroom window," she said.

Suddenly extremely curious about what her father did for work and what he looked like, I certainly didn't want to find out if he was actually going to throw me out of the window or not. So I complied and did what she said. I got down on the floor.

"Set this up fast," she said before handing me the game and unlocking her bedroom door.

Still not questioning it, I pulled open the game and started to set it up. Meanwhile, Eve opened her door all the way before joining me on the floor herself.

"Eve, what the hell are we doing?" I asked in confusion. "Why did we just suddenly get down on the floor to play a game of Mouse Trap? I mean, not that I'm complaining. I love Mouse Trap."

"Hello?" I heard the man's voice say while walking up the stairs. "Anyone home?"

"I'm in here, Dad!" Eve shouted before quietly addressing me. "Look, when he gets in here, you be as polite as possible, understand?"

"I still don't get it," I said. "What's the deal with your dad? Why do I have to—"

"Hello, Eve," I heard her father say from her bedroom doorway.

When I looked over to see who was standing there, I immediately understood why Eve was so nervous.

Mr. Parker stood about six feet, four inches tall with dark hair trimmed to military standards, brown eyes, and a muscular physique. He was decked out in the standard battle dress uniform, complete with the proper decorations of an Air Force Colonel. The moment I saw him, I practically wanted to run for the hills. But aside from his tough exterior, what intrigued me the most about him was his bodily features.

Unlike Eve and her mom, Mr. Parker had dark skin. Of course, that didn't matter to me whatsoever. In fact, I could've cared less. The thing that I was now the most curious about was Eve herself.

If you recall, Eve's mother had dark hair, and her father (skin color aside) also had dark hair. But Eve has natural blonde hair. Which suddenly brought me to a very thought-provoking conclusion of my own. But we'll get to that a little later.

"Daddy!" she excitedly shouted before jumping to her feet and running over to hug him.

"Hello, sweetie. How have you been?" Mr. Parker said.

"Pretty good. How about you? You're home early."

"Yeah, well, I just couldn't stay away from my one and only baby girl."

When he said that, I noticed him glancing over in my direction. I took that as my cue to stand up and introduce myself.

"Mr. Parker, sir," I said, walking toward him with my right hand extended. "It's nice to meet you."

"Who are you? And what are you doing in my daughter's bedroom?" he asked me sternly.

Thankfully, Eve came to my immediate defense.

"Um, Daddy? This is Wes," she said. "We met at the party the other night."

"Is that so?" he asked, eyeballing me from top to bottom and back up again.

"I think your daughter is fantastic, sir," I said.

Holy shit, I was nervous. In fact, I was so nervous that my sweat beads had their own sweat beads forming on them.

"Tell me…Wes," he began with the utmost seriousness. "How old are you?"

"I just turned eighteen, sir," I replied.

"And did you graduate from high school?"

"I did. And I'll be going to Florida State in the fall on a track and field scholarship."

He immediately narrowed his eyes. "Full ride?"

"Yes, sir."

He didn't say anything right away. Instead, he continued to stare at me for the next few seconds.

"And what are your intentions toward my daughter?" he asked.

"Honestly? I don't know," I said. "But I do like her. A lot."

"I see."

"Daddy, to be fair, I like him too," Eve added. "So far, he's treated me with nothing but respect."

"She's right," I said. "You have my word that I won't harm her in any way."

Even though I tried to make myself look like an honest gentleman, I could tell that the Colonel didn't believe a goddamn word I said to him.

"And what makes you think I won't toss your ass out of that window right here and now?" he asked.

"Because I'm a nice guy?" I nervously replied.

"That is not fair, Dad," Eve said. "Look, I really like Wes. As a matter of fact, I like him more than anyone else I've ever met."

The Colonel turned to look at his daughter, almost as if he couldn't believe what she just said.

"Anyone else? Are you telling me that you've met other guys before?" he asked.

"That's not the point," she said. "I mean, you can't just come in here and scare away every guy I bring to my room, which, by the way, Wes is the only one."

"Well then, in that case, it was nice meeting you, Wes. However, I think it's time for you to go." He raised a finger. "As a matter of fact, I want you to go and never show your face around here again." Then he leveled it at me. "And you are to stay away from my daughter. Do I make myself clear?"

"No! Daddy, you can't do this," Eve protested.

I flashed my palms. "That's okay. I think it's time I went home anyway," I said. "It was very nice meeting you, sir." I then turned to Eve. "I'll talk to you later?"

She didn't give me a verbal reply and instead just nodded.

"You won't be doing *that* either," The Colonel added.

I smiled at Eve and gave the Colonel a quick nod before making my way down the stairs and out of the house.

As soon as I hopped in my truck, I started it up and was about to drive off when I suddenly stopped. I peered out the passenger's side window and up toward Eve's bedroom, only to see her looking back at me through her curtains. I waved and smiled, and so did she.

I could tell just by the look on her face that she was sad and didn't want me to go. Of course, I've never been the type of person to come between someone and their parents. Besides, if I wanted the Colonel to like me, then I had to listen and be courteous. However, given how he asked me to leave, I didn't think that was possible.

After I was done waving bye to Eve, I glanced over toward the front of the house and saw her father standing in the doorway. His arms were folded, and he looked just about as happy as someone who was out to get revenge on the bastard who murdered his best friend. Which meant that was my cue to go.

I wasted no time as I quickly threw my truck in drive, stepped on the gas, and made one of the longest rides home of my life.

CHAPTER 13

How about that? I got to meet an actual Colonel in the United States Air Force. I never thought I would ever get to meet someone so high up on the totem pole in my life. Unfortunately, that Colonel just happened to be Eve's father. After meeting him, however, I couldn't help but feel as if something was off.

Something about him made the feeling in my gut send enormously loud signals to my brain. I mean, I'd met overprotective fathers before and have even seen them in movies and TV shows. But him, well, he seemed different.

What struck me the most about him was that he was in the Air Force. Not only that, but according to Eve, he wasn't supposed to be home for another couple of months. Yet, he just happened to show up the very same day I came over to visit, only to tell me that I couldn't see his daughter anymore. Who did he think he was anyway? He didn't know me.

During the drive home, I had plenty of time to think about everything that had happened since the party. I thought about all the weird stuff Eve and I had experienced when we got together. I also thought about her mother's odd looks when I went to pick her up for our date. Well, my date with Eve, not her mother. You know what I mean.

Anyway, now that I'd met her father and realized that Eve looked nothing like either one of her parents, I could only come to one conclusion—Eve was adopted. But why her father was so strict with me, I don't know.

Maybe it was his Air Force training. Maybe he was simply that overprotective of his daughter. Or maybe, just maybe, and this was quite a long shot—maybe he was hiding something. The moment my brain started going into conspiracy theory mode, I quickly shook it off while telling myself that I sounded utterly ridiculous.

I did know one thing, however. I knew that it was now going to be extremely difficult to see or even talk to Eve. I mean, could I have just waited until her father left and went back to wherever the hell he was stationed? Of course. But if we didn't try to sneak around behind her parents' backs and fulfill our suddenly forbidden love, what kind of teenagers would we be? Plus, after meeting her parents and putting two and two together, I also understood why she didn't have a car. They obviously didn't want her driving off whenever she wasn't allowed to do something.

And that just left me with one simple question—Why?

I mean, with all the money they had, they could easily afford some transportation for her. So what were they waiting for? Why did they deny her that opportunity? I guess the only thing left for me to do was go home and possibly wait to hear from Eve.

———

When I got home, I blew past my parents and went straight up to my room to reflect on the past few days. Also, because of everything that had just happened, I wasn't really in a talking kind of mood.

There were still a couple of hours left to go until the sun went down, and I didn't really feel like doing anything but lie in my bed and think. And in order to do that, I had to free my mind.

As I said earlier, when my mind was on the fritz and I needed to take a break from something, I'd usually watch TV, play games, or watch one of the many VHS tapes I had sitting on the shelves in my room.

Starting from just inside the left of my door, I had put up two rows of shelves that hung close to the tops of my walls, forming an L-shape, and ran to the right above my TV, stopping just shy of my closet.

I had a massive collection of films dating all the way back to the mid-'30s. And when I say the mid-'30s, I mean a few of the classics, such as *King Kong, The Wizard of Oz,* and 1942's *Casablanca.* However, I already knew which film I was going to watch.

Because they were all alphabetized, I immediately found the *Ls* and approached one film in particular. It was a film that was released on July 13, 1984, by Universal Pictures. It was called *The Last Starfighter.*

The movie revolves around a teenager named Alex Rogan, who is played by Lance Guest. He lives in a trailer park with his mother and younger brother. After getting rejected for a scholarship, Alex finds comfort from the only form of entertainment the trailer park has to offer—an arcade game called *Starfighter.*

Once he gets the high score, Alex is soon greeted by Centauri, who claims to be the game's inventor. Centauri then takes Alex for a ride in his fancy car, which also happens to be a spaceship. I mean, with a name like Centauri, does that really surprise you?

After a while, Alex learns that the game he was playing was designed to find people "with the gift" and is based on an actual real-life conflict between two alien races: the Rylan Star League and the Ko-Dan Empire.

After getting the high score, Centauri basically kidnaps Alex while leaving behind an android named Beta, who could pass as Alex's twin. Centauri does it, hoping that no one would notice Alex's absence.

From then on, the rest of the movie is a fun ride with some questionable CGI. I won't get into too much detail and spoil everything, though, so I guess you'll just have to watch it yourself to find out what happens.

On a separate note, a few of my favorite books were released later on and were very similar to *The Last Starfighter*. *Ender's Game,* initially released in 1977 as a short story, was written by Orson Scott Card and was later released as a full-length book in 1985. *Armada,* written by Ernest Cline, was released in 2015. Both books featured a teenager playing a video game based on a real-life alien conflict and served as precursors to them going off to fight in some war. Both were fantastic, but *The Last Starfighter* still holds a huge place in my heart.

Once the movie had ended, I pressed the rewind button on my VCR remote. As soon as the tape started rewinding, my mind quickly drifted back to Eve and her parents. But as I was thinking about them, I immediately thought of someone else.

I knew that Eric was headed out on his first date with Anna and wondered if he would notice any of the weird stuff I noticed with Eve. Plus, what were Anna's parents like? Were they similar to Eve's? If so, when they saw Eric, were they going to give him the same bullshit speeches that Eve's parents gave me? I guess I'd find out the next time we spoke. But what was killing me the most was that I now had to wait for Eve to get a hold of me.

I couldn't just call her because there was suddenly a thirty-three percent chance that one of her parents would pick up the phone instead of her. Even if she did answer, the probability of one of them listening in before cutting us off was extremely high. I couldn't text her either because that hadn't been invented yet. So I had no other choice but to play the waiting game.

———————

I decided to call it an early night. I recall falling asleep just as my tape finished rewinding. And because I'd recently met Eve's dad just a few hours prior, my dreams that night were none too pleasant.

I dreamt that I was up in Eve's room, but we weren't exactly playing board games. Instead, we were on her bed, with her lying underneath me as we kissed and fondled each other.

Just as we were about to do the deed, her father kicked her door down, causing it to crash to the floor with a loud bang. He then burst into the room, and after seeing the position Eve and I were in, that was it.

He ran over to me, grabbed the back of my shirt, and yanked me off her with one hand before standing me up against the wall. It was almost like he had some sort of mystical control over my body because when I tried to move, I couldn't. I was stuck in place like a statue. He would look at me and say mean things while Eve just stood there and watched. Then, just when I thought it couldn't get any worse, it did.

The Colonel pulled out his sidearm and fired shot after shot into my body in non-lethal places. After every shot he took, he would laugh while I screamed out in pain. But that wasn't all. After he laughed, Eve would join in on the fun.

After each bullet went clean through one of my limbs, I would cry out and promise him that I would never see his daughter ever again, nor would I tell anyone what he was doing to me. But that wasn't enough.

Once the clip was empty, the gun would magically reload itself before he handed it off to Eve. Then she would have her way with me by doing the exact same thing. No matter how many bullets were fired into me, I never seemed to lose enough blood to die. They just kept taking turns, each firing an entire clip into my body. That must've gone on for about four or five tries each before I finally woke up.

The bright morning sun was now beating down on my face, prompting my bloodshot eyes to open and immediately burn from the lack of sleep I'd gotten. I had no idea what time it was or how long I had been in bed. But I would soon find out.

As I was lying there, I heard my mom call up to me from downstairs, letting me know I had a phone call. So I reached over to my nightstand, grabbed my phone, and brought it over to my bed before picking it up.

"I got it, Mom," I said into the phone.

Once I heard her hang up the downstairs phone, I began to talk. "Hello?" I asked.

"Dude, do you plan on sleeping all morning?" Eric asked.

"It's not that late, is it?"

"It's eleven am. How late were you out last night?"

"Actually, I was in bed pretty early," I said with a yawn.

"You know what? It doesn't matter. I need you to get up, get dressed, and meet me for lunch. We got to talk."

"Talk about what?"

There were a few moments of silence on the other end before he gave me an answer.

"Just meet me at the mall in an hour," he said. "We'll talk then."

"Ten-four," I replied before hanging up the phone.

———

After I got dressed, I hopped in my truck and hauled ass over to Flat Rock Mall. After what had happened to me the day before, I had a pretty good idea about what Eric was going to say and couldn't wait to hear his thoughts about it.

However, on the phone, I noticed he sounded like he wanted to discuss this privately. I also noticed that he seemed slightly concerned about what he wanted to tell me. But if he did want to chat in private, why choose the mall? Why choose a place that would be crawling with so many people?

I met him on the mall's bottom floor (a.k.a. the food court) and saw him sitting at one of the tables in front of Hot Dog on a Stick, a fast-food chain known for its tasty hot dogs dipped in their signature batter. But for all you other folks around the world, they're basically corn dogs.

Besides their signature hot dogs, they also offered French fries and drinks. In my opinion, if you were to walk in there as high as a kite, that place would be the ultimate munchie fix. Not that I've ever tried it or anything, because I haven't. Well, at least, not in the past couple of decades, anyway.

Okay then. Moving on.

After meeting up with Eric, we waited in line to grab some food. Once our trays were full, we sat down and began a much-needed and very critical conversation.

"So how was your date with Anna?" I asked. "Did you guys, well, you know?"

"I wish," he replied. "But other than that, it was…interesting."

"In what way?"

"Well, for one, her mom treated me pretty much the same way Eve's mom treated you."

"Pretty awkward, huh?"

"To say the least," he said before taking a massive bite of his hot dog. "And when I saw Anna, she was glowing, just like she did at the party."

"Did you eventually get used to it?" I asked, stuffing my face with fries.

"It took me a while, but yeah, I did."

"Same here."

We each took a sip of our sodas to wash down the food before continuing.

"So what movie did you guys see?" I asked, curious.

"Well, I followed your advice and took her to see *Honey, I Shrunk the Kids*," he said.

"And what did you think?"

"I got to admit, it was a fun ride. I mean, getting sucked up by the lawnmower and riding a bee was pretty fucking cool. The scorpion was a little far-fetched, though."

"Glad I'm not the only one who thinks so."

I took a giant chunk out of my hot dog while Eric stuffed some fries into his mouth.

"Her glowing in a darkened theater, however, was a little distracting," he said.

"Tell me about it," I said.

"Okay, so here's where it gets interesting." He paused to take a sip of his soda. "After the movie, she totally wanted to skip dinner. So we did."

"Did she take you up to the mountain?"

"Nope. In fact, she took me to Cricket's Field."

My eyes immediately narrowed. "Cricket's Field? Why would she take you there?"

"Every so often, she likes to go there, lie down on the ground, and look up at the stars. I guess she finds it comforting."

I briefly thought about it before nodding my head. "I could see that."

"And after pointing out some of the satellites orbiting the Earth, she leaned over and kissed me."

"All right, man, nice!" I said, raising my right hand to give him a high five. "So how was it?"

"It was kind of hard to describe," he said. "I mean, the moment we started, my body felt like it was melting into the ground."

"See? That's exactly how I felt."

"A few seconds into it, though, something happened."

"Let me guess," I said, raising a finger. "Some otherworldly event?"

"Yeah," he replied before furrowing his brow. "How did you know?"

"Okay. Now, I know that we've been busy, and I haven't had a chance to tell you yet, but do you remember when I asked you yesterday morning if you had felt any earthquakes the night before?"

"Yeah?"

I didn't give Eric a verbal response and just stared at him for a bit before opening my eyes wide and cocking my head slightly, hoping he would catch on to what I was trying to tell him.

"Oh shit!" he said as the light bulb finally turned on inside his head. "You felt an earthquake when you guys kissed?"

"That's not all we felt," I said.

"What else was there?"

I jerked my head toward him. "You first."

"Okay. Well," he continued, "after a few seconds of making out, we started to get hit by a meteor shower."

"There wasn't any meteor shower last night."

"Exactly. Just like there wasn't an earthquake a couple of nights ago."

"So what did you do?" I asked, curious.

"We stopped kissing, got up, and found some cover on the side of the cliff. There was nothing else around, and we figured that would be our best bet."

"Damn!"

"No sooner did we stop kissing and hide at the base of the rock face," he went on, "the meteors stopped. When we went out to survey the damage, it was like it never happened." He then paused as if deep in thought. "I don't know. Now that I've told you my story, and after hearing yours, something doesn't seem right."

I had to hand it to him. He was a lot smarter than I was and seemed to get it a lot quicker as well.

"Well," I said, "if you thought that was weird, then I suggest you buckle up. You see"—I paused to take a deep breath—"a couple of nights ago wasn't the only time something like that happened."

After hearing that last part, he quickly narrowed his eyes and leaned forward a bit, giving me his full, undivided attention.

"I'm listening," he said.

"Okay. So yesterday, while you were on your date with Anna," I began, "Eve and I went roller skating at The Rollaway."

"Dude! You went skating without me?"

"Can I finish my story, please?"

"Sorry. Yes, go ahead."

"Thank you," I said, nodding once. "Anyway, while we were there, we hit the floor for a couples-only skate."

"Wait a minute. You never skate during couples only."

"Are you telling this story, or am I?"

"Sorry. You are," he replied, gesturing for me to continue.

"As I was saying," I went on, "while we were skating, we found ourselves out in the middle of the floor before we started kissing. When that happened, the rink suddenly changed into an empty black void, with us being surrounded by space and stars."

I then proceeded to tell him everything from that moment until we asked the little kid what he saw.

"Of course, after hearing that, we were more confused than ever," I said.

"I would've been too," Eric agreed.

"So we immediately took off our skates, put our shoes back on, and hightailed it out of the rink before going back to Eve's place. But the freaky shit definitely didn't stop there.

"When we got back to her house, we went up to her room," I continued. "She already knew that her parents wouldn't be home and decided to give me a tour of the place. If you know what I mean?" Eric didn't reply and just sat there in stunned silence. "Anyway, while we were making out on her bed—"

"You lucky son of a bitch!" he finally said, interrupting me.

"Trust me. You won't be saying that in a few minutes. As I was saying," I went on, "while we were making out on her bed, I shit you not, we started to float up in the air."

"As in, you guys left the bed?" he asked, pointing upward.

"Exactly. We were hovering about five feet above the bed when, all of a sudden, we heard someone walk through the front door. When we opened our eyes, we fell back down, realizing that it actually happened."

"What happened next? Did her mother come home?"

I shook my head. "Not even close. It was her father."

He immediately narrowed his eyes and jilted his head slightly backward in confusion. "Her father?"

"Yeah. Why do you say it like that?" I asked, curious.

He didn't respond to me right away. Instead, he just sat there, devouring his hot dog while slowly nodding his head, almost as if he was deep in thought. And while I waited for him to answer, I buried a few handfuls of fries myself before washing them down with a couple sips of soda.

"Hello?" I said, hoping he would come to and give me an answer.

When he still didn't say anything, that was when I decided to try to literally snap him out of whatever daze he was in.

"Yo! Earth to Eric!" I said while snapping my fingers.

"Huh? Oh, sorry," he said before shaking his head and rejoining the conversation. "So what did her room look like?"

"Man, fuck the room! Forget that. Go back to her father."

"Oh, right. Anyway, I only asked it that way because when I brought Anna home from our date, her father was also waiting there for us."

"He was?"

"Yeah. And the weird part was, he wasn't supposed to be home for another couple of months."

The moment those words left his lips, the wheels in my head immediately started turning at warp speed.

"He didn't, by any chance, happen to have a military uniform on, did he?" I asked, hoping I'd be wrong.

Eric's response sounded just as curious as my previous question.

"As a matter of fact, he did," he said, his eyes narrowing once again. "How did you know?"

"Let's call it a hunch."

"Well, shit. That's one hell of a hunch."

I took a few more sips of my soda before continuing. "Here's another question," I began. "Did Anna's father forbid you from ever seeing her again?"

"Actually, he did. Why? Did Eve's father tell you the same thing?"

"I wouldn't have asked if he didn't."

"Holy shit." He paused. "Do you think this is all just one big coincidence?"

"Not a chance in hell," I replied while finishing my hot dog.

"Then, if it's not a coincidence, what do you think it is?"

"I don't know. But I'm starting to think something's going on that nobody wants us to know."

"Like what?"

I immediately took a deep breath and stuffed the last of my fries in my mouth. Then I leaned over the table before motioning him to join me.

"Now, this may sound weird, but I've had some time to think about this," I began, using a low, conspiratorial tone. "The way that the girls glow and why we're the only ones who can see it, I have no idea.

"But the weird shit that happens when we kiss them, the odd looks their mothers gave us, and now to hear that both of their fathers are in the military…that's quite the coincidence. Not to mention the fact that both of them came home early, just a few days after we met the girls, nonetheless, only to tell us that we were forbidden from seeing them. Something doesn't add up."

Once I finished telling him my thoughts, I paused to reflect upon what I'd just said. And apparently, so did Eric. But after a few thought-out seconds, he gave me the one response I had hoped he would give.

"But what can we do about it?" he asked.

I flashed him a Cheshire grin. "You know what? I am so glad you asked me that."

"Oh, damn," he muttered, instantly regretting his question while also knowing that with me being me, I already had some kind of devious plan cooked up. "Okay. What kind of shit are you going to get us into this time?"

"Whoa! Whoa!" I said, flashing my palms. "I have never gotten us into any kind of shit in our lives."

Eric, doubting every word I just said, folded his arms and leaned back in his chair while giving me a dubious look.

Okay. So that time at Darren's party in tenth grade wasn't exactly my fault. You know what? No. It was, without a doubt, one hundred percent not my fault. We just happened to be in the wrong place at the wrong time. However, the other times he was referring to were entirely my fault. But we were kids. We didn't yet fully understand the repercussions of our actions. Let me explain…

In seventh grade, we got together with a bunch of our classmates the night before Halloween to go toilet paper our principal's house. So as a joke, they gave us the wrong address. And while the rest of them were toilet-papering the correct house, Eric and I toilet-papered a police officer's house. Of course, when the officer came outside with his gun drawn, we practically shit ourselves before giving in and cleaning it up. Once we were done, we got our revenge by going to each of their houses to "break a few eggs." If you catch my drift?

In ninth grade, Darren, Eric, myself, and some of our other classmates decided to hit up Swanson Country Club after dark. The parents of one of the kids with us worked there, which gave him the easy opportunity to swipe their keys and let us into the main building. Once inside, we each grabbed a set of keys to one of the golf carts. Then we pretty much had at it.

We raced those things all over the greens, the fairways, through the woods, and even drove a few of them into the water. That was, by far, one of the most fun and embarrassing nights of my life. Needless to say, our parents were none too pleased and made all of us do various jobs there until we paid off the damages.

I didn't find it all that bad because being a complimentary caddy had its perks. With all the tips I made, I was able to pay off my share a lot quicker than the other guys. Eric, on the other hand, not so much. He had the unpleasant experience of doing random maintenance, such as sweeping floors, cleaning bathrooms, raking leaves, and keeping the greens and fairways free of debris.

But that was pretty much it. It was nothing too horrible that got us suspended from school or made us do hard time. Yeah, we might've spent a couple of hours at the police station, but all was good.

————

So with that being said, he suddenly had the audacity to ask me what kind of shit I was going to get him into this time? Whatever happened to his sense of adventure?

"Okay, maybe a couple of those were my fault," I said. "But we're still here, aren't we?"

He still didn't respond and just rolled his eyes instead.

"Look, I'm not asking you to do the stuff we did when we were kids," I said. "This time, we're adults. I'm talking about doing some serious recon here."

Eric arched an eyebrow. "Recon? What kind of recon?"

Apparently, that got his attention.

"I'm talking about playing detective. You know, black clothes, sunglasses, walkie-talkies…the whole bit," I said.

"No. That won't make us stand out at all," he sarcastically responded.

"Don't worry. We'll both be using binoculars while keeping a safe distance."

"Oh, well, that makes much more sense," he added, still being a dick.

"You're trying to be funny, aren't you?"

"Not trying. I am funny."

"In your dreams, four eyes."

We then stuck our tongues out at each other while making a stupid face. I know, real mature.

"So are you in?" I asked.

He thought about it some more before taking a deep breath and letting out a monster huff. "Of course, I'm in," he said.

"That's what I'm talking about!" I said, giving him the double finger guns.

He leveled a finger at me. "I better not regret this."

"Trust me," I said, flashing him another Cheshire grin. "You won't."

CHAPTER 14

Reconnaissance, or recon for short. What exactly does that word mean anyhow? Well, if you were to look it up in the dictionary, or by today's standards, Google it, you'd find that the definition of the word recon on dictionary.com is as follows:

1. The act of reconnoitering. (But we'll just skip over that because nobody really cares what reconnoitering actually means.)

2. *Military:* a search made for useful military information in the field, especially by examining the ground.

3. *Surveying, Civil Engineering:* a general examination or survey of a region, usually followed by a detailed survey.

4. *Geology:* an examination or survey of the general geological characteristics of a region.

Basically, what it all boiled down to was that we were about to spy on Anna, Eve, their parents, and their daily activities. Where did they eat lunch? Who did they see or talk to? Were they alone? Shit like that.

As you could've probably already guessed, I was responsible for tailing Eve, while Eric was responsible for tailing Anna. We weren't really focused on what the girls did, but more on what their parents did. I mean, what were they really hiding from us that they didn't want us ever to see their daughters again?

For Eric and me, this task would ultimately lead us to discover just a little more than we actually wanted to. Well, not the task itself, but more or less what bonehead move I made when I couldn't take not seeing Eve anymore. However, once it was all said and done, it was totally worth it.

But before we started anything, we needed to make ourselves look as inconspicuous as possible. And the best way to do that was to buy some new clothes. So the following day, we both drove down to Flat Rock Mall and made our way into the local Sears.

For us, Sears was an affordable, low-cost method to get some new threads, along with a few "other" supplies. Also, do you really think that either of us would buy some regular, everyday clothes? Of course not. Since we were about to officially enter the spy business, neither one of us could resist dressing up like some iconic secret agent or police officer.

I purchased a cheap look-alike version of what Timothy Dalton wore in 1987's *The Living Daylights*. I bought a beige bomber jacket and wore it over a navy long-sleeve button-down shirt. I also purchased a pair of tan khaki pants to complete the undercover-James-Bond look. After thinking about it, though, I decided against the brown loafers and wore my black Converse sneakers instead. Plus, I added a black baseball cap and my Ray-Ban sunglasses to complement the outfit, giving it the complete stalker look. Eric, on the other hand, went for something a little more…Hawaiian.

He bought a short-sleeve button-down Hawaiian-style t-shirt, and that was pretty much it. He already had a pair of blue jeans and a pair of sunglasses. He also decided to skip the loafers and wear his white Converse sneakers. He looked just like Tom Selleck's character, Thomas Magnum, from *Magnum, P.I.* Of course, with those two outfits on, neither one of us looked inconspicuous at all. But man, were we styling.

Eric and I also dug out our old walkie-talkies, which we'd had since we were kids. Because we lived just a few blocks from each other, our parents bought them for us so we could stay in touch. I mean, yes, we could've just called each other on the phone, but the walkie-talkies were way more fun.

After we became best friends, our parents pooled their money together and purchased a pair of Realistic TRC-99c walkie-talkies. Those things were beasts, and each used ten AA batteries apiece to power them. When you held one, it literally felt like you were holding a brick. Regardless, even after all the years they sat collecting dust, they still worked like a charm.

———

The following morning, we got up early and began our not-so-inconspicuous stakeouts. Eric had parked his car somewhere near Anna's house, while I parked my truck near the entrance of Eve's street. Luckily, one of the houses was up for sale and just also happened to be vacant. So I sat right out front, hoping not to draw too much attention to myself.

While we were shopping for some new clothes, we also picked up a pair of cheap binoculars. We didn't need expensive ones, as neither of us would be less than two hundred yards from our intended targets. Not targets for us to kill, but the people we were spying on.

Sorry. I just figured I'd throw in a little spy lingo to spice things up a bit.

Anyway, to try to pass the time, I brought along some of my cassette tapes. That way, in case the whole thing was a bust, I wouldn't get bored out of my skull.

The first one I popped in was Mötley Crüe's 1981 debut LP, *Too Fast For Love*. With such hits as "Live Wire," "Public Enemy #1,"

"Take Me to the Top," "Piece of Your Action," "Too Fast For Love," and "Stick to Your Guns," there was no way in hell I'd be bored.

And yes, I mentioned "Stick to Your Guns" because the cassette I had was the band's original Leathür Records release. Once they signed with Elektra in 1982, that song was dropped, and the album was reduced to nine songs instead of ten. It wasn't until 2003, when the band re-released everything under their own Mötley Records label, that "Stick to Your Guns" finally became available again.

So with "Operation George McFly" underway, we kept a close eye on everything that Anna, Eve, and their parents did. We only decided to give our mission that corny nickname because, while we were stalking them through our binoculars, we literally felt like Crispin Glover's character, George McFly, from *Back to the Future*.

The scene in question is when Marty finds George up in a tree with a pair of binoculars, staring through a window across the street while spying on some lady getting dressed. Although we weren't spying on any naked people (or if we did, that would've been a nice bonus), we still felt like that was what we were doing. Hence, the name.

With the many cassette tapes I'd brought, I also brought a few bags of food so I wouldn't starve. I mean, I could've always stopped and gotten some fast food along the way, but I didn't want to lose track of where anyone was going. I also had a notepad and a pencil to write down where they went, what they did, and what time they did it. Once this whole ordeal was over, we would then compare notes to determine if anything fishy was going on. Or so we had hoped.

It was around eight am, and I had a sharp eye on Eve's house. I only saw one car in the driveway, and with a government-issued license plate on it, I knew it had to be her father's. Her mother must've already gone off to work because she, along with her car, was nowhere to be found.

I wound up listening to the entire *Too Fast for Love* tape, and by the time it was over, nothing exciting had happened yet. So once that was done, I pulled it out and put it back in its case before pulling out Ratt's

1986 LP, *Dancing Undercover,* and popping it into my cassette deck. With hits like "Dance," "Slip of the Lip," and "Body Talk," it was a pretty good album overall. Once the music started playing, I quickly went for my box of cookies and opened it.

With the binoculars in my left hand and the box of cookies sitting in my lap, my right hand shoveled cookie after cookie into my mouth. As a teenager, though, it didn't take me very long to polish off the whole box. However, those were no ordinary cookies.

Big Stuf Oreos were introduced in 1984 and were probably about five times the size of a standard Oreo. You could buy them individually or get them in a box of ten. I wound up polishing off the entire box in just under thirty minutes. Thankfully, my stomach was like a steel trap because if that were anyone else, they would've had no problem redefining the term "toss your cookies."

Those cookies were so big that most people had many problems dunking them into their milk. I usually had to break them in half or even into quarters to fit them inside my cups. Unfortunately, due to their size, they were sadly discontinued in 1991. Damn you, Nabisco! Still love your snacks, though.

"Shit," I said, staring down into the box.

As I pouted at the empty box of cookies, I heard a little bit of static emanate from my walkie-talkie, followed by Eric's voice coming through. And because I was thinking about all that chocolate deliciousness being completely gone, I forgot that the walkie-talkie was even there.

"Wes, are you there?" Eric said.

Once I finished jumping out of my skin, I picked up the walkie and pushed the button on the side to speak into it.

"Dude! How's everything going over there?" I asked before releasing the button.

"Anna's mom isn't here, but she and her dad are," he replied.

"No way. That's the same situation over here."

"How weird is that?"

"Like I said, I don't think any of this is a coincidence. Something is going on, and I want to know what."

It took him a few seconds to respond because I think he was finally starting to come to terms with everything we had recently talked about.

"You know what? I'm starting to think you're right," he said.

"Of course, I'm right," I said. "I mean, when have you known me to be wrong?"

"You really want me to answer that?"

"Actually, forget I ever said anything. In the meantime, let's continue to keep an eye out. If anything happens, we let the other one know ASAP."

"Ten-four."

I then put my walkie back down onto my passenger's seat before continuing the mission.

———

By noontime, my notepad didn't have a lot on it. The only things I had written were the times in one-hour increments down the left side of the paper, followed by what happened at the top of each hour. Unfortunately, nothing was written there.

But it wasn't until around twelve-thirty that something finally *did* happen. By that time, I had already gone through four RC Colas, a box of Big Stuf Oreos, a box of Cinnamon Life, three bags of Sour Patch Kids, and two Hershey's chocolate bars. Again, I was a teenager. I pretty much gave two shits about what I ate.

I saw the front door to Eve's house open up. She came outside first, followed by her father, who was wearing his standard Air Force garb. They then hopped into her father's black Jeep Wrangler before backing out of the driveway and heading straight in my direction. Forgetting that I might get recognized, I quickly dove to my right, disappearing from view just as they were driving by. Once they passed me, I immediately sat back up, started my truck, and began following them.

The moment I got on the highway, I immediately contacted Eric to let him know what was going on. However, since nothing was happening at Anna's house, this was our first official chance to find something out.

While I followed Eve and her dad, I made sure to keep at least four or five car lengths between us so her dad wouldn't spot me in his rearview mirror.

By that point, I had Whitesnake's self-titled 1987 LP playing in my car. That record had such hits as "Crying in the Rain," "Still of the Night," "Give Me All Your Love," "Is This Love," and, of course, "Here I Go Again."

When the music video for that last song debuted on MTV, I think I, along with every other man on the face of the planet, fell in love with the woman in white. Her name was Tawny Kitaen, and at the time of the video, she was dating David Coverdale, the lead singer of the band.

With her auburn-colored hair and her practically see-through white gown, the way she danced and moved in that video made me go weak in the knees. It also didn't hurt that a tiny nip slip happened about halfway through the video. Even to this day, I still think about the way she looked back then.

Oh, Tawny… You will be missed.

Anyway, I wound up tailing them for about five miles until they pulled into the parking lot of a Ponderosa. Still keeping myself out of view, I waited until they went inside before pulling into a convenience store parking lot directly across the street. Once I was in a spot closest to the sidewalk, I turned my car off, grabbed my binoculars, and continued spying.

For the next few hours, I sat in my car, drank the rest of my refreshments, and ate the rest of my food. I also wound up blowing through three more cassettes in the process. Watching them from that lot was just about as uneventful as the time I spent at the end of her street. Since I was in a more populated area, I at least got the chance to do a little people-watching. Unfortunately, that was also boring.

I want to say that for the rest of the day, the Colonel would've done something unusual or possibly gone somewhere I'd never seen before. Or maybe I would even get the chance to see him go all Rambo on someone's ass because they tried flirting with his daughter. However, around five o'clock, they didn't do anything but return home.

So rather than continue my dull day watching nothing, I decided to drive home for a quick shower and something to eat before heading back over there.

About an hour later, after feeling refreshed and ready to go, I left my house in my casual, everyday attire to make my way back over to Eve's street. Don't get me wrong, I loved looking like James Bond, but the clothes were just too damn hot to wear.

Just like earlier that day, sitting down the street from Eve's house was incredibly tiresome. For three and a half hours, nothing even remotely interesting happened. That is, until I saw a glimmer of hope around ten p.m. when Eve started gazing out her bedroom window. She must've been sitting in a chair because it looked like her elbows were resting on the windowsill while her sad, depressed-looking face rested in her hands.

She was pouting and staring off into space, almost as if she had just lost her best friend or maybe even her dog had died. I felt so bad for her because I knew how she felt. At that moment, I just wanted to run up to her house, climb up to her window, and give her the world's biggest hug and kiss. Of course, if I got caught, her father might've killed me, which, again, would've been totally worth it.

Eleven p.m. was approaching fast, and I was about to call it a day. However, since I hadn't heard from Eric in a while, I decided to try to get a hold of him before I did.

"Eric, you there?" I asked, speaking into the walkie.

I waited for a few seconds, but didn't get a response. So I tried him again.

"Dude? Hello?" I asked.

Again, there was nothing.

Since he didn't respond twice and because of the time, I had a pretty good idea about what he was doing.

"*Wake up!*" I shouted.

"Huh? What's going on?" he replied.

That did the trick.

"Dude, did you fall asleep?" I asked.

"What, what time is it?" he groggily responded.

"It's eleven o'clock. How long have you been sleeping?"

"I don't know. Maybe a half-hour."

I groaned. "Anyway, I was reaching out to see if anything had happened. When I didn't hear from you, I got a little worried."

"Nope," he replied before yawning. "It's been like this all day. They didn't leave the house once."

"Damn! Your day was way more boring than mine. And I even went home to shower."

"Wait a minute. You went home?"

"Yeah. To shower and eat."

"And you didn't tell me?"

As soon as he said that, I realized I'd forgotten to tell him and immediately felt horrible about it.

"It must've slipped my mind. Sorry," I said.

"So while you went home to take a break, I was stuck over here doing nothing?" he asked.

Right away, I could tell by the tone of his voice that he was starting to get pissed off.

"Now, when you say nothing, do you mean—"

"Yes! Absolutely, positively, nothing!" he shouted, swiftly interrupting me. "Neither Anna nor her father left the house all damn day! And her mother just got home a couple of hours ago!"

"Shit. That literally was nothing." I paused. "Well, don't worry. I can assure you it'll be better tomorrow."

"It better be," he angrily replied.

"Again, I'm sorry. Look, just go home and get some sleep. I'll talk to you tomorrow. Okay?"

I could hear him sigh on the other end. "I'll see you tomorrow."

We then went radio silent for the rest of the night.

I continued to sit at the end of Eve's street for the next hour, just staring at her house, watching the different room lights flicker on and off as people entered and left. But it wasn't until Eve's bedroom light shut off for the night that I finally decided to call it quits.

———

Eric and I continued our stakeouts for the next three days, sitting and watching every little thing the girls and their parents did. And for three straight days, it was pretty much the same old shit.

Other than Anna and Eve going out for the occasional lunch with their fathers, and their mothers going to their own day jobs, I think Eric and I both gained about ten pounds, consuming all that junk food.. (Figuratively speaking, of course.)

By the end of the fourth night, I was officially desperate. I wanted to see Eve so badly that I actually debated going up to her house and ringing her doorbell. *That* would've been suicide.

But just around midnight on that fourth night, I couldn't help myself. I did something so stupid that I didn't even really think about the consequences that would follow. However, by doing what I did, Eric and I would soon figure out the truth about the girls. But more importantly, we also learned a dirty, nasty little secret that their own parents had been harboring for years.

CHAPTER 15

Midnight, night number four...

I had just awoken from a quick, one-hour nap and immediately began rubbing my eyes. They were all scratchy from the lack of sleep I'd gotten over the past four days.

I was in my truck, dressed in the James Bond gear I'd purchased earlier that week. Eric had already gone home for the night, and because of it, we'd been radio silent for the past two hours.

I looked around and saw that every house on Eve's street was dark and quiet. Everyone had already called it quits and was (I could only assume) sleeping comfortably in their own warm beds, which was where I wanted to be at that very moment. But as tired as I was, I had other plans.

With the street so quiet that the only thing you could hear was the crickets chirping, I opened up the driver's side door on my truck, stepped outside, and gently closed it. Then I quietly ran down to where Eve's house was located.

Why did I run, you ask? Well, if I drove, I would've risked waking up her parents, as my truck's engine would've been too damn loud. Therefore, I ran.

Once I got to her house, I immediately stopped on the front sidewalk and hunched over to catch my breath. Also, because of my clothes, I was sweating like a pig. But I didn't let that stop me. Because after I caught my breath, I quickly ran around to the left side of the house, where Eve's bedroom was located.

I planned to use the same tactic I had when I went to Eric's house the morning after my first date with Eve. So I reached down, grabbed a handful of pebbles from her garden, and slung them up there one at a time.

The first pebble I threw hit her window smack dab in the center. But nothing happened. I waited a few seconds more before trying another one. It was the same thing as it hit the center of the window, prompting absolutely nothing to happen. I pulled my right arm back and was about to throw a third pebble when I suddenly stopped.

I looked at this tiny rock, which was being tightly squeezed by my right index finger and thumb, before looking down at all the other pebbles in the palm of my left hand. I then realized that they all looked about the same size. And seeing as how throwing those tiny pebbles one at a time up at her window probably wouldn't wake her up, I grabbed about four or five of them before hauling them up there.

When they hit her window, it almost sounded like rain was hitting it. Regardless, my plan worked. Because about five seconds after I chucked the pebbles up there, her bedroom light turned on. I then saw her appear in front of the glass, wearing nothing but a pink nightie. The sight of her made me immediately melt in place. However, I still had to keep my cool. And when she saw that it was me, she wasted no time opening the window.

"Wes, what are you doing here?" she quietly whispered down to me.

"I'm sorry, but this was the only way I could see you," I whispered back.

"If my father knew you were here, he'd murder you twice."

"I know. But that's a risk I'm willing to take."

"Wes, I"—she trailed off before continuing—"I'm sorry."

"For what?"

"For not calling you back. You see, my father, he…"

I could immediately tell by how she had closed her eyes, lowered her head, and shaken it that she was upset about something.

"What? What did he do?" I asked, still whispering.

"He..." she started to say before turning and looking back into her room. After a couple of seconds of what seemed like her scanning the house for her folks, she turned back to me. "Hold on. I'm coming down."

"Wait, Eve!" I said, putting my right hand up to stop her.

But it was too late. Before I could say anything else, she had already disappeared from the window.

I just stood there and waited for a moment, hoping she would hear me and come back to the window. However, when her bedroom light shut off, I knew she wasn't coming back. I also knew where she would be going next. So I ran around to the front of the house and waited for her to come out.

A few seconds later, the door opened, and my heart fluttered as she came running over to me with her arms stretched out before wrapping herself around me. The warmth of her body, the scent of her hair, and her overall essence immediately overtook my senses. I reciprocated by wrapping my arms around her, gripping her as tightly as possible.

Over the past five days, ever since her father forbade me from ever seeing her again, something inside of me died. It was almost as if a piece of my heart had been left with her, and I couldn't function without it. But when we hugged, I felt whole again. I felt like my heart had been glued back together and was even stronger than before.

After our hug, which seemed to last for an eternity, we broke apart but continued standing at half an arm's length and stared deep into each other's eyes.

"Oh, Wes," she started to say, a tear running down the right side of her cheek. "I'm so sorry for not calling you back. It's just..."

"Just what?"

When she didn't answer, I could tell she was having trouble getting out whatever she needed to say to me.

"Eve, what is it?" I asked.

"My father warned me that if I was to contact you, then he would move us away from here," she said.

"Why would he do that?"

"I don't know. But if there was any chance of me ever seeing you again, I had to listen to him."

I took my left hand, placed it on the right side of her face, and wiped the tears away with my thumb.

"Trust me, I'm not going anywhere," I said.

She didn't respond. Instead, she just smiled and hugged me once more. After a few seconds, I pulled away.

"Eve, did your father happen to say *why* we couldn't see each other anymore?" I asked.

"No, he never mentioned anything about it," she replied.

"But why would he do that?"

"Maybe it's because you're my first guy friend he's ever met?"

"I highly doubt that's it. Look, I don't care what your father says. There's no way in hell that I'm…"

Before I could finish my thought, I saw a light turn on through the windows of her front door.

My eyes widened in panic. "Oh shit," I blurted out.

She also turned around to see what I was looking at. After she did, she immediately turned back to me.

"Look, Wes, we don't have much time," she said. "Do you know where the Inn at Flat Rock Hill is?"

"Of course," I replied.

"Good. I want you to call Eric and tell him to meet us there tomorrow night at eight."

"What about Anna?"

"She'll be there. Don't worry."

"Why not meet at my house?"

Eve then turned to look at her front door before turning back to me.

"Just meet us there, okay?" she said. "We've got something to show you."

"But what about—"

"Go! Now! Before he sees you."

I looked over her shoulder again and toward her front door before looking back at her. She gave me another smile, followed by a quick peck on the lips, before pushing me away. I stumbled, but not before gaining my footing and quickly running to hide behind one of the parked cars.

No sooner was I out of view, I heard the front door to her house open, followed by a man coming out to join her. It was the Colonel.

"Eve, is everything okay?" the Colonel asked her.

"Yeah. Everything's fine," she answered him. "I couldn't sleep, so I just thought I'd come out and get some fresh air."

"Are you sure?"

"Yeah. But I'm ready to go back inside now."

She folded her arms while he put his right arm around her shoulder. Then they both turned around in unison and immediately started to make their way back toward the front door. Eve went in first, followed by her father.

But right before he closed it, I could see him peek his face out through the crack to give the area a quick perusal, almost as if he was checking to see if anyone was watching him. And once he was satisfied that the coast was clear, he disappeared behind the closing door before turning off the hall light.

Now in the clear, I stood up and took a deep breath before turning around and running back to my truck. On the way, however, I couldn't help but wonder what it was she would have to show me or why she would want to meet us at some shitty hotel. I mean, why not meet at my house? Or even Eric's, for that matter? A hotel didn't exactly sound like the best place to meet. Not unless they didn't want to be found, which, after thinking about it, made a lot more sense.

With a million questions suddenly rolling around inside my head, I couldn't wait to get home to my own bed and fall asleep. Because I knew that the faster I fell asleep, the sooner I could wake up and call Eric.

The following morning, I woke up and was out of bed by seven thirty. I showered, got dressed, and ate some breakfast. Since it was way too early to call, and since I couldn't wait to tell Eric what was going on, I decided to drive to his house instead.

I was out of my house by eight and over at his by eight-fifteen. Once I parked my truck, I got out and sprinted up to his front door. After ringing the doorbell, I only had to wait a few seconds before a woman in her mid-forties, wearing neon green yoga pants and a neon green sports top, answered the door.

Cynthia Jackson (or Cindy, as everyone called her) was a stay-at-home mom. She stood about five feet, five inches tall, had long, dark hair down to the middle of her back, hazel-colored eyes, and a smile as white as the clouds. Besides my own mother, she was by far one of the sweetest people I had ever met. And not to be derogatory or anything, but she was *definitely* a MILF.

I was probably Eric's only friend who kept their thoughts about his mom to themself. I never said anything derogatory about her in front of him or when he wasn't around because, frankly, there was nothing derogatory to say. However, I think he secretly knew I thought his mom was hot, but decided never to say anything to me about it. I mean, come on. That would've been one awkward conversation. Am I right?

When she answered the door, her body was glistening from head to toe in sweat. I then remembered that every morning, she liked to pop in the VHS tape of Richard Simmons' *Sweatin' to the Oldies* to get in a good workout. That was also how she kept her fabulous form. But I digress.

"Well, good morning, Wes!" Cindy said with a smile.

"Good morning, Mrs. Jackson," I responded in kind. "Is Eric home?"

"Of course. Come on in."

She moved off to the side while I walked through the door and straight into his living room.

Eric's house was set up just a little differently than mine. The kitchen in my house was off to the left of the living room, while his was off to the right. Also, unlike mine, his had a dining room.

As soon as I walked inside, Mrs. Jackson made her way over to the bottom of the staircase.

"Eric!" she yelled up. "Wes is here!"

She then made her way into the kitchen and over to the fridge.

"Wes, would you like something to drink?" she asked.

"No, thank you," I replied.

"Okay then. Feel free to have a seat while you wait."

As I sat down on one of the kitchen barstools, she pulled out a pitcher of ice water and placed it on the counter. Then she reached into one of the cabinets to grab a glass. Once she filled it to the top, she put the pitcher back into the fridge before making her way into the living room.

I noticed that the couch and the two chairs were all pushed back a bit. The coffee table was also moved to the side and replaced by a yoga mat. Without missing a beat, she put her water down on one of the end tables, grabbed the VCR remote, hit play, and continued her workout.

While I waited for Eric to come down, I just sat there and stared at her. I won't lie. I was absolutely mesmerized by his mom and the way she moved. The drool was practically hanging out of the corner of my mouth, almost making its way to the floor. In my opinion, watching her workout was a thousand times better than watching scrambled porn.

Okay! I think that's enough of that. Sorry, I was just getting caught up in my own memories. Anyway, let's get back to the story, shall we?

As I sat there, daydreaming about and staring at Mrs. Jackson's firm, round ass, Eric came walking down the stairs.

"What's up, dude?" he said. "You're here early. What brings you by?"

Since I was too busy thinking about his mom and didn't respond, he tried something else to get my attention.

"Wes? Hello?" he said, waving his hand in front of my face.

"What?" I asked, shaking it off and coming too. "When did you get here?"

"Just a few seconds ago."

"Why didn't you say anything?"

"I did. But your eyes were apparently focused elsewhere," he replied, nodding toward his mom.

"Oh. Sorry about that."

He shrugged. "Anyway, what brings you by? I was just about to head out on another pointless stakeout."

"Pointless? In that case, grab a seat. You'll *love* what I'm about to tell you."

"Oh shit. Really?" he asked, quickly plopping his but down on the stool to my right. "What is it?"

"Well, last night, just before I went home, I kind of sort of might have spoken to Eve."

His eyes went wide. "You spoke to Eve?"

"Yeah."

Confusion took over as his brows quickly furrowed. "How did you manage that without her father killing you and burying you in his yard?"

"The same way I get your attention without waking up your folks."

He nodded. "Ah!"

"She wants us to meet her and Anna at the Inn at Flat Rock Hill tonight at eight."

"Did she say why?"

"Apparently, they both have something to show us."

"She didn't happen to say *what* they were going to show us, did she?"

The way he asked that question, I knew exactly what the perv was referring to.

"Dude! Definitely not that," I replied.

He shrugged. "One can dream, can't he?"

"Actually, she didn't say what it was. She just said to meet them tonight."

"What do you think it is?"

"I don't know. But for them to disobey their parents like that, it must be something important."

"Totally."

I purposely waited a bit before continuing so he could take a few moments to think about it.

"So are you in?" I asked.

Eric was silent for less than another second before giving me an answer.

"Fuck it. I'm in," he said.

"You bet your ass you are," I said while nodding and smiling.

After we gave each other a high five, I turned back to focus on his mother. My god, could that woman move.

"So you want to go and grab some breakfast?" Eric asked before noticing what I was doing. "Hey, uh, asshole?" He then smacked my arm.

"I heard you," I said. "No need to hit me."

"Just making sure."

"Actually, breakfast sounds great."

"Cool. And maybe after, we could do a movie marathon. You know, something to pass the time?"

I smiled. "You don't have to ask me twice."

CHAPTER 16

Eric and I ate breakfast at Denny's before going back to his place, where we spent most of the day watching an original *Star Trek* series movie marathon. We decided to skip over 1979's *Star Trek: The Motion Picture* because it was our least favorite of the entire series.

Instead, we started with *Star Trek II: The Wrath of Khan,* released in 1982. We then watched *Star Trek III: The Search for Spock,* released in 1984, before finishing our mini-movie marathon with *Star Trek IV: The Voyage Home,* released in 1986. We would've watched more, but I had to leave and get ready to meet the girls.

While we watched the films, Eric and I speculated on all the possible things they would show or tell us. Ideas ranged from simple things like, *What kind of bugs did their parents have up their asses? And why did their dads suddenly come home?* The more ludicrous ideas were things like, *What kind of secrets were they keeping from us? Did they work for some sort of secret branch of the government?* And, *Would the girls finally have sex with us?*

Okay, that last one was a little more ridiculous than the rest. But as teenagers, incorporating that into any conversation was kind of a given.

––––––––

Once I got home, I ran upstairs to my bedroom, picked out some fresh clothes, took a shower, got dressed, and bolted out the front door before my parents could stop me and ask questions.

I left the house wearing blue jeans, my red Converse sneakers, and a black T-shirt with *Star Wars* written on it in red lettering. The two *S*s formed a box around the words *Revenge of the Jedi*, the original, unused title for George Lucas's classic third film, *Return of the Jedi*, released by Lucasfilm in 1983.

On the way to the inn, I couldn't help but wonder why the girls wanted to meet us at such an isolated place. I mean, the inn itself was about five miles on the northern outskirts of Swanson, located in the middle of nowhere, and didn't exactly boast the heaviest of traffic, as the road was mainly driven by truckers and vacationers.

Why did they want to meet us way out there? And what did they need to show us that they couldn't show us somewhere in town? With those questions running in and out of my noggin, only one stood out above all the rest—*What was so important that they would risk disobeying their parents?*

I mean, as much as I liked Eve, disobeying her parents would cause her father to pick up his family and move them out of town. But not before probably killing me in the process. And if that did happen, I don't think I would ever be able to live with myself.

But the more I thought about it, the more obsessed I became with wanting to see what the girls had to show us. I guess I would soon find out.

I arrived at the inn at exactly 7:55 pm. Again, it was located about five miles north of Swanson, out in the middle of nowhere, and was situated just below a hill with a flat top. Hence, the name.

The inn was shaped like a capital letter *U* and housed about fifty rooms. A gas station with a built-in convenience store where people could buy chips, soda, and other miscellaneous snacks and items was located directly across the street.

Most of the time, the inn was used by truckers traveling toward northern Nevada who needed a place to sleep for the night. There were also a lot of other shady characters who went there to do who knows what. But that was where the girls wanted to meet us, so that was where we went.

I waited in my truck in the parking lot until Eric arrived about two minutes later. Unlike me, he drove a car—a 1988 black Mercury Grand Marquis, to be exact. It was a massive boat of a vehicle that he got dirt cheap from one of his relatives the year before. Lucky bastard.

Once he pulled up and parked, we both got out of our cars to greet each other.

"What's up?" he said. "Long time, no see."

"Yeah, no shit," I replied.

"Have you seen the girls yet?"

"Not yet. I waited in my car until you got here."

He nodded his head before uncomfortably scanning the surrounding area.

"This place really is out in the middle of nowhere, isn't it?" he said.

"It's also the perfect place to get shot or stabbed," I joked. (Sort of joked.)

However, upon hearing my comment, he turned back to look at me with a no-nonsense expression on his face.

"That is *not* funny," he said.

"Dude, that was a joke," I said. "Can you just relax for two seconds?"

"If I wasn't here, out in the middle of nowhere, then maybe."

I quickly agreed with him. "I know what you mean."

As we continued looking around, we noticed a bunch of tractor-trailers parked in the extra-long spaces in the inn's parking lot. We also noticed that our cars were the only two four-wheeled vehicles there.

"How did the girls get here?" I asked. "Aside from the truckers, we appear to be the only ones here."

He shrugged. "You got me. I'm just as clueless as you are."

"Do you think we should go into the rental office and ask them what rooms they're staying in?"

But before Eric could give me an answer, both Anna and Eve burst out of one of the rooms and immediately came running straight over to us. We each embraced our significant others with a hug and held it for what seemed like an eternity.

"I missed you, Wes," Eve said to me.

"I missed you, too," I replied.

As we shared how much we missed each other, I could also hear Eric and Anna mirror our feelings.

Once we finished hugging, I gazed into Eve's big, brown eyes before smiling and kissing her. When we did, that kiss was no different than any of the other kisses we'd shared. Well, other than one slight, minor detail.

The moment our tongues met, the backdrop around us started to spin in circles. It was almost as if we were standing still in the center of a carousel while the surrounding landscape acted as the ride in motion—a super-fast motion.

"Holy shit!" I heard Eric say.

That was when we broke apart and saw the Earth basically slow down to a stop. Once it did, we looked over at Eric and Anna, who were now looking back at us with shock and awe.

"What just happened?" I asked.

"Dude! The earth just spun all around us like a top!" Eric said.

"A top? Wait a minute. You saw that?"

"Fuck yeah, we did! That was awesome!"

Apparently, Eve and I weren't the only ones who could see it. Eric and Anna also saw what had just happened, even though it technically didn't happen to them. My eyes suddenly narrowed as I was more confused than ever.

"So you saw that?" I asked, pointing to the landscape around us.

"We did," Anna replied.

"How is that even possible?" I turned to Eve. "Did you know that they could see what we see?"

She shook her head. "I didn't have a clue."

"Dude, you don't think it has anything to do with…you know?" Eric said, silently motioning to the girls with his head.

"What are you talking about?" Anna asked, curious.

"You know what? I think it's about time we all took this conversation inside," I suggested.

"Good idea," Eric said.

We then grabbed our bags out of our cars and followed Anna and Eve out of the parking lot.

We followed them into room number twenty-three, and once we were all inside, they locked the door behind us before drawing the curtains shut. Eric and I took a seat on one of the beds while Anna and Eve sat down on the other, directly across from us.

"Much better," Eve said. "Now, what was it that you were saying out there?"

From the moment Eric and I first met the girls on the balcony at their birthday party, we noticed something about them that apparently no one else did. Why or how we were the only ones who could see it was also an important question.

We seemed to be the only ones who could see a slight glow emanating from their bodies. We also decided to keep it to ourselves until we figured out the right time to bring it up. I guess that time had finally come.

I looked over at Eric, and he looked back at me before we returned our gazes to the girls. I then took a massive deep breath and let it out before beginning my insane explanation.

"Now, we didn't want to say anything to you because we didn't want you to think we were crazy," I said.

"What…more crazy than we already think you are?" Eve joked.

"Good point. Anyway, when we first saw you," I began, "actually, has anyone ever noticed…you see, what I'm trying to say is…"

Even though I knew it was time to tell them, I couldn't spit it out. I don't know if it was my nerves or if I still thought they would think we were cuckoo for Cocoa Puffs. Who knows? And I know I've already said this, but telling someone that a faint light continuously surrounds their body would most likely make anyone run for the hills. However, as luck would have it, I didn't have to say anything at all.

"Oh, Jesus Christ," Eric said, disappointingly shaking his head. "What my *brave* friend is trying to say here is that you two, well…you glow."

The moment those words left his mouth, we both eagerly waited for them to respond. But there was no immediate response. Instead, they both narrowed their eyes and glanced at each other with confused expressions.

"At first, we thought it was the lighting," I elaborated. "But when it happened while we were in the movie theater, I knew it definitely wasn't that."

"And then, after Wes and I experienced all the weird stuff on our dates, we were even more confused," Eric added.

"Yeah. I mean, we were going to tell you, but we wanted to wait until the time was right to do it."

"And we guess now is the right time."

By that point, we were both anxiously waiting for them to say something in return—anything, for that matter.

To me, it almost felt like I was sitting in the electric chair, strapped down and ready to go, while I waited for them to throw the switch and zap me into wherever it is we go after we die. Thankfully, we didn't have to wait very long for them to glance back at us and give us a response.

"We…*glow?*" Eve asked.

Eric and I nodded in unison.

"You do know how insane that sounds, don't you?" Anna asked.

Again, we just nodded in unison.

"Well, I got to say," Eve said, "you two are the first people ever to tell us that we glow."

"And honestly, we weren't sure if anyone other than ourselves could actually see it," Anna added.

"Look, we know how crazy this sounds, but we didn't want to tell you on account of…" I said before pausing. I then narrowed my eyes and shot Eric a curious glance before looking back at the girls. "Wait, so you two can also see it?" I asked, pointing to both of them.

"Of course," Eve said with a shrug.

I immediately opened my mouth to say something else, but then stopped. Just like the first time we'd met them up on that balcony, I was too dumbfounded to say another word. At least right away.

"Actually, we've known since we met you at the party," Anna said.

"How come you didn't say anything?" I asked.

"We didn't think it was relevant."

"Not relevant?" I said, shooting up off the bed. I then walked to the front of the room. "With all the shit that's been going on…all the weird stuff that we've been experiencing, and you didn't think it was relevant?"

I stood there with my hands on my hips while I waited for either one of them to give us the million-dollar answer.

Eve spoke first. "We just didn't think—"

"How?" I asked.

"How what?"

"How did you know we could see you glow?"

"Through your eyes."

"What do you mean, through our eyes?" Eric asked.

"We can see the glow in your eyes when you look at us," Anna said. "We can also see it when we look at ourselves in a mirror or any other reflective surface."

"Both pairs of your eyes are the first ones we could ever see our glow in when we looked into them," Eve elaborated. "That's how we knew. We're sorry we didn't tell you sooner."

"Yeah. We didn't want to scare you away," Anna added.

I laughed. "Scare us away? You think *that* would've scared us away?"

I continued laughing before lowering my head and shaking it.

"What's so funny?" Eve asked.

"After all the other weird shit that's happened to us," I began, "the fact that you think that telling us we could see you glow would scare us off…is just downright hilarious."

Both Anna and Eve looked utterly confused.

"I don't understand," Eve said.

I went over and sat back down on the bed next to Eric.

"Eve, if all that other weird stuff didn't scare me off, what makes you think that a little glow could finish the job?" I asked before leaning forward and taking her hands in mine. "Look, we drove all the way out here to meet you and even risked getting flayed by your parents. Now, if that doesn't show you how 'not scared' we are, I don't know what does."

"He's got a point," Anna agreed.

"I agree with Wes. We're with you all the way," Eric said.

Eve let out a massive sigh of relief. "That's good to hear."

Eve and I smiled before giving each other a quick peck on the lips.

"Well, now that that's out of the way," Eric said, "how about if we move on to more important matters? So what is it that you girls dragged us all the way out to the middle of nowhere to show us?"

Upon hearing Eric's question, Eve got up off the bed and went over to one of the dressers to grab a backpack with Patrick Swayze's picture on it. I knew it was Eve's because I saw it sitting on the floor in her closet while I was checking out her room.

"Wait a minute. How did you guys get up here anyway?" Eric curiously asked.

"Yeah. Seeing as how your parents don't let you have a car or drive, for that matter, I was kind of curious about that myself," I said.

"We took the bus," Anna answered.

"You girls just got on a bus and rode all the way up here by yourselves? Are you out of your minds? Do you know how dangerous that is?"

"We were well aware of what we were doing."

"Besides," Eve chimed in, plopping her butt back down on the bed, "we're here, aren't we?"

"Why didn't you just have us meet you somewhere?" Eric asked. "We could've picked you up."

"We wanted to avoid any suspicion from our parents," Anna replied.

"Oh, yeah. And the bus was *obviously* the way to go," I sarcastically responded.

"Yeah, yeah, whatever," Eric blurted out, quickly wanting to change the subject. "So where's this thing you wanted to show us?"

With Patrick Swayze sitting on Eve's lap, staring deep into my soul, she unzipped her backpack and reached inside before pulling out a small, black, round object and showing it to us. It was just about the size of a quarter and almost ten times as thick.

I furrowed my brows. "What the hell is that?"

"I don't know," Eve said. "But it fell out of one of my stuffed teddy bears after I accidentally dropped it onto the floor."

I immediately reached over, grabbed the mystery object from her hand, and held it up in front of my face to examine it.

"I've never seen anything like this," I remarked. "You know, from a certain point of view, it looks just like a—"

"A camera," Eric interrupted me before snatching it out of my hand. "A hidden camera."

"A hidden camera? Why would someone want to put a hidden camera in Eve's teddy bear? I mean, the only people who would want to do that are spies or people who want to…"

I didn't finish my thought and quickly trailed off, suddenly thinking that I might have been right about my crazy theory this entire time.

"People who want to do what, Wes?" Eve asked.

"People who want to keep an eye on someone," I said.

Eve looked confused. "Wait a minute. Are you telling me that someone was keeping watch over me?"

I shrugged. "Probably."

"Who?"

"No clue."

"And I'm willing to bet that if someone was spying on Eve, someone was also spying on Anna," Eric said.

Anna immediately turned to Eve. "Which teddy bear did that fall out of exactly?"

"The one I got for my fifth birthday," Eve replied.

"You mean the same ones we got for *our* fifth birthday?"

"You guys were given the same teddy bear for your fifth birthday?" Eric asked.

"Yeah," Eve replied.

"Who gave them to you?" I asked.

"They were a special gift from our parents," Anna said.

Upon hearing her response, my eyes immediately widened as I quickly turned to look over at Eric. He was already looking back at me with the same expression.

"From your parents?" I asked before turning back to the girls.

"Yeah. Why?" Eve responded, curious.

I paused. "Okay. Now, I'm going to ask you a question, and please forgive me if I overstep my bounds a bit. But you're adopted, right?"

Eve shrugged. "Of course. And so is Anna."

"Wait, you're both adopted?" I asked, pointing to them.

"We were adopted on the very same day," Anna said. "What does that have to do with anything?"

"I don't know," I replied, slowly shaking my head. "That's what I'm still trying to figure out. I mean, I do have one theory, but it's not much of a lead, I'm afraid."

"What is it?" Eve asked.

I paused and thought about it for a brief moment. Then I let out a deep breath because I knew it was now time to let the proverbial "cat out of the bag" and tell the girls what crazy things have been churning in my head since day one.

"Ever since we first met you ladies, a lot of weird things have been happening," I said. "Things that we couldn't even begin to explain."

"They're already aware of that," Eric said. "Just skip ahead to the good stuff."

"Right, sorry. Anyway," I continued, "we find it strange that you two glow, and we're the only ones who can see it. We also find it strange that when we kiss, super-cosmic events, which no one else seems to experience except for us, happen right before our eyes.

"Now, the thing that really boggles our minds is that a couple of nights after we met you, both of your fathers just happened to come home early, and at the exact same time, nonetheless, only to banish us from ever seeing you again. However, after seeing this camera lens, I think I finally understand why."

"But that camera was only in my room," Eve said. "There's no way he could've made it home after you being there for just a couple of minutes."

"I realize that. But what I'm trying to say is, if your parents hid a camera in your room, who knows where else they hid them."

"That is an excellent point," Eric said.

"You mean to tell us that our parents have been keeping a close eye on us ever since we came into their lives?" Anna asked.

"Precisely," I replied.

"I mean, I didn't want to believe it either," Eric said. "But when we didn't see each other for a few days, I started to think it was true. And now, after seeing this camera lens, I think that something is definitely going on."

"You don't think it has something to do with what we experienced, do you?" Eve asked. "I mean, what are we, like some kind of genetic mutations or something?"

"I don't know," I replied. "However, I'm willing to bet that your parents know something about you they want kept secret."

"What do you think it is?"

"Again, I don't know." I held up a finger. "But I say we find out."

"Find out?" Eric asked. "We don't even know where to begin, and you want to find out?"

"I have a couple of ideas."

"Oh yeah? Like what?"

"Honestly? I have no idea."

After hearing my response, Eric threw his arms up in disgust.

"Look," I said, standing up off the bed, "I'm pretty tired. What do you say we all get a good night's sleep and discuss this in the morning with much clearer heads?"

"You know what?" Eric said, wagging a finger at me. "That's the best idea you've had in a while."

"Thank you," I said with a smile. "I pride myself on good ideas."

"That's not what we heard," Anna added with a snicker.

I immediately looked down at her, only to see Eve snickering along with her. However, it didn't take me long to glance over at Eric, who I knew was the mastermind behind the girls' laughter.

"What did you say to them?" I asked.

"Nothing," he replied, innocently shrugging and shaking his head. Then he cracked a tiny smile.

"Very funny," I said, pointing at him. "This isn't over."

Of course, I couldn't help it and just wound up smiling myself. Little did Eric know that behind my innocent smile, I was already planning some devious revenge of my own.

———

With Eve and me on one bed and Eric and Anna on the other, we spent the next couple of hours inside the room just relaxing, lying down, snuggling up with the girls, and watching some TV.

As we did, I couldn't help but think about how and where we were going to start looking into this whole thing. I didn't have the slightest clue about where even to begin. I mean, just showing my face to the Colonel would be like committing suicide. Hell, I would've had a much easier chance of breaking into Fort Knox than getting anything out of him.

But even as I lay there and thought about it, a more important question lingered in my mind. And that was, *Is this how we were all going to sleep?* Not that I had a problem with it.

Going back to when we were little kids, Eric and I would sleep over each other's houses all the time. When we did, we usually stayed up all night playing Atari or Dungeons and Dragons. We would also camp out in our backyards and use the most powerful tool anyone could possibly use—our minds.

We would think up all sorts of things to do, like pretend we were fending off dinosaurs, pirates, or even zombies. We would also try a live-action version of D&D, using ourselves as the game pieces. We even built our own weapons and armor out of cardboard and tinfoil. But as we got older, our lives got much busier, and we soon realized that sleepovers were becoming a thing of the past.

I'm trying to say that I didn't mind sharing a room with Eric, nor did I even care. But this time was different because it wasn't just us in there. And with me being a teenager, the only thing on my mind at that very moment was how to get Eve alone. I know. Big shocker, right?

Because her father had burst into the house and ruined whatever fun we were about to have, and since we were all alone at the inn, I figured this would be the perfect time to find out exactly how it would've gone down. The only question left in my head was, *How were we going to make it happen?*

I looked over at Eric and Anna, who were completely passed out on the bed to our left. I then looked down at Eve, who had her head resting on my chest and her left arm draped across me. She was also passed out. I also noticed a door located just to the right of the TV.

Earlier that night, the girls told us that they had rented out two rooms: one for them and one for us. That door led directly into the other room and was supposed to be for Eric and me. And by now, you can probably already figure out where I'm going with this.

So I decided to quietly wake Eve up and get her thoughts on this whole situation.

"Eve," I whispered while lightly shaking her. "Eve."

It took her a second, but she finally opened her eyes.

"Huh? What time is it?" she asked.

I immediately put a finger up to my lips before she got the hint and turned to look over at the other bed.

"How long have we been sleeping?" she whispered.

"About a half-hour," I replied.

She yawned. "Is something wrong?"

"Not exactly. Actually, I wanted to ask you something."

"What is it?"

"Remember earlier this week when we were alone in your bedroom? You know, right before your father came home and interrupted us?"

"Yeah."

"What do you think would've happened between us if he never came home?"

Her eyes narrowed. "What does that have to do with anything?"

"Well, I was thinking," I nervously began, "you know, since we have the other room, and since those two look really comfortable where they are, I was just thinking that…maybe you and I could—"

She took her left hand and covered my mouth, instantly shutting me up while saving me from my own stupidity.

"You talk too much," she said.

She then got out of bed and extended her right hand. I grabbed it and used it to get myself out of bed. Then, as quietly as possible, she led me over to the adjoining room door and opened it up. She turned to smile at me and grabbed both of my hands before backing up and pulling me through. And once we were inside, I quietly closed the door behind us.

CHAPTER 17

I ran out of the inn and through the parking lot as fast as I could, stopping just shy of the road. I looked to my left to make sure no cars were coming before turning to my right. Once the path was clear, I took off across both lanes, making it safely to the other side.

Dan's Quick Stop was the convenience store/gas station located directly across the street from the inn. To the left of that was a small diner called Mom's Kitchen, which served pretty much everything under the sun. After all, since truck drivers and vacationers spent most of their time on the road, they usually had big appetites.

But I wasn't hungry. In fact, I was something else. I was something that only a specific item inside the convenience store could satisfy. So I pulled on the handle to open the door and walked in.

Since it was located across from an inn and was also a place for travelers to stop and shop, it was a relatively decent-sized store. It was about the size of three convenience stores in one and was almost as big as a small grocery store.

As I stood just inside the doorway, I perused the interior to get a good feel for the place. I also wanted to make sure that I could easily find what I was looking for before purchasing it.

To the left was the back of the store, which had all the items to fix and replace most parts on your car or truck, including oil, windshield washer fluid, brake fluid, and power steering fluid.

On the far wall, directly in front of me and past all eight rows of food items, was the refrigerated section. There, you could find all your drinks, dairy, and some miscellaneous frozen goods.

To the right were the cashiers and checkout counters. Behind it, there were shelves upon shelves of alcohol (which I was too young to purchase anyway), cigarettes, rolling papers, aspirin, cold medicine, and everything else that the seventeen-and-under crowd wasn't allowed to buy—except for one thing. And that one thing just happened to be the item I needed. Without it, my night would most certainly suck.

After grabbing a basket, I first made my way over to one of the middle aisles to pick up a few essentials: a couple bags of Doritos, some Twinkies, and some Sour Patch Kids.

Next, I went to the refrigerated section to grab a couple bottles of Coke, some Mountain Dew, and some water. Once my basket was full, I then made my way toward the last item I needed, which was located behind the counter in the front of the store.

When I got up there, both cashiers were busy ringing people out. I purposely stood in the rightmost line, and not because it was the shortest either. I stood in that line because there was a man ringing everyone out.

Now, before you even think about cursing me out for choosing a line based on the gender of the cashier, finish reading. When you're done, you'll hopefully understand why.

Anyway, when it was my turn to cash out, I placed all the items in my basket on the counter. The somewhat young, maybe twenty-eight-year-old, curly-haired, tattooed guy started ringing me out. As he did, he kept looking at me funny, almost as if he was curious about why I was there. It also might have been the way I fidgeted with stuff while I stood there. Who knows?

Once everything was scanned and placed into the bag, he looked at me and noticed that I was looking at the back wall behind him. What I was looking for, however, he had no idea. And that was when he asked me "the question." It also happened to be a question that allowed me to make one of the most important choices I would ever have to make.

"Will there be anything else?" he asked, using a deep, raspy tone.

I looked up at the wall for another couple of seconds before extending my right arm out and pointing to one item in particular.

"I'll also take one of those," I nervously said.

When he turned around and saw the item I was pointing to, he placed his left hand on it.

"You also want one of these?" he asked, making sure he had the right one.

"Yes, please," I replied.

However, when I answered him, he didn't take the item off the rack right away. Instead, he looked at the item, then at me, then back at the item one more time before looking back at me.

"Are you sure you want that one?" he asked with one eyebrow raised.

"I think so," I replied.

He chuckled to himself. "You're new to this, aren't you?"

"You could say that."

He glared at me for what seemed like an eternity before turning back around and pulling an entirely different item off the shelf.

"I've been where you are," he said. "And I remember how it was for me. So if I can give you one piece of advice, it would be to try these instead."

I looked down at the item he had placed on the counter. "Are you sure?" I asked.

He grinned from ear to ear. "Trust me. With these, she'll be begging for more."

I thought about it for another second before giving him an answer. After all, what did I have to lose?

"All right," I said. "Let's do it."

He then rang up the last item and placed it in the bag. After I paid him, I grabbed my change and put it in my pocket before picking up my stuff. But just as I was about to walk away, he said something else to me.

"Have fun," he said before smiling and winking at me.

I politely smiled back before nodding and making my way out of the store.

———————

On the way back to the inn, I saw Eric coming out of his room. He was walking toward the store in the very same nervous manner I'd done just a few minutes earlier.

Once we crossed paths, we stopped to stare at each other. Not only did he stare at me, but he also tried to sneak a peek at what was in my bag. And judging by his overall demeanor, I knew exactly what he was looking for.

I knew that he had woken up and probably spoke to Anna (most likely almost the same conversation I had with Eve) before making his way out here. He was obviously going over to the store to buy some of the same items I'd just bought. After he saw what was in my bag, he simply looked me in the eyes, smirked, and nodded. He knew what I was about to do. I also knew that he was about to do the very same thing. So in kind, I reciprocated with a smirk and a nod of my own. Then he turned back toward the store and kept on walking.

During our brief encounter, we didn't say one single word to each other. We didn't have to. We already knew what the other was going to do, and we also knew that we would brag about it to each other the following morning.

Holding my bag, I stood just outside the door to my room. I hesitated momentarily before going in because I was extremely nervous. I was about to do something with Eve that I'd never done before—with any woman, for that matter. And neither has she. Well, with another man. Definitely not a woman. Although that would be pretty hot.

Sorry, I couldn't help myself.

Regardless of how nervous I was, I gathered all my strength and took a deep breath—probably one of the deepest breaths I had ever taken, before letting it out.

With the moon and the stars high above me in the sky and the three-pack of suggested condoms I'd just bought sitting in my bag, I grabbed the door handle, opened the door to my room, and went inside as I was about to have one of the most magical nights of my entire life.

————

I want you to close your eyes and imagine the apocalypse. Think about what the outcome would be if every possible thing that could destroy human life in one fell swoop happened. Do you have that in your mind? Good. Now take that mental-life-extinction picture and multiply it by ten.

I would assume that if you are, you're probably thinking of the Earth exploding in a glorious fireball, just like Alderran did in *Star Wars* when the Death Star blew it up. That was precisely what it felt like the moment Eve and I started having sex.

Picture yourself beginning that whole process. The moment it started was basically when the first apocalyptic event happened. Then, as we went on, the danger worsened until we both let everything go, causing the Earth to explode.

It was awkward at first because neither of us had any idea what the hell we were actually doing. We basically just did whatever felt natural. Plus, it also helped that we'd both watched a porno or two before then.

However, as the night went on, we started to get more comfortable with each other's bodies and what the other one liked. Needless to say, after eight whole hours and three used condoms later, we were both physically exhausted.

It was a little tricky to concentrate at first. Not because it was awkward or weird, but mainly because all four of us were in the vicinity of one another, and all four of us were, well, you know. And because of that, we were able to see what the other was experiencing. And not in that way, either.

If you recall, when we were all standing outside in the parking lot earlier that night, Eve and I kissed, causing Eric and Anna to see the landscape around us spin like a top. Thankfully, though, after only an hour of us going at it like jackrabbits, we could ignore the apocalypse and focus on the task at hand.

It's evident that everyone remembers a special night in their lives and can relive the moment, almost as if it were yesterday. That night at the inn was mine. And while I may only remember bits and pieces of the rest of my life, I will never, *ever* forget that night until the day I die.

The following morning, after getting roughly four hours of sleep, I opened my bloodshot eyes to find Eve and me sleeping on the bed. My right arm was curled over her as we cuddled in the spoon position.

Because of the night we had, I didn't even care that I was utterly exhausted. And even though I felt like I had just woken up after doing an eight-hour workout with Arnold Schwarzenegger (figuratively speaking), I felt the best I'd ever felt in my life. And you could probably deduce why.

As our naked bodies lay there, pressed tightly up against each other, I smiled to myself before closing my eyes and inhaling her heavenly essence. Either that or it was the half bottle of Rave hairspray she had put in her hair the day before. However, I didn't care. Just being there with her and knowing that we both defied her parents to be together made me happy.

But as excited as I was to be with her, I was even more excited about something else—something that would happen immediately after we got cleaned up and out of the shower—something that would solve my most recent problem—breakfast.

My stomach was growling and ready for some food. After what we'd just done, I could easily fit twenty breakfasts inside of me.

Before my shower and before we all left to head across the street, I quietly got out of bed, hoping not to wake Eve up. I then slipped on my underwear and pants and slowly made my way out of the room.

Standing just outside the door, I lifted my nose to the sky, closed my eyes, and took a huge whiff of the fresh morning air as the warm sun beat down on my face.

I don't know. Maybe it was the fact that I was feeling invincible at the time, or possibly even the fact that I just had sex for the first three times in my life and was suddenly ecstatic. Who knows? But for some strange reason, I felt like I could wake up that morning, get behind the wheel of my truck, play a game of chicken with that thing called life, and win. Because at that very moment, I never felt happier to be alive.

As I stood outside, enjoying my moment, I heard the door to the room next to mine open. I turned to see none other than Eric himself come walking out dressed pretty much the same way I was. The only difference was his glasses.

"Sup," I said, nodding toward him.

For some reason, he thought it would be funny to curiously eyeball me from head to toe before responding in kind.

"Sup," he replied.

We then turned away from each other and looked across the street toward the diner. At least, I was anyway.

"How was your night?" I asked with a smooth, calm, and collected voice.

"It was all right. Yours?" he casually replied.

"Same." I paused. "So uh, how'd you sleep?"

I only asked him that because I obviously knew he got just about the same amount of sleep as I did. I know because I could see what he and Anna were seeing. Plus, when he came walking out of his door, he looked like hell. Besides that, I already knew what his answer was going to be.

"What sleep?" he said.

Upon hearing his response, we slowly turned our heads toward each other while trying to keep our cool. Unfortunately, our "cool" quickly disappeared and was immediately replaced by the smiles of two giddy schoolgirls.

"Holy shit, dude," he said. "Anna and I totally had sex last night!"

"So did Eve and me!" I replied.

Our excitement at that point could not be contained. Needless to say, we wasted no time hugging each other while leaping around in happy circles. And once we realized what we were doing, we immediately stopped and broke apart to compose ourselves.

I cleared my throat. "Sorry about that."

"Don't worry about it," he said.

We stood there silently for a few seconds, waiting for our excitement to calm down.

"I will say this," he added, "I now want to have sex all day, every day."

"Same here," I replied. "However, I don't think there are enough condoms in the world to satisfy my needs."

"I know. Right? I now understand what all the fuss was about." He paused, almost as if a light bulb had suddenly turned on inside his head. "Why didn't we do this sooner?"

"Because if we did, we would've had no choice but to do it with our stalkers."

"Good point. I mean, hey, at least Tammy would've been something to brag about."

"I wouldn't go that far."

"Yeah, right. She definitely would've been a lot better than Sally Vennis."

I pondered that thought for a moment before responding. "Good point."

Eric folded his arms, laughed, and shook his head. "Who would've thought?"

"About what?" I asked.

"After all that talk about us pressuring each other to have sex, we both lose our virginity on the very same night."

"Huh," I said, stroking my chin with my right index finger and thumb. "You're right. I never would've thought. And speaking of which, what was up with the apocalypse?"

"What the hell are you talking about?"

I gave him an intense stare. "You know what I'm talking about."

"Me? I thought that was you?"

"No. *I* was the one seeing the nuclear explosions. *You* were the one seeing the exploding meteors."

He shook his head. "No way. That's where you're wrong. *I* saw the nuclear explosions while *you* saw the exploding meteors."

"Actually," I said, getting an interesting thought, "I think we were both seeing everything."

"How could we see everything when we were…" He trailed off before it suddenly hit him. "Oh! Kind of like what happened in the parking lot last night?"

"Exactly."

"Well, consider that theory confirmed."

"Definitely."

The theory he was referring to was something we had all discussed the previous night in our room while lying down and watching TV.

You see, since neither of us could see what the other couple had experienced until last night, we believed it had something to do with the close proximity of one another. For instance…

While Eve and I were on our date, Eric and Anna couldn't see or feel what had happened to us because they weren't close by. The same went for us, not experiencing what they saw and felt on their date. And after all of us saw the Earth spin around like a carnival ride, we didn't know what to make of it. However, after what happened to all of us the previous night with, well, you know, it seemed our discussions were not wrong.

Aside from that, the one thing still left to discuss was how to proceed with figuring out why a hidden camera was stuffed inside Eve's teddy bear. We initially wanted to wait and discuss that over breakfast so that we wouldn't overload our brains. And speaking of breakfast…

"I don't know about you, but I'm starving," I said.

"Same here," Eric replied.

"Breakfast?"

He thumbed toward his door. "Let's go wake up the girls."

And with that, we both nodded before disappearing into our respective rooms.

———

Mom's Kitchen, located next to the convenience store, was about twice the size of Johnny's Café and was built sometime in the mid-'60s. However, unlike the café's retro feel, Mom's had been updated to reflect the current decade.

The restaurant was shaped like a giant square, with its entrance on the right-hand side facing the store. Inside, two rows of booths, one down the entire right and left sides of the place, accompanied the many square and round tables in between. The kitchen and the to-go counter were set up all the way in the back. The waiters and waitresses were there to take your orders, but it was more or less a free-for-all when it came to seating, as you had to seat yourself.

About an hour later, after getting cleaned up and dressed, we all made our way across the street and over to the restaurant. We walked in and seated ourselves in one of the available booths on the left-hand side in the middle, directly in front of a window facing the inn. In the back right corner, next to the counter, a jukebox played a good mix of everything from the early '70s right up until that point in time.

When we sat down, "Caribbean Queen" by Billy Ocean was playing softly out of its speakers. And because it wasn't entirely busy in there, the waitress came over and handed us our menus almost immediately.

Now, I don't mean to be derogatory or anything, but our waitress was one of those tall, thin, blonde-haired, blue-eyed, ditzy, gum-chewing, oversized breasts that were almost popping out of her shirt type of waitresses who spoke in a southern accent.

Yeah, I know, whatever. You can hate me later. But that was pretty much the only way I could describe her.

"Well, hi there!" the waitress said before popping her gum and handing us the menus. "Welcome to Mom's! My name's Susan and I'll be takin' care of y'all."

We all nodded in unison and said our hellos.

"Can I start y'all off with a beverage?" she asked.

On top of the coffees we all ordered, Eric and Anna each ordered an orange juice, while both Eve and I ordered chocolate milk.

"Perfect. I'll get those in and be right back to take your orders," the waitress said before leaving us to our stomach-rumbling choices.

About twenty minutes later, after all the orders were placed and our food was brought out, we began to chow down like hungry wolves. Four or five songs had also played on the jukebox while we waited, and by the time we finally started eating, "Girls on Film" by Duran Duran had begun playing.

"Okay. Now that I've got some food in my belly, let's talk about that hidden camera you found," I said. "You said it came from one of your stuffed bears?"

"It was from one of the teddy bears my parents gave me on my fifth birthday," Eve replied.

"And both of you got the very same ones?"

"Correct."

I then shoveled in a massive forkful of eggs as I pondered my next thought.

"What does the hidden camera in Eve's bear have to do with Anna's bear?" Eric asked.

I immediately turned to look at him before gulping down the rest of my bite. "Dude, weren't you paying attention last night?" I asked. "If there's a hidden camera in Eve's bear, then there must be one in Anna's."

"And how exactly does that help us?"

I sighed and took a few large sips of my coffee before answering his question. "That helps us *immensely,*" I said. "If we can go back to Anna's house, find her bear, and tear it open to reveal a hidden camera, then we'll know for certain that none of us are going insane."

"I still don't get it," he said.

"Look, I've been thinking about this a lot, and if we can prove that Anna was being watched as well, we can then move forward with finding out why they glow."

By that point, all three of them were just staring at me as the gears in their heads began turning at warp speed.

"Are you saying our parents wanted to keep an eye on us because they know something about us that no one else knows?" Eve asked.

"That's exactly what I'm saying," I replied.

"What do you think it is?" Anna asked.

"I honestly don't know."

"No surprise there," Eric joked.

"*But,*" I continued while giving him the death stare, "it all now makes sense. The hidden cameras, both of your mothers giving us some very odd looks, and both of your fathers coming home early. Not to mention, they're both in the military. Also, with them forbidding us from ever seeing you again, I highly doubt that this is all just one big, strange coincidence. Don't you agree?"

By the time I got done rambling on about my asinine theory, they all just stared at me like I had a screw loose or something. It was almost like the lights were on, but no one was home. To them, I was officially a couple of cards short of a full deck. However, in my mind, I knew I was right. And I just had to somehow prove to them I was.

"Okay," Eric said. "Let's say you're right. Let's say that to prove everything, we need to find a hidden camera in Anna's teddy bear. If that's step number one, then how do you propose we go about getting it? I mean, after all, with the girls being gone for one night without telling anyone where they went, they certainly can't just walk back through their front doors without someone getting suspicious and asking them five million questions. Their parents would see right through them and never allow them to leave the house again."

After hearing his explanation, I slowly nodded my head in agreement. Because, unfortunately, he was right.

"Good point," I said.

"Thank you," he replied. "So with that being said, any other bright ideas?"

"Well, you could always charm your way inside," I joked.

"Very funny."

By that point, I honestly had no idea how we would get into Anna's house without her parents seeing us. I mean, with her being gone, the odds of both of her parents not being home at the same time were slim to none. However, we had no choice *but* to get in there. Finding that other hidden camera was the only way we would know for sure that something fishy was going on.

"Well, we could always crash at the inn for another night while we think about it?" I suggested.

"Or," Eric said, holding up a finger.

"Or what?"

"Or we could simply surrender."

"Are you out of your mind?" I asked, thinking that he'd lost his marbles. "Surrendering is the *last* thing we want to do."

"Maybe you should tell them that," he said, pointing to the window.

When I turned to see what he was pointing at, my jaw crashed through the table while my eyes practically blew out two holes in the glass. The entire area, including the inn and rest stop, was now surrounded by at least one hundred men and women dressed in camouflage clothing.

Humvees, unmarked cars, and a couple handfuls of armored military transport trucks were now parked across the street and directly outside of our window. We were so busy eating and discussing how to get into Anna's house that we didn't even see them approach. Traffic coming from both directions had also been halted. The whole area suddenly looked like it was about to be quarantined or something.

"Oh no," Eve said.

"When the hell did they get here?" I asked.

"Probably while we were eating and discussing your stupid plan," Eric replied.

"Hey, it was all I had at the time."

Not even a second later, we saw another armored transport vehicle pull into the inn's parking lot. Once it came to a stop, the two front doors opened before two men in black suits got out. They then went to the rear doors and opened them up, allowing whoever was in the back to exit the vehicle safely. Both of the exiting men wore the same battle dress uniforms, complete with the decorations of an Air Force Colonel. One of them I didn't recognize, but the other one I did almost instantly.

"It's my father," Eve said.

"Mine too," Anna added.

The moment I saw both of their fathers standing across the street in the inn's parking lot, I knew right then and there that my theory about everything was indeed correct. They were definitely hiding something from us, and I was suddenly more curious than ever to find out exactly what it was. I mean, why else would they send an excessive amount of military personnel to come and capture us? Also, how in the hell did they know we were there?

Regardless, we were now trapped, with no way out. If we tried, we would indeed get captured. If we gave ourselves up, well, then they might go easy on us.

"You don't think they're here for us, do you?" I asked.

No sooner did that question leave my lips, I saw Eve's father reach into the back seat of the car and pull out a megaphone before holding it up to his mouth and speaking.

"Wesley, Eric, Anna, and Eve," he began. "We know you're here. Please come out now so we can talk. If you do not comply, we will be forced to go in after you."

I immediately turned to look at Eric, Anna, and Eve with a defeated yet cocky expression on my face.

"So," I said before leaning back in my seat and folding my arms, "who's the crazy one now?"

CHAPTER 18

We hadn't even finished our breakfast yet when an entire squad of U.S. military personnel decided to grace us with their presence. It also could've been more like a platoon or even a brigade. I can tell you one thing, though—whoever they were, they certainly weren't there to enjoy the scenery.

I didn't know why, but I assumed it was because Anna and Eve were with us, and their fathers somehow knew about it. And now they were there for our heads.

Okay, maybe not our heads, but they were definitely there to get their daughters back. And take our heads.

As we all stared out of the restaurant window, we had no clue what to do. I mean, should we try to make a run for it? Probably not, because we were too far from civilization, way out in the middle of nowhere. We could always try to sneak over to the cars and speed our asses out of there. Nah. That wouldn't work either because, again, they had the whole place surrounded and the roads blocked off.

I then pictured myself sneaking out there before disabling one of the soldiers and grabbing his machine gun. I imagined myself opening fire on everyone, blasting them all to smithereens while becoming the hero. Of course, that thought quickly dissipated before I then imagined myself getting shot down in slow motion, just like Willem Dafoe's character, Sergeant Elias, in the 1986 film *Platoon*.

Just like in the movie, I immediately fell down a couple of times before getting back up and taking gunfire to my back. And once I couldn't go on any further, I raised my arms in the air and lifted my head to the sky before falling forward and succumbing to my injuries.

I guess being the hero was ultimately out.

So if we couldn't escape and I couldn't be the hero, then the only option left was to give ourselves up. I mean, we hadn't done anything wrong, well, other than defile their daughters. But as far as we were concerned, we were all adults, and we all consented to it. However, if that subject were to come up, I wasn't so sure the Colonels would see it that way.

I also thought that there was no way in hell they could possibly harm us. Why? Well, for one, we were all civilians. And two, again, we didn't do anything wrong. Not to mention, we hadn't even started acting out our plan yet.

And speaking of which, at that moment, I suddenly became very curious as to what the Colonels would tell me when I asked them about the hidden camera in Eve's teddy bear. But since they worked for the government, they would most likely deny everything.

By that point, all the other patrons in the restaurant had shifted over toward our side of the building. They were now staring out the windows while quietly discussing amongst themselves what was happening.

"What do we do now?" Eric quietly asked.

I shrugged. "Your guess is as good as mine. I mean, how did they even know we were here?"

Immediately after asking that, Eric and I gave each other a quick glance before turning to look at the girls.

"Hey, don't look at us," Eve said. "We didn't say a word."

"Do you really think we'd tell anyone where we were going?" Anna added. "We're not stupid."

"We never said you were," I said. "We're just trying to figure this thing out, that's all."

"But seriously," Eric said. "If you didn't say anything to anyone, then how did they find us so fast?"

"Believe me, we'd like to know the same thing," Anna replied.

Since none of us responded to the Colonel the first time, he lifted the megaphone to his mouth and spoke into it again.

"We know the four of you are here," he said. "Again, if you don't come out to talk, we will be forced to come in and find you. You now have exactly one minute to decide."

"One minute?" I said, nervousness echoing in my voice. "One minute isn't even long enough to take a piss."

"Maybe for you," Eric remarked.

"Hey, not all of us have tiny, pea-sized bladders."

"Yeah, well, not all of us have—"

"Guys! Can we just focus here for a minute?" Eve angrily interrupted.

"He started it," I said.

Eric didn't reply and just scowled at me before punching me in the arm. I was about to punch him back, but Anna decided that she'd finally had enough of our childish behavior.

"If you two don't stop, you'll both be getting my fist," she said. "And it won't be in the arm."

We both covered our faces in defense.

"It won't be there either," she added.

That was when we realized that she meant a punch in the jewels would be in order. So we stopped.

"Thirty seconds!" the Colonel yelled out through the megaphone.

I lowered my head and shook it as I sighed in disgust. "Shit," I muttered.

We really had no choice. With the whole place surrounded, all the roads blocked off, and all the soldiers armed to the teeth with machine guns, knives, and pistols, we had but one option left. It was time to face the proverbial music.

"Well, it was nice knowing everyone," I said before attempting to leave the booth.

"Where are you going?" Eric asked.

"Dude, look around. We can't escape, and we have no place to go. I just think it's about time we went out there."

"Are you out of your mind? Who knows what they have in store for us?"

"Come on, we're eighteen years old and fresh out of high school. What are they going to do, shoot us?"

All three of them didn't say a word and just gave me a look, almost as if to say, "Probably."

"Besides," I continued, "if doing this means that we won't have to face any consequences, then we have no other choice."

"But what about the girls?" Eric asked. "You would rather give yourself up just to risk never seeing them again?"

"If sacrificing my own freedom means that they'll be safe, then yeah."

Eric let out a disgusted sigh of his own. "Unfortunately, you're right," he said.

"Wait a minute," Anna said. "Doesn't anyone care what we think?"

"Yeah. What if we don't agree with this?" Eve added.

"You don't have a choice in the matter," I said.

Eve scowled. "Who made you boss?"

I leveled a finger at her. "First of all, Springsteen is the boss. Second of all, I already know for a fact that you two will be unharmed. As for me, well, that's just a risk I'm willing to take."

After hearing what I had to say, the girls quickly turned to Eric for his answer, almost as if they knew he would disagree with my suggestion.

"What?" he said. "Don't give me that look."

"Well?" Anna asked.

"What do you want me to say?"

"We want you to tell him that this is a stupid idea."

"I wish I could. But unfortunately, Wes is right about this one. I'd rather give myself up knowing that you two are safe than have them come charging in here."

"Ten seconds!" The Colonel shouted before counting down. "Ten…nine…eight…"

Eve sighed. "I suppose you're right," she said. "However, if you're going to go through with this, then we're all going out there together."

"And when we do, we'll try and talk to them about keeping you two safe," Anna added.

I smiled and nodded at the girls. Then the three of them got up out of the booth, with me following closely behind.

With Anna holding Eric's hand and Eve holding mine, we all looked at one another and took a deep breath before walking toward the restaurant door. Once we got over there, we briefly hesitated before glancing around at one another one more time. Then we pushed the door open as the four of us marched right outside to meet our would-be captors face to face.

———————

The moment we stepped out of the restaurant, every person outside who had a gun (which was literally everyone) raised their barrels and pointed them directly at us. I'll tell you, with about a hundred guns pointed directly at my face, my life immediately flashed before my eyes. It was and wasn't something I would highly recommend anyone else try, either.

"Don't shoot!" I heard the Colonel say through the megaphone. "Everyone, lower your weapons!"

Upon hearing his orders, no one wasted any time lowering their guns.

"All four of you walk over to me right now," the Colonel said.

With all of us still holding hands, we slowly made our way out of the restaurant parking lot and toward the inn. On our way there, the soldiers who stood around took a couple of steps back so that we could freely walk past them. That was the first time I had ever seen anything like that happen—other than in the movies, of course.

I don't know about the other three, but as we walked past them, I felt a sense of dread wash over me. I had no idea what was going to happen the moment we were all taken into custody or what would become of us. I was scared, anxious, and slightly nauseated at the fact that I didn't know what was going to happen next. Was what we did so wrong that it was worth the big show? Who knows? But we would soon find out.

After we crossed the street, we made our way to the inn's parking lot and over to where the Colonels' vehicle was parked. Eve's dad was glaring at me with a dead-serious look, almost like he wanted to rip my arms right off my body and beat me senseless with them.

I had to give the guy props, though. Somehow, he wound up keeping his composure. I mean, if it were me, the guy doing that with my daughter wouldn't stand a chance in hell. Also, it was at that very moment that I finally got to lay eyes on Anna's father.

He was about as tall as Mr. Parker and had the same build, haircut, and uniform. However, that was pretty much where their similarities ended.

Unlike Mr. Parker, Mr. James had light skin, blue eyes, and dirty blonde hair. After seeing him for the first time, it finally made sense that Anna and Eve, who looked absolutely nothing like their parents, would be adopted.

Stopping just about five feet away from them, both Colonels signaled to each of the other soldiers they were driving with. The moment they did, the drivers came right over and snatched the girls away from us.

"What the hell do you think you're doing?" I screamed.

I immediately tried to advance and make my way to Eve, but was quickly stopped by Mr. Parker, who had his hand on my chest, holding me back.

"Mr. Tucker," he said. "I wouldn't do that if I were you."

"What's going on here? What are you going to do with her?" I asked.

"Don't you worry about her. Both of the girls will be safe and sound. As for you two…"

He shook his head, telling me my chances didn't look so hot.

The girls didn't say a word or put up much of a fight. Eric and I could do nothing but stand there and watch as they got placed in the back of one of the Humvees.

"Allow me to introduce myself, Wes. I'm Mr. James, Anna's father," Mr. James said.

"Yeah. I kind of figured that one out on my own," I sarcastically responded.

Upon hearing my remark, he narrowed his eyes and glared at me for a moment before continuing.

"Eric, allow me to introduce Eve's father, Mr. Parker," Mr. James said.

"So you're Wes's best friend?" Mr. Parker asked.

Eric, in kind, decided to give him a sarcastic response of his own. "Come to that decision all on your own, have you?" he asked.

The Colonels just snickered to themselves, almost as if we were missing out on a hilarious joke.

"I thought we made it clear that both of you stay away from our daughters," Mr. Parker said.

"Oh, you did," I replied. "But after figuring a few things out, there was no way in hell that was going to happen."

"Oh? And just what have you *figured out?*"

"Don't play dumb with us," Eric said. "We know about the hidden camera in Eve's Teddy Bear."

After hearing Eric's comment, both Colonels briefly glanced at each other before turning and looking back at us.

"We have no idea what you're talking about," Mr. James said.

"Bullshit!" Eric replied. "And I'm willing to bet that there's one in Anna's room as well."

"Oh, really? Then tell me," Mr. James said before leaning up against the vehicle and folding his arms. "Why do you think there'd be a hidden camera in Anna's room?"

"I don't know. But that's what we're going to find out."

"Yeah! We're also going to find out why you both came home early instead of a couple of months from now," I said. "Trust me. The lying, the sneaking around, the weird things that happen when the girls are with us…we know what's going on here."

It wasn't until I accidentally let slip the thing about the girls that Mr. James immediately stood upright, unfolded his arms, and was back to being the stoic person he was. Mr. Parker gave us his full attention as well.

"What do you know about the girls?" Mr. James asked with an all-too-serious expression on his face.

However, with him asking me that question the way he did, a small red flag rose to the top of an invisible flagpole inside my head.

"I don't know," I responded before curiously furrowing my brows. "What do *you* know about the girls?"

"I asked you first."

"I'm not telling you a thing."

"It appears then that we've come to an impasse," Mr. Parker said.

"It appears so," I said, folding my own arms.

"Which means, if you won't tell us, then you leave us no choice."

Before I even had a chance to figure out what the hell was going on, I suddenly felt a small prick on the right side of my neck. The pain lasted for but a second before my body started to get the sweats. My right hand instantly went up to feel where the sharp pain had just come from, while my eyes began dancing around in circles. I looked over at

Eric, who now looked like the same drunken fool as me, before turning back to the Colonels.

"What…what did you…do to me?" I asked, my speech suddenly slow and tired.

It felt like my entire body had instantly turned into a walking pile of jelly. My legs started shaking, my limbs started to go numb, and I felt like I wanted to go to sleep.

Without any warning, and before either one of them would give us an answer, my body gave out and crashed to the ground like a brick. And that, unfortunately, was the last thing I remembered until waking up sometime later.

CHAPTER 19

One moment, Eric, Anna, Eve, and I were enjoying a nice breakfast at Mom's Kitchen. The next thing we know, we're surrounded by at least a hundred or so armed soldiers, including the two Colonels. They had ordered us to surrender so they could speak to us peacefully.

What a bunch of bullshit.

In the middle of our conversation, we were suddenly injected with some kind of numbing agent and almost instantly passed out. The next thing I know, I'm waking up in some room, very similar to an interrogation room at a police station, strapped to a chair.

It was a metal chair complete with metal restraints. The restraints were bolted to the chair and were on a hinge so they could easily lift and come down to wrap around my wrists and ankles. They were also secured in place by a small lock, which I wished I had the keys for.

There was a dim light above me and a mirror in front of me. I assumed it was a two-way mirror so that the people standing behind it could hear any conversation without being seen. But I would later find out that it was, in fact, just a mirror.

I couldn't even begin to tell you how long I was out for, and I wouldn't find out until a few minutes after coming to. The one thing I did know was that I was by myself, all alone in a room with walls made of concrete.

I tried to wiggle my hands and feet in hopes that I would be able to shimmy myself out of the restraints. Yeah. No luck whatsoever. Those things were rock solid.

I then tried to rock the boat to see if the chair would somehow tip over, hoping to break or snap off one of the restraints in the process. I didn't realize until after I tried that the chair was bolted to the floor. Silly me for not thinking about that sooner.

So, not knowing where I was or what the hell was going on, I did what any other normal person would've done in that situation.

"Hello?" I called out. "Is anybody there?"

I waited a few moments, hoping someone would get back to me. When nobody did, I just slumped down in the chair and waited some more. I must've waited for a good half an hour before someone finally came into the room to greet me.

The door to my left opened, and a lone man walked in. It was the Colonel. Well, Eve's dad. But you probably already figured that part out yourself.

Anyway, he closed the door behind him before walking over to stand directly in front of me. His legs were spread out and shoulder-length apart, while his hands were joined together behind his back.

He didn't say anything right away, though. Instead, he just glared at me, almost as if looking deep into my soul. But he didn't look angry. He looked more intrigued by how our conversation was about to go. If I had to guess (which I didn't need to), I knew that it was more or less what kind of information I was harboring about the girls.

"Where am I?" I asked

"We'll get to that shortly, Mr. Tucker," the Colonel replied.

"Please, just call me Wes."

"How about if I don't? And if you wish to know where you are, then I suggest you answer my questions first."

"Not a chance. Where's Eve?"

He shrugged. "Okay. If that's how you want to play it…"

The Colonel took his right hand and brought it down to his right hip before placing it on his firearm. After unbuttoning the strap, he pulled it out and held it down by his side. In that moment, I thought, *There's no way he'd pull his gun on me. I'm just an innocent civilian.* I mean, after all, what was he going to do, shoot me?

"Will you answer my questions now?" the Colonel asked.

"Hell, no," I replied. "And I already know you're not going to pull that trigger."

Without hesitation, the Colonel cocked his gun and aimed it at me. He obviously only did it to scare me because a few seconds later, he shifted it up toward the ceiling to my right and pulled the trigger, shooting out one of the lights. As a natural reflex, I flinched and watched the tiny glass shards come crashing down to the floor.

"Jesus Christ!" I shouted. "Are you insane?"

"*That* was your only warning," the Colonel said.

Okay, so maybe he was going to shoot me. However, I definitely didn't want to take the chance to find out. Regardless, his scare tactic worked because I immediately gave in.

"Fine!" I said. "I'll answer your questions first."

Upon hearing my response, he immediately holstered his gun and secured the strap. An evil smirk rested upon his face as he stood back at ease.

"Thank you," he said with a single head nod. "Now, first things first. Who am I?"

I narrowed my eyes and just stared at him like he had two heads or something. "Is this a trick question?" I asked.

"Answer it, or I will break your fingers one at a time," he replied.

"Okay, okay," I said, wanting to keep my hands in working order. "You're Eve's father, Mr. Parker."

"Colonel Parker, to you."

I let out a disgusted sigh. "Fine. *Colonel Parker.*"

"Much better. Now, tell me…what do you know about the hidden camera that was found in Eve's room?"

"Well, nothing…yet."

"Yet?" he asked, intrigued by my response.

"Yeah. I mean, we were going to see if Anna had one in her room before coming to any radical conclusions. But now that I'm here with you"—I gave the room another perusal—"there's really no need."

"Very good. On to my next question, then." He paused briefly. "What do you know about Anna and Eve? And I want you to be as honest as possible, no matter how ridiculous it may sound."

The last part of his question told me that he already knew a little something about what I was going to say. But how or why *he* already knew was a completely different story.

"You want the truth?" I asked.

"Correct," he replied.

"No matter how crazy it sounds?"

"Yes."

"Okay. You asked for it. You see, since I've been with Eve," I began, "a lot of weird stuff has been happening to us. However, for some strange reason, only we can see it. To everyone else, it looks like a simple magic trick."

"I see. Is that all?"

"Not quite." I paused to take a deep breath before continuing. "Also, for some strange reason, when we look at the girls, we can see them, well…glow."

He raised a curious eyebrow. "You can see them *glow?*"

"That's what I said."

"Okay, Wes. Now, I'm going to ask you one more question, which happens to be a big one. Also, if you lie to me or don't give me the answer I'm looking for," he said before the tone of his voice changed to pure evil, "I will make your life a living hell."

My eyes quickly flew open, as I was more scared now than when he shot out the light. And with him seeing me scared shitless, a barely noticeable smile graced his face before his voice changed back to something a little more soothing.

"Did you and my daughter…" he began before trailing off, unable to finish the question.

With his mouth hanging open, practically catching flies, I knew he was having a hard time asking me whatever it was he wanted to ask. Unfortunately, with everything I'd learned about the girls, along with what we'd done and seen since meeting them, I couldn't even begin to fathom a guess as to what it was.

The Colonel took a deep breath before trying once again. "Did you and my daughter…" he began again before pausing, almost as if finishing the question made him want to throw up. "Did you two…have sex?"

Ho—ly—shit.

Now *that* was a question I *definitely* didn't expect him to ask. I mean, I did. And in my mind, I was totally prepared for it. But actually hearing him ask it and me suddenly having to give him an answer were two completely different things.

So before I told him, I looked up to the ceiling, took a deep breath, and in my mind, prayed to the maker that the Colonel wouldn't kill me after hearing my answer. And once I was finally ready, I looked him directly in his eyes.

"Yes, sir," I replied, my face a stone mask. "But we were totally safe. I swear."

Now, I honestly didn't know how he would react to me telling him that. Actually, that's not true.

The moment he heard those words leave my lips, I pictured his eyes glowing bright red while he sprouted bat wings and a devil's tail. Then I imagined him pulling out his gun and unloading the entire clip into my body before dragging me down to hell himself. However, the reality was that when I gave him my answer, his posture changed almost immediately.

Instead of being the hard-nosed Colonel I saw, he suddenly looked almost like a rage-induced father. And after seeing him change, I could instantly tell that he knew what saying yes to him meant. But nothing, and I mean absolutely nothing, could've prepared me for what happened next.

Without saying another word to me, he went over to the door, opened it up, and stepped outside, closing it shut behind him. And I think that scared me just as much as him pulling his gun on me because I suddenly had no idea when he would be coming back, or if he would be coming back at all, for that matter. Plus, by that point, I had an entirely new problem to deal with.

"Um, Colonel?" I called out. "I have to pee!"

When he didn't answer me, I called out for anybody who would hear my pleas to use the bathroom. "Hello? Anyone? I really have to pee!"

———

A couple of hours and one pair of pee-soaked jeans later, I was still sitting in the very same room, waiting for someone to come in or answer my cries for help.

"Anybody? It's starting to smell in here!" I yelled out, referring to my pants and the giant yellowish puddle on the floor.

I didn't know where the Colonel went or how long he would be gone. I did know, however, that it was only a matter of time before he eventually came back for me. *When* that was, I had no idea. Thankfully, though, I didn't have to wait much longer.

No sooner did I cry out, the Colonel walked back into the room. But this time, he wasn't alone. This time, he had a pair of armed escorts with him.

"I'm sorry I had to leave you like this, Wes," he said.

"I bet you are," I replied.

After hearing my response, I could see the steam practically billow out of his ears. I knew that if I pissed him off enough, he would have no problem ripping my head clean off my body. To keep himself from doing that, he just closed his eyes and took a couple of deep, calming breaths before continuing.

"Anyway, I had to go and check in with Colonel James," he said. "And as it turns out, both you and Eric gave us almost the exact same story."

"Almost?" I asked, curious.

"Let's put it this way…*you*, we believe. Him"—the Colonel shook his head—"not so much."

"Why? What did he say?" But the Colonel didn't answer. And when that happened, I feared the worst. "Where is he? What did you do with him?"

Hearing the tone of my voice, the Colonel responded by flashing his palms. "Relax. He's fine." I instantly let out a sigh of relief. "But that's not important. What is important is your knowledge of my daughter and Anna."

"What does that have to do with anything?"

The Colonel didn't answer my question. Instead, he pulled a set of keys out of his pocket and reached down toward me, unlocking the locks on my ankles first, followed by the ones on my wrists. Once I was free, I massaged my wrists with my hands as I looked up at him and awaited his orders.

"You may stand up now," he said.

As you could imagine, I wasted no time standing up and stretching. And man, did that feel good.

"Here," he said, tossing me a pair of clean, dark blue khaki pants.

I caught them and looked down at them before looking back up at him.

"What? No underwear?" I asked.

"Just put those on, and we'll get going," he said.

But I didn't move. Instead, I just stood there and stared at them, hoping that he and his escorts would catch my drift and turn around while I changed.

"Can I get a little privacy, please?" I asked.

"No," the Colonel replied.

Giving all of them the stink eye, I turned myself around and stripped off my jeans and underwear while "accidentally" mooning them in the process. Once my new pants were on, I zipped up and turned around.

"Okay, there," I said. "Now, could you please tell me why my knowledge of your daughter is so important?"

"I could tell you, but you probably wouldn't believe me," the Colonel replied. "Instead, how about I give you a little tour of our facilities?"

My eyes narrowed. "After you show me, you're not going to kill me, are you?"

His reply was a simple, villainous grin as he motioned to the door. And with me suddenly being scared for my life (again), I did as he suggested. I walked through the door first, followed by the Colonel and then his escorts.

———

Once we were out in the hallway, we immediately turned left and started to make our way toward who knows where. As we walked, we passed many other rooms, just like the one where I was held. That gave me a pretty good idea about what went on in them. Or at least, so I thought.

The feeling of that entire place was a little creepy, to be honest. The building itself had that whole *Day of the Dead*, underground bunker-type feel. Minus the zombies, of course.

Once we got down to the end of the hallway, the Colonel motioned for me to take a right. So I took a right and started down that hall, passing even more rooms similar to the one I was in.

And that made me start questioning other things in my mind, like, *Why do they need all these interrogation rooms? And just who the hell are they interrogating?*

At the end of the hall stood three doors: one to my left, one to my right, and one directly in front of me. Unlike the other doors, however, the one in front of me had a keypad located to its right.

The Colonel immediately went in front of me and punched in six digits, all of which I couldn't see because he blocked my view. I only knew it was six because I managed to count the beeps while he was punching them in. The seventh beep, however, sounded much different than the previous six.

After the seventh beep, I heard the door unlock and then saw it open by itself. The Colonel then stuck his right hand out, motioning for me to go in. So I did. But when I opened that door to go inside, I was amazed by what I saw.

The room I walked into must've been the control room for the entire place. Of course, I hadn't really seen everything yet, but the sheer size of it told me that wherever I was, it was pretty fucking huge.

The room we were in looked almost identical to the control room where Matthew Broderick had the supercomputer play tic-tac-toe against itself to stop global nuclear war in the 1983 movie *WarGames*. Not only did it look identical, but it was probably about five times the size.

Almost every computer in there had someone sitting in front of it, working on lord knows what. Men and women of all ages and races were hard at work. What they were doing, however, I had no idea.

"Holy shit!" I said in amazement while scanning the room from left to right. "What is this place?"

"This is our command center," the Colonel replied.

"And just what exactly are you commanding?"

"You'll find out in due time. But first, I would like to show you something else."

"I don't know how it could get any more impressive than this, but lead the way."

After taking one more quick look around the command center, we exited and immediately went straight back down the hall.

We walked past the corridor that we initially came from before finally making it down to the very end. There sat a single elevator. The Colonel wasted no time pushing the DOWN button. Of course, that was the only button on there. There was no UP option.

After a few brief moments, the doors opened, and we all got on. I watched as he pushed the *U* button.

U? I thought. *How many levels are in this place, anyway?*

U is pretty far down on the alphabet ladder and just happens to be only six away from *Z*. But the letters in that elevator only went from *A* to *U*. After that, there were no more. And once the doors had closed, we officially began our descent down to hell.

"Where are you taking me?" I asked.

"Don't worry. You'll find out soon enough," the Colonel replied.

I suddenly couldn't help but wonder if where we were going had anything to do with my knowledge of the girls. I would soon find out, though.

———

Once we finally arrived on level *U*, the doors opened, and we all stepped out into a brightly lit hallway. Albeit a very short, brightly lit hallway.

It had five doors that led out of it: two on the left, two on the right, and one straight ahead. The first one the Colonel took me to was the first door on the right, closest to the elevator.

He stuck his hand out to punch in a code on the control pad, located to the right of the door. Come to think of it, all the control panels in that place were on the right-hand sides of the doors. And if I had to guess, it was probably because they wanted everything to be—uniform.

Get it? "Uniform?" Because they were all wearing—never mind.

Anyway, just as the Colonel was about to punch in the door code, he suddenly stopped. And that was when he turned around to face me.

"Before we go inside, I must warn you that whatever you see in there cannot be unseen and must be kept a secret," he said.

"Well, if I'm not supposed to see it, then why are you showing it to me?" I asked. "And what'll happen after I do?"

"Because it may help with our research. And to answer the second part of your question, that all depends on you."

"Great," I sarcastically remarked.

"Are you ready?"

Was I ready? I mean, what other choice did I have?

I stuck out my left hand, motioning for him to input the code into the control pad. He once again blocked my view as he punched in another six digits. And again, after the seventh beep went off, I could hear the door unlock before seeing it open slightly ajar.

Once we went inside and I saw what was in there, my heart started pounding, my skin crawled, sweat began to seep out of every pore, my eyes bugged out, my jaw hit the floor, and my adrenaline went into overdrive. I was suddenly looking at something I never thought would ever have existed in my lifetime.

Before that day, I had a slight suspicion that what I saw might be real. But actually getting to see it up close and personal, well, to be honest, I practically shit myself.

CHAPTER 20

"What in the holy fuck is going on here?" I asked, absolutely stunned at what I was looking at.

"I know this may come as a shock to you," the Colonel said.

"Shock isn't exactly the word I would use."

"Wes, welcome to our A.M.U."

"A.M.U.?" I asked, confused.

"Yes. Our Alien Medical Unit."

I was looking into a massive, long room lined with concrete walls. Two rows of tall tanks, each similar to the Bacta tank that Luke Skywalker was in after Han found him on Hoth in *The Empire Strikes Back,* sat on each side of the room. Except, unlike the movie, the liquid inside them wasn't clear. It was more of a yellowish, light green color.

There were ten tanks in total—five on each side, each standing roughly twelve feet tall. Also, to my utter surprise and the sole reason for me practically wanting to shit myself, four of the tanks had something in them.

"Aliens?" I asked, shocked. "Are you for real right now?"

"I am very real right now," the Colonel replied. "Go ahead. See for yourself."

With my jaw sweeping up the dirt on the floor, I quickly walked over to the first tank on the right.

Through the somewhat murky liquid, I could see a tall shape, maybe around seven feet or so, just floating in there. It was a grayish, greenish, brown color and was thin, almost like a malnourished basketball player. It had four toes, four fingers, and a head that was about twice the average person's size. I couldn't see its eyes because they were closed and reduced to nothing but slits. Its mouth was also closed, and it looked like someone had drawn a line on its face. The other three in the tanks looked similar to that one, except that the colors and heights varied.

"So," I quietly began, placing my right palm against the glass, "we're really not alone."

"No, we aren't," the Colonel said.

"How long have you had these things?"

"Two of them have been here since the mid-sixties. But the other two have been here since the late forties."

"Holy shit," I whispered before realizing what he had just told me. "Wait"—I turned to face him—"did you just say the late forties?"

"I did."

"Are you trying to tell me that the Roswell incident *actually* happened?"

The Colonel slowly bobbed his head from side to side, almost as if he was trying to think of the right words to tell me.

"Yes and no," he said. "You see, the Roswell incident was merely a cover-up for what really happened."

"So then it wasn't a weather balloon?" I asked.

"What that rancher found was indeed a weather balloon," the Colonel explained. "But something collided with it to make it crash, sending both objects to the desert floor. The spaceship that the aliens were flying landed just a few miles away. Luckily, we were able to clean up both messes. The rancher only found a few pieces of the weather balloon. Thankfully, though, the ship itself was fully intact when we recovered it."

"What about the other two?" I asked with the utmost curiosity.

"They must've hit the mountains nearby. We found their downed ship not too far from this facility. Because the two ships look similar, we assume that they must've been looking for the other two."

"So the facility we're in is in New Mexico?"

He took a second to answer me. "Not quite."

"Then if we're not in New Mexico, where the hell are we?"

"Unfortunately, I can't tell you."

My brows immediately furrowed. "Why not?"

"This way," he said, altogether avoiding my question.

And before I could get anything else out, he quickly turned back around and exited the room. I took one more glance at the tanks before following him out and back into the hallway.

Once we were out of the A.M.U., we made our way over to the door directly across the hall. Again, he punched in the six-digit passcode, and after the seventh beep, I watched as the Colonel pushed open the unlocked door. Through there was something else that, again, I never thought I'd ever see in my lifetime.

We stood inside of what looked like a massive hangar bay, probably big enough to hold ten 747 jet airplanes. However, sitting inside that hangar were definitely no airplanes.

Inside sat two massive spaceships, one on each side, each one basically mirroring the other. They were long—maybe the length of two passenger jets—and twice as wide. They were silver in color and hovering about ten feet off the ground. As far as I could tell, there was only one window per ship, located at the front, presumably where the cockpit was. Ladders and computer equipment surrounded the two ships while about six dozen military personnel (three per craft) worked to figure out how they operated. Or so I had only assumed.

"These are their spaceships?" I asked, my face looking just like it did when I first saw the aliens a few minutes earlier.

"Correct," the Colonel replied.

"And they fly?"

"To our knowledge, they do."

"Holy shit. But again, why show all of this to me?" I curiously asked.

"As I said before, you hold some knowledge that might be helpful to us. I just wanted to prepare you for what you are about to hear."

"So showing me aliens and spaceships is just the tip of the iceberg?"

"Pretty much."

"Well then, if this is just the tip," I said before extending my right hand out toward the door, "then I'm ready to see the whole damn glacier."

The Colonel apparently didn't find my analogy very funny because his face never cracked a smile. Still, he turned around, and I followed as we exited through the door and back out into the hall.

We avoided the doors next to the hangar and the A.M.U. altogether. Instead, we headed toward the door at the end of the hall— or the one straight ahead when we got off the elevator.

When we got to that door, he punched in his six-digit passcode into the keypad before it beeped and unlocked itself.

"Wait, what's behind those other two doors?" I curiously asked.

"That's not important," he replied. "Now, are you ready?"

After having just seen the impossible, the only response I could give him was a simple head nod. And once he had my answer, he put his right hand on the door and pushed it open.

The room we walked into was nothing like I imagined it to be. Honestly, I didn't really know what would be in there, but I never expected to see an oversized hospital room. I mean, after being questioned, seeing the control room, aliens, spaceships, and now this, I suddenly couldn't help but think of the film *Hangar 18,* which was released in 1980.

After a satellite was launched, it collided with an alien spacecraft, forcing it to land somewhere in the Arizona desert. The craft was successfully recovered and then taken to Hangar 18, located inside a Texas Air Force base. Once there, the scientists and other technicians could study it a little more closely. And after seeing everything so far, I suddenly felt like Eric and I were in the same situation as two of the film's main characters, Steve Bancroft and Lew Price.

After Bancroft and Price are blamed for the death of one of the astronauts (who just happened to be in the launch bay of the satellite at the time of the collision), they set out toward Hangar 18 in search of the truth. However, during their quest, they immediately become targets of the U.S. government. Sound familiar? Of course, the movie's ending completely differed from what happened to me.

On an unrelated note, "Hangar 18" was also a Megadeth song, released on their *Rust in Peace* album in 1990.

Sorry, I couldn't help myself. Okay, back to the story.

Anyway, there were twenty beds (ten per side) in this oversized hospital room, each complete with its own monitoring equipment, surgical utensils, and other miscellaneous drugs and medicines. But that wasn't what shocked me. What shocked me was seeing both Anna and Eve lying down, strapped to separate beds. They were also unconscious, each with an IV drip going into their left arm.

"Eve!" I shouted while attempting to run to her.

But before I could make it more than five feet, the two escorts jumped in front of me and raised their guns, pointing them at my chest.

"Let him go," the Colonel said.

Both men obeyed his orders and immediately stood down.

Seeing her lying on that bed, all helpless and vulnerable, I wasted no time hauling my skinny ass over there.

"Oh my god. Eve," I quietly said, placing a hand on her cheek.

Lying on that hospital bed, she had three belt straps across her: one at her legs, one at her waist, and one just above her chest. And even though her hands were down by her sides, she also had metal cuffs on both her wrists and ankles. Those particular restraints were all attached to the bed using a heavy-duty chain.

"Isn't this a little overkill?" I asked.

"This is what we were told to do," the female doctor replied.

I addressed the Colonel. "She's your daughter. Why all the security?"

"It is a necessary precaution," he replied. "But you'll understand why soon enough. However, for the time being, we wait."

"Wait for what?"

He held up his left wrist to look at his watch. "We are waiting for three…two…one."

The second he finished counting down, the door leading in and out of the room beeped. After it opened, Colonel James, along with his two escorts and a very bloodied-up Eric, walked in. Eric's face looked like it had been hit one too many times with a baseball bat. Bruises, cuts, and blood covered his entire face, except for his right eye.

"Here they come now," Mr. Parker said.

"Sorry, we're late," Mr. James said. "But this one was being a little stubborn."

"Eric!" I shouted. "Are you okay? What the hell happened?"

With the escorts holding him up by his armpits and his feet dragging across the floor, in his current condition, Eric's answer sounded more or less like gibberish.

"Why…don't you…ask…them," he mumbled.

I immediately turned to Mr. James, anger dripping from my tongue. "What the fuck did you do to him?" I asked.

"What was necessary," he replied.

"You son of a bitch! I'll kill you!"

In a fit of rage, I immediately charged toward Mr. James, completely forgetting that both of the Colonels had their own sidearms. And as you could've probably already guessed, he pulled his out and pointed it at me, instantly halting my advances.

"If you want, I could make you look like your friend here," Mr. James said. "Your choice."

I turned back to Mr. Parker. "How come you didn't do that to me? Although you did threaten to shoot me."

"Because *you* cooperated," he replied.

"Your friend seems to have a mouth on him," Mr. James said before addressing the escorts. "Lay him down gently on the bed. The staff will patch him up."

I watched as the other two escorts carefully laid Eric down on the hospital bed directly across from Eve. Once he was settled, I quickly ran over to him.

"Jesus. Is he going to be okay?" I asked, wincing at the sight of his face.

But before anyone could give me an answer, I saw Eric's right arm slowly rise. Then he balled up his fist and gave me a thumbs up.

I smiled. "Damn right."

He mustered up whatever smile he could before dropping his hand back down to the bed.

"All right, enough of the bullshit," I said, turning back around. "And no more of this good cop, bad cop routine either. Now that Eric's here, can someone finally tell me what in the hell my knowledge of the girls has to do with anything?"

Both of the Colonels immediately turned to look at each other and nodded before turning back to me.

"I suppose you've waited long enough," Mr. Parker said. He then clasped his hands behind his back and slowly began pacing back and forth. "Ever since the first aliens were found back in the late forties," he began, "we've been curious about them and why they were here. We did nothing but study their anatomy while trying to figure out where they came from. It wasn't until the other two came to us that we finally made a breakthrough.

"Once we had two more to study, we began different kinds of tests...things you wouldn't usually see in the real world. We started experimenting with humans.

"You see," he continued, "we discovered that their alien DNA is very similar to our own. Don't get me wrong. There are still many differences between the two, but since they are similar, we thought we could successfully combine both DNAs into one. Basically, we tried to grow our own alien/human hybrids. Over the years, however, we were very unsuccessful. That is, until Anna and Eve came along. They were the first humans whose DNA had successfully merged with the injected alien DNA. Thus, a completely new breed was born.

"Over the years, we studied them to see if their bodies would form any special abilities. Unfortunately, our findings were inclusive. At least until you and your friend came along. Thanks to the alien technology, we were able to put implants into the girls' bodies, allowing us to monitor their vital signs and tell us where they were at all times."

"So *that's* how you found us so quickly," I said. "You were able to track them down."

"Correct," Mr. Parker said. "We first noticed their vital signs jump off the charts when they met you and your friend. That was also why Colonel James and I showed up when we did."

"I don't get it," I said, confused.

"What don't you get?"

"If you were so interested in seeing what they could do, why did you forbid us from seeing each other? Why not let us stay in touch and just keep monitoring them?"

"Because…" he said, trailing off and lowering his head.

"Because what?"

That was when the Colonel stopped pacing to look back up at me.

"Because we got scared," he said.

"You? Scared?" I asked, completely shocked by his answer. "Why?"

"We noticed that when you and Eve or Eric and Anna got together," he began, "the girls' vitals would spike so high that we couldn't get an accurate reading. The technology inside their bodies would just transmit as static. When that happened, we got scared and didn't know what else to do. We figured that by breaking you up, you wouldn't see each other anymore, and therefore, you wouldn't be down here talking to me at this very moment."

After hearing his explanation, I was suddenly more confused than ever.

"Wait a minute," I said. "So you wanted us to break up because you care about our safety?"

"Not quite," Mr. Parker replied. "We only care about the safety of our two daughters."

"Gee, thanks a lot."

"And upon reviewing the footage of what was captured on Eve's teddy bear, we had strict orders to bring you here. However, that part of the plan was only meant as a last resort. Unfortunately, since you were too stubborn to listen"—he stretched his arms out wide—"here we stand."

I pointed to the Colonel. "I *knew* you were spying on us!"

Holy shit. I couldn't believe it. Well, actually, I could. But at that moment, I realized that I was right about everything.

If you recall, I knew that something was up with Eve. And when Eric confirmed my theory after hearing about what had happened during his date with Anna, I knew we just had to find out. I also thought that because of their fathers coming home and banning us for life from seeing them, they must've been hiding something.

But after being down there with them, I knew why the Colonels couldn't be honest with us from the start. Because if they had just told us all this when we first met them—yeah. That would've gone over really well.

Even after all that, I still had just a few more questions bouncing around in my head. And hopefully, after I asked them, I wouldn't end up in a body bag.

"Who are their parents?" I asked.

"Can you be more specific?" Mr. Parker replied.

"Who are their birth parents?"

"Ah," he said with a nod. "That. Well, actually, both sets of their parents volunteered to give them up."

"They volunteered? Why?"

"Simple…they were only teenagers who weren't ready to be parents. So when we learned about two mothers wanting to give up their babies on the same day, we stepped in and took them. And as always, we generously compensated them for it."

By that point, and after everything I had just learned, the anger inside me was building up so fast, I was like a smoking volcano getting ready to blow. But I'll get to *that* in a moment.

"Let me get this straight," I said. "You took innocent kids off the street and decided to perform experiments on them just so you could create the perfect alien/human hybrid?"

"Correct," Mr. Parker said.

"Why?"

"Because the aliens requested it, that's why."

"The aliens requested it?" I asked with one eyebrow raised.

"They did. You see," Mr. Parker began, "we have no idea where they came from or how far they traveled. What we do know is that when the last two crashed here in the sixties, they communicated with us using a very broken form of Morse code.

"They told us their homeworld was dead and that they were the last two survivors. Their dying wish was to have us try to integrate their DNA with our own in hopes that their species would live on through us."

"But how did they know our two species would be compatible?"

"Just before the first two died," he continued, "they were able to transmit all their findings back to their homeworld. Unfortunately, the last two survivors didn't arrive until much later."

"And you believed them? Are you out of your fucking minds? I mean, how many people have you experimented on, anyway?"

"Since the mid-sixties…about one hundred and fifty."

I was absolutely flabbergasted by the Colonel's answer. And along with everything else he'd just told me, I didn't really know how to respond. Actually, that wasn't entirely true. Of course, I knew how to respond.

"Okay. I think I understand now," I said. "So the government set up this secret facility and probably funded billions of dollars to its cause, just so you could appease a dying alien species by experimenting on our own race? These are human lives we're talking about. That's the stupidest idea I've ever heard in my life!"

Remember the volcano analogy I mentioned earlier? Well...

"Are you all out of your fucking minds?" I angrily asked. "These two girls are innocent! And *then*, you bring me and my friend down here to see all of this, only to probably do who knows what to us while trying to keep us quiet. Sorry, but that ain't happening! When I get out of here, I'm telling this story to the whole world. And as far as I'm concerned, everyone down here can go straight to hell!"

That felt amazing to get off my chest.

The Colonel's response, however, after hearing my tirade, wasn't exactly how I envisioned him responding. Instead, he had the gall to stand there and laugh his ass off.

"What's so funny?" I asked.

"If you really think you're going to be leaving this place, then think again," he said.

"You can't keep me down here. I don't care how long it takes. I'll find a way out. And when I do, you'll all be sorry."

The Colonel immediately stopped laughing. "You're really not going to give up, are you?"

"Not until I get to see all of you burn."

He glared at me for a moment. "I'll tell you what I'm going to do, Wes," he said, holding up a finger. "I'm going to make this easy for you. You now have two choices, and only these two. You can either work with us by telling us what you know about the girls, or we can wipe your memory and leave you with no record of ever having met Eve or us. But I highly implore you to take the first one."

I looked at him as if he'd lost his damn mind. "Wipe my memory? Are you insane?" I said. "This isn't some cheesy, B-rated science fiction movie. This is real life. What you're saying is physically impossible and can't be done."

"Oh, but it can," he said. "You see, with the new alien technology, we now have the ability to erase people's minds. And if you do decide to take that option, let me just say that by the time we're finished, you'll be wishing it was *you* who was in hell."

I think I was a little more shocked by the whole memory-wipe thing than by seeing the aliens. However, with my options basically dangling in front of my face, I had a massive decision to make.

I mean, could I forget what I saw down there and be perfectly okay with it? You bet your ass I could. But losing any memories I had of Eve would be devastating. Of course, if I did lose those memories, it would be like it never happened in the first place. But I think you get the picture.

Besides, with Eric and Anna down there as well, I would feel awful if something happened to them. After all, it was his stupid idea to go to that party in the first place. Actually, now that I think about it, this was all his fault. I can see that now. Nah. Just kidding. We were both equally responsible for our own actions.

With everything going on, there was really only one option I could take. After all, I wanted to make it out with all my friends and live. Also, I suddenly wanted everyone else down there to pay for their actions. And the only way I could do that was to form a plan—a really good plan. Scratch that—the perfect plan.

CHAPTER 21

After making my choice, I spent a very sleepless, dreamless night on one of the hospital beds. They initially offered me a room in one of the many living quarters they had down there, so I could rest easy on one of the beds. However, I didn't want to leave Eve's side.

Regarding my choice, I told the Colonel I would help and share everything I knew about the girls. I only agreed to do it so that I could delay getting a memory wipe. I figured that would give me plenty of time to formulate a plan to get us all the hell out of there. Unfortunately, that part of the plan was very slow-going.

I was tasked with helping out a couple of the doctors who worked in the medical lab, all while under strict supervision from a couple of armed guards, of course. I was also informed that they wouldn't hesitate to shoot me if I stepped out of line. So much for the memory wipe.

One of the doctors I worked with was a male, while the other was a female. Both of them probably had many degrees and certifications, most likely from some high-profile medical school. I never bothered to ask, and frankly, I didn't really care either.

The military also trained them to use multiple forms of hand-to-hand combat. Plus, just like the rest of the medical staff, they were armed. So even if I wanted to try something, I most likely wouldn't get the chance to do it.

Doctor Blumb, whose first name was Michael (or Mike for short), was about my height and was built like a flagpole. He had light skin, dark hair neatly parted on one side, blue eyes, and wore the most gigantic-rimmed glasses I had ever seen. The one thing he did have going for him, however, was his perfectly white smile.

Doctor Harbor, whose first name was Sherri, was very thin but had curves in all the right places. She had light brown skin, brown eyes, and long, flowing dark hair, which she kept up in a ponytail. She stood only a couple of inches shorter than Doctor Blumb.

On a side note, Doctor Harbor also wore glasses. But hers were very similar to what Hayley Mills' character, Miss Bliss, wore in 1987's *Good Morning, Miss Bliss*. And if you just happen to be a die-hard *Saved By The Bell* fan, you'll know exactly what I'm talking about.

Even though they never came out and told me, I could tell that Blumb and Harbor had a thing for each other. The way they flirted and touched each other while working was a dead giveaway. Even a blind man could've seen what they were doing. It also might've been something more than flirting. Who knows? It wouldn't be until later that I would actually confirm that.

Anyway, I was tasked with telling them everything I knew and what I'd experienced with Eve while we were together. Though how much detail I wanted to delve into was a decision only I could make.

With Eric knocked out and having a shit load of drugs being pumped into his system, I was pretty much on my own. As for Anna and Eve, they were being kept under heavy sedation. Strictly for safety reasons, of course. And because of that, I think everyone knew much more about them than they wanted to tell me.

So to begin, I started telling them everything from the moment we met the girls right up until we got banned from seeing each other. I told them how we could see a slight glow emanate from their bodies and that when we kissed, weird, unexplained phenomena would happen that only we could see. I didn't go into all the details and just gave them a simplified CliffsNotes version.

With all the information I'd given them, they wanted to review their own notes on what the aliens could do before comparing them to mine. Apparently, the aliens that crash-landed there had their own set of strange abilities.

The scientists first discovered what they could do when the two aliens that crashed here in the late '40s could move things with their minds. Yes, they may have died on impact, but the alien ship brought some technology we weren't used to seeing at the time. Or ever, for that matter.

They'd hooked up the two dead aliens to some kind of machine, which they had taken off the ship. The machine would basically kickstart their brains and allow them to function, even though their physical bodies weren't alive. The scientists could then dive into their innermost psyche and speak with them to try to understand them a little better.

Along with moving things with their minds, the aliens could also briefly stop time and transport themselves to different parts of the base. I was told that the last one was a lot of fun because the doctors had to go and find them after they did. Then they had to bring them back down to the lab and reconnect them to the machine.

As for the girls, because their DNA had been successfully fused with the alien DNA, nobody knew exactly what they would be capable of. However, thanks to the alien communication they could understand, the one thing they did know was that once the girls turned eighteen, their abilities would kick into high gear. But it wouldn't be until something else happened that they would be fully unlocked. And that brings me back to the day before, when the Colonel was questioning me.

He asked me one question in particular that I was very hesitant about answering. However, when I gave him my answer, I saw his posture change drastically. The question in question was whether I had sex with Eve. And of course, I said yes. I think he only asked me about it because he already knew what would happen if we did.

You see, according to the aliens, once the members of their species turned eighteen, only a select few of their abilities could actually be used. But it wasn't until they consummated their relationship that their abilities became fully functional. That was why I was there. I was going to use my knowledge of the girls to see what they could do. But to do that, we had to wake them up. Well, in my case, just Eve.

———————

Doctor Blumb and Doctor Harbor, along with me, stood over Eve's body. Blumb held a syringe in his right hand, ready to inject it into Eve's IV. Since they used alien medicine to put them to sleep, they needed to use a different type of alien medicine to wake them up. And since the girls were part alien, they knew it wouldn't hurt them.

Blumb looked at Harbor, and they nodded in unison, letting each other know the procedure could be started. That was when Blumb took the needle and injected it directly into Eve's IV. And not even five seconds after injecting it, Eve's eyes slowly began to open.

"Where…where am I?" she quietly asked, still groggy from the medically induced coma.

"Just relax, Eve," Doctor Harbor said. "You're perfectly safe."

"Where's Wes?"

"I'm right here," I replied, grabbing her hand.

Eve's eyes shuffled from side to side as she tried to get a good look at her surroundings.

"What happened? Where are we?" she asked.

"That's kind of a long story," I said. "But for right now, why don't you just focus on waking up first?"

She tried to move and sit up, but couldn't because of the restraints.

"Why can't I move?" she asked.

"Because you're strapped to the bed," I told her. "They said it was for your own good."

"My own good?"

Still not understanding what we were talking about, she tried to gently wiggle her arms, legs, and the rest of her body free. When she wasn't having any luck, her calm movements soon turned into panicked, jerking thrusts.

"Calm down, Eve! We'll get you out," I said before turning my attention to the doctors. "I promise you, she's no threat. Can you please unstrap her?"

"I'm sorry," Blumb said. "But without her father's permission, we can't."

"Unstrap her!" I heard a voice say behind me.

When we all turned to look in the door's general direction, the Colonel was standing there. Upon seeing him, both doctors and the two armed guards all immediately stood at attention.

"At ease," the Colonel said, flashing his palms.

The armed guards immediately relaxed while the doctors quickly got to work, unstrapping Eve. Once she was free, however, the first person she hugged wasn't the first person I initially thought she would hug, which completely caught me by surprise—sort of.

"I missed you," she said, throwing her arms around me.

"I missed you, too," I replied, squeezing her tightly.

Why was I surprised? Well, to be honest, I thought she would hug her father first. You know, because he's her father, and up until that point, she had known him much, much longer than she had known me.

"Where are we?" Eve asked before turning to her father. "Daddy, what's going on?"

"It's all right," the Colonel said. "You're safe and sound inside a secure underground facility."

Her brows immediately furrowed. "Underground?"

She then surveyed the room. That was when she noticed the armed guards and doctors. However, once her focus hit the other side of the room, she stopped when she saw Eric and Anna lying there unconscious.

"Anna!" she said, attempting to get off the bed.

The doctors immediately put their hands on their pistols and were ready to draw them. But the Colonel signaled for them to stay calm, prompting them to back off.

Once Eve's feet hit the floor, she almost immediately collapsed, as her body was still a little weak from the heavy sedation. I saw this and quickly bent down to catch her before helping her back up and onto the bed.

"Well, it looks like that upcoming triathlon is out," I joked.

She smiled. "Maybe I should recover first."

"Good idea." I then turned to face the Colonel. "So now that she's awake, I think it's about time you told her the truth, don't you?"

That question garnered Eve's full and undivided attention.

"The truth about what?" she asked.

The Colonel slowly made his way over to the bed and stood next to her. "The truth about who you are," he said.

––––––––

For the next half hour or so, Eve listened to every little detail the Colonel had to say. He told her everything, starting from when the aliens crash-landed here on Earth (twice) all the way up to when she and Anna were adopted and injected with alien DNA. He then finished his explanation with why we were all captured and brought down there in the first place.

"So…I'm an alien?" Eve asked.

"Not quite," the Colonel said. "You're still human, just with a little something extra to boot."

"And these abilities you speak of…I have them?"

"Honestly, we're not sure. But that's why you're here. So we can figure it out."

"How?"

"From what Wes has already told us," the Colonel proceeded to tell her, "your abilities seem to come out only when the two of you are together. Now, whether or not it only happens when you're intimate, we don't know."

By that point, Eve still looked confused. I mean, can you really blame her?

"I still don't understand," she said.

"Yeah. I'm a little lost on that one myself," I added.

"As you already know," the Colonel began, "aside from our many different rooms and floors in this facility, we also have many different types of living quarters as well. We want to put you two in one of our apartments so we can monitor what happens while you…you know."

"*Eww,* gross!" Eve said, disgusted by the Colonel's comment. "You want to spy on Wes and me while we…"

The Colonel immediately flashed his palms. "Let me try this again," he said. "We will have ways to monitor everything that happens to you while you're in there. However, there are no cameras. And we won't be able to hear you. You'll have total privacy."

"You won't be able to see us?" Eve asked.

"That's correct."

With my left hand resting on my hip, I raised my right index finger.

"Let me get this straight," I said. "You want to put Eve and me in one of these 'apartments,' just so you can monitor her abilities if and when they happen?"

"Correct again," the Colonel said. "And as much as I despise the thought of you two going in there, I have direct orders to make it happen."

"Yeah, well, pardon me if I don't believe you, but remember the hidden camera in Eve's teddy bear? And what about Eric and Anna?" I asked, thumbing toward them over my right shoulder.

"You're absolutely right. But this time, you will have total privacy. And when Eric wakes up, we will also wake up Anna and tell them everything we've already told you."

"What if they refuse?" Eve asked.

The Colonel was quiet for a moment while he thought about what to tell us.

"I honestly don't know," he said. "But I assure you, they won't be harmed."

"How do I know you'll keep your word?" I asked. "I mean, just yesterday, you offered for me to either help you or, if I refused, you threatened to wipe my mind."

"I swear to you on Eve's life that they won't be harmed."

"That's not saying much. After all, you did keep your daughter sedated for the past two days."

"And for that, I am sorry," the Colonel said while staring at Eve.

I briefly glanced down at Eve before looking back up at the Colonel.

"Okay. Let's say we do this and get to go to one of these 'fancy underground apartments,'" I said. "How long are we going to be down here? I mean, I'm starting school in the fall, and there's no way I'm missing it."

"I do apologize, but you will be down here for as long as it takes," the Colonel replied.

"As long as it takes? What about my parents? My life? Everything I have?"

"Again, you could always take the memory wipe."

"Memory wipe?" Eve asked, looking concerned. "What memory wipe? What's he talking about?"

"If I refuse to help out," I told her, "they'll use some of the alien technology to erase everything I know about you, your father, and this place. And trust me, I'm not going to lose you."

"Don't worry. We will handle all of your affairs up on the surface," the Colonel said.

And with that, I suddenly had an even more important decision to make than I did before.

My choices were simple—I could stay down there, live in an underground apartment with Eve while they monitor her abilities, and never see the light of day again. Or I could easily take a memory wipe and forget everything that had happened over the last couple of weeks. Hmm, tough decision. Still…

With my options being tossed around in my head, there was a ninety-nine percent chance I would stay with Eve. Okay. Maybe more like a one-hundred percent chance I would stay with Eve.

Regardless, one thing was still bugging me. There was one piece of information I was still looking for regarding the girls. And by now, I'm pretty sure that you're probably wondering the very same thing.

"Before I give you my answer," I began, "I just have one more question. Why is it that I'm the only one who can see Eve glow?"

If you recall, earlier on in this story, when we were all at the party, Eric almost immediately called dibs on Anna. At the time, he claimed it was because she looked like Elizabeth Hurley. However, I knew for a fact it was because he could see her glow.

Still slightly confused about everything? Well, keep reading. Hopefully, by the time you finish this next part, you'll understand.

After hearing my question, the Colonel nodded his head. "An excellent question," he began. "According to the ancient alien texts, they refer to that as finding their 'other being.'"

"'Other being?' What the hell's that?" I curiously asked.

"It took us some time to figure it out ourselves as well. But here on Earth, I believe that their version of an 'other being' is also referred to as finding someone's soulmate."

The moment he finished his explanation, my eyes narrowed in confusion as I immediately turned to glance at Eve.

Okay, so do you remember when Eve and I were up on the mountain, and I thought that the feelings I had for her at the time weren't love but something else entirely? And do you also remember how I wouldn't get to my theory until much later in the story?

Welcome to much later.

Up until that moment, the whole idea of someone finding their soulmate was, in my mind, nothing but a big pile of bullshit. I mean, the idea that someone could find their one true love was utterly ridiculous. After all, having multiple partners because they're unsatisfied with just one person is quite commonplace.

But the idea that someone could find that one person out of a possible eight billion on the planet's surface in their lifetime is a complete farce. Especially if two pairs of people find it at the exact same time.

However, knowing that real-life aliens exist and that we're not, in fact, the only living beings in the universe, I had no choice but to believe what he said.

"My…soulmate?" I asked, making sure I heard him correctly.

"So they say," the Colonel replied.

"Well, that would explain why I'm the only one who can see her glow."

"That could also explain the fast, strong connection we've had," Eve added.

"So, Wes, what's it going to be?" the Colonel asked.

By then, I honestly had no intention of staying down there and playing their little games. However, I didn't want to be without Eve either.

So I glanced down at her and looked her right in the eyes. I could instantly see it in her big, beautiful browns that she didn't want me to leave. However, she also knew that I shouldn't just give up my life to be with her. And because of that, I could see the sadness in her eyes as they began to well up with tears.

I grabbed her hand and smiled at her without saying a word while she smiled back. She then nodded her head, almost as if to tell me, "It's okay. Go and be with your family."

And that was when I knew.

With my mind officially made up (as if I was going to pick choice number two), I looked back up at the Colonel and gave him my answer.

"I'm staying," I said. "And if you wouldn't mind taking care of everything up on the surface for me, I'd be grateful."

"I had a feeling you'd make that decision," he said.

I let out a huff of air. "So what happens now?"

"Now"—he paused to eyeball both of us. Then, as he turned back toward me, he smiled—"we begin."

———————

A little while later, after leaving the hospital room, Eve and I followed two armed escorts and the Colonel into the elevator, where he then pushed the button for level *T*. Once it arrived, the doors opened, and we all got out before following them down the hallway.

Living in an underground apartment (or our own personal living quarters, as they called it) was just downright creepy. Not only did it look and feel very real, but half of the time, we couldn't even tell we were underground.

The living quarters for the personnel who worked there were kept separate from those of Eve and me. Theirs was up a few levels higher. Ours was located on the floor just above the hospital.

When we exited the elevator, we immediately entered a hallway containing ten doors, five on each side. At the very end sat door number eleven. That led directly into a computer room, which was just about the size of a classroom.

Inside, computer equipment was explicitly set up to monitor each of the ten rooms. Some of the equipment looked like it was built here on Earth, but all of it seemed to be integrated with a majority of the alien technology. About fifteen men and women worked on those computers to document the activity inside the rooms. An armed guard was also stationed outside each monitored room. While we were there, only two of the rooms were being used. And you could probably take an educated guess as to who was in each one.

Once we left the computer room, the Colonel took us to the first door on the left (or the last room on the right after exiting the elevator). After he opened the door, we all stepped inside, where the lights automatically turned on.

Each set of living quarters was about the size of a two-bedroom apartment. This was mainly because each one had two bedrooms. They also had a living room, a kitchen, a bathroom, and a small dining nook.

Now, when I said that we couldn't even tell we were underground, it was because of the faux windows they had in there. They were all made to look like lit-up pictures. There was a lamp behind each one that would turn on during the day and shut off at night. The daytime windows would have pictures of trees, grass, birds, and everything else you would see outside, including the sun. The nighttime windows would replace the sun with the stars and the moon. The lights on the outside of those photos gradually lit up in the morning and dimmed at night to give you the complete dawn-to-dusk feel.

The apartment was also filled with furniture, tables, chairs, clothes, and electronics. For obvious reasons, the only thing it didn't have was a telephone.

Our cabinets and cupboards were stocked with food so we could make our own meals. If we wanted something else (say, like pizza or Chinese food), we would have to let one of the guards standing just outside our door know. Then they would have to let one of the grunts know. The grunt would then travel to the surface and out to a restaurant to get what we needed. By the time the food got back to us, though, it was usually around two hours. So if we wanted anything special, we had to order it way in advance. But that was pretty much it.

For the next few days, we would be calling that place home. Yes, you read that right. Unfortunately, it took us a little longer than I would've liked to form a plan and get out of there. However, our "plan" wasn't actually a plan at all. It was more like a discovery. And perhaps, it might even have been mixed in with a little bit of luck. But we'll eventually get to that.

"I think you'll find these quarters to your liking," the Colonel said.

I immediately glanced around the place and noticed that our quarters looked like it was designed to house teenagers and young adults.

Included in the electronics were a Nintendo (with every game ever made up until that point), a VCR (with a vast selection of horror, science fiction, comedy, and romance movies), and some kind of TV screen I'd never seen before. I had a feeling that whatever it was, it came from within the alien ship because most of the writing on it was in a language not from this Earth. Junk food, candy, and a whole slew of other foods that weren't good for you were also present in one of the cupboards.

"This'll work," I said while looking around the place and nodding.

"I'm your daughter. You can't do this to me," Eve pleaded.

"I don't want to do this to you either," the Colonel said. "But I have orders, and it's for your own good."

"To hell with your orders!" Eve shouted. "You have to understand, I'm not a threat to anyone."

"I know," he said with an understanding nod. "But just remember, if you need anything at all, simply knock on the door and tell one of the guards."

The Colonel turned around and started to make his way out of the apartment. But just before shutting the door, he turned back to look in at Eve. He didn't smile at her, though. Instead, he took a deep breath before quietly letting it out. Then, after a quick moment, he turned around, closed the door, and was gone.

The moment he left, Eve turned to look at me and couldn't help herself as she started to cry. I quickly comforted her by running over and holding her in my arms, hoping to ease her pain and get her to calm down.

Now, I don't know if my eyes were playing tricks on me or not, but when the Colonel turned back around to look at Eve, he almost looked genuinely crushed that he had to do this to his daughter. It wouldn't be until all hell broke loose during our escape that I would find out what his true intentions really were.

We continued to stand in the middle of the living room for the next few moments. I figured letting Eve cry it out a bit would be best before I started talking to her.

"Eve? Are you okay?" I quietly asked.

"Why would he do this to me? To us?" she asked, still sobbing.

"I honestly don't know."

"I thought he loved me."

"I'm sure he does."

However, after the look he just gave her, I wasn't so sure.

"He's definitely got a funny way of showing it," Eve said.

"Look, why don't we go over to the couch and sit down?" I suggested.

Eve looked up at me and nodded. Then I brought her over to the couch and sat us down.

"There. Feel better?" I asked.

"Not really," she said.

"Well, don't worry. We'll get through this together. I'm not going anywhere."

She sniffled several times before lifting her head to look at me. "Can I ask you something?" she asked.

"You can ask me anything," I said.

"I hope you don't take this the wrong way, but why did you stay?"

My eyes narrowed. "What do you mean?"

"What I mean is, why did you stay with me instead of taking the memory wipe and going back to your old life?"

And there it was.

That was a question for which I would have to give her an honest answer. The answer was also something I'd never told anyone else before in my life, except for my parents and family members, of course.

But after remembering what the Colonel had explained to us about how the aliens refer to "other beings" as soulmates, I knew, in my heart, that my reason for staying with her was the right one.

"The reason why I opted not to take a memory wipe is because," I began, my heart practically pounding out of my chest and my hands turning into a sweaty, clammy mess.

Not only were my hands a mess, but I was, too. This was the first time I had ever felt this way about any of the girls I'd ever dated. But no matter how nervous I was, I knew that deep down, she would feel the same way. Or at least, so I had hoped.

"The reason I didn't take the memory wipe," I tried again, "is because…I love you."

The moment I said that, I felt like a massive weight had been lifted off my chest. However, my nervousness quickly turned into sheer fright as I waited for her response.

"Oh, Wes," she said, her lower lip quivering while a tear ran down the left side of her cheek. "I love you, too."

When I said those three magical words and she repeated them, all her fears and sadness about what her father had just made her do immediately disappeared.

Eve looked genuinely happy as her eyes practically sparkled with excitement. It was almost as if I had just given the poorest girl in the world the most expensive piece of jewelry money could buy.

With her still in my arms and the "love barrier" officially broken, I wiped the tear from her cheek before smiling and kissing her.

CHAPTER 22

Day one…

Since all we had to do was stay in there and basically "live while they monitored us," that was precisely what we did.

After saying those three magical words, Eve and I sat on the couch for the next few minutes and kissed each other with a fiery passion we hadn't yet felt. And because we were living in one of the apartments designed for people our age, along with all the other goodies they had stocked up on, condoms (lots and lots of condoms) were among them. And before you even read on, I'm pretty sure you could already guess what we decided to do first.

After we finished making love while the apocalypse falsely destroyed everything around us, we went out to the kitchen to see what breakfast foods they had. Technically, by that point, it was lunchtime, but we both wanted some breakfast. Well, she wanted lunch, and I wanted breakfast. So I did my best to convince her that I could make a killer breakfast.

"So what would you like for breakfast?" I asked.

"Breakfast? Don't you mean lunch?" she said.

"No. I mean breakfast."

"But it's just a little after noon."

"So? What's wrong with having a little breakfast for lunch?"

"Well," she began before pondering that notion, "nothing. But I still want some lunch."

"Come on," I said. "It'll be fun. Besides, once you've had my breakfast, you'll want it all the time."

She immediately furrowed her brows and pointed at me. "You can cook?"

"Is that so hard to believe?"

"Actually, yeah, it is."

"You don't really think I just worked as a waiter, do you?"

"I don't know. Wait, where did you work again?"

The moment she asked that, it immediately dawned on me. I realized that I never actually got around to telling her where I had worked. With me forgetting my head when I was around her, along with all the other weird shit going on, it completely slipped my mind.

"Oh shit. That's right," I said. "I never told you where I worked."

"You were going to, but then, for some reason, you never did," she said.

"Sorry about that. I used to work at Johnny's Café as a waiter. But before that, I was a cook."

"Was that in your town?"

"Located right next to my favorite arcade."

Eve didn't give me an immediate response. Instead, she just folded her arms and glared at me, most likely trying to decide whether or not she was going to give my cooking a chance.

"Okay then. Let's see what you got," she said with a smirk.

I smiled. "With pleasure. And trust me, you *won't* be disappointed."

―――――――――

Two hours later, Eve told me that she'd never had a breakfast quite like that one. We then joked about my cooking before she apologized for doubting me. And after cleaning everything up, she decided to compliment the chef—twice. If you know what I mean?

After we got dressed and made our way back out into the living room, Eve plopped down onto the couch while letting out a loud sigh. I could tell something was bothering her. It was also written all over her face that she looked pretty depressed. But really, could you blame her?

I mean, her own father, the man who had taken care of her for her entire life, just basically imprisoned her without even giving it a second thought. If that were me, I'd be just as pissed and would want to find a way to get some kind of revenge on him. Thankfully, I was there to boost her confidence and tell her everything I'd been planning since day one.

Ever since we got taken into custody (so to speak), I'd been thinking of many different ways to get us out. They all ranged from using my smarts and sneaking our way out to knocking out one of the doctors or guards, taking their guns, and then going on a heroic rampage. However, as you already know, the heroic rampage would've probably ended just like the scenario in *Platoon* I'd described earlier.

But after hearing the Colonel tell me what some of the aliens' abilities were, I thought that if I could help Eve unlock some of her own abilities, then we'd be able to escape with no problem. Unfortunately, thinking about it was a lot easier than doing it.

"Are you okay?" I asked.

She shrugged. "Not really."

I took a seat next to her on the couch. "Want to talk about it?"

She hesitated for a moment before turning to face me. "Why me?" she asked.

I cocked my head back in confusion. "What do you mean?"

"Why inject Anna and me with the alien DNA and not someone else?"

When she asked that, it immediately dawned on me that her father might have forgotten to tell her a valuable piece of information, probably fearing the consequences if he did. Luckily, that same information just happened to be something he told me while she was unconscious.

"Oh shit," I whispered.

"What's wrong?" she asked.

"Eve, I'm sorry, but…you two weren't the only ones injected with the alien DNA."

She narrowed her eyes and slightly tilted her head sideways. "We weren't?"

I shook my head. "No."

"Well then, how many others like us are out there?"

"Actually? None."

"What do you mean none?" she asked. "You just said we weren't the only ones?"

"From what your father has already told me, since the mid-sixties, about a hundred and fifty people have been experimented on."

"A hundred and fifty people?" she asked, her eyes wide from shock. "Holy shit! What happened to them?"

I shrugged. "I don't know. He never told me that."

She then got quiet for a moment.

"I loved him. And all he ever did was lie to me," she said.

I placed a hand on her shoulder for comfort. "Eve, I'm sorry."

"You have nothing to be sorry for. None of this was your fault."

"True. However, look at me now," I said before smirking and spreading my arms wide.

When she saw my innocent-looking grin, she couldn't help but snort.

"Yeah. You're now stuck down here with me when you could be up top living a normal life," she said.

I moved my hand from her shoulder to her cheek. "I'm right where I want to be," I said, leaning in and giving her a quick peck on the lips. "Besides, I have a plan to get us all out of here."

"You do? What is it?"

"It's probably going to take a little bit of time and patience, but I figured we could try and use some of your abilities to do it."

"My abilities," she said, disgusted, while shaking her head. "We don't even know if they're going to work."

"That's why I said with time and patience."

Eve got quiet and trailed off as she finally came to a harsh realization.

"Eve, what is it?" I asked, noticing her troubled look.

"After all these years…I actually thought he loved me," she said.

"I'm sure that deep down, he still does."

"No, he doesn't." She turned to face me. "Wes, I thought he was supposed to be my father. Instead, I'm nothing to him but a…a fucking science experiment."

I honestly didn't know what to say to her at the time except, "I'm sorry, Eve."

She didn't say or give me anything. Instead, she just sat there, her arms folded, while staring off into space as if lost in her own thoughts. Her silent gaze almost reminded me of how someone would look right before they started planning the perfect revenge scheme. Either that or she was now a rage-induced homicidal maniac ready to kill someone. I hoped for the first one.

"You know what?" she said, standing up off the couch. "If my father thinks he can keep me down here and use me as a guinea pig, then he's sorely mistaken."

I opened my mouth and lifted a finger to say something, but she quickly cut me off.

"Fuck him!" she continued. "I'm his daughter. And if he thinks that he can use me to unlock some bullshit abilities, he'd better think again. Because we aren't giving him anything." She paused as if she was finished. She wasn't. "As a matter of fact, we're just going to stay down here until he gives up. Then he'll have to let us go."

Okay? Not exactly the answer I was looking for, but it was something.

Even though she just told me that she wasn't going to do a damn thing, she continued to stand there with her arms folded while a fire burned in her eyes. And although she had basically just given up, she suddenly looked angrier than I'd ever seen anyone in my entire life. So I used that as my cue to chime in.

"I think that would be a big mistake," I said.

"How so?" she asked.

I also stood up off the couch. "Actually, I think you should do what he says."

"Do what he says? Are you out of your mind?"

"Maybe I am. But in my opinion, the key to getting out of here is unlocking what you don't know."

She then said something to me that I hoped she would've said right before she started going off on a tangent about her father.

"Explain," she said.

"Okay. So here's my thinking," I proceed to tell her, very happy to do so. "We're in an underground base, trapped by who knows how many armed guards. And other than you learning your abilities, I can already tell you that the only way any of us are getting out of here is by taking a memory wipe. But I don't want that.

"You see, I don't want to forget you or any of the time we spent together. If that happened, I would never be able to forgive myself. Of course, I wouldn't really remember anything that happened between us, so—"

"Will you just tell me already?" Eve interrupted me.

"Right, sorry. Eve, I love you," I continued. "And I've never felt this way about anyone before. Your dad may see you as just an experiment, but not me. I see you as a smart, kind, beautiful woman and could give two shits about what you can do." I walked up and took her hands in mine. "I'm here for you, and you alone, abilities or not."

"Wes, what are you saying?"

"I'm saying that we work together to try to unlock whatever it is your dad wants you to. Then, when we're confident enough that you have the power to get us all out of here, we burn this whole place to the ground and never look back. I mean, it may take a little while, but I think we can—"

I was interrupted yet again. But instead of Eve's words doing the interrupting, this time, it was her lips. With her right hand on the back of my head, she pulled me down for a kiss that practically made the whole installation shake to the ground.

"Let's do it," she said with a smile.

"Really?" I asked, surprised by her answer.

"Really. If it's possible, let's show these assholes what I'm really made of."

I smiled. "I love you."

"Well, if you love that, then you'll certainly love this."

She then flashed a flirtatious little smile before taking my hand and leading me straight into the bedroom.

———————

We spent the rest of the day going at it like rabbits. In between sessions, we would go out to the kitchen to grab some food, drink, or whatever. For the next three days after that, it was pretty much the same thing.

We couldn't figure out why, but we both suspected that the reason for all the sex was because of her alien-infused DNA. I just thought it was because we were horny teenagers. But when I thought of all the times my friends said they were having sex and compared it to us, I knew it definitely couldn't be that. However, I certainly wasn't complaining.

For the next three days (between our romps in the sack), we would try to have her focus on one of the abilities the Colonel or the doctors mentioned to us.

First, she tried to move things with her mind, kind of the same way a Jedi would. Unfortunately, she had no luck.

Next came trying to stop time or even random objects I threw across the room. We also tried to have her think of a different place in the base she wanted to be transported to—still nothing.

But it wasn't until our fourth day, when Eve and I were completely out of ideas, that we tried something different. It was a last resort, and we honestly didn't think anything would come of it. But when we decided to suck it up and give it a shot, we got a lot more than we bargained for. On that fourth day, Eve finally found the secret to unlocking her full alien potential.

CHAPTER 23

We'd been stuck in that apartment for three days without seeing a single person. The only other person we saw was Eve's father, just before he left us alone on day one. I mean, we could've had the guards ask one of the grunts to go topside and get us some takeout, but we were pleased with the food we had. I will admit, though, the time we did spend down there wasn't all that bad.

In between trying to get her abilities to come out, eating, and having loads of sex, we spent a lot of time watching some of the vast array of VHS tapes they had. On the second night there, we wound up watching one of my favorite films of all time. And since Eve had never seen it before, it was something I knew we just had to watch.

They Live was released in 1988 and was directed by the great John Carpenter. Roddy Piper, the ex-WWE wrestler, stars as Nada, a drifter who finds himself in Los Angeles. While there, he finds a box of sunglasses buried within a church wall. Once he puts the sunglasses on, however, he discovers a horrible truth—some of the people on Earth are not actually people at all but aliens who disguise themselves as humans to go about their daily business. Nada then goes on a quest to discover who these aliens are and why they're there.

Along the way, he meets a few allies, who help him discover that the aliens are there to take over the world. (Big shocker, I know.) Of course, the hero does wind up saving the day, but not before suffering some significant casualties.

When the movie ended and the credits started rolling, I turned to Eve to get her opinion.

"So what'd you think?" I asked.

It felt like an eternity had passed while I anxiously sat there and waited for her to say something. I mean, a film like that usually only has a cult following. So I honestly had no idea what her reaction would be.

She didn't answer me right away. Instead, she just sat there, slowly nodding her head.

"I will say this," she calmly said before turning toward me and smiling, "that was fucking awesome! How come I've never seen that before?"

After hearing her answer, there wasn't a doubt in my mind.

With that one confession, I absolutely believed, one hundred percent, that we were soulmates. Because if she liked that movie, then she'd most likely love all the other movies I liked as well. Of course, that happy moment was two nights ago.

Day four…

Eve was angrily screaming at the top of her lungs because everything she had tried to get her abilities to show themselves led to dead ends. I mean, there we were three days later, and neither of us was even remotely close to figuring anything out.

Since I met her, I don't think I have ever seen her angry, let alone scream out profanities into the air. I will admit, though, when I heard her do that, I was a bit scared. And even though she sounded like a she-devil, I knew she wouldn't do anything to hurt me.

"Maybe you should sit down for a bit," I suggested, motioning to the couch.

"Sit down?" she said, almost as if she was about to bite my head off.

"Yeah. I just think that taking five will clear your mind."

"Wes, we've been down here for four days. Clearing my mind is the *last* thing I want to do. I just want to unlock my potential so I can get the hell out of here."

"You mean so that *we* can get the hell out of here?"

When I said that, she didn't need to respond. Instead, she just looked at me with tightened lips and narrowed eyes. I honestly thought she was going to use some dark, unheard-of Jedi force power to make my head explode with her mind.

"I'm sorry," I said with flashing palms.

She sighed. "No, I'm sorry. There's no reason for me to get mad at you. I was way out of line."

"It's okay. Besides, I probably would've yelled at me, too."

She smiled and shook her head before turning around, taking a seat on the couch, and groaning.

"We've tried everything under the sun to get my abilities to come out," she said.

I went over and took a seat beside her. "Hey, none of this is your fault," I told her, placing a comforting hand on her shoulder. "Besides, it's not like you asked for any of this."

"I know," she said. "But now I feel as if I'm the one keeping us from leaving."

"Take as much time as you need. As long as I'm here with you, that's all that matters."

She turned her head to look over at me and smile. "How do you do it?"

"Do what?" I replied.

"How do you always seem to cheer me up when things are bad?"

"What can I say?" I said before leaning back on the couch, spreading my arms across the top of it, crossing my right foot over my left leg, and smiling. "It's a gift."

She smiled at me again before playfully nudging me with her elbow. I then stuck my arm behind her and pulled her toward me, laying her down in my lap.

As I caressed her head with my hand, we sat there silently. At that point, I think a little quiet time was precisely what we both needed—the past few days had been so hectic. Other than sleeping, we never really got a chance to stop and just enjoy the moment.

While we sat there, my mind started to drift as I immediately began thinking about my family back up on the surface. My mother and father were probably worried sick about me, and by now, they must've sent out at least five dozen search parties. I just hoped that the Colonel would be able to hold true to his promise about taking care of everything up there.

Then I started thinking about other things, like what we missed. *What haven't we tried yet? Is there something so blatantly obvious that we're just trying way too hard and not seeing it?* It wasn't until I asked myself that last question that I noticed it.

My eyes immediately drifted over to the TV-looking thing with the alien writing on it. It looked just like a twenty-five-inch TV, only without the controls or knobs. Up until that point, we ignored it, probably because we had no idea what the hell it was. That and the fact that it was covered in a language no one could possibly understand. So with all other options exhausted and nothing left to try, I figured, what the hell?

"What about that thing?" I said, pointing to the strange, alien TV.

"Wes, we don't even know what that *thing* is," Eve reminded me.

"I know. But at this point, what have we got to lose?"

She briefly thought about it before sitting up.

"Well," she said before shrugging and turning to me, "it's worth a shot."

We quickly got off the couch and made our way over to the far right corner.

The unknown alien device sat on a small wooden table. When we got over there, I quickly plopped my butt down in the office-type chair and immediately got to work.

"So where's the on switch?" I asked while examining it.

I must've looked that thing over, front to back and top to bottom, at least three times before coming up blank.

"Maybe you're just missing it," Eve said. "Here, let me try."

No sooner did I stand up, she sat down almost twice as fast.

"Maybe if I just…move over here…there's got to be something I can…" she said, not finding a single thing on it. "This really is strange. I've never seen anything like this before."

And that was when it happened.

When Eve's right hand touched the screen, the device turned on. Instead of the screen being black, it was suddenly filled from top to bottom with nothing but white static. Not expecting that to happen, both of us immediately jumped back.

"What happened? What'd you do?" I asked.

"I don't know," she replied. "But now it's all staticky."

My eyes narrowed as I leaned in closer. "I don't think that's static."

Upon closer review, I noticed that the static now filling up the screen wasn't static at all. Once I was practically on top of the thing, I could see lines upon lines of the tiny alien language broadcasting and masking itself to look like static.

"Holy shit," I said. "Do what you did before."

"All I did was this," she said, placing her hand back on the screen.

When she did, our eyes widened as the alien language suddenly disappeared, only to be replaced by multiple windows, each containing different items.

At the time, that kind of technology was unheard of and wouldn't be invented by humans until the mid-2000s. At least not in the capacity in which we were about to use it. But from what I could tell, and because I was also a big video game nerd, I think I knew exactly what we were looking at.

"Wes, what is this?" Eve asked.

"I think it's some sort of a…a touch screen computer," I said.

She turned to look at me like I'd lost my mind. "A touch screen computer?" She shook her head and faced forward. "Yeah, right."

"No, seriously. Watch."

I placed my right index finger on the screen to activate one of the boxes. But when I did, I was quickly confused about why nothing happened.

"I don't understand," I said. "When you touched it, it activated." I then attempted to touch it a few more times in different spots, with no luck, of course. "Damn! I was sure that this was a highly advanced computer."

"Maybe you're doing it wrong," she said.

I gave her a skeptical look. "Seriously? How can I touch a screen the wrong way?"

"I don't know. Maybe you just need the right kind of touch."

She also attempted to touch one of the boxes on the screen. But when her finger touched the glass, something unexpected happened.

The boxes that were there quickly disappeared and were instantly replaced by a single line of alien text. But that wasn't the shocker. The shocker was that the text had transformed itself and was no longer displayed in its native language. It was displayed in English.

That one line of text now sitting on the screen, which we were suddenly able to read, simply said:

DNA RECOGNIZED

It appeared briefly before disappearing, and was once again replaced by the individual boxes. However, the text within the boxes was also no longer displayed in the alien language. They were displayed in English as well.

"Or maybe it just needed *your* touch," I said, still stunned by what I'd just seen.

The boxes on the screen each contained something different, as we now had access to everything the aliens had: their history, culture, technology, language, planet, galaxy of origin, and even the different types of abilities they had.

I didn't know it then, but the kind of storage capacity the alien computer needed to hold that much information wouldn't be invented until the late '90s or early 2000s. For us (at the time), that was way beyond our comprehension, and it literally felt like we were living in a science fiction film.

"I've never seen anything like this," Eve said.

"That's because this kind of technology doesn't exist," I remarked. "From what I can tell, this appears to be some form of advanced, touchscreen computer."

"Again, with this touchscreen computer. Do you know how crazy that sounds?"

Eve wasn't a big nerd like I was. So I half expected her to doubt me.

"Let me get this straight," I said, "knowing that aliens exist and also knowing that you are one is perfectly okay. But seeing a touchscreen computer isn't?"

"Good point," she said before taking a deep breath. "So where do we start?"

I wasted no time and immediately pointed to the box titled ABILITIES.

"Are you sure? Don't you want to know where they come from?" she asked.

"Not really," I said. "I just want to unlock what you got and get the hell out of here."

"Fair enough." She paused. "But I kind of want to know."

Hey, since she had to deal with the burden of carrying around alien DNA in her body, I figured she had every right to take a quick look.

"Sure," I said while nodding.

So instead of pressing the ABILITIES box, Eve held up her right index finger to the screen and tapped the one labeled ORIGIN. When she did, all the other boxes disappeared and were instantly replaced by lines and lines of information about where the aliens came from, including a map of their planet's location.

From what we could tell, they weren't all that far from the Milky Way. It appeared that they had come from just a couple of galaxies over. It was a galaxy whose name was unpronounceable, along with a planet whose name was also unpronounceable.

It wouldn't be until 2006 that a small galaxy, roughly 0.43 million light-years away, would be discovered and named. That very same galaxy also happened to be the one the aliens came from. If you're an astronomer or someone who likes to study the stars as a hobby, then you know this galaxy as Hercules Dwarf.

"Holy shit. They traveled so far to get here," I said.

"According to this," Eve read, "it says that their homeworld, the only livable planet there, was overrun by dark matter, which made it completely uninhabitable."

"Your father was right," I whispered.

Upon hearing my comment, she turned to face me with furrowed brows. "My father was right?"

If you recall, when the Colonel was telling me about the two spacecraft that crashed here, he also mentioned how those aliens were the last of their kind. And while he was telling me all of that, Eve was still unconscious on the hospital bed. So she heard none of it.

"That's right," I said, remembering she wasn't a part of that conversation. "You were still out of it when he told me."

"Told you what?" she asked.

"Your father told me that the reason why humans started getting injected with the alien DNA was because the aliens themselves requested it. They also told him the reason for their request was because their homeworld was dead, making them the last of their kind."

"So if they came from a now-extinct species," Eve began, "then that means…"

She paused and quickly trailed off, deep in thought. And after a few moments, her eyes grew wide. She looked petrified.

"Means what?" I curiously asked. When she didn't answer me right away, I tried again. "Eve?"

And that was when she looked up at me, her eyes still wide, and her skin almost a paler shade than it was just a few seconds prior.

"It means that Anna and I are now"—Eve swallowed hard—"officially, the last of their kind."

It took us both a moment to process that information. Maybe it was because we didn't want to believe what she just said. Or maybe we were tricking our minds into thinking that. Who knows? But as much as we didn't want to believe it, unfortunately, she was right.

With the alien DNA coursing through their veins, Anna and Eve were (hypothetically speaking) the last of a now-dead alien race.

"Oh my god," I whispered. "You're right."

"Okay, now I'm scared," she said, practically hyperventilating.

"*Now* you're scared? Are you telling me that you weren't scared before?"

"You know what I mean."

"Eve," I said before standing up and throwing my arms in the air, almost as if I'd just scored a touchdown, "this is great!"

"How is me being the last of an alien race great?"

"Don't you see? You're now one of a kind. Well, if you count Anna, two of a kind."

"Wes, I just don't know if I can handle that kind of pressure."

"What pressure? As soon as we get out of here, no one ever has to know."

She thought about that for a moment. "The military would know."

"Trust me," I said. "By the time we get out of here and are able to burn this place to the ground, I can guarantee that they'll never bother you again."

"But how can you be so sure?"

"Do you honestly think that the military would want to kill or experiment on the last two members of an alien race? I certainly don't. Plus"—I bent down to give her a quick kiss—"I love you. And I'll be with you every step of the way."

She smiled. "How can I doubt that?"

I immediately stood up, my face sporting a cocky expression. "Because this is me we're talking about."

"I know. And *that's* what scares me," she said, grinning.

"Smartass," I replied.

"I know."

We smiled at each other for the next few seconds before our little moment soon passed. When it did, we quickly realized what we needed to do next.

"How about if we check out those abilities now?" I suggested.

She didn't even have to say a word as she turned around and placed her right index finger on the screen, closing the box that said ORIGIN. As soon as it disappeared, the screen instantly filled with all the other boxes. After she found the one that said ABILITIES, she touched it with her finger. Almost immediately, we were finally one step closer to officially getting the hell out of there.

CHAPTER 24

The moment Eve touched the ABILITIES box on the screen, a list of everything the aliens could do (which was practically five miles long) showed up in front of our faces. Telekinesis, the ability to briefly stop time, transportation (the aliens' version of teleportation), and telepathy were just a few of the things the aliens could do. A whole slew of others also appeared on the screen, but there were simply too many to name them all.

Once we had the list somewhat memorized, we continued scanning the page for the all-important, missing piece of the puzzle—how exactly does Eve get her abilities to work? *That* was the big question. The *answer* was found on the very bottom of the page, underneath everything else.

If you recall, with the girls giving off a glow, and because we were their apparent soulmates, only Eric and I could see it. Also, when Eve and I were together, whether we were kissing or having sex, that was the only time the weird stuff actually happened.

The earthquake on top of the mountain, floating in space while roller skating, and then the apocalypse at the inn were just some of the unexplainable things we had experienced. So when we read about how her abilities supposedly worked, it all made perfect sense. The key to making everything work for her was me. Let me explain…

According to the ancient alien texts (now that's something I never thought I'd ever hear myself say), the key to someone using their abilities was their "other being," or soulmate. As long as they were nearby, all they had to do was think of them while trying to use one of their powers. Yeah, we didn't quite understand it at first, either. But it didn't take us all that long to figure out.

When Eve and I weren't together, none of the weird stuff I explained a few minutes ago would happen. So for the past four days, when she tried to use one of her powers, she would think of just that one ability while trying to get it to work. But that was all she thought about. Ever since we learned that she had to think of me while trying to manifest one of her powers, we were extremely satisfied with the results.

Now you're probably wondering, *If all she had to do was think of you, then why didn't her powers manifest when you two weren't together?* Well, I just happen to have a simple explanation for that.

You see, when we were apart, we always thought about each other. But the reason why Eve's abilities didn't manifest themselves was because she wasn't trying to use them. Plus, we had to be within a certain proximity of each other. However, we discovered that levitation was one of the things she could do. Hence, the time we rose from her bed shortly before her father came home and banished me. So with the how-to all figured out, we jumped right into the testing phase.

She was easily able to move objects with her mind, which ranged from small items like pens, pencils, and cups all the way up to big things like the table, the chairs, the TV, and even me.

Stopping objects in mid-air? No problem. Transporting herself from one room to another? Piece of cake. Of course, watching her vanish into thin air right before my very eyes took a little bit of getting used to.

Briefly, stopping time? When she did that, I was somehow unaffected by it and even managed to count to twenty before time resumed. I will say this, though, throwing an object into the air and watching it stay put for twenty seconds was pretty fucking creepy, but still amazing.

As far as the telepathy went, that was a little weird. Having someone project a question or comment into my head, then thinking of something to say in return, only to have them tell me what it was, was also quite interesting. Plus, I figured that would give us a little bit of an edge. I mean, she obviously wouldn't use her telepathy on someone she didn't know or didn't want to speak with. We would only be able to use it with each other. That way, none of the military personnel would know what we were thinking.

And just to clarify, I don't have telepathy. I'm only telepathic when Eve projects herself into my mind, which would, in turn, give me the same ability, but only for as long as she was using it. It was a little weird talking to someone in my head, but again, still pretty fucking cool.

After we discovered what she could do, planning our escape immediately became our top priority. Mapping it out, we thought the best time to escape from the underground facility would be at night, when most of the staff and personnel had either gone home or fallen asleep. That way, just in case something did go wrong, there would be fewer people to cause us harm.

So to kill a couple of hours, we had planned on eating some dinner, having some more mind-blowing sex, taking a shower, and changing back into the clothes we had on when we were initially brought down there. However, within two minutes of us finishing our last test, we heard a knock on our door. Before either one of us even got a chance to say anything, it opened, and in walked one of the scientists from the monitoring room at the end of the hall. She was also accompanied by two armed escorts.

So much for killing a couple of hours.

"Good evening, Wes. Good evening, Eve," the scientist said while one of the escorts closed the door behind them.

"Good evening," I replied with a confused look on my face. "What brings you down here?"

"We noticed that Eve finally figured out her abilities. So here we are."

Shit! I thought.

We were so hell-bent on having Eve learn her powers, just so we could get out of there, that we completely forgot we were being monitored. And once everyone got wind of Eve having learned her newfound abilities, it wouldn't be long before they came down to get us, which they did—almost immediately.

"Oh, right," I said. "So I guess you're now here to take us down the rabbit hole?"

Trying to keep her professionalism in check, the scientist couldn't help but let out a silent chuckle. "I suppose that's one way to put it."

"Then what are they here for?" I asked, pointing to the two escorts.

As if I didn't know.

"They're here to make sure *you* don't do any funny stuff," the scientist replied.

I immediately put my left hand over my heart and opened my mouth wide, feigning shock.

"I'm appalled that you would even think we'd try and do something funny," I said. "I mean, we're in an underground facility, surrounded by armed individuals. Come on. How stupid do you think we are?"

The way that I replied to her, I think she could easily see right through me. And so could the two escorts. I only know this because, by the time I was done delivering my laughable speech, the two escorts had their machine guns raised in the ready-to-fire position. And even though her firearm was still in its holster, the scientist had her left hand on hers.

"I have to admit…that was pretty good acting on your part," the scientist said.

"Really? You think so?" I asked, already knowing I'd set off the bullshit alarm.

"No. However, you do have to come with us now. And no funny stuff."

I looked her right in the eyes. "Funny stuff? I wouldn't dream of
it."

Then, without hesitating, Eve quickly stared down all three of
them, and I could see the fright in their eyes as they stood there like
stone statues, unable to move. The scientist and the two escorts were
pinned in place like scared little mice. I just looked at them and grinned
while giving a nod of approval.

"But she would," I said before turning back to Eve. "Nice job."

"Thank you," Eve replied.

"Now, do you think you can knock them out without physically
knocking them out?"

"Piece of cake."

Within two seconds of my asking Eve to do that, all three of them
fell to the floor like bricks and were completely unconscious.

My eyes widened. "Holy shit! How did you do that?" I asked.

"Easy," she said. "I simply ventured into their brains and cut off
their oxygen supply. But we have to hurry. They won't be out for
long."

"You made them pass out?"

"Hell yeah, I did."

"Good thinking. I just hope the rest of our encounters are this
easy, and we can get out of here without hurting anyone."

Little did we know that neither one of us would have any idea how
wrong we would actually be. Because with guns, bullets, grenades, and
other military weapons down there, the chances of us escaping a
fortified, underground base would certainly not be easy without causing
a few casualties.

As I said earlier in this story, Eve and I wanted to see that place,
along with everyone in it, burn to the ground. But before it did, the
good-natured sides of ourselves attempted to take the high road.
Unfortunately, we were quickly driven off it.

"Come on, let's go," I said, attempting to make for the door.

"Wait!" Eve shouted.

I stopped dead in my tracks before turning around to face her.

"What's wrong?" I asked.

She didn't immediately answer me and just stood there, staring at the three bodies. I didn't really understand what she was doing until I saw the barrels on both machine guns start to bend like pretzels. The pistol that the scientist was carrying didn't bend like the other two. It was crushed, almost like Superman had squeezed it with his bare hands.

"There," Eve said. "At least we know that when they wake up, their guns will be out of the picture."

"Have I told you that I loved you?" I said.

"Many times," she replied with a smile. "Now, let's go across the hall and rescue our friends."

"Yes, ma'am."

I then turned back toward the door, grabbed the door handle, and was just about to open it when Eve stopped me again.

"Wait!" she said, flashing her right palm.

"What now?" I asked, slightly peeved.

"What about the guys in the hall?"

I shrugged. "What about them? You can just take them out the same way you did these three."

"True. But you're forgetting about one thing."

"And that is?"

"There may not be any cameras in here, but there are everywhere else, including the hallways."

"Oh!" I said, understanding her. "So the second we open that door, and they see us by ourselves, they'll react, which would leave you with no choice but to take them out where they stand."

"More guards will come, and our time will be severely limited."

"Well, you could always try to use your transport."

"Do you think it'll work?" she asked.

"It has to," I said. "I think it's our only way out."

We just stood there and thought about it for a moment, hoping to come up with any other way of getting across that hall without causing the need to sound the alarm (if there really was an alarm). But with us being down in a heavily fortified, underground military base, I would've bet my right nut there was.

"Let's do it," she said. "Now come over here and take my hand."

I wasted no time and quickly approached her, grabbing her hand.

Just like telepathy, I couldn't use the transportation ability myself. That required some form of assistance from Eve. And we discovered that if I were to hold onto any part of her body, she could simultaneously transport both of us. The way it worked was probably best described as getting into an elevator.

After you get in, the doors close, and then you move up or down to reach a different floor. Once you arrive at the floor you've selected, the doors open, and you're free to get out.

Unlike an elevator, however, the entire transport process takes less than a second. Your eyelids basically acted as the elevator door. You blink, and the door closes. When you open them, well, I think you get the picture. Trust me, it was weird the first time I did it, too.

So with me standing there, holding Eve's hand, I took a deep breath and let it out.

"Are you ready?" she asked.

"As ready as I'll ever be," I said.

"Let's go get our friends."

Wasting no time, she closed her eyes and concentrated on where she wanted to transport us. Then, within a second, we disappeared from our apartment.

———

We instantly reappeared out of thin air directly into Eric and Anna's living room. Once we were no longer in the existence of, I don't know, we'll just call it the "space between spaces," we took a second to catch our bearings before looking over at the couch. They had fallen asleep in their pajamas while watching the 1984 cult classic *Night of the Comet*. (Fun movie. You should watch it.)

I looked over at Eve, and she looked back at me before we both quietly snuck around to the front of the couch. She quickly used her telepathy on me and started to communicate many of the different ways we could wake them up without having them piss themselves. Once we were finally settled on how to proceed, we leaned in and placed our hands over their mouths. My hand covered Eric's mouth while Eve's hand covered Anna's.

The moment we did that, their eyes shot open. They were immediately startled, which made them practically jump off the couch. Mine and Eve's index fingers from our free hands were placed over our own mouths, merely letting them know not to scream. And after a quick head nod from both, we removed our hands.

"Dude! What the fuck are you doing here?" Eric quietly asked. "And how did you get in?"

"Long story," I replied before turning to Anna. "Did you figure anything out yet?"

"Not yet," she said. "We've been going at this for three days and haven't discovered shit. But by the looks of things, I take it you have?"

Although Eve and I had been trying to figure out her abilities for four days, Anna had only been doing it for three. I didn't find out until later that it took Eric an extra day to recover from the injuries he sustained while being questioned by Colonel James.

"We have," Eve said. "Look, we don't have a lot of time, so I'll make this quick. In order for you to use your abilities, you must think of Eric while you do. Otherwise, they won't work."

"And he has to be near you as well," I added.

"How did you figure that out?" Eric asked.

I pointed to the alien computer. "See that box over there? That is a computer that holds every bit of information about the aliens. What they can do, where they come from…it's all in there."

"A computer?"

"A touchscreen computer, to be exact."

He laughed. "A touchscreen computer? That's the stupidest thing I've ever heard of. That kind of technology doesn't even exist."

"Not on Earth, it doesn't," I replied, my expression more straight-faced than he'd ever seen.

"Oh shit. You're serious?"

"As a heart attack."

"But only Anna can use it," Eve said. "Somehow, the machine only reacts to the alien DNA in our bodies. When I touched it, it saw me as one of their own."

"Can I go over there and use it now?" Anna asked.

"Didn't you listen to a word we said? We don't have a lot of time."

"Look," I began, "after we used it, we started testing out all of Eve's abilities. The moment we stopped, however, we got a visit from one of the scientists, along with two armed escorts."

"I used my powers to render them unconscious," Eve said. "Then we transported ourselves over here."

"Yeah. And both the guards outside our doors still think we're all in there."

"Holy shit," Eric quietly said, stunned by what we just told him. "Well, what happens when they call for help?"

"What do you mean?"

"You did disable their walkie-talkies, correct? Because when the others realize that they've been gone for too long, they'll try to contact them. And when they don't answer, they'll send more people to find them."

Son of a bitch! I shouted out loud in my head.

We were so anxious to get out of there that we completely forgot about their walkie-talkies.

"Shit," I muttered.

"Nice thinking, Einstein," Eric said.

"Nice thinking? We're the ones doing all the work, *asshole!*"

"I mention one little mistake, and suddenly, *I'm* the asshole?"

"Guys," Eve interrupted. "We don't have time for this. We have to think of a way out of here, remember?"

"Besides, both of you are already assholes," Anna joked.

Eric and I looked at each other.

"She does have a point," I said with a smile. "It's good to see you."

He wound up giving me a smile of his own. "You too, buddy," he replied.

He then stood up from the couch and embraced me with a hug.

"*Awe!*" both girls said in unison, their hands crossed over their hearts.

"Now, why don't the two of you kiss and make up so we can get out of here?" Eve said.

I turned and sneered at her. "Very funny."

"Yeah, I don't think I want to see that either," Anna added.

So with everyone back on each other's good side (not that we ever left), the four of us were ready to go.

"So does anyone have any ideas?" Anna asked, standing up off the couch.

"Well," I said, "Eric did bring up a good point about the walkie-talkies." I paused, then turned around, before slowly pacing back and forth. "If someone does try to get a hold of them and they don't respond, they'll most likely send more people to check up on them. And since the only way off this floor is by the elevator, I think we could use that to our advantage."

"How?" Eric asked. "I mean, what if they send more scientists?"

"With a few armed escorts being unresponsive, I got a feeling that they'll send more armed escorts."

"Which means they'll have no choice but to use the elevator."

"Correct. The moment that thing stops, the doors will open. And once they all get off, we'll have to be quick about it."

"Can you try to speed this up a bit? I think I'm starting to get some gray hair."

I scowled at him. "What I'm trying to say is that when those doors close, we all transport into the elevator. Then we can ride it up to the surface."

"There," Eric said, folding his arms across his chest. "Was that so hard?"

"That's a pretty good plan," Anna said. "But what'll happen when we get to the top floor? I mean, we'll still have to contend with everyone up there."

"Well," I started to say before slowly turning my gaze toward the girls, "that's where you two come in."

Not having used her powers yet, Anna looked at me with a confused expression.

"What do you mean, that's where we come in?" she asked.

"I think he means that we're going to use our abilities to get past everyone," Eve told her.

"First of all, I haven't learned how to use any of my abilities yet. And second, are you out of your mind? You want me to just learn them on the fly?"

"She's right," Eve said. "Besides, I think I can handle this on my own."

"Are you sure?"

Eve placed a hand on Anna's shoulder to reassure her. "I'll be fine. Trust me," she said with a smile. "Now, you two should go and get dressed. They'll be here any second."

Anna smiled at Eve before turning around and heading into the bedroom. Eric followed suit with a smile of his own and a nod before making his way into the bedroom shortly after.

Frankly, I was a little jealous. I was jealous because they actually had the time to go and put on any clothes they wanted. I didn't get a chance to change and was stuck wearing whatever clean clothes they had provided for us in the drawers. I mean, don't get me wrong, what I was wearing wasn't all that bad.

I found a slightly faded black T-shirt with an upside-down pentagram inside a circle. MÖTLEY CRÜE was printed in red letters above it, while SHOUT AT THE DEVIL was printed in red letters below it. Thankfully, I was still wearing my red Converse sneakers. As for my *Revenge of the Jedi* T-shirt, unfortunately, I never saw it again.

A few minutes later, Eric and Anna came out of the bedroom, dressed and ready to go. As I said, they were lucky enough to wear the same clothes they had on when we were all brought in.

"We're ready," Eric said.

"Good. Now we just have to wait for the elevator to arrive," I said.

"Do you know how long it'll take?" Anna asked.

No sooner did she say that, we could all hear a loud *ding* come from out in the hallway, followed by the elevator doors opening up.

"Now," I said with a smile.

"Okay. I want you two to grab onto one of my shoulders," Eve told Eric and Anna. She then turned to me. "And, Wes…"

"I know the drill," I said, grabbing her outstretched hand.

"Now, are you ready?" Eve turned to look at both Eric and Anna, who just nodded their heads. "Okay. Hold on!"

"I still don't understand how—" Eric began.

But before he even got a chance to finish what he was going to say, Eve closed her eyes. Then all four of us instantly vanished from their living room, leaving no trace behind.

CHAPTER 25

As all four of us reappeared inside the elevator, only one thought had crossed my mind—*Our escape from this hellish place is finally underway.*

The moment we were all able to reorient ourselves, Eve and I looked over at Eric and Anna, who were both looking back at us with surprised expressions on their faces, most likely due to what had just happened.

"Holy shit!" Eric said. "Did we just do that?"

"Pretty cool, huh?" I replied.

"*That's* one of our abilities?" Anna asked.

"Told you it wouldn't be that hard," Eve said. "But don't worry, we'll work on yours when we get out of here."

"As for right now," I said, "we need to get our asses back up to the surface."

"I couldn't agree more," Eric said.

And with that, I wasted no time pushing the button for level *A*, the very top floor.

When the button lit up, and to our esteemed delight, the elevator started moving. However, our happy faces quickly turned to panic as we realized that, instead of going up, the elevator started going down.

"What the fuck, dude?" Eric said. "You pushed the wrong button!"

"No, I didn't," I said, pointing to the highlighted *A*. "The top floor is lit up."

"Then why are we going down?"

"I don't fucking know."

Our arguing immediately stopped the moment we all arrived on the ground floor. Or listed on the elevator as level *U*.

Did I just make a huge mistake by pushing the wrong button? There was no way. I couldn't have. I know I pressed the button for the top floor because level *A* was lit up green. But why did we start going down instead of up? I don't know. Maybe it was already in the process of going down. That, of course, was the most logical answer.

But now that we were going down, who was about to get on with us? More scientists? More armed escorts, this time with bazookas instead of machine guns, coming up to blow us all to smithereens?

Okay, that last one might have been a bit over the top. There was no way in hell they'd kill the only two people whose DNA had been successfully merged with the aliens' DNA.

However, when those doors opened, the six of us (yes, I said six) were wide-eyed. Our jaws hit the floor with a loud thump. Also, I'd be lying if I said that a little bit of hilarity didn't ensue. After all, with Eric and me in the same elevator, it was practically a given, no matter the circumstances.

"Eve?"

"Daddy!"

"Anna?"

"Dad!"

"Wes!"

"Mr. Parker!"

"Eric!"

"Mr. James!"

Eric and I then faced each other.

"Wes?"

"Eric!"

After Eric and I included ourselves in that whole bit, both girls turned around to give us what I could only describe as looks of death. The only way we could respond was with an innocent shrug and smile.

"What? We couldn't just leave each other out," I said.

Disgusted by our childish action, the girls rolled their eyes and shook their heads in unison before turning back to their fathers.

"How did all of you get out?" Mr. Parker asked. "And where are your escorts?"

But before anyone could respond, the elevator doors started to close. Both Colonels reacted quickly and stuck their arms in to keep them from shutting. They then grabbed their daughters and yanked them out of the elevator. As the doors started closing a second time, Eric and I managed to stick our arms out, preventing them from closing before exiting ourselves. And at that point, unfortunately, no one would be going to the top floor anytime soon.

Once we were out, we found ourselves surrounded by the two Colonels and eight additional armed escorts, all of whom stood there pointing their guns at our heads.

"Shit," I said, quickly putting my hands up to surrender.

Eric also did the same.

"Daddy, don't hurt them," Eve pleaded.

"Yeah, leave them out of this," Anna added.

"Oh, don't you worry about them," Mr. James said. "The moment we leave, these guards have explicit orders to take them out."

"Since you two now know how to use your abilities, the boys are no longer needed," Mr. Parker added.

"I wouldn't bet on that, Colonel," I said.

"Oh yeah? And why is that?"

"Because without us, the girls are powerless," Eric added.

"Is that so?" Mr. James asked, questioning our truism.

"It's true," Anna said. "Without them, Eve and I can't use our abilities. It has something to do with the guys needing to be nearby for us to use them."

"And just how did you figure that out?"

"I was able to use the alien computer you put in our room," Eve told him. "It seemed to only respond to me. Probably because I'm carrying the aliens' DNA."

"Hmm. Well, that would explain why none of us could figure it out," Mr. Parker said.

"And that's why you need us alive," I said.

There was an immediate pause while the two Colonels pondered that thought. Also, judging by the looks on their faces, they didn't seem very keen on the idea of keeping us alive or down in the base any longer than they needed to. I had a feeling that if it were up to them, they'd give us an involuntary memory wipe and send us on our way.

"I guess we'll just have to make do then, won't we?" Mr. James said.

Before any of us had any time to react, both of the Colonels pulled out a needle and stuck them into their daughters' necks, injecting them with whatever was inside. It was most likely the same liquid they injected all of us with outside the inn.

"No!" I screamed.

Within two seconds, both girls' bodies went limp while their fathers held them up. I started to step forward, but was quickly reminded of the half dozen guns still being pointed at my head.

"One more step, and I'll have my escorts decorate these walls with your brains," Mr. Parker said.

"Geez. That's a little dramatic, don't you think?" I asked the insane psycho Colonel.

"Now that the girls have been knocked unconscious," Eric said, "how are you going to test out their powers?"

"These needles were originally intended for you two," Mr. James told us. "However, after seeing the four of you standing here, we had to deviate from our plans a bit. After all, we couldn't have the girls using their abilities on us now, could we?"

"So then, what are you going to do with us?" I curiously asked.

"Since you two refuse to cooperate, we're going to have to put you in with the rest of our prisoners until we figure out what to do," Mr. Parker said.

"The *rest* of your prisoners?"

"Don't worry, you'll see," Mr. James said, a villainous grin residing on his face.

Just then, the door to the hospital room swung open, and out walked Doctor Blumb and Doctor Harbor, along with two other doctors I hadn't seen yet. All four of them immediately came walking over to the Colonels.

"Please strap Anna and Eve down to the beds like the last time," Mr. Parker told them. "And keep them under heavy sedation."

All the doctors nodded before grabbing Anna and Eve. They then took them back inside the hospital room before disappearing behind the closing door.

"As for you two," Mr. Parker said, addressing Eric and me, "follow me."

With the girls knocked out and a small battalion of guns still pointed at our heads, Eric and I had no choice but to do as they said. But we didn't follow the Colonels into the elevator, though. As a matter of fact, we followed them over toward the two doors we had initially walked past when we were down there earlier that week.

If you recall, there was a door next to the A.M.U. and the spaceship hangar. I never got to see what was behind either one of them, as I was quickly shuffled past them and into the hospital room. However, by the time they did show us what was in there, I quickly regretted ever wondering.

As we started walking toward the room on the left, everyone suddenly stopped. Mr. James ordered half of the escorts to follow him and Eric over there while Mr. Parker took me and the remaining escorts to the door on the right.

"Wait! What the hell are you doing?" I asked before looking over at Eric. "Eric!"

"Wes!" he shouted back.

"Don't you worry about him," Mr. Parker said. "Just like you, he'll be in good hands."

Yeah. Somehow, I didn't quite believe him.

And with that, I just stood there and watched as Mr. James punched in the keycode for the door. I then heard the familiar beep as the door unlocked. But before I could say anything else, Mr. James grabbed Eric by the arm and pulled him inside. The escorts followed suit, and the door swiftly closed behind them. Eric was now gone, and soon, I'd be joining him. Just not over there.

"You are going to love what we have planned for you," the Colonel said, sporting a devilish grin spanning from ear to ear.

"Why? What's in there?" I asked, curious.

"Let's put it this way…by the time we figure out what to do with you, you'll wish we *had* erased your memory."

I immediately swallowed hard and thought, *Oh shit.*

The Colonel punched in his code on the keypad before the seventh beep sounded, followed by the door unlocking. After he pushed it open, I followed him inside, along with the escorts, before the door slammed shut behind us.

I honestly didn't know what I expected to see behind those doors. Maybe another room full of dead aliens. Or perhaps, another hospital room. But what they actually had in those rooms was basically something straight out of a horror film. The immediate smell of dead bodies washed through my nose like a tidal wave.

Before that summer, I had never seen a corpse in my life. Because of that, my stomach had a sudden urge to take all the food I'd recently eaten and bring it up to the surface.

Because the room was also a little dark, I could barely see anything. The only things I could make out were just a few shadows. I could also hear what sounded like very quiet moans and groans. It almost felt like I had just closed my eyes during a movie scene depicting a bunch of sick people lying down on hospital beds. However, when that light came on, my eyes were looking at something from no movie I had ever seen before.

The room I was now in was about half the size of the A.M.U. and set up almost the same way. But instead of massive tanks being on either side, there were massive cages. And three of them even had people inside. The smell of urine, dead bodies, feces, and rotten food filled both of my nostrils. The only thing I could do was cover my nose, hoping the smell wouldn't get me.

"What is this place?" I asked.

"What you see is a room full of half-empty cages that once housed the people we experimented on," the Colonel said. "Well, the ones who survived, anyway."

"You kept your experiments locked up in cages?"

"Only the ones who couldn't get their abilities to work. Which was pretty much all of them."

"What the fuck is wrong with you people? Do you know how sick and twisted this all is?"

"It's all part of the job," the Colonel said.

"All part of the job? I mean, look at these people," I said, motioning to the lot of them. "They're barely alive."

"Sadly, yes. And now, unfortunately, you will be joining them. Unless, of course, you opt to take the memory wipe?"

"You know I can't take the memory wipe. You need me."

"That is an excellent point."

"Plus, what about them?" I continued. "It's like a fucking zombie freakshow down here. Did you give them the option to take the memory wipe?"

"Because they have already been injected with the alien DNA, no."

Without even having to ask, I already knew what my only option was. Knowing that the Colonel needed me and that a memory wipe was officially off the table, I immediately took action.

"No way," I said, shaking my head. "Fuck this. And fuck you! There's no way in hell I'm spending the rest of my life down here!"

Outmanned and outgunned, I quickly did the only thing I could think of at the time. I turned around and charged toward one of the escorts, hoping to grab a gun, a knife, or anything else to help me out.

But before I could even make it two feet, I felt a thud on the back of my head. Then everything else around me, almost instantly, faded to black.

───────────

I woke up sometime later to the same putrid, dead-body odor that had overpowered my nose when I first walked in there. However, this time was different from when I first smelled it—this time, whatever was sitting in my stomach, probably coupled with the fact that I'd just recently received a near concussion, came out in a fountain of glory. By the time I was finally done, though, there was nothing glorious about it.

As I continued to sit there on the concrete floor, I looked around and noticed that I was in one of the cages. Each one measured about twenty feet by twenty feet—a perfectly shaped, square cube of torment. The only thing inside it was me and a bucket. (Guess what the bucket was for?)

All the cages were spread out just enough, probably about six feet apart from one another, so that no one could interact with any of the other prisoners. Not like there were many to talk to anyway.

As I scanned the room, I could see three people who looked different in terms of race and gender. One of them sat directly across from me and seemed somewhat fresh. But the other two (the one next to him and the one next to me) looked like shriveled-up raisins, too weak to move.

In a way, their bodies kind of reminded me of the half-female zombie corpse that they captured, tied up, and questioned in 1985's *Return of the Living Dead.* At that point, I was waiting for one of them to screech out, "I need your brains to take away my pain."

After scanning the room and thinking back on the information the Colonel had told me before knocking me out and throwing me in there, I honestly didn't know what I was more shocked about—the fact that some of those people actually survived or the fact that after being injected with alien DNA, not a single one of them ever made it back up to the surface. Thankfully, though, because Anna and Eve were the very last ones to be injected, the three people left in there were no younger than their early twenties.

The one good thing about being in there was, well, actually, there wasn't anything good about being in there. I was about to spend the rest of my life down there, rotting away into nothing. However, they were kind enough to leave the lights on for me. Either that or I had been out for so long that it was now morning. But since there were no windows down there, the first one was my initial guess.

I noticed that I was in the second cage on the left, away from the door. Once I regained all signs of life, I immediately stood up and tried to feel around the steel cage, hoping to find any type of flaw or exploit I could use to escape. Unfortunately, the way the cage was built, I wasn't going anywhere.

"Damn," I whispered.

"Good luck trying to get out of there," I heard a semi-weak male voice say.

I immediately turned to look in the direction the voice was coming from. That was when I saw the somewhat healthy-looking male sitting directly across from me on the other side of the room—the one exception I mentioned earlier.

The clothes he had on looked like shredded rags. His hair had all but practically fallen out, and his skin didn't look like (from what I could tell) its regular dark color. His teeth were yellow and half missing, while his eyes looked almost glossed over.

"Holy shit," I whispered before walking to the front of my cage and addressing him. "How long have you been down here?"

"I honestly don't have a clue," he responded with a slow, weak tone.

I then looked at the bodies in the two other cages before turning back toward him. That was when I realized that aside from me, he was the only other person sitting upright. He was also the only one left with enough strength to speak or move.

"Jesus. Don't they feed you?" I asked.

"They bring us food only once a day," he said.

"Once a day? No wonder why it's like death down here."

After saying that out loud, I repeated it to myself a few times in my head before quickly pondering the possibility of starving to death. But I immediately shook it off because I didn't have any time to waste thinking about it. The only thing I was thinking about was rescuing my friends and getting the hell out of there.

"If I may ask, what's your story?" I asked him.

"What do you mean?" he replied.

"I mean, I obviously know that all of you were injected with the alien DNA. But why did they really put you down here?"

"It's just like the Colonel said," he replied before coughing. "Because we were unable to manifest any abilities."

"Did they also have you in one of those apartments?"

"Yeah."

"For how long?"

He took a deep breath. "I was up there for about two months before they sent me down here."

"Two months? And you have no idea how long you've been down here?"

"That depends."

"Depends on what?" I curiously asked.

"What year is it?"

Okay. Usually, when someone in that position asks you what day it is, or possibly even the time, you know that they've been out of it for a little bit. That only tends to happen after waking up from just one night or even days of drinking. But when someone asks you what year it is, you know they're out of the loop.

So instead of asking him why he'd want to know the year and remembering everything else the Colonel told me, I just swept my thoughts under the rug and answered him.

"It's nineteen eighty-nine," I said.

He immediately let out something reminiscent of a laugh as I could see the wheels turning inside of what was left of his brain.

"Well, holy shit," he said. "I can't believe it's been ten years."

"Ten years?" I blurted out. "Damn!"

My eyes were wide as I seriously couldn't wrap my head around the fact that he'd been down there for ten years. Just by looking at the guy, I would've guessed much, much longer.

"Were you injected with the alien DNA?" he asked.

"No. But the Colonel's daughter was," I replied.

He immediately lowered his head and shook it, saddened by my response. "That poor girl."

"Look, I know that you've been down here for a while, but there must be a way out of here. I have to get to her."

"You'd be much better off taking the memory wipe."

"You're right. I would be," I said. "Unfortunately, that's no longer an option for me."

An intrigued expression immediately hit his face. "Why not?"

"Because without me, her powers are useless."

Apparently, my mentioning that Eve could use her powers instantly made him perk up.

"How did she unlock her abilities?" he asked.

"We figured out how to activate the alien computer in our room," I told him. "And when we did, we learned that the secret to Eve using her abilities was what the aliens referred to as their 'other being.' Or as we've come to believe here on Earth, their soulmate." I pointed to myself. "That's me."

"Well, I'll be damned."

"That's also why I can't take the memory wipe," I continued. "If they were to send me back up to the surface, her powers would become useless."

"It appears then that they have you right where they want you."

"Yeah. No, shit."

The man coughed again. "So friend, what's your name?"

"Wes," I told him.

"Well then, Wes, it's nice to meet you. My name's John. And if I were you"—he let out a little laugh, followed by another cough—"I'd get *real* comfortable."

CHAPTER 26

While I was in my cage, I thought about one thing and one thing only—Eve. Also, what John had said to me about getting real comfortable, I found to be absolute bullshit. I mean, he may have already accepted his fate about being down there, but I wasn't ready to give up—not by a long shot.

I hadn't seen Eve in some time, and judging by how long I was out, I'd say maybe just a little over twelve hours. As far as I knew, they were keeping her and Anna under heavy sedation on one of the hospital beds just next door. And all I had to do was get to her. But how?

I already knew I wasn't breaking out of my cage. Not unless I was Superman or the Hulk. So that was already out.

I could always try to fake being sick so that they would take me to the hospital wing. However, looking around at all the almost lifeless bodies in those cages quickly made me rethink that plan.

Regardless, they still needed me alive. And if that was the case, maybe I did have a slight advantage over the other prisoners. Let me explain…

The only reason those people were down there was because they didn't know how to unlock their own alien abilities. Plus, keeping them locked up was much easier than giving them memory wipes and sending them back up to the surface. After all, having alien DNA loose up top would most certainly make the five o'clock news in any country.

But when Eve and I discovered how to use them, Eric and I became instant hot commodities. If we were to die or take a memory wipe and go back up to the surface, the girls' powers wouldn't work. And that would make everyone else down there start back at square one.

So that just left me with one critical question. *If they did need me, why would they put me in here knowing that I might starve to death and die? Did they have some bigger plans for me that I didn't know about?*

Okay, technically, that was two questions. But who's counting?

Anyway, I sat in my cage for the rest of the morning, just thinking about all the different answers to the two questions I just mentioned. I also thought about the Colonel and what his true motives really were. But more importantly, I thought about Eve.

I thought about her face, her smile, her body, and just her overall kindness toward me. I also thought about how much I loved her, which was a lot. So much so, in fact, that I was ready to die for her.

But when I started to think about us getting out and spending the rest of the summer together before going off to college, I smiled so much that I thought my face would freeze that way. If it did, then I could paint it white and dye my hair green. Maybe even get a purple suit and a matching fedora to boot.

Sorry, I couldn't help myself.

"Well, it's almost lunchtime," I heard John say, still speaking in a weak, quiet tone.

"Oh, joy," I sarcastically responded.

"I bet your tone will change the moment you start eating."

"I highly doubt that."

Then there was silence. On any other day, it probably would've been a little too silent for my liking. But considering the predicament I was in, that suited me just fine.

However, it didn't take long before I thought I could feel two holes being burned into my head. Sure enough, when I looked over at

John, there he was, just staring at me, almost as if he was trying to project his own thoughts directly into my head.

"Is there something else?" I asked him.

"Can I," he said before coughing. "Can I make a suggestion?"

"Sure."

"Judging by what you told me, it seems like they really need you."

I shrugged. "So?"

"You could use that to your advantage."

"How?"

"Make yourself sick."

"Make myself sick?" I asked, confused. "I don't understand."

John took a couple of deep breaths, almost as if he was about to read me a ten-line paragraph from start to finish without taking a break.

"They need you for something, correct?" he asked. I nodded. "In that case, fake being sick."

I opened my mouth to respond, but he could tell I was still confused and quickly began to elaborate.

"You see," he continued, "there are always two guards that come in here to deliver the food. If they were to find you unconscious on the floor, one would stay with you while the other would go get help." He coughed some more. "If they needed to keep me alive, I would've tried that a long time ago."

By the time he finished his long-winded explanation, I wished he would've just gotten to the point because the look on my face said that I still had no clue as to what in the holy fuck he was talking about.

"I can see that you're still confused," he said.

That was an understatement.

"When they find you unconscious," he continued, "one guard will leave to go and get some help. When that happens, you'll have to somehow grab the other guard's gun."

"Are you insane?" I said. "If I take one of their guns, then they'll kill me for sure."

"You said they need you, correct?" I nodded. "Then it's logical to assume that if they truly need you, they'll refrain from killing you."

When he said that, my eyes widened, and my jaw just about broke on the floor. I mean, holy shit. Thank you, Doctor Spock!

He had basically just reached into his pocket (well, if he had any pockets), pulled out a truth grenade, pulled the pin, tossed it over to me, and watched it explode in my face. What he just told me made perfect sense. I could go on an actual suicide run without committing suicide.

"How do you know one of the guards will leave?" I asked.

"Look at all of the death in this room," he said, slowly using his head to motion toward the rest of the cages. "I've seen it before."

"If that's true, then how do I get one of their guns?"

"That's up to you to decide."

And that was that.

Reflecting on everything John had just told me, I thought his idea held some actual merit. Which meant I now had a big decision to make. Well, not really. It was a surprisingly easy decision to make. Would I possibly get a bullet in the leg or arm in the process? Maybe. But after hearing what John said, it was worth taking a risk. And again, I just had to figure out how.

———————

We spent the rest of the late morning in silence, waiting for the guards to bring us our lunch. As we did, I carefully looked around the room before stopping and staring at the two shriveled-up bodies. As I looked them over, I winced and thought about how they were ripped from their lives above the same way I was. I mean, by that point, I was only in there for less than twenty-four hours, and I already couldn't stand it. But to be down there for years on end, basically, until the day you die, with only one meal per day, I couldn't even begin to fathom how much torture they all went through.

If I had to guess, some were probably taken as babies, while others were taken as young kids, teenagers, or adults. But the bigger question that entered my mind was, *Why?*

How did the assholes down here decide who was to be taken from above? Were they criminals, conspiracy theorists, or just regular folks who discovered what insane experiments they were doing and, therefore, needed to be kept quiet?

But if that was the case—if all three of those were the reasons why people were down here in the first place, then why choose two young, innocent babies to inject with alien DNA? What was their plan? Did they figure something out that I didn't know about? And more importantly, why were the girls the only two people they ever sent topside? What were they hoping to achieve by doing that? By the time our lunch had finally arrived, I was more confused than ever.

After the code was punched into the keypad, the door beeped, and in walked two armed guards with a three-tier, metal cart filled with food. Cage by cage, they delivered one tray to each so that its corresponding occupant could eat. The problem was that half of the occupants couldn't even lift their hands to grab something and put it in their mouths.

My lunch consisted of mashed potatoes, a couple of slices of bread, some fruit, and some kind of meat—most likely steak, ham, or a pork chop. I honestly couldn't tell. We were also given a glass of water. It was actually a giant plastic cup of water. I mean, they couldn't have the prisoners breaking the glass to make weapons now, could they?

Other than my water, I only ate the meat and wound up tossing the rest over to John, who almost instantly wolfed it down like a starving animal.

Once the guards finished handing out the trays, they removed the old ones and stacked them on the cart before leaving the room. Half an hour later, they would then come back into the room, this time to check on the prisoners. The ones that were dead would be taken away one at a time. After my first day down there, sadly, the four of us had been reduced to three.

Their cages would then be washed and cleaned. Not well, mind you, because the dead body odor never left. Once that was all said and done, the guards would leave again and not return until lunchtime the following day.

This process lasted seven days as I watched the guards come and go. I studied their every move, how they acted, and who they spoke to. I also kept a close eye on their outfits, how they were dressed, and which side their guns were located. Plus, during those seven days, I also noticed that John wasn't lying. Once the remaining shriveled-up person died, the guards followed the exact same procedure he had previously described.

One of them would stay while the other one left the room. The one who stayed would radio someone in the hospital to let them know one of the guards would be coming to escort them over. I honestly don't know why they did that, seeing as how they weren't in any real danger to begin with. But they did. Most likely, it was some type of ancient protocol put in place when they first opened the facility. Who knows? Regardless, John was right. Faking being ill was my only shot at getting out of there.

So I waited—and waited—and waited—patiently, while I planned my escape.

My second day in the cage was pretty much like my first. I just sat there while John and I chatted about anything and everything regarding what we had done with our lives so far, what we liked to do for fun, and what kind of jobs we've held.

I discovered that John was forty years old and had served in Vietnam. But by the time he returned from the war, he had nothing left. His wife left him, taking the kids with her. His parents had also died in a tragic boating accident that took their lives, along with the lives of five other people. His house had even been foreclosed on and taken by the bank. So the only possessions he had left were basically the clothes on his back. Talk about losing everything. He also told me that he just drifted around the country for the next few years, going from shelter to shelter.

But it wasn't until June of 1979 that he was approached by two men, Colonel Parker and Colonel James, who happened to notice him hitchhiking through Henderson, Nevada, going west. They stopped to ask him a few questions and, after finding out what his deal was, offered him a chance to rejoin the U.S. military, just not in the way he'd hoped.

The Colonels then took him to the underground facility, where they pumped him full of drugs and injected him with the alien DNA. And after two months of him trying to manifest any abilities, well, you know the rest.

After hearing his story, I felt so bad for him. And that just made me want to get out of there even more. After all, I was going to school in the fall and didn't want to spend any more time down there than necessary. Of course, it was only my second day behind bars, and I was yet to formulate any escape plan.

On the third day, it was pretty much the same thing. John and I talked, ate, and that was pretty much it. I ate my meat and drank my water while I tossed the rest of my stuff over to him. And in doing so, my nose caught a whiff of something else—something I thought was just the smell within the room. But it wasn't until I started to sniff around that I discovered it wasn't the room that smelled like that at all. It was me.

After being down there in that stench-infested death pit for three days without a shower, I was starting to become a little ripe. And even though I wasn't anywhere near John, I couldn't even begin to imagine what he smelled like. The thought of it actually made me want to barf.

I mean, ten years without showering? I'm surprised there weren't any flies buzzing around him.

By day number four, the stench of my own body pretty much blended in with the smell of the entire room. In which case, I began to not even notice it. However, I did start to notice something else.

After giving John the rest of my food for the past four days, minus my meat and water, of course, I noticed that he wasn't looking as thin as he was when I first went in there. He started to look much fuller and a little healthier. I also noticed him getting up and walking around his cage a little more, almost as if he had a newfound outlook on life.

Days five and six were pretty much me getting stir-crazy. By the time day number six had come to an end, I began to lose it. Shitting and pissing in a bucket, eating only meat and water, not getting a shower, and having to sleep on a concrete floor started to get the best of me. Thankfully, John was there to talk to me. Because if he wasn't, I think it would've been a lot worse.

But when the guards came in to deliver my lunch on day number seven, that was when I finally decided to put my extremely sloppy plan into motion. After not sleeping much for the past week and missing Eve more than ever, the time for discourse had officially ended.

CHAPTER 27

When the guards came in to deliver our lunch, they immediately noticed me lying motionless on the floor. To them, however, they probably thought I was only sleeping or maybe even on the verge of death. Luckily, since I was the first cage they delivered to, and the fact that there were only two of us in there, I didn't have to wait very long for them to get to me.

"Hey, wake up! It's time for chow!" the male guard shouted.

Of course, I didn't move. So he tried again, this time while banging on the bars.

"I said, wake up! It's time for lunch!" he shouted.

When I didn't move after the second time, his demeanor quickly shifted.

"Shit," I heard him say.

"What's the matter?" the other guard, a female, asked.

"Something's wrong with this one. You better go and get one of the doctors."

"Damn. Never a dull moment around here."

Barely through the door, the female guard immediately turned around and left the room, while the male guard stayed put. But he didn't open the cage like I thought he would. He just stood there, waiting for the female guard to return to the room with one of the doctors in tow. Apparently, John was only partly right about how they handled situations like that. However, I had a feeling that because it was me and I was still reasonably healthy, they decided to take a little extra precaution.

Less than five minutes later, the female guard returned to the room with Doctor Harbor running in behind her. Once she stood before my cage, the male guard quickly unlocked it and let her in.

"What happened to him?" Harbor asked while running over to me.

"I don't know," the male guard responded. "When we came in here to feed them, I found him like that."

Inside my cage, Doctor Harbor quickly got down on her knees before pulling out a small flashlight.

"Oh, no," she said, worry emanating from her mouth. "Colonel Parker is going to have a meltdown if anything happens to him."

She opened my eyelids one at a time as she moved the light back and forth, shining it into each eye multiple times.

"Why is this one so special, anyway?" the male guard asked.

"You are not authorized to know that kind of information," Harbor snidely responded.

"I meant no offense. I mean, if we have to look at him every day, I just think we ought to know."

"Well, if you'd like, you could always bring it up with the Colonel the next time you see him?"

The male guard almost immediately flashed his palms. "I'll take your word for it."

Harbor then looked me over some more while performing a variety of standard medical tests.

She used a stethoscope to check my heartbeat. She also used her fingers to check that my pulse was in proper rhythm while she counted silently. Once she was finished with that, she then gave me a quick once-over to make sure I wasn't bleeding or bruising.

Since the first guard didn't open the cage like John said they would, and since the doctor was in there instead, I had to improvise. I wound up doing the same thing to her that I would've initially done with one of the guards. Only now, I had three people to contend with instead of two.

So with the two guards sort of lax and the doctor busy checking me over, I briefly opened my left eye to get a good view of her sidearm. I noticed that it was strapped to her right side. And since I was right-handed, I had to be patient and wait for the right moment to grab it. Luckily for me, my opportunity came in the form of a distraction.

Even though I couldn't see John from where I was lying, he was obviously watching this whole thing go down from his cage. And when he noticed that I hadn't made any moves yet, he figured he would help me out. And what better way to do that than by throwing a piece of bread at the back of the male guard's head.

"What the fuck?" the male guard said.

Not only did he turn around to see John smiling at him, but the female guard and Doctor Harbor also looked in his direction. And that gave me the perfect opportunity to take action.

With everyone distracted and focused on John, I immediately stood up before reaching my right arm out and pulling Doctor Harbor's gun out of its holster. I then used my left arm and wrapped it around her chest, pulling her in toward me. Once her back was flat against my body, I pointed the gun directly at her temple. Our little scuffle caught the other two guards' attention, and they immediately turned around to see what was happening. In turn, they went for their guns. But I quickly reminded them why they shouldn't do it.

"You touch those guns, and I'll pull this trigger," I said, threatening to blow the good doctor's brains all over the bars of the cage. "And don't even think about touching those radios either."

"Wes, what the hell are you doing?" Harbor asked me. "You know you can't make it out of here. You'll be dead before you leave this room."

"Shut up!" I then ordered the guards again. "Both of you put your hands in the air!" When they didn't comply, I got slightly angrier. "*Now!* Or I blow her fucking head off!"

"Don't shoot! Do as he says," Harbor told them.

Complying with the doctor's orders, both guards quickly raised their hands into the air.

"That's better," I said. "Now, give me the code to the door so I can get out of here."

"Even if we did tell you what it was, you wouldn't get that far," Harbor said.

"I don't care. I want that code so I can get my friends and get the hell out of here."

"Wes, there are other ways out of this. Look, just give me the word, and I'll wipe your memory. Then you're free to go."

I laughed. "Nice try, doctor. You know, as well as I do, that the Colonel isn't just going to let me walk out of here. And you also know that he needs me to stick around so he can study Eve's powers."

"That part is true, yes. But maybe if you let me go, he'll—"

"He'll what? Have pity on me?" I laughed and shook my head. "You're all just as fucked up as he is. Now, give me the code so I can—"

Before I could finish my sentence, I was interrupted by two gunshots ringing out from the very same room I was in. Once I realized what was going on, I looked over to see both guards lying on the floor.

Each one of them had a bullet hole in the back of their head. Blood was oozing from their wounds and had started to pool around their lifeless bodies. When I finally got up the nerve to see where the shots came from, I simply couldn't believe my eyes.

I saw John standing upright and commanding inside his cage. I then looked over at his right hand and noticed that he was holding a gun, most likely one of the guards' guns. The smoke was still freshly rising out of its barrel.

"John? What the hell did you do?" I asked, my eyes wide from shock.

"I did what needed to be done," he said, his voice still a little weak.

"But you killed them."

That was the first time in my life I had ever seen someone die in front of my own eyes. As I stood there to soak in what I was looking at, I still couldn't believe it.

And because I didn't have a mirror, I assume that the expression on my face looked very similar to how Gordie, Chris, Teddy, and Vern's faces looked in the 1986 movie *Stand By Me*. After they discovered Ray Brower's body buried underneath the brush next to the railroad tracks, they couldn't believe it either. In the movie, that was the first time they had ever seen a dead body as well.

"You would've done the same thing," John said.

I didn't respond to him right away. Instead, I continued to stare at the guards' corpses while trying to see everything from his point of view. And you know what? He was right.

Being locked in a cage with only one meal per day while people and food just lay there, rotting all around him, he had every right to kill them. After all, what comes around goes around. Plus, none of them down there really seemed to care about what happened to the prisoners anyway. Because if they did, that room would've been much livelier.

"Now, stand aside so I can kill the doctor," John said.

"No way," I said. "I need her to help me."

"To do what? Free your girlfriend?" He shook his head. "You know that the doctor won't help you."

"Maybe not. But I still have to try."

Just then, and before our conversation could continue any further, the lights briefly went down before some red, spinning emergency lights came back on. Shortly after, a loud warning klaxon started blaring throughout the entire facility.

"What the hell's that?" I asked, looking around at the new light show.

"It appears that your secret is out," Harbor said.

"Shit!"

"Wes, you have to let me out," John shouted over all the noise.

"Don't do it, Wes," Harbor said. "You don't know what he'll do."

"Frankly, doctor, I trust him more than I trust you," I said. "Now move." I then ushered the doctor over to the front of John's cage. "Open it!" I ordered. When she didn't budge, I moved my gun closer, pressing it directly up against the side of her temple. "I said, open it."

When she refused to do it a second time, I immediately looked over at John and nodded, prompting him to raise his gun and point it directly at her forehead.

"You now have a choice," I told her. "You can either do as I say and open this cage, or my friend John here will blow your brains out. Then once you're dead, I'll take your keys and open it myself."

Apparently, the thought of her own death must not have sat too well in her mind. Because the moment I finished presenting her with some options, she quickly pulled out her keys and unlocked his cage.

I couldn't even begin to describe the elated look on John's face the moment he stepped out and onto that floor. Tears immediately started forming in his eyes. Well, whatever tears he could form. Due to the lack of hydration, it was a little difficult. But I could tell that the man was overjoyed. However, his freedom would, sadly, be short-lived.

"Wes, it's time for you to go," John told me. "Guards will be swarming this place shortly. Take the doctor, get to your friends, and then get the hell out of here."

"What about you?" I curiously asked. "You're coming too, aren't you?"

"As good as I feel right now, I'm still very weak. I won't stand a chance."

"No. You're coming with me. End of story."

"If you want to live, go now." He paused to catch his breath. "I'll stay here and distract them."

"But you'll die."

"I've been down here for far too long. My time is up. But yours isn't."

"John, I'm not just going to leave you down here. We can help you," I said, hoping to change his mind.

"Just promise me you'll get out of here. Because if you don't, then my death will be for nothing."

In that moment, I knew that no matter what I would or could've said to him, he wasn't coming with me.

My thought was that he was going to stay behind and try to take out as many of the guards as he could before they ultimately killed him. And as much as I didn't like that plan, he was right.

If I were him and had been taken away from the world, injected with some strange alien DNA, brought underground, and caged for ten years, I would probably want some kind of revenge as well. Hell, I was only down there for just over a week, and my thoughts mirrored his to the letter. However, unlike John, I had someone waiting for me.

John placed a hand on my left shoulder before taking a couple more deep breaths and nodding. "No matter what happens to me," he said, "just know that you saved my life."

I could only muster up a faint smile. "Thank you, John," I said.

"Good luck, Wes."

I nodded and immediately took the doctor over to the door. Once we were standing in front of it, I suddenly remembered that I still had no idea what the door code was. And since I knew the doctor wouldn't tell me, I was royally screwed. Or was I?

"Zero six…two two…seven one," I heard John say right before coughing up a lung.

I immediately turned to look at him with a very stunned expression on my face.

"Being down here for as long as I have also gave me plenty of time to listen and pay attention," he said.

I then turned back around and punched the numbers into the keypad. However, as I did, I couldn't help but wonder why that code sounded so familiar. And just as the door opened, that was when it hit me.

0 6 2 2 7 1 weren't just any random numbers that everyone used to unlock the doors in the facility. Both Colonels must've agreed on that code before giving it to everyone. Those numbers represented June 22, 1971, Anna and Eve's birthday. After thinking about it, I was slightly disappointed that I didn't think of it myself.

Once we were out the door, I glanced back inside to get one last look at John, the man who would graciously give his life to save mine, even though we both knew I wasn't going to die no matter what I did.

I looked in and gave him another quick smile and a nod while he did the same. Then I lowered my head and closed the door, leaving him in there to defend my freedom.

As I said before, the time for discourse was officially over. And from here on out, I hated to be in the shoes of anyone who got in my way.

CHAPTER 28

The thought of John risking his own life to save mine didn't quite sit right with me. However, as much as I didn't want to admit it, he was right. If he had tried to come with me in his weakened condition, he would've only slowed us down.

With my arm still wrapped around Harbor, we took a right out of the door and made our way to the hospital room. The prospect of being just a few yards away from Eve made my heart skip a beat. I couldn't wait to go through that door, wake her and Anna up, rescue Eric, and then get the hell out of there. The sooner we did that, the sooner this nightmare would be over.

I punched in the code on the panel located just to the right of the door. After it beeped, the door unlocked. I then pushed it open, headed inside, and closed it behind me. Once we turned around, however, Doctor Blumb, who was already in the process of caring for the girls, was standing there, just staring at me. The pair of guards, who were stationed in the room, were also staring at me.

The moment we all made eye contact, the guards drew their weapons and pointed them at us. That made me grip the gun I had just a little tighter as I kept it firmly pressed to the right side of Harbor's temple.

"Don't even think about it," I said. "You make one wrong move, and she dies."

"Sherri, are you all right?" Doctor Blumb asked.

"It's okay, Mike. I'm fine," she replied.

"If you lay one finger on her, I swear to god I'll—"

"What? Kill me?" I asked before shaking my head. "I don't think so. I already know you need me alive. And I'll just go out on a limb here and say that you're also not allowed to harm me. Am I right?"

"You're certainly not wrong," Blumb said. "But we do have orders to incapacitate you if necessary."

Just then, I heard the elevator doors open from out in the hallway, followed by what sounded like a whole brigade of troops getting off it. In actuality, it was more like a dozen.

"Looks like the cavalry has arrived," I said.

While I kept an eye on everyone in the room, I listened through the door. I heard the guards go from door to door, inspecting everything while ensuring everyone else was okay. Little did they know that they'd be in for a huge surprise.

They first opened the A.M.U. before going inside and doing a clean sweep of the room.

"Clear!" I heard one of the men shout.

They then went over and checked the inside of the hangar where the two ships were located.

"Clear!" he shouted again.

Since they were already on that side of the hallway, they decided to go in and check out the room where Eric was being held.

"Hey, what the hell's going on?" I heard Eric ask.

After hearing his voice, I silently thanked the maker in my head that he was alive. The guards, of course, just ignored him. And once I heard them give the all-clear, they then made their way across the hall and over to the room where John and I were being held.

I could hear them punch in the code, followed by the door beeping and them going inside. However, the moment they all stepped foot over that threshold, all hell had officially broken loose.

I heard gunshots, yelling, and even a few explosions. I couldn't help but wonder if John had also managed to get a hold of the two guards' machine guns, along with the other guard's sidearm. In his weakened condition, however, I doubt he would've managed to get very far.

The fighting went on for a whole minute or so before everything suddenly went quiet. I then heard screams of agony from a few of the guards who had been shot. Either that or the ones left alive were screaming for the ones who were killed. I honestly couldn't tell.

After a couple more seconds, I finally heard someone give the all-clear. And that was when I knew they'd soon be coming for me. Which meant I was now in deep shit. Unless I thought of some way to keep the hospital room door magically locked.

I'd seen it countless times before in many of the movies I watched. Someone would shoot a lock on one side of the door while rendering the whole thing completely inoperable. But with the fifteen or so bullets I had in my gun, taking out two doctors, along with a dozen armed soldiers, was way beyond my skill set. So I decided to take a shot—literally.

I slid myself and the doctor over a few steps to our right before briefly turning around, aiming my gun at the keypad, and pulling the trigger. I turned away as the bullet coursed right through it, causing it to spark like a firecracker. Once the crackling stopped, I turned back to look at it, only to notice it was now destroyed.

When the guards on the other side of the door finally made it over there, I could hear them jamming their fingers on the keypad. As they did, nothing happened—no beeps or sounds. The only way they could get through it was to blow it up, which they could've easily done. But they probably had orders not to risk injuring anyone of importance—namely, me and the girls.

"There," I said. "Now, no one gets in here."

"You're making a big mistake," Blumb said.

"You only wish I was making a mistake."

"What do you want?"

"I want you to wake her up," I said, nodding toward Eve. "Wake both of them up."

"Are you crazy?" Harbor asked. "If he wakes them up, who knows what they'll be able to do?"

"I know what they'll be able to do," I said. "Now, wake…them…up."

I stood there and waited for Blumb to wake the girls, hoping he would take me seriously. But of course, he didn't. He basically just stood there with his thumb up his ass. So I decided to give him a little bit of motivation.

When he didn't comply, I pointed my gun directly at him and held it there for a few seconds before pointing it at one of the guards and shooting him in the leg. The male guard screamed out in pain and dropped to the floor like a brick while holding his right leg just above his kneecap.

"Holy shit!" Blumb screamed. "You shot him!"

"Yeah. And if you don't wake them up, my next shot will be in someone's head," I told him. "Possibly, your own."

His eyes narrowed. "You wouldn't?"

"Wouldn't I?"

Of course, I wasn't about to let him doubt me. So I shifted the gun and pointed it at the female guard before pulling the trigger and shooting her square in the forehead. Her body tumbled backward like a domino before slamming against the concrete floor.

As she lay there, her body suddenly devoid of all life, I just stared at her. I honestly don't know what came over me. I was in total shock at the fact that I'd just killed a living person. I mean, watching someone die at the hands of someone else and making the killing yourself are two completely different things.

Sadness, dread, a rush of excitement, and maybe even a little bit of pride quickly overtook my emotions. It felt pretty damn good to get revenge on someone who willingly went along with hurting people. But actually killing someone, not knowing if they had a family of their own, really hit my emotions hard.

I could only imagine what I would be going through if I found out that my parents or kids had died and that I would never see them again. And that's what hurt. But as much as I wanted to feel bad for them, I couldn't. Because really, they all did this to themselves, not me. The only thing that currently mattered was getting me and my friends the fuck out of there.

After I finished processing my emotions and realizing that it was now kill or be killed, I quickly came to and pointed the gun directly back at Blumb.

"All right! All right!" he said, flashing his palms. "I'll do it. Just don't shoot anyone else."

"Thank you," I said, nodding once. "But before you do, I want you to slide your gun over to me. Then I want you to take the guns off of them"—I motioned to the guards with my head—"and slide them over to me as well."

"Whatever. Just don't shoot anyone else."

Doctor Blumb immediately pulled his gun out of its holster before ducking down and sliding it across the floor toward me. He then made his way over to the guards and grabbed each of their machine guns and sidearms before sliding them over to me one at a time.

With all the guns now sitting in a pile just below my feet, I pushed Doctor Harbor away from me and over to Doctor Blumb, where they embraced with a long hug, followed by a kiss.

"All right, enough of the mushy shit," I said. "Just wake them up."

Blumb and Harbor immediately stopped kissing, gazed lovingly into each other's eyes, and smiled. Then they quickly got to work, waking up the girls.

Blumb went over and took care of Eve, while Harbor took care of Anna, each turning off the girls' IV drips in the process. Then they each took a syringe from one of the tables and injected it into each girl's IV tube. Once they were done, both doctors took a step back.

"Is that it?" I asked. "Nothing's happening."

"You have to give it a second for the medicine to take effect," Harbor said.

So that was what I did. I stood patiently by Eve's side while I waited for her to wake up. And after about four long, grueling seconds, she did.

She started to move before her eyes slowly began to open. I could then see her glance around the room, almost as if she had a hard time deciphering whether or not she was actually awake. After a couple more seconds, she turned to meet my gaze.

"Wes?" she said, still groggy from the medicine.

"I'm here," I said, holding her hand.

"What happened? How long have I been out?"

"They had you under heavy sedation for the past seven days."

"Seven days?" She slowly looked around the room once again. "Where am I?"

"You're in the hospital. We're still in the facility."

"Why can't I move?"

"They have you strapped down like before."

Without saying another word, I saw Eve close her eyes, take a deep breath, and calm herself. At the time, I just thought she was trying to catch her breath or possibly regroup her thoughts. What I wasn't expecting was for her to instantly vanish from the bed before reappearing next to me.

She stumbled a bit from being still slightly out of it. But I caught her before she hit the floor. The shocked expressions on the doctors' faces and the remaining guard pretty much summed up what they'd just witnessed.

"That's one of your abilities?" Blumb whispered, his eyes wide from shock.

Blumb, Harbor, and the remaining guard didn't say another word as they just stood there with their mouths agape. It wasn't until a few moments later that the shock finally wore off.

Blumb shook his head. "Holy shit!" he said, checking back into reality. "What else can you do?"

What else can they do? I couldn't believe the balls on this guy.

"You kept them under heavy sedation and kept me locked up in a cage, yet you have the cajónes to ask what else they can do?" I said, peeved. "I don't think so."

"But that was amazing!" Harbor added. "If we had known that, we would've—"

"What? You would've set us free? Helped us escape?" I shook my head. "You're all out of your fucking minds, do you know that?" I then turned to Eve. "Do you think you can help Anna get out of there?"

She nodded before we walked over to Anna's bed, where Eve reached down to take her hand.

"Eve," Anna said, letting out a sigh of relief. "I thought we'd never get out of here."

"I would never leave you," Eve said.

"Neither would I," I added.

"Wes," Anna said with a smile before perusing the immediate area. "Where's Eric?"

"He's still locked up. But don't worry, we'll get him next."

I then motioned to Eve, giving her the go-ahead, before stepping back a bit. As soon as I did, both Anna and Eve closed their eyes and took a deep breath. In a flash, they instantly disappeared before reappearing directly next to me. I was ready for it this time and immediately caught a weak, stumbling Anna before she hit the floor.

"Thanks," she said.

I nodded. "Now, let's go get Eric and get the hell out of here."

"What about them?" Eve asked, thumbing toward the doctors and the guard.

"They sedated you two and locked us up in cages," I said. "They die with everyone else. But kill the guard first, just so they know what to expect."

Almost immediately, the quirky, expressive girl I once knew completely disappeared right before my very eyes and was replaced with pure evil. The expression on Eve's face quickly went from happy to unbridled rage in less than a second. And knowing what the full extent of her abilities entailed, I won't lie. It scared me—a lot.

With a raging fire now burning in her eyes, she slowly turned to face the doctors and the guard. But before anyone had a chance to take another breath, Eve took action.

I saw the male guard get lifted off the ground and hurled against the back wall like a rag doll. Once his body hit with a thud, Eve just held him there in mid-air as she stared him down and thought about what to do with him next. Thankfully, it didn't take her long to decide.

The male guard's body stiffened suddenly, as if it were a piece of wood. Then horror besieged both doctors' ears and eyes as they heard what sounded like breaking tree limbs. Both of the guard's legs immediately snapped like twigs in the complete opposite direction of each other, causing him to scream out in agony as his body suddenly looked like an upside-down capital letter *T*. But because he was suspended in mid-air, he couldn't do a damn thing about it.

Eve held him there for just a few seconds more while she continued to watch him like some maniacal overlord who loved watching their victims get tortured. Then once she was done, she let go, and the guard immediately fell hard to the floor. But Eve wasn't done.

With the guard screaming out in pain, he tried to lift himself up with his arms. And when he lifted his head to look over at us, that was it. Just like a dark lord of the Sith, Eve stuck out her right hand and turned it clockwise, snapping the guard's neck, causing his lifeless body to instantly fall to the floor.

"What the hell did you do?" Harbor asked, shocked by what she had just witnessed. "That was completely unnecessary!"

"At least he won't be bothering us again. Now," Eve said, focusing her gaze on the two doctors, "what to do with you?"

Both doctors, frightened beyond belief, ran toward each other and embraced.

"Please, don't hurt us," Harbor begged.

"Oh, don't worry," Eve said. "I'm not going to hurt you."

"You're not?"

"Of course not. I'm going to kill you."

"Kill us? Why?" Blumb asked.

"Well, let's see…you sedated us, caged us, treated us like prisoners and lab rats…would you like me to continue?"

"We were just following orders," Harbor said. "We're sorry."

"*Now* you're sorry?" I asked. "I think it's a little late for that."

"Look, you can't just kill us, all right?"

"Unless you give me one good reason why, I'm not helping you," Eve said.

Harbor opened her mouth and looked like she wanted to tell us something, but couldn't. For whatever reason, she was struggling to get it out. I had a pretty good feeling it was something important. Either that or it was something she was trying to keep secret. Who knows? But by that point, we were becoming very impatient.

"I'm waiting," Eve said, not wanting to wait for an explanation.

And that was when Doctor Harbor decided it was finally time to drop a bomb on us all.

She turned to Doctor Blumb and smiled. "I'm pregnant," she said.

Well, holy shit. Talk about life throwing you a curveball.

"You're pregnant?" Blumb asked, the anticipation on his face growing by the second. Harbor nodded. "That's wonderful!"

Blumb then pulled Harbor in and squeezed her tightly, not wanting to let go.

As the two doctors embraced, I could see the tears of joy and excitement streaming down their faces. That was when I turned to Eve and placed a hand on her shoulder, hoping she wouldn't do anything rash. However, her mind was already made up.

After hearing what Harbor had just told us, I could see the rage on Eve's face swiftly dissipate as she suddenly had no intention whatsoever of hurting them.

"Congratulations," Eve quietly said.

"You're not going to hurt us, are you?" Harbor asked.

Eve shook her head. "No."

Both doctors let out a massive sigh of relief.

"Thank you," Blumb said. "And we're truly, very sorry for what we did to you."

Somehow, after hearing his apology, deep down in my gut, I believed him.

"Just do me a favor," I began to say. "When this is all over, promise me you'll find different jobs?"

"You don't have to worry about that. You have our word," Blumb replied.

"If we get you out to the elevator, will you two be okay to leave?" Eve asked. They nodded. "Good. Now, come over here and hold on to my shoulder."

Without hesitation, both doctors came over and stood behind Eve, each grabbing onto a different shoulder. I took one of Eve's hands while Anna held the other. Then, after a quick breath, all five of us disappeared from the hospital, instantly vanishing into thin air.

———

We all reappeared directly in front of the elevator. Once I finished reorienting myself, I looked to the right and stared at the door to the room where I was being held. I so desperately wanted to head over there to check if John was okay. However, before any of us had any time to react, we noticed that the guards John didn't kill were standing there, just staring at us.

Once they all got over the shock of seeing us appear out of thin air, they quickly raised their guns and pointed them at us.

"Don't move!" one of them said.

I instantly recognized that voice as the same one I heard while the guards went from room to room just a few minutes ago.

"One false move, and we'll shoot you where you stand!" the guard said, stepping forward. That was when he noticed the two doctors standing behind us. "Doctor Blumb, Doctor Harbor, are you okay?"

They both nodded. "We're fine," Blumb said.

"Good. Now, if you two will step out from behind them and walk toward us, we can take care of them," the man said.

"I assure you, we're in no danger," Harbor said.

"Please, just slowly make your way over to us so we can proceed. You don't know how dangerous they—"

But before the man could finish what he was saying, he and all the other remaining guards were instantly frozen in place like stone statues. All the barrels on their guns slowly started to bend and form a U-shape, ultimately rendering them useless. Blumb and Harbor were both stunned and intrigued by what they were witnessing. However, their looks of intrigue quickly turned to panic as we all could feel the ground start to quake beneath us.

"What the hell's going on?" Blumb asked.

The wall behind the guards—the same one that separated the hallway from the hospital room—started to shake. A crack began to form on both sides, beginning where the wall met the floor and ending in the middle, just above the door. The wall then split and emerged, lifting to sit flat directly over the guards' heads. And before anyone had time to blink, it came crashing down to the ground, crushing and killing everyone underneath it. We all took a moment to shield our eyes and mouths from the dust and silt that came hurtling toward us.

"I guess that takes care of that," I said while coughing and waving my hands in front of my face.

Doctor Blumb also coughed. "You killed them," he said, shocked about what had just happened.

"It was either them or us."

"But you didn't have to kill them."

"I don't have to remind you about—"

"What he meant to say was," Harbor said, swiftly interrupting me, "thank you for not hurting us."

"Just make sure that baby grows up and doesn't repeat your mistakes," I told them.

"Don't worry, we will."

They both smiled awkwardly at us before turning around and pushing the button to call the elevator. Luckily, the doors opened immediately, as it was still sitting there and hadn't left.

Both doctors got on and stood there, hugging each other, while Doctor Blumb pushed the button for the top floor. They both faintly smiled at us, and I returned the gesture by nodding and smiling back.

"Good luck," I said.

"Thank you," Harbor said. "And we are forever in your debt."

Then, before anyone could get out another word, we all watched as they both disappeared behind the closing doors.

I won't lie. Letting the doctors go made me a little sick to my stomach. If it weren't for the fact that Doctor Harbor was pregnant, we definitely would've killed them. However, killing an unborn child was just not in the cards for us. I mean, yes, we wanted to kill everyone down there and watch that place burn in the process, but the child that was growing inside of her had nothing to do with it. At that point, it was just an innocent life waiting to start its journey. Besides, we're not total monsters.

"Well then, now that they're gone, can someone please shut off that fucking alarm?" I asked, utterly annoyed by the noise.

Eve quickly scanned the hall before finding the source of the noise. Once she located the speaker, and without hesitation, she used her abilities to rip that sucker right off the wall.

"Thank you," I said. She smiled and gave me a quick peck on the lips. "Now"—I turned to face the door on the far left—"let's go rescue Eric."

CHAPTER 29

All three of us quickly made our way over toward the door on the far left. As we did, we practically had to play a game of hopscotch to make it over some of the fallen wall debris, along with a few miscellaneous body parts.

When we got over there, I punched in 0 6 2 2 7 1 on the keypad before hearing the door unlock. I then put my hands on the door and slowly pushed it open, erring on the side of caution. The moment we all walked inside, Eric immediately stood up and was suddenly like a dog, happy to see its owner come home after being away all day.

"Holy shit! Am I glad to see you guys!" he said.

"Come on now. You didn't really think we'd leave without you," I said.

He didn't reply to me. Instead, he turned his gaze to Anna.

"Anna!" he said, a smile gracing his face.

Anna immediately ran up to the cage to hug him. Well, as much of a hug as they could do with the bars between them.

"I thought I would never see you again," she said.

"You can't get rid of me that easily," he replied. "Now, can someone please get me out of here?"

Eve quickly walked over to the cage and extended her right hand out toward him.

"Take my hand," she said.

Eric happily obliged while Anna and I stepped back, allowing Eve to free him from his prison. Eve then closed her eyes and took a deep breath as the two of them vanished into thin air right before our very eyes.

Almost instantly, they both reappeared directly next to us. Once they were able to reorient themselves, Eric embraced Anna with a hug, followed by a kiss.

I groaned. "Get a room, will you?"

Upon hearing my comment, they both stopped and turned to glare at me. But they knew I was joking. Eric flashed me a grin before hugging me as well.

"Just so you know, I'm not kissing you," I said.

"That's okay," he replied. "I heard you're a terrible kisser."

We broke apart, and I smiled at him.

"Plus, you smell like shit," he added, waving his hand in front of his face.

"You're one to talk," I told him, making the same motion.

"Guys," Eve said, shifting her gaze between the two of us, "you both smell like shit."

"I couldn't agree more," Anna said.

"Yeah, well, not all of us had the luxury of receiving a daily sponge bath," I said.

Then it went silent. None of us said another word as we just stood there, smiling at one another.

It felt amazing to be back together again. However, our joy would be short-lived, as we still had to get out of there alive and in one piece.

"Let's blow this popsicle stand," I said.

Cheesy, I know. But hey, it was the '80s.

We all wasted no time leaving that room and making our way back out into the hall. Eric, Anna, and Eve all immediately started heading toward the elevator. But I didn't go with them. Instead, I made my way across the hall and over to the room where I was being held. Since the door was left open—correction—since it had been blown completely off its hinges, I could walk right inside.

There was a tiny part of me that was curious to know if John had survived. After all, he stayed behind, so I would have plenty of time to leave. At the time, I knew that what he was saying was all bullshit. It wasn't just about him saving my ass. He wanted to get some revenge of his own and take out as many of them as he could before going down himself. It was basically his own suicide run.

I walked through the door and looked inside, only to see that the room looked like a battlefield. Pieces of the cages were blown apart and scattered across the floor. The two guards John killed were still lying there, along with a slew of other dead guards, most of whom were missing a few limbs—probably due to the explosions I heard.

I scanned the room as best as I could, trying to find any evidence of what had happened to John. Unfortunately, I couldn't find him. And because of that, a couple of theories about what actually happened suddenly crept into my head.

My first thought was that he managed to kill some of the guards before miraculously escaping. My second thought was that if he didn't escape, it was his body I was looking at splattered all over the far wall. I didn't even want to think about it.

So with John gone, or perhaps turned into a wall painting, I left the room to join everyone back over by the elevator.

"Where'd you go?" Eric asked.

"I had to check up on someone," I said.

"And?"

I shrugged and shook my head. "He's gone."

"Sorry about that, buddy."

"Don't worry about it."

I paused for a moment and took one last look toward the door to remember John and what he did for me before turning back to my friends.

"Now, let's get the hell out of here," I said.

Eric nodded and pushed the button to call the elevator back down to our floor. While we waited for it to come, however, a thought had quietly slithered its way into my mind.

If we were about to leave and never come back, I didn't want anyone else to go through the same kind of torture we recently went through. No one should ever have to suffer or fall victim to life as a lab rat.

"Hold on a second," I said while walking away from them.

"Where are you going?" Eric asked.

Without saying a word, I walked straight over to the room where I was being held and grabbed as many grenades off the dead guards' vests as I could possibly carry, which wasn't many because I could only find three. Then I walked back out into the hallway and over toward the elevator.

"What the hell are you doing?" Eric asked. "We don't have time to fuck around. We've got to get out of here."

"I know that. But I don't want anyone else to go through what we just went through," I said. "Also, living out your life in a cage for something you didn't even do"—I shook my head while looking plenty disgusted—"never again."

"Okay? So then, what's your plan?"

"Since I only have three grenades," I began, "we'll have to do this methodically." I handed Eve and Eric one grenade each while I kept the third. "You two are going to open the doors to the hangar and the A.M.U." I then turned to face Anna. "And I want you to hold our ride. Once those elevator doors open, we'll pull the pins on our grenades, chuck them inside, and haul our asses back here. Then we all get the fuck out of here. Before we become barbecue, that is."

"But that'll destroy everything," Eric said.

"That's the idea."

Eric paused to think about what he was going to say. And although I already knew what his answer would be, he still decided to be dramatic about it.

"Will you just say yes already?" I said.

"You don't have to be so pushy about it," he said. "Of course, I'm in."

"And you already know how we feel about all of this," Eve said.

Anna nodded in agreement.

I smiled. "Let's go blow some shit up."

While Anna waited for the elevator to arrive, the three of us went over and opened our assigned doors. Eve took the hangar, Eric took the A.M.U., and I wound up taking the big hole in the wall leading to the hospital.

For the next few seconds, we all stood patiently outside our respective doors (and holes), grenades in hand, as we waited for the elevator to arrive. And once it finally did, we all took simultaneous action.

With the grenade nestled in my right hand, I used my left hand to pull the pin out before hurling it into the hospital. Eric then launched his grenade before closing the door to the A.M.U. Eve also did the same before closing the hangar door.

After all our grenades were tossed, the four of us hauled ass into the elevator, where I wasted no time pushing the button for level *A*. Once its doors closed, we immediately started our quick ascent back up to the surface. And not a moment too soon, either.

As the elevator rocketed to the top of the facility, almost at warp speed, I suddenly felt like I was riding in one of the turbo lifts aboard the USS *Enterprise*. Or at least, that was what I hoped it would feel like. I only thought about that to take my mind off the explosions I was suddenly hearing coming from where we just were.

Apparently, tossing grenades into a hangar containing two spaceships, each equipped with a power source comparable to one small nuclear warhead, was not the best of ideas. The explosions wound up weakening the rest of the floors above it, ultimately causing them to slowly collapse in succession.

On the way up, as we passed each level, we could still hear the explosions happening below. But the farther up we went, the more we realized the explosions weren't just happening on the bottom level. The explosions that suddenly sounded pretty damn close to us were happening on each subsequent level above it. It was now a race to the top between us and the collapsing floors. Who would win? Who would get there first? Since I'm the one telling this story, obviously, it was us.

———————

We managed to arrive on the top level without stopping at any of the other floors. We mainly had Eve to thank for that. She used her abilities in the elevator to keep it from stopping. That enabled us to bypass each additional level, giving us a one-way ticket to the top. And I don't even want to think about what happened to the personnel on the floors we passed.

The second those elevator doors opened, we all sprinted out of there like Olympic runners taking off after hearing someone fire the starter pistol at the beginning of a race. And because the rest of the facility was collapsing, the top floor was where most of the chaos was happening. (Figuratively speaking, of course.)

We all ran straight down the hallway, with me leading the charge. We passed many rooms on the left and right-hand sides, all of which were open and vacant. Most of the guards up there didn't pay much attention to us because they were all too busy running for their own lives. But the ones who actually did try to stop us just wound up getting tossed against one of the hallway walls by Eve.

Halfway down the hall, we took a right and ran past the room where I had been held and questioned when we had first arrived. As we went by, I briefly looked inside, only to see that it was vacant as well.

Now, if you recall, when we were first brought there, all four of us had been sedated. So none of us knew where the exit was. I only took us in that direction because that was the only part of the facility we hadn't seen yet, which meant that the exit had to be around one of those corners.

At the end of the hall, we could either go left or we could go right. We opted to go right because at the very end, about fifty yards away, nestled comfortably above the farthest door, was a glowing, red exit sign. We could quickly run down there, go through the door, and be done with this whole ordeal before any of us would even have a chance to sneeze. But as our luck would have it, none of us would be breaking out the tissues just yet.

We were literally about ten feet from stepping through the door when we heard a very familiar voice ring out from behind us.

"Hold it right there!" the voice shouted.

All four of us stopped dead in our tracks before turning around to see who it was. When we did (and to no one's surprise, I'm sure), we saw both Colonels, along with a couple dozen guards, all standing there with their guns drawn and pointed at us.

"You're not going anywhere," Colonel Parker said. "No one is leaving this facility."

I laughed. "And who's going to stop us, you?"

"If we have to," Colonel James answered.

Eric laughed as well. "I'd like to see you try."

"If you two had just minded your own damn business when we told you to, none of this would've happened," Colonel Parker said.

"If we had minded our own damn business," I said, "then we wouldn't have found out what sick and maniacal things you people were doing down here."

"Why did you do it?" Eve asked.

"As I said, we were under strict orders," Colonel Parker answered.

"From who?"

"That is not your concern."

Just then, we all felt a rumble beneath our feet. Most likely, the collapsing floors below ours creeping ever closer upward. And if that was the case, then we needed to leave, or we'd be the ones falling to our deaths.

"This whole place is coming down, Colonel," I said. "We need to get out of here now!"

"Daddy, if you really love us," Eve said, "then you'll let us go."

"If we really loved you," Colonel Parker said, "then we wouldn't have injected you with the alien DNA in the first place."

After hearing Colonel Parker's response, I couldn't help but want to charge toward them and snap both of their necks myself. The fact that he would even say that told me something about them I pretty much already knew. They never really loved those girls at all. They were nothing more to them than orders handed down by their superiors.

I turned to look at Anna, whose face slowly changed into a rosy color before she started to cry. Eve did the exact same thing. Luckily, Eric and I were there to comfort them in our arms.

"As you can see, none of you are leaving," Colonel James said.

He turned his head quickly to his right before turning it briefly to his left. After checking to make sure that the guards were ready, he bent his right elbow, pulling his hand up to the side of his head. And as quickly as he brought it up, he brought it down just as fast, motioning toward us. That was their cue to come and take us into custody. But before anyone could take a single step, Eve broke from me and acted.

With Eve standing to my left and her face still red from crying, she immediately stared down the couple dozen guards that stood on either side of and behind the Colonels, freezing them in place. Then what came next was like something straight out of a horror film.

In unison, I saw two dozen heads twist to the side. I also heard two dozen necks snap like tree branches before watching all the guards collapse dead onto the floor. Both Colonels looked around at the dead bodies in horror as they just stood there, shocked by what Eve had managed to accomplish.

"You just killed two dozen soldiers!" Colonel James said.

"It wouldn't be the first time," Eve replied. "How do you think we got up here?"

Of course, she was referring to the guards who were crushed underneath the hospital wall on the bottom level, not to mention the damage we caused to the rest of the facility by blowing it up.

"Let's try this again," I said. "Let us leave, or you will die."

The Colonels almost looked as if they weren't sure how to proceed. But after just a few short seconds of deliberation…

"Judging by what we just witnessed," Colonel Parker said, "it appears that you are an even bigger threat than we initially thought. And for that, we cannot allow you to leave."

Then, before any of us had any time to react, it happened.

Both Colonels immediately pulled out their sidearms and proceeded to unload them on us. Eric quickly ducked down with Anna and covered their heads with his arms, hoping to become a human shield. (It's not like doing that would really stop a barrage of incoming bullets anyway.)

Of course, I tried to make my way over to Eve to do the same thing. I threw myself in front of her and closed my eyes as I waited for the bullets to pierce through my skin and kill me instantly. But instead, nothing happened. It got silent.

When I opened my eyes and turned around, I saw the Colonels, the bullets, and the collapsing facility, all frozen in time. My jaw crashed through the floor, and my eyes shot open like window blinds as I just stared in amazement.

It was almost as if someone paused an action movie right in the middle of a massive battle scene. I could see each bullet, just frozen there in mid-air. It looked like the Colonels had suddenly been turned into porcelain figures, placed in their respective spots to complete a scene in some lifelike diorama. As for Eve, she was already busy using that ability to her advantage.

The three of us looked on in curiosity as she went over to each and every bullet, grab hold of them in mid-air, and turn them all around. Instead of all the bullets facing us, they were now facing the two Colonels. Once Eve was done, she quickly made her way back over to us.

"You might want to hit the floor," she said, motioning for us to drop flat onto the ground.

By that point, I had a pretty good idea about what she was trying to do. And even though Eve hadn't tried it yet, manipulating the laws of physics was one of the aliens' abilities. She hoped to focus on the still bullets and send them back toward the Colonels once time had unfrozen. Regardless, we all flattened ourselves like pancakes, just in case it didn't work.

Now, I know what you're probably thinking. You're thinking, *If the aliens can manipulate the laws of physics, couldn't they just shoot the bullets back at them without turning them around?* Well, the short answer to that is no.

The aliens could only manipulate an object's trajectory by facing it in the opposite direction of its travel. If they didn't do that first, then it wouldn't work. Stupid, I know. But it was all right there in the texts.

And before you decide to yell at me about how lame that is, don't. Yell at the aliens. They're the ones who had these stupid abilities in the first place.

Anyway, after I got to a count of sixteen, even though it was supposed to be twenty (remember, I spent about four seconds standing in front of Eve with my eyes closed), time around us suddenly resumed, and all the bullets hit their marks.

As we all lay flat on the floor, our eyes widened in shock. Both pairs of the Colonels' eyes were also wide, as they appeared to be in shock as well. But for them, it was a different kind of shock, almost as if they'd just seen a ghost. However, it didn't take long for them to look down and notice the little blotches of blood now soaking their uniforms.

Holy shit! I thought. *I can't believe that actually worked!*

All the bullets that were fired pierced through the Colonels' bodies like paper. After they noticed their wounds, they immediately dropped their guns to the floor before looking back up at the four of us. Then they both fell to their knees before collapsing onto their backs. The three of us then got up off the floor and ran over to get a closer look.

"Holy shit!" I said while staring down at their blood-soaked uniforms.

"Eve, I'm sorry," Colonel Parker said.

"You're sorry?" Eve asked, surprised by his apology. "You've been lying to me, to us, our whole lives. Sorry doesn't even begin to cut it."

"I know it probably doesn't mean much, but I'm also sorry," Colonel James told Anna. "We should never have injected you or anyone else with the DNA. Our orders—"

"Your orders?" Anna interrupted him, looking thoroughly pissed off. "Fuck your orders! I'm a human being, not some lab rat. If you had any shred of human decency, you would've known better." She closed her eyes, took a deep breath, and lowered her head. "Having us locked up down there the way you did, not to mention sedating us for seven whole days"—she shook her head before lifting it to look her father in the eyes—"I'm now convinced that neither one of you ever had a soul, to begin with."

"That's not true," Colonel James said while coughing up blood. "I do love you, Anna."

"He's not lying. We really do love you girls," Colonel Parker added.

Eve scoffed. "You really expect us to believe that, don't you? I mean, I can't speak for Anna, but at this point," she said, shaking her head, "I don't even consider you *ever* having been my father."

"The same goes for me," Anna added.

In that brief moment, I could tell that utter disappointment and some emotional wreckage hung over Anna and Eve's heads.

Those two men, who were supposed to have been their fathers, weren't. And neither one of the girls made those last statements because they didn't love them, far from it. They did love their fathers. And even though the Colonels may not have loved them back, the girls only said that to purposely twist the proverbial knife as deep as it could possibly go.

"Eve…I…" Colonel Parker called out.

In his last moment of desperation, he raised his right hand, hoping Eve would take it. But she never did. And about one second later, Colonel Parker's arm fell to the floor as he succumbed to his fatal injuries. He was now dead.

Colonel James saw it all happen and just shook his head before letting out a saddened sigh. Unfortunately, he didn't have much time to mourn his friend because he knew he would soon be joining him. And that was when he quickly refocused his attention back on Anna.

"My sweet girl," he said before coughing up some more blood.

Anna shook her head. "No. I was never your sweet girl," she said. "I see that now. Apparently, the only thing I was to you was just some bogus science experiment that you agreed to keep watch over."

"You're right. And I regret all of it. Again, I'm sorry."

Trying to ignore the Colonel's apology, Anna briefly closed her eyes and took a couple of deep breaths. And once he was ultimately out of her head, she reopened them.

Now wheezing and breathing hard to try to stay alive, the Colonel didn't say another word. He didn't have to. He knew that his time was up. And so did Anna. Knowing that he was about to die, she met his gaze for the final time.

"Goodbye…*Colonel*," she said.

And then, he was dead. The only thing that the girls could do was hug and comfort each other.

Now, I can't really speak for Eric, but I was in complete and utter shock over what I heard both of them say. I mean, to live your whole life with someone and know them as nothing more than your parents, only to turn around at the last possible moment and tell them they weren't, was probably one of the biggest *Temple of Doom* moments that anyone could've ever done.

Confused? Here, let me explain…

In a span of less than a few seconds, both girls basically reached into their fathers' chests, ripped out both of their hearts, and held them up in front of their faces to show them how black and rotted they were.

Those two men, lying dead on the ground, were supposed to be their fathers, parents, mentors, and people they could've both looked up to or come to when they needed to have a question answered. Instead, they both turned out to be nothing more than just two regular men working a high-end government babysitting job for the last eighteen years. To put it simply, their fathers were nothing more than a couple of frauds.

As much as we both wanted to stay there and let them mourn, we knew we couldn't. With the floors underneath us still collapsing faster than the Empire of China, we had to quickly haul our asses out of there before our own bodies became a permanent fixture amongst the debris.

"Come on," I said softly, touching Eve's shoulder. "We have to go."

Eric followed suit by placing a hand on one of Anna's shoulders. "He's right," he said. "If we stay any longer, then we're pancakes."

Knowing we were right, the girls immediately stood up. They then took our hands, and all four of us quickly made our way down the hall toward the exit. Once we reached the door, I wasted no time and immediately punched in the six-digit code. After it beeped, the door unlocked, and I pushed it open.

But just before we went through, Anna and Eve turned around to get one last look at their fathers' bodies. Unfortunately, their final memory of them (aside from knowing that they were lying bastards) would involve seeing both of the Colonels' bodies, along with the other dead guards, fall through the collapsing floor and disappear out of view.

We hightailed it up the twenty or so stairs before I punched in the last code I would ever need to use in that godforsaken place. Once the door unlocked, we pushed it open and went through.

Standing in the open air with the hot sun beating down on our faces, we were relieved to have finally made it out. We also had to shield our eyes because none of us had seen daylight in over a week and a half. However, we had very little time to waste, as we needed to get as far away from that place as quickly as possible.

"Take my hand," Eve said to me before turning to face Eric and Anna. "You two each take a shoulder."

Anna immediately grabbed Eve's right shoulder while Eric grabbed her left. After Eve took one more quick glance at the three of us, I nodded. None of us had barely enough time to blink because no sooner did my head move, all four of us instantly vanished without a trace.

We all reappeared about a half-mile away and stood atop a small foothill. It wasn't until we were standing in that very spot that we could see everything.

Off in the distance, we could see the smoking, crumbling facility we had just escaped from. We could also see an even larger facility located directly to its right. Along with those two installations, a runway and what looked like a massive dried-up lake were the only other things out there.

"Holy shit," I said, not believing what I was looking at. "That's not what I think it is, is it?"

"No way, dude," Eric said while shaking his head and having almost the exact same reaction as me. "That's impossible. It doesn't even exist."

"Then what the hell am I looking at?"

"I have no fucking idea."

Still in disbelief, we all just stood there for a moment, staring at the ghostly military base.

Until that point, we had only heard about it briefly on the news and had only seen it depicted in movies. But to actually stand there and see it in person while looking at it from afar was definitely an indescribable experience. And even though we still had our doubts about what that place was, our theories would eventually come to fruition. Just not yet.

After taking a second to soak it all in, Eve turned to look at me. "Wes, I'm so sorry you got dragged into all of this," she said, her eyes tearing up again.

"It's not your fault," I said. "You didn't know any of this was going to happen."

"I know. But I still feel responsible."

I pulled her in for a consoling hug. "You know what? If I had the chance to go back and do it all over again, I wouldn't change a single thing."

After hearing my remark, Eve lifted her head, met my gaze, and smiled before burying her face back into my chest.

"What about you?" Anna asked Eric. "Would you do anything differently?"

Eric briefly looked over at me and smirked before turning back and looking Anna in the eyes.

"No way," he said. "I'd still be right here standing next to you."

"Good answer."

She smiled and gave Eric a quick peck on the lips before leaning in and hugging him.

After a few seconds, we all broke apart and just stood there, looking out over the lifeless, wide-open, vast desert landscape. My arm was wrapped around Eve, and hers around the middle of my back. Eric and Anna were also standing the same way. I then looked down at Eve and smiled as she returned the sentiment.

As I stood there, getting lost in her vision, I couldn't help but think to myself how lucky I was to have met her. Half alien or not, I could've given two shits about that or her abilities. At that very moment, I was just happy to be with her. I also knew that pretty soon the summer would be over, and both of us would be going away to college. Actually, all four of us would be going away to college. And that scared me.

It didn't scare me because we would all be in different states at different schools. It scared me because even though Eve and I were supposed to be soulmates, I knew that long-distance relationships hardly ever worked out. I mean, what if she met someone else while she was gone? Hell, what if I met someone else and we never saw each other again? That last thought, I think, scared me the most.

But I couldn't think about that now. Because the reality of it was, we still had the rest of the summer to be with each other and do whatever the hell we wanted. And no matter what would happen to us over the next couple of months, or even after we all split up and went our separate ways, one thing was definitely sure.

All our future adventures, including going to college, getting married, having kids, growing old, and even dying, would *never* compare to, or even come remotely close to, the incredible adventure we all had during that epic summer—the summer of '89.

EPILOGUE

After spending just about a week and a half in the underground alien experimentation facility, the first thing we did was hitchhike back to the Flat Rock Inn. I know. It wasn't very smart of us. I mean, we could've had Eve transport us short distances at a time, but we didn't want anyone to notice what we were doing. (For obvious reasons, of course.) Plus, our vehicles were still in the parking lot, and we desperately needed showers. Well, mainly just Eric and me.

After we were all the cleanest we'd ever been, we finally returned home to our parents. Eric took Anna back to his house while I took Eve back to mine. There wasn't a chance in hell we would even think about bringing them back to their mothers. But don't worry, you'll find out why shortly.

Once we'd arrived home, we soon found out that neither of the Colonels had held up their end of the bargain by contacting our folks. (Surprise, surprise.) Plus, we weren't too shocked when our parents told us that they reported us missing and sent out a search party to find us. Needless to say, they were super pissed. Which meant we needed to come up with one hell of an excuse.

As far as Eric and I went, we got away with telling them that we went on some epic road trip over on the California coast.

According to our story, we visited Los Angeles, Hollywood, Santa Monica, and Long Beach, all in an effort to meet some famous actors or musicians. Of course, we failed miserably. And the best part was, they totally bought it.

To quote my father, after we told him all about it, he said, "So you boys decided to take a little road trip and party before going off to college, huh? Good for you. But don't forget, the party doesn't have to stop there." Eric's dad also said something similar to him. Our mothers, on the other hand, carried a completely different tune.

They were worried sick that something might have happened to us while we were gone. They thought that we might have gotten shot or kidnapped or something. Honestly, though, I don't blame them. After all, it was the end of a decade notoriously known for its sex, drugs, and rock and roll.

As for Anna and Eve, we accompanied them home to help them deal with their own parents. More specifically, their "mothers."

They each returned to houses infested with members of various branches of the U.S. military. As it turned out, their "mothers" knew about everything. (Again, surprise, surprise.) And because of what had happened, they were immediately discharged from their "service of caring for the girls" and were taken away. After that, none of us ever saw them again.

Both of their houses were also sold at auction, along with all the items inside, minus the contents of the girls' rooms, of course. And since their whole lives basically resided within them, they were allowed to keep anything they wanted.

Except for the few knick-knacks, posters, and clothes they decided to keep, the rest was either sold or thrown out. I mean, if you were lied to your whole life, would you want to keep anything from it? Yeah, me, either.

Until their living arrangements got settled, Eve was allowed to stay at my house, while Anna was allowed to stay at Eric's. Of course, since we were teenagers and all, we had to follow a few ground rules while they were there.

They ranged anywhere from not sleeping in the same bed or in the same room, all the way up to not drinking alcohol and having sex. Regardless of all the rules, however, we still snuck around as much as possible.

———

Eric and I spent the rest of our summer finally going to the movies and watching all the films we had initially intended to see in the first place. However, our plans had changed slightly as we didn't have to watch them alone. Instead of going by ourselves, we saw them with the girls.

By the end of the summer, all four of us were packed and ready to head off to college. I attended Florida State, while Anna and Eve attended Princeton in New Jersey. Eric was the lucky bastard who didn't have to live in a dorm and got to commute from his house to the University of Nevada, Las Vegas. I flew back and forth between New Jersey and Florida to visit Eve during our holiday breaks. Over the summers, we all just wound up flying back home.

And speaking of college, as you already know, I wound up getting a full ride, while Eric did not. But about two weeks before we were all slated to leave, Eric's parents received a letter in the mail saying that his tuition had been fully paid. After reading the letter, they were very curious about where the money came from and who gave it to them.

As it turned out, after we destroyed the underground facility and escaped, the government decided to pay us all off to keep us quiet. Knowing what the girls were capable of and how much damage they could do, the top brass simply didn't want anything to do with us. However, I will admit that the mysterious money donor they used was pure genius.

Eric's and my parents received letters in the mail from some bogus lottery office. And even though they were completely fooled, we both had a pretty good idea about where the money *actually* came from.

The government deposited a cool ten million dollars into our parents' bank accounts. I'll tell you, when they checked to make sure everything was 100% legit, both of our mothers almost had coronaries. Since the girls didn't have any parents left, they got their news from a very unexpected source. As it turned out, we weren't the only ones who were offered a shitload of hush money.

Shortly after our parents were informed, Anna and Eve were contacted by Michael Blumb and Sherri Harbor, the two doctors who kept them sedated in the hospital room on the facility's bottom level. They were tasked with telling each of the girls that they would also be compensated for their troubles. But that wasn't all. Along with their own hush money, Blumb and Harbor also requested one additional thing.

After what they did to the girls and after we graciously let them go, they figured they owed them. So they requested to be given the files of Anna and Eve's birth parents, along with their last known locations. And when the girls received them, they were in complete and total shock. Also, with that one little gesture, we were all finally able to forgive Blumb and Harbor for what they did to us—to a point.

Along with the girls' parents' location, they also shared something else with us. They answered a few of the questions that had been burning holes in my brain ever since I was thrown in the cage.

According to what they remembered, everyone who had been experimented on was no one special. They weren't criminals, or thieves, or even people they just wanted to keep quiet. Everyone who was experimented on down there was just random folks who were kidnapped and taken off the street. Some were bankers, some were students, and some were even members of their own military. They were just regular people, ripped from their everyday lives purely for the joy of science.

Once we learned *that* little fact, I suddenly didn't feel too bad about what we did to those people down there. They deserved everything we gave them. Unfortunately, I just wish we had taken a different path. Because the deaths of all those whom we killed still haunt me. As for Blumb and Harbor (now Mr. and Mrs. Blumb), we still keep in touch with them and their two kids to this very day.

———

After their first year of college, the girls finally set out to find their birth parents. They chose not to do it before they started school because seeing them would've been way too much for them to handle with everything else going on. Plus, they didn't want to get too distracted with the first few days of school.

Eve tracked her birth mother to San Francisco, where she lived with her husband and two kids. Eve's birth father died shortly after she was born. After he found out that Eve had been given up, he went berserk and committed suicide.

Anna wound up tracking her birth parents down to Houston, Texas, where they lived along with their one son. Apparently, after they made the mutual decision to give her up, they ultimately stayed together and wound up getting married sometime later.

Over the years, Anna and Eve kept in touch with their birth parents, but not before explaining that they needed nothing from them and that their relationship would be strictly based on friendship. And even though the girls told them that their bank accounts were loaded, their parents never once asked them for anything in return.

———

As it turned out, the underground facility we utterly annihilated was all part of a larger secret military installation. And although none of us were ever told where or what it officially was, we had a pretty good idea.

It wasn't until later that year that a gentleman named Bob Lazar came forward and told the media that he had worked with alien spacecraft at an underground installation called Sector Four, located inside the Papoose Mountain range. He had also mentioned that Sector Four was a secret project spearheaded by (get ready to have your minds blown) Area 51! Big surprise, I know.

———————

Anyway, Eric's mother is still alive and well and currently lives in a nursing home on the outskirts of Las Vegas. His father, unfortunately, died about ten years ago.

After college, Eric married Anna and had two kids: a daughter and a son, who were just two years apart. Currently, they all live in Astoria, Oregon, and love it.

Now, he's told me many times throughout the years that it's merely a "quaint little town with a great atmosphere." However, even though he'd never mentioned it, Anna, Eve, and I aren't stupid and know the real reason why he moved there—two words—*The Goonies.*

As for me, well, both of my parents died a few years back. My dad went first, and then my mom just a couple of months later. But before they left us, they got to spend many, many years together with their two grandkids, who are now both adults themselves.

My wife and I currently live in Bar Harbor, a quiet island in Maine that boasts many visitors each year. The winters are a little hellish, but the summers make up for it by having about five million different ice cream shops open for business.

I became an author shortly after moving here and do all my writing in my second-floor study. Since we live pretty much in the middle of nowhere, the silence enables me to work and focus on my thoughts without getting distracted.

But as I sit up here on my balcony, I can't help but think back to that epic summer of 1989 and how we met the girls. Witnessing their abilities for the first time and getting locked up in a secret underground base would surely set off a memory tidal wave for anyone.

Maybe it's the nostalgia of wanting to relive the best summer of my life. Maybe it's the fact that as I'm writing this, I'm currently listening to one of my old Mötley Crüe tapes. Yes, you read that right. Tapes!

Or maybe it's even the upcoming anniversary of that event that's prompting me to finally tell my story. Who knows? The government certainly won't admit to it because, even to this day, they still deny everything that happened.

Regardless of whether you believe my story or not, I want you to know that if you're just as curious as I was about what's out there among the stars or even what's happening in your own backyard, then look harder. And if you want your own epic adventure, I say go for it. As for me, my adventures are over.

I don't have to look up at the stars and ask myself if we're all alone in this universe because I already know the answer to that question. And I can safely say that after all these years, I am one hundred percent positive we're not. Plus, you never know. The person standing next to you might just be some half-alien hybrid hiding in plain sight. I mean, after all—I married one.

ACKNOWLEDGMENTS

First of all, I wish to give a very special thanks to Jon Burgos, Sara Winniman Rossman, and one of my best friends, Eric Davidson, for reading this and providing me with valuable reader feedback.

Second, I'd like to thank my artist, Ethan, for doing yet another kick-ass job on the cover. If you like it and would like to see more of what he does, feel free to contact or follow him on Instagram at **@hexbatt** to see more of his stunning artwork.

Lastly, I would like to give a very special shoutout to all the directors, producers, actors, and musicians who made the '80s what it was: the best decade ever for watching movies and listening to music.

ABOUT THE AUTHOR

Rob J. LaBelle lives in the middle of nowhere, Massachusetts, where he spends most of his time with his wife and two sons.

When he's not writing, you can find him doing a plethora of activities, including watching movies and TV, playing video games, playing his drums, spending time with his family, and working on computers (which he currently does to make a living).

For more information, along with current and upcoming works, please visit www.robjlabelle.com.

This is his second novel.